W9-BLQ-448

BOUNDLESS

THE LOST FLEET ◇ OUTLANDS

BOUNDLESS

THE LOST FLEET ◇ OUTLANDS

JACK CAMPBELL

ACE
New York

ACE
Published by Berkley
An imprint of Penguin Random House LLC
penguinrandomhouse.com

Copyright © 2021 by John G. Hemry
Penguin Random House supports copyright. Copyright fuels creativity, encourages diverse voices,
promotes free speech, and creates a vibrant culture. Thank you for buying an authorized edition
of this book and for complying with copyright laws by not reproducing, scanning, or distributing
any part of it in any form without permission. You are supporting writers and allowing
Penguin Random House to continue to publish books for every reader.

ACE is a registered trademark and the A colophon is a trademark of Penguin Random House LLC.

Library of Congress Cataloging-in-Publication Data

Names: Campbell, Jack (Naval officer), author.
Title: Boundless / Jack Campbell.
Description: New York: Ace, [2021] | Series: The lost fleet: Outlands; 12
Identifiers: LCCN 2020040643 (print) | LCCN 2020040644 (ebook) |
ISBN 9780593198964 (hardcover) | ISBN 9780593198988 (ebook)
Subjects: GSAFD: Science fiction.
Classification: LCC PS3553.A4637 B68 2021 (print) |
LCC PS3553.A4637 (ebook) | DDC 813/.54—dc23
LC record available at https://lccn.loc.gov/2020040643
LC ebook record available at https://lccn.loc.gov/2020040644

Printed in the United States of America
1   3   5   7   9   10   8   6   4   2

This is a work of fiction. Names, characters, places, and incidents either are the product of
the author's imagination or are used fictitiously, and any resemblance to actual persons,
living or dead, business establishments, events, or locales is entirely coincidental.

To Palin Spruance, a different generation of quiet warrior. A gentleman whose presence made the world brighter and who is deeply missed.

For S., as always.

THE FIRST FLEET OF THE ALLIANCE

ADMIRAL JOHN GEARY, COMMANDING

FIRST BATTLESHIP DIVISION
Gallant
Indomitable
Glorious
Magnificent

SECOND BATTLESHIP DIVISION
Dreadnaught
Fearless
Dependable
Conqueror

THIRD BATTLESHIP DIVISION
Warspite
Vengeance
Resolution
Guardian

FOURTH BATTLESHIP DIVISION
Colossus
Encroach
Redoubtable
Spartan

FIFTH BATTLESHIP DIVISION
Relentless
Reprisal
Superb
Splendid

FIRST BATTLE CRUISER DIVISION
Inspire
Formidable
Dragon
Steadfast

SECOND BATTLE CRUISER DIVISION
Dauntless
Daring
Victorious
Intemperate

THIRD BATTLE CRUISER DIVISION
Illustrious
Incredible
Valiant

FIFTH ASSAULT TRANSPORT DIVISION
Tsunami
Typhoon
Mistral
Haboob

FIRST AUXILIARIES DIVISION
Titan
Tanuki
Kupua
Domovoi

SECOND AUXILIARIES DIVISION
Witch
Jinn
Alchemist
Cyclops

TWENTY-SIX HEAVY CRUISERS IN FIVE DIVISIONS
First Heavy Cruiser Division
Fourth Heavy Cruiser Division
Eighth Heavy Cruiser Division

Third Heavy Cruiser Division
Fifth Heavy Cruiser Division

FIFTY-ONE LIGHT CRUISERS IN TEN SQUADRONS
First Light Cruiser Squadron
Third Light Cruiser Squadron
Sixth Light Cruiser Squadron
Ninth Light Cruiser Squadron
Eleventh Light Cruiser Squadron

Second Light Cruiser Squadron
Fifth Light Cruiser Squadron
Eighth Light Cruiser Squadron
Tenth Light Cruiser Squadron
Fourteenth Light Cruiser Squadron

ONE HUNDRED FORTY-ONE DESTROYERS IN EIGHTEEN SQUADRONS
First Destroyer Squadron
Third Destroyer Squadron
Sixth Destroyer Squadron
Ninth Destroyer Squadron
Twelfth Destroyer Squadron
Sixteenth Destroyer Squadron
Twentieth Destroyer Squadron
Twenty-third Destroyer Squadron
Twenty-eighth Destroyer Squadron

Second Destroyer Squadron
Fourth Destroyer Squadron
Seventh Destroyer Squadron
Tenth Destroyer Squadron
Fourteenth Destroyer Squadron
Seventeenth Destroyer Squadron
Twenty-first Destroyer Squadron
Twenty-seventh Destroyer Squadron
Thirty-second Destroyer Squadron

FIRST FLEET MARINE FORCE
Major General Carabali, commanding

3,000 Marines on assault transports and divided into detachments on battle cruisers and battleships

ONE

THEY had left behind the star system known to humanity as Unity Alternate, left behind the wreckage of the battleships *Amazon* and *Revenge*, the debris that had once been the battle cruisers *Leviathan* and *Implacable*, the remnants of cruisers and destroyers and the massive orbiting facilities secretly constructed to prolong a century-long war if defeat had finally loomed. The fleet brought all of the dead they could recover with them, as well as many wounded in a fight that no one had expected to survive.

Behind they also left the ruin of the entire badly misnamed Defender fleet, warships crewed and commanded only by "reliable" artificial intelligences that had come close enough to self-awareness to go insane and begin attacking the Alliance they were supposed to defend. Stopping them had cost a lot of lives. The Alliance had been saved again, this time from its own folly.

Once, the sailors aboard these Alliance warships had been certain what lay ahead. They'd fought the Syndicate Worlds all their lives, thinking that war would never end. Today they knew only what lay behind them. The Syndics had finally been beaten, and then the Defender fleet foolishly created to deal with future threats to the Alliance had been faced and destroyed when it also became a danger. Now, though, the future seemed both limitless and unknowable.

For Admiral John "Black Jack" Geary, on his flagship, the battle cruiser *Dauntless*, that meant that he couldn't help wondering if this time he had saved the Alliance only to destroy it.

They'd jumped from the twin stars of Unity Alternate to the star called Drezwin. From there, most of the surviving ships of the fleet had jumped for the base at the star named Varandal to resupply and repair damage. But *Dauntless* and the attack transport *Mistral* had jumped in another direction to reach a star system with a hypernet gate that could bring them to the star that held the capital of the Alliance. The capital long ago named Unity in hopes that it would inspire harmony among the many star systems and peoples who made up the Alliance.

Soon, a moment dreaded by countless people (and hoped for by countless others), would finally happen. Geary, the Alliance's greatest hero, back from the dead, would be arriving at the Alliance capital in his flagship. That action alone might trigger the collapse of a government stressed to near the breaking point by the recently ended century-long war with the Syndicate Worlds. Even if the government survived that, the evidence being brought to the capital aboard the attack transport *Mistral* might well shatter the Alliance.

And yet, in the end, he had no choice. The same sense of duty that had led him to save the Alliance when it trembled on the brink of final defeat now forced him to take the actions that could destroy it anyway.

"Five minutes until arrival at Unity Star System." Lieutenant Castries's announcement carried easily across the bridge of *Dauntless*.

"You look like you're going to another funeral," Captain Tanya Desjani remarked. Her ship's command seat sat next to Geary's own fleet command seat on the bridge, so she could speak in a low voice.

"We may well be doing just that," Geary said.

"You're doing what has to be done."

"I know." He scowled at the display before him, which showed an image of the outside that revealed nothing. The jump space accessed using the older jump drives that had opened the galaxy to human exploration and settlement (and war), appeared as an endless, formless gray. But when using the newer hypernet gates, ships traveling from gate to gate were literally nowhere, surrounded by nothing. The blank emptiness outside the ship made him think of the dark beyond life, which did nothing good for his mood. "I'm not bothered so much by what might happen to me," Geary added, "as I am thinking about how many men and women have died to protect the Alliance. Am I betraying their sacrifices?"

Tanya didn't answer for a moment, then shook her head. "I knew Kostya Tulev for a long time. And I spent much more time around Victoria Rione than any sane person would want. I have no doubt at all that both would agree with what we're doing." She paused. "Though that woman would've surely expressed her agreement in the most disagreeable way possible."

He knew that last sentence was an attempt to distract him from his thoughts, which dwelled on the dead in body capsules on many of the ships that had gone to Varandal. Those sailors would be given the most honorable burial possible, consigned to space, their bodies launched on trajectories that in time would bring them to the star itself, to be consumed by the light. Some far-distant day, the star would explode, hurling outward atoms and elements forged partly from those bodies, to help form new stars and worlds and all that existed on those worlds. But the spirits that had once animated those bodies were already gone, hopefully having been received into the arms of their ancestors. "I'll never get used to it," Geary said. "We did our duty, but so many paid the price this time."

"A lot more would've paid the price if you hadn't made the right decisions," Desjani said.

"And if Victoria Rione hadn't sacrificed herself to save the rest of us."

"We were all willing to do the same," Desjani pointed out. "I honor her sacrifice, because it saved the rest of us, but we all would've died to protect those depending on us. Don't forget how many lives were *saved*, Admiral."

"I—" Geary broke off his reply as he heard the brief whistle that alerted him to an urgent incoming message. He called up the message screen before realizing that there shouldn't be any incoming messages while the ship was still inside the hypernet. "Captain Desjani, why did I just get a message supposedly sent from an outside source?"

Tanya frowned at him. Getting up, she leaned close enough to gaze at his message display. "That's impossible."

"The time of receipt says it arrived on the ship one minute ago."

"That's—" She paused before speaking again. "Did you take a look at the originator?"

"No, not yet." Wondering why Tanya was focusing on that, Geary found the line identifying who'd sent the message. He felt a chill run down his back. "Victoria Rione?"

"It's not her ghost," Tanya said, angry. "That woman must've somehow planted the message in *Dauntless*'s comm system in a way that kept it invisible until now. That's also supposed to be impossible."

"Should I read it?"

"Not until we figure out why it's here," she said. "And if it really is from her. If it was hidden that well, it might be from anyone, and might contain anything." Reaching past him, she tapped the quarantine command for the message. "Comms!"

"Yes, Captain?" the communications watch stander responded.

"The comm system says the ship just received an external message."

The lieutenant took a moment to process her words, bafflement appearing on his face. "Captain, we're still in the hypernet. It's impossible to receive external messages."

"I know that. You know that. The comm system apparently doesn't know that. I've quarantined the message. I want to know where it's been hiding in the system, who put it there, and whether it contains any malware or other hazard."

"Yes, Captain!"

Two minutes until arrival at Unity.

Geary looked over at Tanya as she settled back into her ship's command seat. "I've noticed something about you and this ship."

"What's that, Admiral?"

"You never have to say 'do this now' or 'get this done fast.' Your crew can tell when something needs done quickly just by the way you give the order. They can tell what you want, so they get it done without confusion or delay."

She glanced from the display before her to look at him. "I'm the ship's captain. That's how it's supposed to work. Why is that finally getting a smile from you?"

"Because from anyone else that'd be a boast, but from you it's just a statement of what you think is expected of you."

"Standing by for arrival at Unity," Lieutenant Castries called.

No one could miss the impact of leaving jump space, a jolt that would momentarily rattle the strongest mind. But in that way, too, the gates were different. *Dauntless* exited the hypernet gate on the edge of Unity's star system without any physical effect humans could sense. What they could feel was the sense of relief as the nothingness beyond the ship was replaced by an infinity of stars.

The virtual display screen before Geary came to life, space traffic and other information multiplying as fast as the sensors aboard *Dauntless* could spot the information, process what they saw, and display it in forms easily grasped. Less than a light second away, *Mistral* had also arrived and was broadcasting normal status. The nearest other ship was a ponderous Alliance battleship orbiting a light minute from the hypernet gate, apparently on guard. No alarms sounded or appeared on the display to indicate potentially dangerous situations.

"Do we head for the primary world?" Desjani asked.

Geary nodded. "Unless and until we receive orders otherwise."

"Lieutenant Yuon," Desjani ordered. "Give us an intercept to the primary world. Use point two light speed."

"Yes, Captain." Yuon's hands flicked over his own display. "Ready, Captain."

The projected course appeared on Geary's display as well. Intercepting something in a fixed orbit, such as a planet, was child's play for the navigation systems. A long arc curved through the star system, heading in toward the star and the planet orbiting about ten light minutes from it. Given that Varandal was a bit larger and a bit hotter than Sol (the star that still warmed humanity's ancestral home world, Earth) the surface of the primary world was mostly comfortable for humans. But it also meant that the intercept was about five light hours away from where *Dauntless* and *Mistral* were at the edge of the star system. Even at two-tenths the speed of light, or sixty thousand kilometers per second, which was the sort of velocity warships could achieve in a reasonable time, that distance would require more than twenty-five hours to cover. "I'm good with it," he said. "Make sure *Mistral* has it, then execute."

"Yes, sir," Desjani said. "Lieutenant Yuon, send to *Mistral* and get their receipt for the signal."

"Yes, Captain. *Mistral* acknowledges and reports ready for the maneuver."

Geary tabbed his comm controls, comforted by the routine. "*Dauntless, Mistral*, this is Admiral Geary. Immediate execute, turn starboard zero one five degrees, down zero two zero degrees, velocity point two light. Over." Space didn't have an up or down, an east or a west, so humans made up standard directions based on the star. "Starboard" meant toward it, "port" meant away, while the plane in which the star's planets orbited defined "up" as above it and "down" as below it.

"*Mistral*, aye," the reply came back.

"*Dauntless*, aye."

Desjani moved her fingers lightly across her controls. Thrusters fired along the hull of the battle cruiser, pitching the vessel's bow toward the star and down relative to the plane in which the star's planets orbited. Moments later, as the bow lined up on the right vector, the main propulsion units aft kicked in, hurling the ship toward the star, *Mistral* matching *Dauntless*'s movement.

Geary kept his eyes on the image of the world they were headed for. To the naked eye, it was a barely visible point of light, billions of kilometers distant. He was seeing where it had been five hours ago. At the speed of light, it would be five hours before the people on that world saw that *Dauntless* and *Mistral* had arrived. Against the size of space, even light seemed to move slowly.

But he knew how people might react when they saw that *Dauntless* had arrived here. So he called up the status report he had carefully crafted during the trip from Unity Alternate, fully aware that the fate of the Alliance might rest on whether he used one word or another in any part of the report. The report had a huge attachment, containing what seemed to be the most important evidence collected at Unity Alternate.

He tapped the send command, feeling as if he'd just pulled the trigger on a weapon.

"Captain," Lieutenant Castries said, "we're receiving a challenge from *Audacious*."

Geary tried not to grimace as the name of the nearby battleship was announced. Since awakening a century after his supposed last battle, he hadn't gotten used to the frequent reuse of the names of destroyed ships, which had become routine in a fleet that suffered appalling losses all too often. The last time he'd seen a battleship named *Audacious* it had been a badly battered hulk at a star named Lakota, where his fleet had fought the Syndics twice. The memories the name brought up weren't happy ones. "Inform *Audacious* that I'm aboard and we're heading to the primary world to deliver important individuals and documents to the government."

"*Audacious* is guarding the capital of the Alliance," Tanya Desjani observed to him. "What orders do you think they might have in case you turned up?"

"Hopefully nothing extreme. Can he intercept our track from where he is?"

She frowned at her display, her fingers rapidly testing maneuvers. "Maybe. *Mistral* is a bit slower at acceleration than we are. I doubt you want to leave her behind."

"No," Geary said. "Recommendation?"

"Stall him. For . . . ten minutes. Then we'll be far enough along that any intercept by him will be a stern chase. Even *Mistral* can outrun a battleship under those conditions."

"Fleet Headquarters should have known that," Geary said. "Why put a single battleship in orbit here knowing my flagship could outrun it?"

"Because it's a battleship," Tanya replied. "The biggest, most powerful type of ship the Alliance has. They put *Audacious* here because it looks like they're using the strongest defense available."

"Does anyone at Fleet Headquarters ever do the right thing? Instead of doing what looks right to outside observers?"

"Maybe by accident," she said.

Sometimes having light speed limiting communications speed was a good thing, especially if you wanted to stall. It took another couple of minutes for *Dauntless*'s reply to *Audacious* to be received and the battleship's answer to cross the light minute between the ships. A window appeared on Geary's display, showing the commanding officer of the battleship on his ship's bridge. "This is Captain Zhao of the *Audacious*," that officer began, his tone of voice and appearance seeming more nervous than welcoming. "Admiral Geary, I have standing orders that if you arrive at Unity your ship and any accompanying ships are to assume orbit near my ship and await orders from headquarters. Adjust . . . please adjust your course and speed to take up position one kilometer from *Audacious*. Zhao, over."

"He did say please," Desjani commented, sounding amused.

"Yeah." Geary tapped reply, determined to try to keep the situation from escalating as he tried to stall. "This is Admiral Geary. Captain Zhao, the circumstances under which I arrived here are exceptions to your standing orders." He didn't know that, but Zhao would now have to check his orders for any exceptions, which would buy a little more time. "My flagship and the attack transport that we're escorting will proceed onward to the primary world so that vital personnel and materiel can be delivered to the government. Once there and upon instructions from the government I will proceed to Fleet Headquarters for further orders. Geary, over." He could've ended the message with an "out," but instead wanted to encourage Zhao to keep talking, each exchange of messages requiring at least a couple of minutes.

"Do you really think he's going to be brushed off that easily?" Desjani asked.

"No. How much longer do I need to stall him?"

"Eight minutes."

"Eight? We've already stalled him for several minutes."

"And he's maneuvering," Desjani said, pointing. "Not full propulsion yet, though. He's probably worried about scaring us into bolting at full acceleration and walking away from him."

Geary laughed despite the tension inside him. "So he's trying to stall us?"

"He's trying to get us to stop accelerating." She shook her head. "That's his only real option. He'll answer you again."

Sure enough, three minutes later another message arrived, Zhao now trying to project sincerity as he spoke.

"This is Captain Zhao of the *Audacious*. I regret that I am unable to find the exception you speak of in my orders. But I don't want to make any errors where another Alliance warship is involved. It won't require much time for you to close on my ship so we can resolve any issues. Please do so. I've always wanted the opportunity to speak with you, sir. Zhao, over."

"Seriously?" Desjani grumbled.

"How much more time do we need?"

"Seven minutes."

"Three minutes ago we needed eight minutes!"

"Do you want to be certain that he can't catch *Mistral*, Admiral? He's shifted vector slightly to intercept her instead of *Dauntless*."

"I shouldn't have told him *Mistral* had valuable things aboard her," Geary said, angry with himself. He composed his expression before tapping the reply command. "This is Admiral Geary. Captain Zhao, your interest in avoiding errors is commendable. In that regard, I suggest you review the top secret annex to your standing orders for the situations under which exceptions occur. As you say, we don't want to make any mistakes that would reflect negatively on either of us. Geary, over."

"How do you know his standing orders have a top secret annex listing exceptions?" Desjani asked, raising an eyebrow at him.

"I don't," Geary said. "But now he's got to search for one, and be as certain as possible that no such annex exists. Otherwise, if such an annex existed and he violated orders, he'd see his chances of making admiral go spiraling into a black hole."

"That's good," she said approvingly. "Four more minutes and *Mistral* will be clear. He'll never be able to catch us before we reach the primary world."

How long would Zhao spend searching for an annex that didn't exist? Geary watched his display, where the tracks of the spacecraft slowly altered as they accelerated, and the intercept point for *Audacious* moved farther and farther away. A blinking alert drew his gaze to the battleship at the same time as Lieutenant Castries called out. "*Audacious* has lit off full propulsion. She's accelerating at maximum."

"*Audacious* can still intercept *Mistral* at our closest point of approach," Desjani said.

Oh, hell. Geary touched another comm circuit to call *Mistral*. "Commander Young, can *Mistral* give us any more acceleration?"

Commander Young appeared totally unruffled as she replied. That wasn't surprising, since she'd shown few signs of worry even when things had seemed bleakest at Unity Alternate. "We've got some new mods. If ordered, we can boost at override for about thirty seconds max before the engineering controls mandate going back to normal levels to avoid blowing up the ship or having the inertial dampers fail. I can't guarantee the extra boost will last that long, though. At those levels, main propulsion units don't behave predictably."

"Consider yourself ordered to boost at override," Geary said. "Hold it as long as you can, but don't risk your ship."

"Understood, Admiral."

"*Mistral*'s propulsion has increased output," Lieutenant Castries reported. "She's accelerating at ten percent beyond safe parameters."

"If she holds that for thirty seconds, will we be clear of that battleship?" Geary asked Desjani.

She frowned, then slowly nodded. "Twenty-five seconds at that rate will get *Mistral* beyond intercept. We are going to face other warships deeper in system, though."

"By that time the government will have received my arrival message, and hopefully sent out some orders of its own."

Desjani turned a slight smile his way. "You still believe in the government."

"I have to," he said as another message came in from *Audacious*.

Captain Zhao had now adopted a determined look to match the harsher tones of his voice. "Admiral, I must order you to comply with my instructions. Immediately adjust your course and speed to take up position one kilometer from *Audacious*. My orders authorize me to take all necessary measures to enforce my instructions. Zhao, over."

"How are we doing?" he asked Desjani.

"Almost—"

"*Mistral* is throttling back to one hundred percent acceleration," Lieutenant Castries said.

Desjani paused, eyeing her display while Geary waited, tense.

She smiled.

"That did it, Admiral. *Audacious* is in a stern chase. Intercept probability has gone to zero."

Geary sighed with relief before touching the reply command. "This is Admiral Geary. Captain Zhao, I regret to inform you that I judge my mission to be of extreme importance to the Alliance, such that delays would be inadvisable. I should also note that I am under no obligation to follow orders issued by an officer of lower rank. *Dauntless* and *Mistral* will proceed toward the primary world. *Audacious* is welcome to follow, but I strongly encourage you to check with Fleet Headquarters for further instructions before leaving your patrol orbit. Geary, out."

"You were easy on him," Desjani complained.

"He's stuck in a bad place," Geary said. "That's not his fault. He can't stop me, and if he keeps chasing us he can't catch us; *and* he'll leave the hypernet gate unguarded. I've given him a perfect out from that dilemma by recommending he call headquarters. Just calling in for instructions and getting an answer will take at least ten hours, and by then we'll be almost halfway to the primary world."

"*Audacious* is reducing propulsion," Lieutenant Castries reported. "She's firing thrusters. Estimate the battleship is returning to her patrol orbit."

"And there's our answer," Geary said. "He's taking the only approach left that covers his butt."

Desjani shrugged. "He probably already worked his butt off to get that command by kissing up to everyone with higher rank than him. Who else do you think Fleet Headquarters would choose to protect it?"

"You're an awful cynic," Geary said, watching his display to see if *Audacious* would continue back to her orbit and leave off the now-futile pursuit of *Dauntless* and *Mistral*.

"War does that to you," Desjani said.

SWEATING out the next ten hours wasn't easy, wondering what the Alliance government would do with the information he'd provided. There were some senators who wouldn't be surprised by the news of what had been going on outside normal channels (though unpleasantly surprised to see it uncovered), but hopefully most of them had remained ignorant of the malfeasance and would act to deal with those who'd decided that laws and rules were things for other people to worry about.

He called Commander Young on *Mistral* for an update on the status of her ship. He took the call in his stateroom, both for privacy and to give the bridge crew a break from having the admiral underfoot. "No problems to report with the ship, sir," Young said. "My only real problem is that most of the former prisoners we liberated at Unity Alternate are mad as hell because I'm still treating them as security risks."

"You have to," Geary said. "Once we release them to the authorities on Unity, the government is going to have to decide whether to charge them with crimes or let them go."

Young gestured toward a display to one side of her. "I've looked over the files of a few of the people who were disappeared to Unity Alternate cells on suspicion of being terrorists or traitors during the war with the Syndicate Worlds. I'm no lawyer, but there doesn't seem to be very much there. I guess that's why they disappeared them, because they didn't have enough evidence to charge them."

"Meaning they didn't have enough evidence to know whether they really were guilty of the crimes they were suspected of," Geary said. "That'll be the government's job to figure out, how to handle the former disappeared, and how to handle the people in the government who approved and ran a program like that contrary to the laws of the Alliance." The idea of building a secret, alternate capital for the Alliance government to flee to if necessary had probably seemed wise as the war dragged on for decade after decade, but in retrospect those secret facilities had also been the perfect place to hide things from even the Alliance government itself.

"I'm glad that's above my pay grade, Admiral," Commander Young said. "Colonel Rico is standing by to give you an update on the Marines aboard *Mistral*."

Rico reported that all was well with his Marines, aside from complaints about their having to act as prison guards. "That's good, though,

Admiral," Rico said. "As long as they're grumbling about little stuff like that, it means nothing big is wearing at them."

"Are the prisoners giving you any trouble?"

"No, sir. Nothing to speak of. The mercenaries who were being employed as security guards at Unity Alternate are very unhappy about having been abandoned to their fates by the people running Unity Alternate. They've been spilling their guts to my interrogation specialists, telling us everything they can." Rico paused. "My Marines will ensure all the evidence we have is turned over to the authorities. Some of my people have asked me about what we found at Unity Alternate."

"What have you told them?" Geary asked.

"I've told them that we're upholding our oaths to defend the Alliance. That what we're guarding and delivering is the truth, and the truth matters. We're Alliance, not Syndics. I understand 'truth' in the Syndicate Worlds is whatever the people in charge declare it to be."

"That's right," Geary said. "That's why we fought the Syndics, because we believed in things like the truth. Thank you, Colonel."

"Admiral, can I ask about those aliens? The ones who helped us at Unity Alternate?"

"The Dancers," Geary said, using the name sailors had given the species because of the grace with which they maneuvered their spacecraft. "What about them?"

"They're our friends, right?" Rico asked.

That was a question Geary himself had spent considerable time wondering about. "They've helped us more than once," he said. "Whatever their reasons, the Dancers have helped us."

Rico nodded, his expression as serious as if Geary's vague answer had been detailed and complete. "They were going home, right, Admiral? Do you suppose the Dancers made it home safely?"

"They said they could make a jump that far," Geary said. "Why does that worry you, Colonel?"

"Well . . ." Rico hesitated. "They're sort of comrades-in-arms, right? They fought alongside us. You know Marines never leave any of our own behind. I just think the Dancers deserve the same kind of consideration, to know they made it back safely from battle."

"I have every reason to believe they will make it home safely," Geary said. "They seem to have been a step or two ahead of us ever since we first encountered them."

The link ended, Geary's primary display shifted to a view of local space, the projected track for *Dauntless* and *Mistral* curving through the star system until it intercepted the primary inhabited world on its orbit about the star. *Audacious*, steadily getting more distant, had remained in its orbit, but a pair of heavy cruisers lingering near the primary world could pose a danger if things went wrong.

He sat in his cabin, gazing at the tracks showing all of the other space traffic in this star system, trying not to speculate in endless circles about what would happen when the evidence was delivered. About how the message he'd sent on arrival would be received. About whether after all was said and done he was really doing the right thing.

Tanya Desjani's arrival was a welcome distraction. As always she left the hatch to Geary's stateroom open after she entered. That remained the rule when they were on her ship and on duty. Off the ship, they could be a married couple. Aboard it, there couldn't be a hint of them acting as anything other than admiral and captain. If anything, Tanya's insistence on abiding by regulations was even stronger than Geary's.

She wore an expression that combined admiration with annoyance as she dropped a data coin on the desk. "We isolated that message and my code monkeys took it apart. There's no malware hidden in it."

"Did they find out how it was activated?" he asked, picking up the coin and turning it so the light glinted off one side and then the other.

Desjani blew out an angry breath. "It had a subroutine monitoring the ship's navigation system to tell it if we were close to arriving at Unity. That's supposed to be impossible, by the way, for an outside program to monitor the navigation systems without being detected. My code monkeys would love to meet whoever that woman got that program from, but there aren't any fingerprints on it, real or virtual. Anyone capable of coding that well is capable of hiding their own presence."

"Is there any reason I shouldn't activate the message?"

"Not that I know of. I'll leave."

"Why should you leave? I want both of us to see what Rione thought was important enough to send to me this way."

But he hesitated with the data coin just above the read panel. All of the recent losses were too fresh, too painful. This was certain to rip the bandage off of emotional wounds that were still far from healed.

It had to be important, though. He dropped the coin and waited.

He couldn't help staring at the image of Victoria Rione that appeared on the display, gazing outward at him as if she were still alive and contacting him in real time.

For a moment, he wondered if she was, somehow, really still alive.

"Admiral," Rione said, her words carrying a heaviness despite her attempt at a light tone, "if you're seeing this message, it means I'm dead, and your ship will soon arrive at Unity. Needless to say, I don't want either of those things to happen. But I've long lived with the possibility of both, though my fear of what you might do at Unity has been considerably lessened."

Rione paused as if gathering her words.

"This was made within a few weeks of us heading for Unity Alternate," Desjani said. "That's her as she was very recently."

"All I can do," Rione finally said, "is offer what advice I can. Never forget that just by going to Unity you create the conditions that could shatter the Alliance. Others will interpret your actions in the ways they want to. Everything that you do and say must be carefully thought out. If you want to save the Alliance, and I believe that you do, you have to express support for the ideals behind it even while pressing for actions against those who betrayed those ideals, no matter their reasons, and no matter their positions. This cannot be about one man or one woman. Not you. Not anyone else. It has to be about the principles, the ideals, that have always justified the Alliance. Make it clear that you believe that you are just as subject to the guiding spirit of the Alliance as any other person, and just as subject to the laws that govern it."

Another pause, this one brief. "As a rule, you should trust no one, but there are a few exceptions in the Alliance Senate. Senator Navarro is bitter enough to see through whatever must be done. Senator Unruh will not betray you though she remains wary of you. Your most important ally in the Senate, though, is Senator Sakai. He will do his best to hide his leanings toward you, and his reputation for impartiality will make any statements and actions on your behalf seem all the more significant. Do not tell anyone Sakai is an ally of yours. He will act when and how he deems best.

"There will be many people who want to suppress any evidence of violation of laws. They'll use the official classification system to do that if they can. It's only supposed to be used for matters of Alliance security, but people long ago learned that classification can also conceal matters that might embarrass those in power. Ensure that whatever evidence you have is known to the public. If the public nonetheless rallies to demagogues who tell them what they want to hear, the fault won't lie with you."

Rione seemed to be looking straight at him, Geary thought, her eyes dark. "This last advice is the most important of all. Tanya Desjani. Keep her close. She will tell you the truth, she will tell you what she thinks you need to know, even and especially when you don't want to hear it. Everyone with power needs someone like that. You have her. Listen to her."

Her image on the display leaned closer, tense. "The legend claimed that Black Jack would save the Alliance when it most needed saving. I have come to believe that Admiral Geary may be able to do that. Don't let me down.

"To the honor of our ancestors. Goodbye, Admiral."

Rione's image froze as the message ended.

He stared at the unmoving image a few moments longer before lowering his gaze. Geary rubbed one hand across his eyes and forehead, trying to calm the tumult in his mind.

He heard Tanya say one word. "Huh."

"What does that mean?"

"It means I think you should pay attention to that advice," she said. "Especially the last part."

"Thank you, Captain Desjani." He dropped his hand, looking over at her. "Anything else?"

"You've already done some of what she advised," Desjani said, crossing her arms and gazing steadily at him. "Your arrival message was coded, of course."

"Of course," he repeated, already knowing where she was going.

"You apparently didn't notice that the code you used to encrypt that message is old, and was compromised some time ago. Every news organization in the star system will be able to read your message almost as fast as the Alliance government and Fleet Headquarters can."

"Oh . . . that's . . . unfortunate," he said, trying to avoid sounding guilty. "It's my responsibility to spot things like that, so the fault is clearly mine."

"Sure." She shook her head at him. "If I didn't know how much you must've wrestled with your conscience before doing that, I'd be worried about you deciding not to play by the rules in that case. But you knew as well as that woman did that a lot of very powerful people would do all they could to make sure what we found at Unity Alternate got buried so deep in the classification system that a black hole couldn't suck it out again. That's now impossible."

"Yeah." Geary sighed and rubbed his eyes once more. "If the truth still matters, I had to do what I could to bring it out."

"But, technically, all you did was use an outdated code," Desjani said. "Inside an Alliance star system. They can't hang you for that, even if you weren't Black Jack. Were you disappointed?"

The sudden change of topic threw him. "By what?"

"Her farewell."

"Tanya . . ." Geary frowned at the display. "She said what mattered."

"What mattered to her, yes." Desjani kept her eyes on the image of Rione as she spoke. "There's something I've wondered about for some time, and I think that woman just confirmed it. Why did she take up with you in the first place soon after you assumed command of the fleet? She never seemed to be in love with you, or like the sort of person who was attracted to power."

"Excuse me?" Geary shifted his frown in Tanya's direction. "What are you implying?"

"I'm not *implying* anything, Admiral. I think Victoria Rione wanted to be close to you not only so you'd be within reach of her knife if necessary, but also so she could serve as the person who'd tell you the truths you might not want to hear." Tanya straightened, eyeing him. "But then she saw you developing feelings for me, realized I'd tell you those truths, and backed off."

His frown deepened. "We're not supposed to discuss personal matters while on duty."

"Is that why you're upset at what I said?" Desjani shook her head. "That woman wasn't the sort to give up when she wanted something. If she'd wanted you, she'd have fought for you."

Geary bit back an angry retort, wondering whether it would've been born of dismay at her words or embarrassment at the idea that Rione had only bedded him to further her own aims. He'd long since reached that same conclusion, but didn't like hearing it from someone else. "Victoria Rione had honor," he finally said.

"I'm not denying that. As a single woman, she had every right to make the choices she did. But you saw her with her husband when we found him. You saw how it hit her when she learned he'd been alive all the time and a Syndic prisoner."

"Yes." That had been one of the few times Rione's shell had cracked, revealing the depth of the pain she kept shielded. "There's no doubt she loved him, and never stopped loving him." He let out a small, self-mocking laugh. "I guess I'm just as egotistical as anyone else. I don't want to dwell on the idea that she was motivated by other reasons than . . ." Geary stopped, realizing he'd just dodged an incoming rock by avoiding saying he wanted to think she'd really been attracted to him.

Tanya Desjani raised her eyebrows at him. "What was that?"

"What was what?"

"You didn't finish your sentence."

"I was thinking. And we're still on duty." He nodded to the display. "Any other comments?"

"Not at the moment. Well, one other comment. I'm glad that woman was on our side." Desjani grimaced. "Especially at Unity Alternate. I'll light another candle for her later."

"I'm sure her spirit will appreciate that."

"Her spirit will probably try to trip me as I'm leaving the room." Tanya offered him a casual salute. "I'll see you on the bridge later, Admiral."

"Thank you, Captain."

Before she made it to the hatch, alerts sounded from her comm pad and his desk. Geary checked his display as Desjani checked her pad.

"Eyes only message for Admiral Geary, highest priority," Desjani said. "From the Grand Council of the Alliance Senate. Want me to hang around a little longer?"

"Yes," he said, reaching to accept and read the message.

TWO

THE message, heavily encrypted and text only, offered clear direction but few clues to what his reception would be at Unity. "We're to proceed to orbit about the primary world," Geary told Desjani. "Once there, I'm to come down in a shuttle to meet with the Grand Council."

"That's it?" She leaned over to view the message. "What makes that eyes only for you?"

"I don't know." He sat back, rubbing his face. "Strange. I know exactly what Rione would be saying if she was here. They're idiots for keeping this message so secret. If everyone knew I was coming there on orders from the Grand Council it would quiet a lot of speculation."

"So, we keep on?"

"Yes, Captain Desjani. Maintain our current vector."

But as she was almost out the hatch, Desjani paused to look back. "That message doesn't give any clue as to what will happen when you land there."

"They won't . . ." He let the sentence die, unfinished.

But she figured out the rest. "They won't do anything stupid? Were you really going to say that?"

"Tanya . . ." Geary let his eyes go to his display, where the field of endless stars outside the ship was visible once more. "I still have faith in the Alliance. Faith that enough of those elected to serve it will live up to their responsibilities."

She nodded. "I hope you're right. But even if you're wrong, I'll be beside you all the way."

THEY were still six hours from reaching orbit about the primary world, the star for Unity a small disc to the naked eye rather than a spot of light. They could now see where the planet had been an hour ago, and hear messages or other transmissions sent an hour in the past.

During a restless walk through the passageways of *Dauntless*, meeting and greeting sailors who seemed cheered up by seeing him, Geary encountered General Charban, the retired officer who'd become the primary speaker with the alien Dancers. A nearby break room was empty, so they both grabbed coffee and sat down in the regulation chairs that rumor said had been carefully designed to become uncomfortable after a few minutes to keep sailors from lingering on break.

"Have you been keeping track of the news reports?" Charban asked, grimacing as he took a drink. "I thought fleet coffee was supposed to be better than what the ground forces got, but it tastes just as bad to me."

"Believe me," Geary said, "I've had coffee that was a lot worse than this. I think it's a fleet tradition. No, I've been avoiding the news."

"So has your intelligence officer," Charban said. "Lieutenant Iger knows the laws that forbid military intelligence to collect against civilian Alliance targets, and he's ethical enough to not try searching for loopholes he could claim allowed it in this instance." He set down his coffee, gazing at the battered surface of the table. It had been repaired using a variation on an ancient means of fixing broken items with bright strands of gold to highlight the former break and turn it into a form of art. Like everything else on *Dauntless*, the table had been built with the expectation that the ship would have a combat life span measured in months, because that was what the war had come to. But Geary, bringing back prewar tactics forgotten in the century-long bloodbath, had considerably raised the combat survival rate of ships, creating an unexpected problem as they outlived the life span of their components. While critical systems had been overhauled to keep *Dauntless* working, things like break room tables hadn't been replaced for lack of time and the money spent on more important things.

"I'll summarize them for you," Charban continued. "Some senators, by I'm sure pure coincidence those prominently named for wrongdoing in the evidence you compiled, are asserting they are in fact innocent and everyone else is guilty."

Geary nearly choked on his own coffee, managing to swallow without ruining his uniform. "That isn't working, is it?"

Charban smiled sadly. "The Big Lie is an old, old tactic. Make a lie so huge that no one would believe anyone would dare try such a massive distortion of the truth. And there's a portion of the Alliance's population who've stopped caring about the truth after hearing so many lies. So, it is working in some places among some people. Beyond that, there's a lot of tension about you coming to Unity. What it means. What you intend. Here. I saved this one. It's typical of what's being said."

Charban displayed his epad, which showed two women and one man sitting in casual chairs arranged in a semicircle so they faced the screen and each other. "John 'Black Jack' Geary," one of the women said, looking out to address her audience. "One hundred years ago he stopped the first Syndic attack on the Alliance in the famous battle at Grendel, where he was believed to have died saving as many of his crew as possible. For a century, he inspired everyone in the Alliance with his heroic example. Over time, his reputation kept growing. People began claiming that he would return someday when the need was greatest, and save the Alliance. In fact, though believed dead, Black Jack was found frozen in survival sleep in a damaged escape pod, lost amid the battle debris, and revived after nearly a century just before the Alliance fleet launched a daring and dangerous attack deep in Syndic space."

"An attack which resulted in a disastrous ambush," the man in the group said. "Black Jack took command of the surviving Alliance warships and in an incredible series of battles, brought them back home. No one else could have done that!"

"And then," the second woman said, "he took the fleet back into Syndic space and finally defeated the foe we'd been fighting for a hundred years. Not content with that, he soon discovered three intelligent alien races. And now he arrives at Unity, with news that secret government programs imperiled the Alliance they were intended to defend. That the legendary Unity Alternate location for the Alliance government to retreat to if the war had gone badly enough did indeed exist, and was used for more than one secret project that violated the laws of the Alliance."

"Black Jack saved us all. Again!" the first woman said.

"But why is he here at Unity?" the man asked.

"Maybe he's decided the next place the Alliance needs to be saved is here," the second woman said.

"Can we trust him?" the first woman said. "Unity is the heart of the Alliance. Great men and great women have often had great ambitions."

"Black Jack *is* the Alliance," the second woman answered as the man nodded in vigorous agreement. "He didn't bring the fleet here as a conqueror would. Just his flagship and one other ship."

"That might be all Black Jack needs to do what we wants," the first woman said. "All we can do is wait and see what he does."

Charban tapped the vid recording to end it. "That speaks for itself, doesn't it?"

Geary nodded, grimacing. "That was all about me but it felt to me like they were talking about someone else."

"Black Jack," General Charban said. "Your mythical counterpart who always knows just what to do."

"I wish I could ask him for advice," Geary said. "You know I can't make a public statement about my intentions without approval."

"I know." Charban paused. "But maybe you should. Until you speak, others can claim to speak for you. Some already are." He raised one hand to stop Geary's response. "Wait, please. I know. It's a violation of regulations. A minor violation, as long as you don't call for mutiny or the overthrow of the government or something like that. Measure that against the major problems that can happen if you stay silent in public. Read more of the news. A rumor that you'd been arrested might set off riots. A rumor that you'd arrested the Senate might cause something even worse."

"It's that bad?"

"I think so. That newscast I showed you is very middle of the road, and you heard the questions they posed. Some of the other reporting out there is . . . very speculative and seems designed to incite trouble." Charban sounded regretful as he continued. "Admiral, sometimes you have to bend the rules a little for important reasons, as long as those reasons aren't for your personal benefit."

Geary sat thinking, frowning down at his coffee, trying to find reasons to debate Charban, and realizing he had none except for his own distrust of stretching the rules because he could. "I'll assess the situation on the ground when I land," he finally said. "I'll make a decision then."

"I can't ask for more than that," Charban said. He took another drink of coffee, grimacing only a little this time at the taste. "What do you need from me? I'm supposed to make a report based on my status as an observer with you."

That one was easier to answer. "I don't think you should get involved in any aspect of the political drama," Geary said. "You're the person who's had the most contact with the Dancers. Communicated with them most frequently. It's important that whatever you say be listened to. If you get identified with one political faction or another, a lot of people might not listen. I know you were thinking of going into politics yourself, but for the time being there's a more critical need for you to be perceived as completely nonpartisan."

Charban looked at the small table, running one finger along the twisting gold line where the break had been repaired. "It looks like we're both giving the other advice we'd rather not hear. I'm not the sort to keep my head down when others are charging into danger. It's not in me."

"How'd you survive this long?" Geary asked.

"The living stars may know, but I have no idea." Charban raised his gaze, meeting Geary's eyes, and smiled a bit. "Maybe to do something important, like improving communications with the first alien species that will willingly talk to us. I won't lie in my report. I saw too many lies in official reporting and too many lives lost as a result of such lies. I will be truthful as to what I saw and what I experienced. If anyone takes truth as a partisan political issue, then I doubt anything I said would make a difference to them."

"Fair enough." Geary stood, feeling tired. "I should try to get a little rest before we reach the planet."

"Remember what I said, Admiral."

"I will."

FROM near orbit, the world called Unity looked like many other planets. Patches of darker and lighter land, green where vegetation bloomed, white where ice or snow lay, a very broad ocean and some slender seas, and rafts of cloud cover sailing between the surface and space. The native vegetation on the planet was lighter in shade than species from Old Earth, with a silvery sheen, so the forests and grassy plains bore a strange gloss where the light of the star fell upon them. One city bore the name Unity as well, but there were other cities, and many citizens whose work and lives weren't directly tied to the fact that this planet held the capital of the Alliance.

Tanya Desjani walked him to *Dauntless*'s shuttle dock. "Be careful."

"You, too. Keep an eye on *Mistral*. There are people who'd love to see all of that evidence destroyed."

"I'll be watching." They walked into the dock, where a large display showed the planet below. She nodded toward it. "I read that once this star had another name. The first colony planted here was bombarded from space, though. They never did find out who was responsible."

He looked at the planet, imagining it as it must have been on that long ago day when death fell upon it from orbit. "Why mention that now?"

"Because even at the time a few people speculated aliens might've been responsible." Tanya gave him her most serious look. "We've learned some alien species were making tentative moves into this part of space when humanity came flooding in. And we've learned that one of those alien species, the enigmas, wouldn't have hesitated to try to stop the human expansion. And we know they had malware hidden in all of our fleet's systems. There might still be some hidden dangers down there, because the enigmas still don't want us at peace and we don't know what else they might have planted before we discovered them. Don't assume all of your dangers will come from known sources."

"Good point. I'll contact you as soon as I can."

"Yes, Admiral." She saluted him, still solemn. "We might develop some comm problems of the blind eye to the scope variety, though. Depending on events."

"I understand." He returned the salute, praying that everything would be fine and he'd see her again, before turning to walk up the ramp into the shuttle.

Orbital space was busy, filled with maneuvering traffic and satellites of many kinds as well as human habitats and stations. But the shuttle was given a clean path down, other spacecraft scattering to clear the way.

"We've got company," the pilot announced, her voice echoing in the passenger compartment where Geary sat. The display on the forward bulkhead shifted to highlight several contacts swerving in to match vectors with the shuttle. Aerospace craft, deadly and swift. Hopefully an escort to protect the shuttle, and not guards with orders to keep the shuttle from deviating from its trajectory.

The shuttle swooped down, coming to rest on the surface with the unnecessary but graceful élan of a human pilot showing off their skills.

The VIP landing field was clear, security barriers and what seemed to be hundreds of police holding back a crowd of spectators that appeared to number in the tens of thousands, filling the open public areas that ringed the landing field.

Geary stood up, straightened his uniform, and nodded to the two members of *Dauntless*'s crew who'd come down in the shuttle with him. Marine Gunnery Sergeant Orvis and Master Chief Gioninni, both resplendent in dress uniforms, nodded back. Tanya Desjani had suggested sending down *Dauntless*'s entire Marine contingent in full battle armor as escorts, but the impression that sort of show of force would create would send precisely the wrong message. Aside from displaying professional background, Gunny Orvis would spot any open threats being aimed at the shuttle, while an expert schemer like Master Chief Gioninni should be able to detect any covert dangers. Geary didn't think anyone would be authorized to take steps against him, but he had to worry about those who might be worried enough about protecting themselves that they might try something.

The shuttle ramp dropped, letting in the air of Unity's atmosphere, as well as the distant rumble of thousands of voices. As Orvis and Gioninni walked down the ramp and took position on either side of the bottom, the noise dwindled rapidly, not even the sound of wind rising over the silence, as if the entire planet were holding its breath.

Geary walked down the ramp, trying to look calm and professional despite the worries filling him.

As his right foot touched the surface of the planet, noise erupted from the watching crowds. He nearly froze as the sheer mass of sound from so many people rolled past.

But he did pause, looking out across the landing field, nerving himself for what was to come.

It was one of those moments that he knew would be forever branded in his memory, the smallest details clear no matter how many years passed. On this part of the planet, the sun was just rising, its rays lighting up the bottom of a swath of clouds so that they looked like a sheet of molten gold flung across the sky. The air smelled of cut grass and distant flowers and the thousand faint scents put off by people and their machines and their buildings. A flock of something birdlike was circling the landing field, repelled by the measures used to keep wildlife off the field, but stubbornly still trying to find a way in.

There was something else in the air, something indefinable, that made him want to back away. The same feeling the air got before a huge storm, the same sense that immense danger hovered just out of sight but was bearing down and would soon strike with overwhelming force. These crowds held a terrible potential, which if unleashed would rage against anything and everything in its path. In that moment he knew with absolute certainty that Charban had been right.

"At least they're cheering, Admiral," Master Chief Gioninni remarked as he and Gunny Orvis saluted. But the way Gioninni said it, the way he ran wary eyes across the crowds, made it obvious that he, too, could feel the ominous atmosphere. A good con artist had to be able to read their audience, and Gioninni was a very good con artist. "Sir, you might want to watch your step."

Gunnery Sergeant Orvis nodded in agreement with Gioninni's words, his eyes scanning the crowd as if they were a threatening enemy force. "I *think* they're cheering you, sir."

"Let's hope you're right, and that they don't change their minds," Geary replied. "You two wait in the shuttle and keep an eye on things until I get word about how long I'll be on the planet."

"Yes, sir," Orvis said. "Should we seal the shuttle and remain ready to lift?"

"Yes. If a mass of people comes charging onto this field, you're authorized to lift."

"What about you, sir?"

"I will hopefully be in a more secure area than this."

Orvis nodded. "Light off your beacon and get to the top of a building, and we can lift you off. If you can't get to the top, get to a window and we can get close enough to get you. The pilots flying this bird are the best in the fleet."

"Thanks, Gunny." Geary tried a smile he hoped looked reassuring. "I doubt that it'll come to that. Those are all citizens of the Alliance," he added, waving to indicate the crowd.

Gunnery Sergeant Orvis shook his head, his expression grim. "Admiral, with all due respect, if things go to hell, we won't be dealing with citizens of the Alliance. We'll be facing a mob. Mobs are people who've forgotten they're human, and forgotten that other people are human. A mob will do things none of them would imagine doing in other circumstances, because they've forgotten they're human. I've seen it, and wish I hadn't. Even disciplined military units can turn into a mob if they have poor leadership or are pushed too hard for too long. Civilians . . . hell, Admiral, you know as well as I do that there are politicians who've been encouraging these people to turn into mobs."

"Not all of the politicians," Geary said. "A great many are doing their best."

"I concur, Admiral," Orvis said. "But it only takes one match that doesn't care what gets burned in the blaze it sets off for its own profit."

He couldn't think of any words to answer that, because everything Orvis said was true, so Geary just nodded wordlessly before turning to walk to the waiting ground vehicle, an armored limousine. A single guard waited at the door, another Marine, who saluted as Geary approached.

He got in, finding a single occupant waiting. "General Carabali. It's nice to see you again." Nice and reassuring. He'd been working with her since Carabali had been the senior surviving Marine in the fleet he'd assumed command of deep inside Syndic space, and knew he could trust Carabali in any matter. The government knew that as well. Had sending her to meet him been a subtle sign of encouragement?

"And you, Admiral." Carabali gestured to the guard. "Seal us in and get this thing moving."

"Yes, General." The heavy door sealed with a reassuring thunk, cutting off the sustained roar of the crowds. The display screen on the front end of the passenger compartment gave a view of the guard getting in next to the driver, who was also a Marine.

"A fully armored limo?" Geary asked as the ground car surged into motion. The side screens, positioned as if they were windows instead of panels inside strong armor plate, showed the crowd waving and shouting, the sound still blocked. "But no other ground escort?"

"No, Admiral," Carabali replied, her eyes studying the outside view. "I was told they didn't want to create the appearance of you being detained by force, or the appearance of you coming in to take over, and a lightly armed honor guard also acting as an escort would've been too exposed if the crowds erupted. They don't want anything happening to you, but they can't do anything that might trigger unpleasant reactions."

"At least they're thinking things through. Are there any specific concerns?"

Carabali gave him a startled look. "They didn't provide you with that information, Admiral?"

"No." Geary tried to sit back and relax a little. "All I've been told is to come down here in the shuttle and report to the Grand Council."

"I see." Carabali gritted her teeth, clearly unhappy. "There've been reports of plans to harm you to create a distraction. Nothing specific as to time and place and means, but credible enough to cause concern."

"A distraction?"

"Sir, if the Alliance is dealing with massive mobs rampaging through its capital, things like following up on what you found at Unity Alternate will go way down the priority list, giving the guilty parties a lot more time to work up their strategies, and making anything they did look minor compared to what the mobs might be doing."

Geary gave up trying to appear relaxed and sat straight, fighting a feeling of despair. "It feels like I'm dealing with Syndic CEOs again."

He looked at the crowds outside again as the limo left the field and began moving down a broad boulevard, empty except for the car, but the sides lined with more guards and security vehicles. Beyond security stood a swarm of spectators, craning their heads to look at the limo as it passed.

"Do you have any idea what they expect?" Geary asked, indicating the crowds on either side.

"Each of them expects you to give them what they want," General Carabali said. "And they all want different things. But there've been a lot of stories circulating in the last few days. Stories about your loyalty to the Alliance, and statements you've made about following orders from the government. Measured against that are stories claiming you're coming to finally clean out the government. And some really crazy stories that you've sold out humanity to the aliens."

"Which aliens?" Geary asked, his eyes on the faces in the crowds, trying to read their moods and feelings. "The enigmas, the Dancers, or the Kicks?"

"The Dancers. Of course. They're the ugly ones so they must be evil, right? You can't argue with some people about that. My Marines, who fought the Kicks face-to-face, have been really surprised to see how popular the Kicks are. Nobody wants to hear how dangerous the cute little Kicks were." Carabali shook her head in disgust. "We finally find truly alien intelligences and people just want to plug them into our own little human categories, as if they were some kind of toy or exotic animal. Are we going to screw up alien contact that badly?"

"I hope not." Geary looked back at her. "Any problems with security in the government?"

"Lots of baskets being turned over and lots of people expressing shock at what was under them. No one's tried anything obvious, though. The special agencies are almost paralyzed because most of their people didn't know what was going on in the hidden programs, and now they have no idea who to trust with anything." Carabali shrugged. "But no open threats," she repeated. "Everyone seems to have thought they were being loyal, even the ones who deliberately worked around the rules."

Geary shook his head. "The road to hell is still paved with good intentions, isn't it?"

"I can't judge intentions, Admiral." Carabali shifted her gaze to look to the west. "Also, some senior officers at Fleet Headquarters are on house arrest since your arrival message was received. Admiral Otropa is one of them, as is Admiral Tosic. There are others."

"Who's enforcing the house arrest?"

"My Marines."

That was simultaneously reassuring and worrisome. What had it come to that Marines had to be used as prison guards for senior officers?

"How far is it to where we're going?" Geary asked.

"You've never been to Unity, Admiral?" Carabali gestured ahead. "Not much farther."

The landing field hadn't been far from the seat of government. Geary saw the street they were on end at the plaza outside the soaring building that housed the Alliance Senate. Every image Geary had seen of that plaza showed many people entering and leaving, but as the armored limo came to a halt no one else could be seen between the car and the entrance. More security forces and police formed lines keeping the crowds clear of what was formally known as the Plaza of the People of the Alliance. He gazed somberly at the empty Plaza of the People, no people allowed on it at the moment, thinking there was no better metaphor for the problems facing the Alliance.

Carabali got out of the car with him and gestured toward the entry. "I'm supposed to let you enter alone, Admiral."

"All right. I'd be the last to tell you not to follow orders." Geary smiled at Carabali. "But there's something else I should do next."

Instead of walking straight to the building, Geary walked at an angle toward a large fenced-off area crowded with people bearing press badges and cameras. Cameras hadn't had to be large enough to be easily seen for a long, long time, but after privacy violations got bad enough and frequent enough the laws had been changed to require any recording of others to use equipment that was clearly visible.

Some of the security officials, seeing him deviating from the middle of the path, ran to intercept Geary. But he adopted a ship's captain attitude, striding forward as if nothing and no one dare stand in his way. He had to direct a single look at one official who planted himself in his path but gave way under that stare.

He didn't stop until at the fence separating the press from him, trying not to frown at the symbolism of that. One of the founding principles of the Alliance had been to allow as few restrictions as possible on the public's ability to learn what the government was doing. When had the Alliance started fencing off the press whose constant vigilance was necessary in a democratic system?

The reporters stared at him, poised to shout questions but waiting to see if he'd speak.

"I have something to say," Geary said, speaking calmly. "I want to put to rest any rumors or worries. I came here on orders from the Alliance government. I will follow the orders of the Alliance government as long as I wear this uniform, because I still believe in the Alliance. I don't know how many men and women have given their lives over the centuries to defend the freedoms the Alliance has protected, but I've seen many of them die fighting under my command. I will never betray their sacrifices. I ask everyone who hears this to refrain from any actions that would harm others or the Alliance. Our ancestors gave us a very precious gift, a government shared among many to ensure their safety and freedom. I will never support any actions that would undermine that."

As far as he could see, the members of the crowd near enough to listen were intent on his words, while farther off people's attention was focused on their individual pads as his words were broadcast as fast as they were spoken.

He paused, and a reporter's voice leapt into the tiny gap. "Are you here to see justice done? Will you clean house in the Senate?"

Geary didn't have to feign a frown of puzzlement. "I'm not part of the legal system. I've done what I can to ensure all evidence of violations of the Alliance's laws were brought to the government. I will answer whatever questions the Senate puts to me. And I will trust the government to take the right and necessary actions to deal with those who have violated their oaths and responsibilities."

His response appeared to stun them for a moment. Geary noticed that the buzz of conversation beginning to rise from the crowd had suddenly dropped back to silence. Was that a good or a bad thing? Did it mean they were thinking about his words, or rejecting them?

The quiet was broken when another reporter called out, her voice harsh. "Won't you vow to immediately deal with corrupt and law-breaking senators? Will you immediately bring them all to justice?"

"No." He let the word sit alone for a moment before continuing. "I will let the courts and the legal system do that. Abandoning due process in the name of justice is insane. Do you only want someone to blame, or do you want those who did wrong to be held to account for their actions? These are your courts, your laws, which exist to protect every citizen. Casting them aside would not produce justice."

How were they taking that? Geary tried to unobtrusively look over the nearest portions of the crowd to read their reactions, but it was very hard to pick out a single expression in the mass of people without obviously focusing on one individual at a time. The quiet might mean anything, agreement or stunned disapproval. Whether the silence meant they were listening, truly hearing what he was saying, he couldn't tell.

Another reporter spoke up, her voice more measured. "Do you have anything else to tell the people of the Alliance?"

He hesitated, not wanting to risk saying the wrong thing, unsure how his earlier words had been received, but his memory suddenly produced a vision of Rione's last transmission at Unity Alternate, and that broke something inside of him. *Save the Alliance.* Every moment since he'd awoken from survival sleep, other people had been expecting him to save them, to fix everything for them. He was worn out from those expectations. Frustration fueled his words as Geary looked at the reporters, letting the words come.

"Yes. I wish that all of the people of the Alliance would stop listening to lies, stop believing that everything wrong is someone else's fault, and stop believing that someone else will fix everything. There aren't any easy, simple, painless answers. I can't save the Alliance! When Victoria Rione sacrificed herself to save my fleet and to save all of you, she asked me to tell the people of the Alliance to stop blaming others and to look in the mirror for the solution to our problems. Only that person, the one you see in that mirror, can fix what ails the Alliance. She died doing not what would benefit her or people just like her, but doing what would save us all. She knew that anything good requires a willingness to sacrifice for others, to believe the best of others no matter how difficult it is. I believe that her ancestors welcomed her, and that all of our ancestors would approve of her actions."

He realized that if she were here, Rione would probably be rolling her eyes in open scorn of the idealistic words. But she had lived them, in her own way.

"Thank you," Geary said in the silence that lingered following his words. He turned and walked away, followed by a crescendo of more shouted questions. His mind was already worrying over what he'd said and how he'd said it. He could only hope those words helped things instead of making them worse.

He had only taken several steps when a single small drone flashed into sight and zipped toward him, so low it skimmed the surface of the plaza, somehow evading a volley of defensive fire as well as whatever unseen electronic countermeasures were being hurled at it.

Running would be senseless. The drone was faster and quicker than he was. Geary stood watching it, not knowing what else he could do. It wasn't fatalism, just a realization that his best and only chance would be a last-moment dodge that the drone wouldn't have time to adjust for before racing past him. The same tactics that he'd use in space, but on a much, much smaller and much, much slower scale.

It didn't seem slower, though, not when standing here as the drone tore through the air toward him.

He was bracing himself to leap to one side, the drone only a couple of meters away, when a shot finally connected, shattering propulsion units on one side of the drone and causing it to flip wildly up and to one side. As the drone staggered, trying to regain control, several more shots slammed into it and the device broke into several pieces.

The remnants of the drone tossed off fragments as they fell, but he still stood just watching, feeling foolish even though no amount of dodging would have made him any safer.

He realized that the shot that had crippled the drone had come from the same security officer who'd tried to stop him from getting to the press. He and other officials were trying to use their bodies to screen Geary from the drone's debris.

Geary took a deep breath, realizing that in the wake of the shots the crowds had fallen silent. The attack had happened too quickly for the crowds to panic, and now the images being broadcast by the press were telling everyone the danger was over. He raised one arm and waved, turning so that everyone could see him. Lowering his arm, he walked to the security officer whose shot had crippled the drone and extended his hand. "Thank you."

The officer, face still filled with strain, stared at the hand, then reached to shake it. "It . . . was my . . . honor, sir."

Turning, Geary waved again to the crowd, who inexplicably had erupted into cheers. A senior official ran up, looking near tears. "Sir, I'm very sorry for this security breach. I—"

He held up a hand to halt the apology. "It's over. Just make sure you find out how it got past your defenses so the next one can be stopped." With another wave to the world in general, Geary headed once more for the building. He'd been dreading walking inside those doors but now looked forward to being cut off from the masses of people watching his every move.

He reached the building without further incident, grateful when the entry door closed behind him to seal off the crowds who all expected something, but not the same thing, from him. Halting to take a long, slow breath, Geary looked around.

Everyone had heard of the great hall just inside the front entry of the Alliance Senate. Everyone had seen images of it in all of their virtual reality glory. But, as with so much else, actually standing in that hall felt very different. Especially when he was apparently the only person here in a place normally crowded with those who had business with the Senate or tourists visiting what was effectively the home of the Alliance.

The walls of the great hall were lined with works of art, mostly paintings or poems, but occasionally interrupted by sculptures or other creations. Geary walked past some of them, reading the names of the artists. Da Vinci and Wheatley. Hokusai. Kahlo, Kipling, and O'Keeffe. Sher-Gil. Phidias and Behzad. People from every part of humanity, who'd all put their own special mark on art that spoke to many even now, very far from Old Earth and very long after their creations were made. He paused before one work, marveling at it, slightly extending one hand in the human instinct to reach the amazing before halting himself.

"You can touch them," someone said.

Geary turned to see a lean woman had approached silently and was watching him with a slight, knowing smile. She was old enough for it to be apparent despite the medical advances that could hold back signs of aging until near the end. Her clothes were a rich, bright purple, standing out against the more subtle shades of the art surrounding them. He felt a vague sense of familiarity as he looked at her, as if they'd once met briefly or he'd seen her image somewhere. "Touching them seems wrong," he said.

"If they were the originals from Old Earth, it would be a terrible crime to touch them." She waved in a broad, graceful sweep taking in the entire hall. "All of these are reproductions, as exact as could be made, but using far more durable materials. That particular painting isn't on canvas even though it looks like it to the eye. It's a ceramic material. Almost indestructible."

He winced in embarrassment. "I knew that. I forgot when I actually saw these, though."

"A lot of people do." She looked around. "The greatest artistic creations of all of humanity. Our ancestors look out at us through these images and these words, which show far more than any digital picture could ever capture. Some of the originals no longer exist on Old Earth, destroyed by time or accident or war. But they live on here." The woman eyed Geary. "I always feel humbled in their presence. People come and go from life, here and gone, perhaps little remembered. But these works have lasted far longer than their creators, because they were judged worthy of being preserved. I often wonder if I'll ever do anything half so worthy."

"Me, too," Geary said.

"Do you mean that? The great Black Jack?"

"I never claimed to be great."

"Really?" She nodded around her. "This hall was designed to humble those who looked upon it. To show them what humanity could create, what we all shared, and how small we all are compared to what we aspire to. The founders of the Alliance wanted it that way. They passed on a warning to their descendants, that anyone who could walk through this hall untouched by it, anyone who didn't feel diminished in comparison to the greatest art of humanity, was not someone to be trusted with power."

"I'd never heard that." He tore his eyes from the works of art to look more closely at her. "Are you my escort?"

"If you want to call me that," she said.

"And this is another test?" Geary asked, gesturing around the room.

"Everything is a test. I'm Senator Nakamura."

The name was surprisingly familiar. "From Kosatka?" Maybe that was where he'd seen her.

"Yes. One of my ancestors played a role in the founding of the Alliance. He was the one who put the warning about this hall into our family lore." Her smile shifted slightly, but her eyes remained sharp. "My family also goes a long ways back with the Desjani-Ochoas."

"I see. Do you know Tanya?"

"I'm her godmother."

"Oh." Couldn't Tanya have mentioned the possibility that he might run into her godmother on Unity? "She never told me about that."

"I'm not surprised. Tanya was never comfortable with being part of an Old Family on Kosatka. She always believed that the only things which mattered were those she earned by her own efforts."

"That's Tanya," Geary said. He rubbed his chin as he gazed at Senator Nakamura. "I assume there's a reason that you in particular were sent to meet me."

"Yes." She nodded slowly, as if deciding whether to say more, before finally speaking, her eyes locked on him. "It was hoped you might be more candid with me than with anyone else."

"Candid?"

"About your motivations, your plans."

Geary sighed, the sound making a strange, sibilant echo in the vast hall. "I gave my reasons for being here in my message when my ship arrived. I judged it vital to provide an armed escort to *Mistral* to ensure she arrived safely at Unity. Once here, I received orders to land and provide my personal report to the Senate Grand Council. After that I expect to report to Fleet Headquarters for further orders."

"Really, Admiral?"

The note of skepticism stung. He felt his face hardening. "As I just said out there, I will not betray the sacrifices of those who died to preserve the Alliance by acting otherwise. Those sacrifices include the men and women who died at Unity Alternate to save the Alliance.

Those names may be faceless to you, but to me every single one is a person who gave their future to preserve the future of the Alliance."

Senator Nakamura said nothing for a long moment, her face as rigid as if carved from stone. "I knew the face of Victoria Rione," she finally said. "I didn't like her, but I respected her. On your honor, Admiral, is your account of her sacrifice complete and accurate in all details?"

"If you've seen the evidence included in my arrival report, you've seen the copy of her final transmission attached to it. I would not dishonor her by lying or trying to alter that transmission," Geary said, hearing the strain in his voice as he fought to control his temper. "And I would very much appreciate not being implicitly accused of that again."

After another long pause, Senator Nakamura shook her head. "I can't promise that, Admiral. You say she destroyed the Defender fleet, what you called the black ships, by causing the hypernet gate at Unity Alternate to collapse."

"I'm not saying anything," he replied. "I sent you the evidence. That's what tells you what happened."

Senator Nakamura appeared unimpressed by his statement. "It is absolutely prohibited for any person to have a copy of the software that can cause a gate to collapse in that fashion. Where did Rione get it?"

"I have no idea."

"The original work to develop that software was done in *your* fleet by one of *your* officers at *your* orders."

He got mad. He couldn't help it, even though that was surely what Nakamura was aiming for, to provoke him into making some incriminating statement. But he could be angry and still watch his words. "Which you know because I reported it. And you know that software was a by-product of trying to find a way to ensure the collapse of a gate wouldn't cause a hugely destructive pulse of energy to be released. That's what I ordered my officer to do. And it was members of the Alliance Senate who suggested using that software as a weapon against the Syndics, not me. If you're looking for where former senator Victoria Rione got that software, maybe you should look closer to home." Whatever he would have said next went unsaid as Geary spotted worry in the senator as a result of his last statement. "You're afraid that your name is among the rest of the evidence aboard *Mistral*, aren't you?"

Any remaining trace of camaraderie fled as Senator Nakamura spoke with careful control. "Those of us entrusted with the safety of the Alliance have to take necessary actions. Actions which can be easily misinterpreted by those lacking the same perspective and responsibilities."

"Responsibilities? Perspective?" Geary realized his hand had clenched into a fist, and willed it to relax. "Would you like to compare your responsibilities to mine, Senator?"

"You have no right to act as judge of us!" Senator Nakamura said, her eyes wide.

"I won't judge anyone, but I will tell the truth, Senator. If the truth worries you, then perhaps you'd better consult with your ancestors. They're the ones who'll be judging you in the end, not me."

"You really do think you're the great hero who deserves to rule the Alliance, don't you?"

The words might have stung if he hadn't more than once mocked the idea. "If I did, I would've arrived here with a fleet," Geary said. "Are you going to escort me to wherever I'm supposed to go?"

She glared at him before turning and walking off at a quick enough pace that he had to hurry after her. Geary watched her stiff back, wondering how well Tanya and her godmother got along.

Senator Nakamura halted before a massive door guarded by two Marines. The Marines wore sidearms, but otherwise weren't in battle readiness. The sight of them in dress uniforms was reassuring, a sign that no one thought the situation was dangerous enough for more extreme measures.

Inside he found himself facing not just the Grand Council seated along one side of a broad table, but also the rest of the Senate in rows of seats ranked behind them, all facing toward the long desk at which he was clearly supposed to sit. Senator Nakamura walked past the desk without any gesture to Geary, heading for a seat among the front row of senators not in the Grand Council. He stood beside one of the chairs at the desk, uncertain what to do.

Senator Navarro was back on the Grand Council, and apparently serving as its head once more. He nodded in welcome. "Thank you for coming, Admiral. Would you please take a seat?"

"Thank you, Senator," Geary said. He realized again that it wasn't easy to sit down with a lot of people watching without feeling awkward as he sat. The movement simply didn't lend itself to feeling graceful or smooth.

He couldn't be certain what the mood in the large hall was. The senators, used to keeping their feelings masked or only projected to serve a purpose, were watching him without clear signs of either hostility or welcome.

Were they on trial, or was he?

THREE

NAVARRO looked around at the other senators, made a face, and then focused on Geary again. "Admiral, I wish we were meeting under better circumstances. We're going to handle this first session informally, but it is on the record. Do you want to say anything before we begin asking you questions?"

Feeling emotionally drained from the walk to the building and his talk with Senator Nakamura, Geary shook his head. "All I have to say at this point is that I did my duty to fulfill my oath to the Alliance. The Defender fleet project, the artificial intelligence–controlled warships we destroyed in battles culminating in the fight at Unity Alternate, was kept secret from anyone who could've questioned the wisdom of placing so much firepower under the control of software. As a result of the Defender fleet running amok, attacking Alliance and neutral star systems as well as Syndicate Worlds star systems, hundreds of Alliance sailors died doing their duties to protect the Alliance, as well as uncounted numbers of innocent neutral citizens in star systems like Atalia. In some cases, our sailors died without any chance to protect themselves because the systems they relied on to support and defend them instead were corrupted as part of ill-considered programs kept secret from them. If we are to keep faith with those who died, the individuals responsible for those deaths, for violating the laws of the Alliance, should be held to account."

"You are lying to us!" Senator Wilkes shouted. "To us and to the people of the Alliance!"

Instead of shutting off Wilkes's outburst, Navarro looked at Geary.

Geary fought down an urge to yell back. His nerves were on edge facing the senators, trying not to let his anger at what had happened, at how many had died, color his words. Most of these men and women weren't his enemies, but the ones who were surely wanted him to lose control. "Everything I have said and done is backed up by physical evidence and the testimony of many other individuals. I don't think anyone has the right to question my honor."

"This is a conspiracy to undermine—!"

"Senator Wilkes!" Navarro said, his voice sharp enough to cut off the rest of Wilkes's statement. "You will abide by the rules of the Senate or you will be expelled from this session."

"You don't have the votes for that!"

"Would you like to find out if I do?"

Wilkes looked about, apparently didn't see the support he was hoping for, and subsided.

"Admiral," Navarro said, "in your own words, please briefly describe the events that led you to Unity Alternate, and what occurred there."

Recalling the events wasn't hard. He'd spent every day since going over them in his mind. Describing them all briefly, while avoiding inflammatory language, was a lot harder. Especially when he had to talk about the ships and sailors lost at Varandal and in the battle at Unity Alternate. But he made it through, then waited.

Senator Sakai was allowed to speak first, probably because he was believed to be impartial. "Admiral, am I correct that military sensors, communications, and other systems were breaking down at Varandal?

That as a result portions of the Alliance military were in danger of attacking other Alliance personnel?"

"That is correct," Geary said. "If not for individuals questioning what their sensors were showing them, questioning the validity of orders supposedly from their superiors, many more could have died. The destroyers *Mortar* and *Serpentine* were massacred at Varandal, with only seventeen survivors, as a result of false orders and the inability of their sensors to see the Defender fleet ships targeting them."

Another senator jumped to his feet—"These matters have not been established as fact"—only to be interrupted when yet another senator bolted out of her seat. "Most of the crew of *Mortar* came from my home world! The people of my world want someone to answer for their deaths at the hands of supposedly friendly forces!"

"I was not—!"

"And," the woman senator shouted, "my people will not accept punishment of minions who thought they were following proper orders! We want the heads of those who gave the orders! *And we will have them!*"

The Senate dissolved into a mass of loud arguments as Geary sat, watching them and trying not to let his feelings show. At least the chaos allowed him to judge how many senators were either trying to or willing to avoid accountability, how many more senators were ready to face them down, and how many looked like they simply wished they didn't have to make public stands on the matters.

It took more than ten minutes for Senator Navarro to regain order, until he finally employed sound-deadening systems to literally silence all of the arguing senators. "I will remind everyone present," Navarro said, his own voice unnaturally loud, "that this entire institution, the entire Senate, is on trial in the eyes of the people of the Alliance. It is our duty and our responsibility to handle this in a legally and morally defensible manner. If we do not, the Alliance may not survive, and all of the finger-pointing in the universe to try to lay the blame elsewhere will not alter the fact that *we* failed in our responsibility. Senator Sakai, do you wish to continue?"

"Not at this time," Sakai said, appearing totally unruffled by the tumult unleashed by his first question.

"Senator Dara?" Navarro said.

Dara stood up, her face lined with the history of old worries. "I do not understand something basic. The war with the Syndics is over. I was told military expenditures were being greatly cut back. Yet constructing the ships of the Defender fleet must have cost a great deal, and the facilities at Unity Alternate to support them were also large and expensive. Why was the Defender fleet built at such a time?"

Geary waited to see if anyone else would jump in with an answer, but once again everyone was looking at him. "I don't have full knowledge of the decisions made," he finally said. "From what I have been able to determine, certain elements in the government and the Alliance fleet were . . . concerned about the loyalty of the fleet's officers and sailors. Apparently it was believed that warships controlled by artificial intelligence would never pose a threat to the government, and could counter any threat from human-crewed warships. Judging from the meant-to-be-secret attack on the Syndicate Worlds Indras Star System by part of the Defender fleet, it was probably also believed that AI-controlled warships would never compromise any secrets they were aware of and could be used for missions that were meant to be kept from public knowledge."

"This is pure speculation," Senator Telontaskee objected.

Senator Navarro shook his head. "The evidence we've so far reviewed supports Admiral Geary's assessment. Not only he, but most of us here in the Senate, were regarded as unreliable by those who hid the Defender fleet program."

"What," Senator Dara demanded, "were the grounds for regarding Admiral Geary as unreliable? I am unaware of any actions he has taken against the government. Admiral, why did these people distrust you?"

Geary paused to think through his words. "I have a great deal of popular support," he said. "I would never misuse that, but some people fear that I will."

"Fear." Senator Dara almost spat the word. "Have we not spent enough time living in fear? Has fear become the way the Alliance thinks? That is not a question for you, Admiral, but one for my colleagues." She sat down.

Senator Suva gestured for attention. She gave Geary a look that held neither friendship nor hostility, just carefully presented neutrality. "Admiral Bloch was in command of what he called the Defender fleet?" Senator Suva asked.

"He said he'd been in command, but had lost control of the artificial intelligences on the ships," Geary said.

"Did Bloch say who'd placed him in that command?"

Geary shook his head. "I don't think he ever spoke of that during the brief time he was able to get messages out."

"Did you try to pursue that question?" Suva pressed. "Try to find out who had given him that much power and authority?"

"I'm sorry, Senator, no, I did not. It didn't matter at that point, because Bloch no longer had any power or authority over the black ships. I was focused on trying to defeat those ships and save my own. Bloch was . . . irrelevant, an impotent prisoner on his own supposed flagship."

"At one point he offered you a deal in exchange for a promise to rescue him?"

"Yes, Senator," Geary said. "No one, myself included, believed he could provide what he offered, and in any event we had no choice but to try to defeat all of the black ships of the Defender fleet by every means possible. No one suggested agreeing to his deal."

"What did Bloch say when you refused his offer?"

Geary once more shook his head. "We weren't able to tell him. We couldn't communicate with him after his own ship cut off his comms."

"For the record," Senator Suva said, "there is no record of any official assignment of Admiral Bloch to that command. It was done outside of official channels, and never approved by the full Senate. Does that surprise you, Admiral?"

Geary inhaled slowly before replying. "Not at this point, Senator."

A low murmur arose from the ranks of senators facing him, a murmur that threatened to grow louder until Senator Navarro turned and directed a meaningful glare around the chamber.

Navarro turned back to face Geary. "Admiral, preliminary analysis of the evidence brought from Unity Alternate shows a pattern of actions which avoided using normal channels and procedures in the Alliance government. Why did those responsible do that over and over again?"

Senator Sakai interrupted the renewed murmur that arose among the Senate on the heels of Navarro's question. "I must object to Senator Navarro's question. He is asking Admiral Geary to speculate as to the thinking of those responsible for these actions."

Navarro spread his hands. "I concede the error. Admiral, what were the practical results of avoiding using normal channels and procedures to authorize and supervise the actions you uncovered at Unity Alternate and elsewhere?"

Geary took a moment to frame his reply, trying to avoid anything that might sound like an accusation aimed at a specific individual. "The practical impact of avoiding normal channels and procedures was to hide those actions from the oversight and legal restrictions on what the government is allowed to do. Those people who oversee what the different parts of the government do were cut off from knowing what was going on."

"So, in your opinion, the problem wasn't in the oversight," Navarro said. "It wasn't in the rules and regulations governing how the Alliance works. It was in those people who decided that bypassing all of that would enable them to do things they knew would never be approved by those charged with ensuring the government worked properly."

Yet another murmur arose among the senators, punctuated by one of them calling out loudly, "Are you summing up the case for the prosecution, Senator Navarro? I thought at this point we were trying to determine what happened, not conduct a trial to convict anyone."

The chamber seemed on the verge of once more erupting into loud argument.

"My apologies for my unartful phrasing," Navarro said to disarm the tension, despite sounding not the least bit apologetic. "Senator Costa?"

Costa leaned forward, her glare at Geary apparently intended to convey determination. "Admiral, what would your attitude be toward those who, after you've achieved victory, question your actions in achieving those results?"

He shook his head. "Senator, I assume every action I take will be examined and questioned. I know some of my actions prior to this have been questioned by members of the government. If my actions are found to be improper, my reasoning incorrect, I fully expect to be held to account by those responsible for oversight. I have had a great deal of authority. I was taught that the greater the authority, the greater the need for oversight. That's what we were taught a century ago." The unspoken implication of his last sentence, that something important had been lost in the intervening century, hung between them as Senator Costa's glare deepened.

"Even if you consider such questions to be misinformed?" Costa demanded. "To be based on after-the-fact knowledge and assumptions? To be grossly unfair given the conditions under which you labored?"

Senator Unruh laughed. "Are you summing up your defense against charges that haven't yet been brought?"

"I want the admiral to answer the question!"

Geary tried to keep his voice and face neutral as he answered. "I repeat, I assume any actions I take will be examined and questioned. If I am not willing to defend those actions in open debate, then I will not take them. I am not above the law. No one in the Alliance is above the law. That means *everyone* must be willing to answer for their actions, openly and publicly, and if necessary be judged for their actions."

It went on like that, and on like that. Geary soon realized that the reason Navarro was running the proceedings was because no one else had wanted the job. Some senators, such as Wilkes and Costa, kept insisting that the evidence was fake or didn't even exist despite all proof to the contrary, including an exasperated Senator Navarro's offer to bring the disappeared who'd been confined at Unity Alternate to physically stand in the chamber. Other senators, outraged by the deaths of men and women from their home worlds, often seemed ready to exact vengeance then and there. A third group of senators seemed only intent on establishing that they'd personally been both unaware of what was going on and innocent of any wrongdoing themselves.

For her part, Senator Nakamura contributed little to the discussion, acting as if the debate were beneath her.

Eventually, how late in the day Geary couldn't even guess, Senator Sakai asked to speak once more. "Admiral, the material you brought from Unity Alternate indicates some serious breaches of trust by some members of this body—"

"That has not been established!" Wilkes cried.

"One more word from you," Navarro said, "and I will call the vote to expel you." He seemed to have a worse headache than Geary did at that point. "Please continue, Senator Sakai."

"Thank you," Sakai said. "Given these breaches of trust, why did you bring this evidence to us?"

Geary frowned, trying to sort out the possible answers. "Are you asking me why I trust the Alliance Senate to handle the matter?"

"Yes."

He inhaled deeply, thinking. "Because if the Alliance Senate cannot be trusted to deal with breaches of trust by some of its own members, then the Alliance is doomed. I have to trust you, Senator, and the other senators, to do what is right regardless of politics. If the Senate can't do that, the Alliance has already begun to fail. The sacrifices of our military, of all the families who have served the Alliance government in civilian positions, would be in vain. I'm not willing to concede such a thing. I think what we fought for, worked for, still matters enough to follow the rule of law. And I hope most of the Senate feels the same way."

Sakai nodded, deliberately drawing out the time between his next statement to let Geary's words resonate. "I was never informed of some of the programs this evidence reveals," Sakai finally said, his voice growing noticeably angry. The other senators, and Geary, listened with surprise, since Sakai rarely displayed strong emotions. "I am certain that the evidence will bear out my statement. Even though I am a senior member of the committee assigned oversight of Unity Alternate, I was never informed of the activity there. Instead, I was repeatedly assured that everything at Unity Alternate remained dormant and inactive. I was lied to. So were many other senators, and so were the people of the Alliance."

As Sakai paused to take a breath, Senator Costa leapt to her feet. "I will not be accused of—"

"I have not yielded the floor!" Sakai shouted before Navarro could act.

Costa, as shocked as the other senators, abruptly sat back down.

"We will be told that these actions were necessary, that these programs were for the good of the Alliance," Sakai continued. "But, if so, why did those who approved and oversaw these programs take such extreme measures to keep them secret? To keep all knowledge of them from not only the people of the Alliance but from their own comrades who have equal responsibilities for the welfare of our people and our worlds? To make certain that the watchdogs in the government who ensure our actions are legal and appropriate were kept in the dark? Because of this behavior, allegedly for the good of the people, many of our brave people died, others engaged in actions they thought had been legally authorized but had not, and the Alliance itself trembles on the brink of dissolving. I vow before everyone here that I will not rest, nor permit this Senate to rest, until justice has been done, no matter where that leads. And if those who elected me to this post disapprove and choose not to vote for me again, I will proudly step down, knowing I did not dishonor our ancestors by my words and actions."

The applause that followed from many of those present sounded sincere enough, but Geary was too tired to tell for certain.

"Admiral Geary," Senator Kim said. "You've been testifying all day as to fact. I want your opinion on something. Of everyone here, everyone in the Alliance, you are the only one who remembers life when the Alliance was not at war. Obviously, danger has not been eliminated from our galaxy. But danger also existed before the war began, and still that prewar Alliance focused on other matters. What do you believe those matters were? What did our ancestors want to accomplish that united them?"

It was a decent question. A more than decent one, causing Geary to think for a long moment before replying. "I remember a sense that we were still growing. That even though Alliance space was bumping up against regions already occupied, such as those controlled by the Syndicate Worlds, and gaps between stars that jump drives couldn't span, such as the great rift, there were still frontiers to explore. New things to learn, new things to accomplish. We were still learning how many things we had yet to learn, and eager to search for more answers."

"Are you saying the Alliance didn't see physical boundaries as insurmountable?"

"We thought we could do anything we turned our minds to," Geary said. "There was debate about where to allocate money and resources. There's always debate about that, and there should be, I believe. But I think it's fair to say that our gaze was turned to new challenges and new opportunities. We were united in believing the future could be better, and our efforts could make it better."

Senator Kim nodded. "Thank you, Admiral."

"I believe that is a good note to end on," Senator Navarro said. "It's been a very long day. All in favor of concluding this session? The motion passes. Thank you, Admiral."

The senators all began talking among themselves, while Geary sat, wondering what he was supposed to do now.

The answer came in the form of a staffer who walked up to Geary's seat and beckoned. Geary followed into a side room that contained a fairly fancy conference table, comfortable chairs around it, and large displays on the walls that showed nothing but generic scenes of Alliance member worlds.

He stood, waiting, for a couple of minutes, feeling tired and grouchy.

The door opened again and Senator Unruh entered. She gestured toward a seat. "Please sit down, Admiral. You must be tired after all of that."

Geary didn't move, eyeing Unruh closely. "Who am I talking to, Senator?"

"Do you mean who do I represent?" Unruh spread her hands. "From one perspective, the chosen representative of those determined to see this through, call to account those who abused their power and positions, and end the excesses in secrecy once excused by the war. From another perspective, I'm one of those who allowed it all to happen. Did we fail to ask the questions that we should have? Did we fail to insist on our rights as representatives of the people? We need to call ourselves to account as well, I think. The question is, what about you?"

He'd interacted with Unruh at other meetings before this, and Rione had vouched for her. Both of those things gave him reason to trust Unruh. "I thought I'd made it clear that I'd done what I had to do, and would now leave it up to the Senate."

Unruh quirked one eyebrow at him. "Surely you realize that as long as you're at Unity, many people will assume that you're directing all of the actions here. No matter what you say. And, as long as you're at Unity, the pressure will keep increasing on you to direct the actions here. Too many would willingly trade their freedoms for obedience to the whims of Black Jack."

He closed his eyes for a moment, wanting to shut out that reality. Opening them again, he fixed the senator with a grim look. "I've already, numerous times, withstood the temptation to do whatever I wanted because I could get away with it."

"Yes, you have." For a moment, Senator Unruh let her tiredness and sadness show. "But, if you were here, would you be able to refrain from acting? What if it seemed that some senators and other officials guilty of misconduct, guilty of ordering the actions that led to the deaths of some of those under your command, were about to wriggle free? If it looked like they were going to be able to avoid being held accountable due to legal niceties or political influence, would you try to prevent that?"

"Probably," Geary said. "I'd try to do something."

Unruh nodded, her eyes on him. "Keeping you here would not only create the wrong impressions, it would subject you to endless temptation to compromise your own beliefs. Am I wrong?"

"No," he said. "I don't expect to stay here, though. I'm subject to orders. I'm sure that Fleet Headquarters already has some orders ready for me."

"Oh, you can be sure of that!" Senator Unruh said. "But some of the names in the evidence from Unity Alternate are those of senior fleet officers."

"I've been told that some were under arrest."

"And more may follow as the evidence from Unity Alternate is analyzed. Their ambitions overrode any sense of loyalty to their oaths." Unruh sat down herself, rubbing her eyes. "There's been a lot of that. I can't imagine our ancestors are happy with us. Admiral, in light of . . . concerns regarding the fleet's senior officers, some of whom are already under arrest, a majority of the Senate believes that for now your orders should come directly from the Senate, to avoid any appearance of impropriety. To make it clear that you are doing what the government says." Unruh gazed at him, her expression growing somber. "What will you do?"

"Why are you asking me that?" Geary demanded. "I've already made it clear that I'll follow lawful orders."

"And you've made it clear that you'll resign your commission if you believe your orders are contrary to the principles of the Alliance," Senator Unruh said. "You do realize what would happen if you resigned your commission? Black Jack would be casting down the gauntlet, telling everyone that he disapproves of the government's actions. That shouldn't matter, that one officer disagrees with his orders. But you're Black Jack, you *are* the Alliance in the eyes of many, so if you resign your commission, the government will surely fall under pressure from the public. If that happens, I don't think the Alliance will rise again. We'll once more be a mass of squabbling independent star systems."

How should he answer that? He'd tried denying it after learning who the people of the Alliance thought he was, but he'd be a fool to keep pretending her words weren't true. "Senator, please give me orders that I can accept in good conscience."

She surprised him with a slight smile. "I hope we have just that. For now, return to the fleet base at Varandal Star System and oversee the repairs to your ships. There's an independent commission going over military expenditures, so you should start getting more of the funding you need, while money being wasted on projects like the Defender fleet and a new class of admirals' gigs will be devoted to better uses." Turning to one side, Unruh touched a panel to activate a starscape that appeared over the table, the tiny stars winking in the air between her and Geary. "After that . . . Admiral, when the Alliance was founded humans were flooding into space. We'd discovered the jump drive, and the galaxy was open to us. The future seemed to be limitless in every sense of the word."

He nodded, his eyes on the stars. "I wish we could remember that time. So much today seems to be about fear and drawing back, not hope and exploration of new things."

"Exactly." Senator Unruh pointed to one edge of the starscape. "Going beyond our previous limits. You've done that already, exploring through alien-controlled space. And as you pointed out, that once gave the people of the Alliance something to pull together for. We need to keep doing that. There are two missions the Senate wants you to undertake."

"The Senate?" Geary asked. "All of it?"

"Oh, the vote was far from unanimous," she said. "But there was a clear majority. Mission one is to make it easier to reach alien space. Our access to those regions of the galaxy is through Midway, and Midway is a long ways from the Alliance. Getting there requires crossing some very dangerous areas of space, and then using the Syndic hypernet, knowing the Syndics can block our access to it." She indicated those far-off stars again. "A team of scientists and engineers has developed what they think is a means to link the Syndicate Worlds hypernet gate at Midway to the Alliance hypernet, allowing us direct access to Midway."

"What? I thought it was impossible to change the characteristics of a gate once it has been activated."

"Science is about learning things once thought impossible, and engineering is about making the impossible work," Senator Unruh said. "They think that they can do this, and the Senate wants to see if they can."

Geary stared at the starscape, rubbing his chin as he thought. "Midway will have to agree, won't they?"

She nodded. "That's why you have to lead the expedition. Yes, a majority of the Senate wants to get you far away from Unity so you don't seem to be pulling our strings, but that's only part of our reason. If anyone can convince Midway to let Alliance engineers play around with their hypernet gate, it's you. I've seen the intelligence reports from former Syndicate star systems. They believe that Black Jack is 'for the people' and the only Alliance official they can trust. That's mission one. Mission two is that once you've delivered our team to Midway and gained Midway's agreement, we want you to reestablish connections with the Dancers." Senator Unruh paused. "What do you think of the Dancers, Admiral?"

He considered his words before replying. "I think they're willing to work with us, and they're willing to help us. They helped us fight against the Kicks, they helped us get back to Alliance space afterwards, helped defend Midway, and showed up to help defeat the Defender fleet."

"But why are they willing to do those things?"

"The Kicks are a common enemy, but beyond that I'm not sure," Geary admitted. "No one is."

"Exactly." Senator Unruh nodded toward the display of tiny stars. "We want you to escort a ship to Dancer space, a large passenger ship modified to act as a long-term research and diplomatic vessel. It'll carry scientists and representatives of the government to act as an Alliance embassy to the Dancers."

"Will the Dancers accept that?" Geary asked.

"The only way to find out is to try it and see how they respond. The embassy ship will be unarmed except for close-in defenses. It will carry only a small honor guard, not a full military unit." She bit her lip, eyeing the stars as if they were pieces in an immensely difficult game. "The Dancers seem to know a great deal about us. We need to know a lot more about them." Her eyes went back to Geary. "Are your orders acceptable, Admiral?"

The question startled him. Thinking of the tasks ahead, he'd mentally gone far beyond the initial talk of his intentions. "Of course, Senator. Since you ask my opinion, I think both actions are important to at least attempt."

"Good." She smiled again, though her eyes remained serious as she watched him. "I assume protocol requires you to visit Fleet Headquarters. You can do that tomorrow and inform them of your orders from the Senate."

"I won't be asked to testify again tomorrow?"

"The evidence you brought speaks for itself." Unruh sat back, looking tired. "Today was about everyone staking out public positions. Having you there forced every senator to make their own stand clear. But we don't want this process to become about you. As long as you sit in front of the Senate, it looks like you're judging us. I assume that you want that as little as we do. No, you're, um, 'free' tomorrow to deal with military matters."

"Senator," Geary began, reluctant to bring up a question that could easily be seen as insubordinate, "Fleet Headquarters undoubtedly already has other orders for me, and for the ships currently under my command."

She shook her head. "You are being tasked directly by the Senate. Your orders come from the Senate."

"What about the ships under my command, and the people on those ships?"

"The same," Unruh said. "Until our investigation of all of the material you brought from Unity Alternate is complete, you and those under you answer directly to the Senate. We'll try to give you what you need for the missions we've assigned you. If you don't get it, we want to know."

"Thank you, Senator," Geary said, feeling a little dizzy and realizing he hadn't eaten for a long time. "I'm not sure what time of day it is here."

"About nine in the evening."

It had indeed been a long day. "I don't think Fleet Headquarters will be expecting me to show up right now."

"That's why I said you can go there tomorrow. Get some sleep," Senator Unruh said. "There are apartments in this building for visiting specialists and dignitaries. Comfortable and safe. I'll have someone show you to one. You can order a meal from the cafeteria. It's open all day because this is far from the first time our work continued into odd hours. Have you been told that a trusted investigative group is being established to go over the evidence and hear testimony from those aboard the other ship with you?"

"*Mistral*?"

"Yes. We can work out procedures for that. We don't want anything to happen to what's aboard that ship."

Geary held up a hand as Unruh started to leave. "Can I speak with my flagship?"

"Certainly. There'll be a comm unit in your room. Of course, all conversations on official comm units are monitored and recorded."

Unruh moved to leave, then paused again. "Admiral . . . I meant what I said. We failed in our duties. People died as a result. Most of us are resolved to ensure that we don't fail again. Please trust us."

HIS room turned out to be comfortable but not luxurious. It would've severely disappointed those who enjoyed complaining about spoiled government officials living high on the backs of Alliance taxpayers. Similarly, the meal he ordered from the Senate cafeteria was good, but hardly gourmet. Exhausted, Geary spent little time awake once he'd finished eating, falling asleep quickly after communicating with Tanya to ensure she knew what was happening. As tired as he was, he made sure to tell her about the Senate's orders overriding any orders from Fleet Headquarters.

Early the next morning, General Carabali showed up again, this time to escort him to Fleet Headquarters. As the armored limousine covered the distance from the government building, Geary noticed the crowds on the streets appeared to be those normal for a city going about its business. "Nothing blew up?" he asked Carabali.

"No, Admiral, nothing blew up." Carabali glanced from the views of the streets to him and back again. "What you said seemed to do the trick as far as a big chunk of the public is concerned. That and your standing firm like a rock when that drone tried to take you out."

"I was going to dodge," Geary protested.

"But you didn't look like it." General Carabali grinned. "It's not often a fleet officer impresses Marines."

"At least some good came of it. Did they find out who sent that drone at me?"

Carabali's smile vanished as she shook her head. "The latest report this morning said they still couldn't find any clues to exactly who tried to kill you. It was a very sophisticated effort, though. All the latest countermeasures and equipment on it."

Geary felt like he had tasted something sour. "Isn't that a clue? Who has access to that sort of thing?"

"Not that many people who could squirrel it away without being caught. All of those people are being checked out," Carabali said. "If one of them was involved, I'm assured it will be found out. Have you been watching media?"

Everyone asked him that. "No. Should I be?"

General Carabali gestured in annoyance. "Faked vids of you are showing up by the thousands, and being shut down as fast as they appear. Everything from you supposedly declaring that you're taking over the government to supposedly showing you running in panic from the local version of a rabbit instead of standing waiting for that drone attack. As far as authentic vids, it's mostly your declaration to the press yesterday, segments of your testimony at the Senate afterwards, and segments of what various senators said, all of it heavily slanted toward different audiences." She paused. "You're expected to show up at Fleet Headquarters. No one knows the time, but the place is obvious. Anyone aiming for another shot at you will probably try there."

"But we're prepared for that," Geary said.

"Hopefully. We were prepared yesterday," Carabali said. "You understand, Admiral, that when engaged in personal combat, displays of courage have their place, but as a rule it's still wise to dodge or fall flat or otherwise seek cover."

"But . . ." Geary frowned, realizing that seeking cover hadn't even occurred to him.

Realizing that when the drone came at him he'd split-second analyzed the entire situation in the same way he would've a battle in space, using the same assumptions and preconceptions, even though he was in a totally different environment.

"Admiral?" Carabali was watching him closely. "Is anything wrong? I mean, anything *else* wrong?"

"I was just realizing how very much out of my element I am," Geary said. What did he need to know to protect himself here? "Know your enemy" was one of the first rules. "Do we know what the motives are of people who want to kill me?"

Carabali shrugged. "There are a number of motives, Admiral. Some people want the biggest possible distraction, as I said yesterday. Some want to kill you to ensure you don't become a dictator. Other people want you dead so they can hopefully themselves become dictators in the ensuing chaos. One cult, thankfully a very small one, altered the prophecy about Black Jack a bit to include saying his return would herald the end of the universe. So now that you're back they want to kill you so the prophecy will be complete."

He stared at General Carabali. "Why would they want the universe to end?"

"Something about 'we'll all bask in the light of the living stars after that,'" Carabali said, herself looking puzzled. "Everyone's supposed to end up there eventually after we die, so I don't know what their particular rush is. That's not the strangest quasi-religious cult after you, by the way."

"It's not?" Geary weighed whether to ask the next question, deciding he needed to know the answer. "What's stranger?"

Carabali made a face. "Oh, there's one cult that believes you weren't sent back from the dead, but rather *escaped*. They think the only right thing to do is send you back as soon as possible so the living stars won't be offended."

Geary sat back, wondering why he felt an urge to laugh. "You know, we've had a lot of trouble understanding aliens like the enigmas, and even friendly enemies like the Dancers. But I don't envy any aliens trying to make sense of humans. I don't know how I could explain the ways some people think."

"You know the old saying about the difference between friends and family," Carabali said. "You get to choose your friends. Whereas we're forced to claim kinship with every Homo sapiens in the galaxy."

Geary forgot what he was going to say next as a massive structure came into view, extending a long ways to either side and far enough back that he couldn't be sure where it ended. Multiple stories soared into the air, and he knew important facilities would be buried in more stories extending underground. "That's Fleet Headquarters?"

"That's Fleet Headquarters."

"It's . . . huge." Geary tried judging the size of the building again. "How many people are assigned to Fleet Headquarters?"

"I doubt that anyone could tell you," Carabali said. "There are people assigned to different offices and commands and bureaus. You know how headquarters staffs are. Black holes that just keep sucking in more and more resources as staffs keep expanding in an endless game of mine-is-bigger-than-yours by senior officers. Staffs for frontline commanders shrank during the war, but I think Fleet Headquarters expanded every year of it."

"Great." Coming into view were scores of Marines in dress uniforms but carrying weapons. They formed two lines from the road leading into the headquarters complex. "That's a lot of Marines. Is it a full company?"

"A reinforced company," Carabali said. "It's officially just an honor guard, but I managed to convince the necessary people that a proper Marine honor guard needed to be heavily armed." She gestured around them. "There are a lot of buildings looking down on this area. A lot of potential firing positions. I wanted the Marines to be in full battle armor but was told that would look too much as if you were coming to take over. To be honest, I wanted you in battle armor as well to help protect you. If anyone is going to make another try at you soon, it'll be here."

Beyond the Marines, Geary could see groups of people scattered along the street and sidewalks. Their clothing all had a hard-to-explain similarity that somehow broadcast security agent. Maybe it was the dark glasses they all wore, or the way they were all loitering and at the same time paying a great deal of attention to their surroundings. Parked here and there were apparently civilian vehicles that were carefully positioned to cover the entire street and the visible airspace over it. Higher up, a half-dozen police air cruisers were doing slow figure eights, and even higher beyond them were the unmistakable shapes of aerospace fighters hovering on overwatch.

It all should've been a reassuring sight, except for the disturbing fact that a lot of people were clearly certain that this level of security was needed to protect him. It wasn't the sort of spectacle he had ever imagined at Unity, or anywhere else in the Alliance.

Carabali was one of the few people Geary felt comfortable sharing his thoughts with. "One of the reasons I haven't visited many places in the Alliance," he said in a low voice, "is because I was afraid I'd see more signs of how things had changed in the last century. As long as I didn't actually go back to anywhere, I could pretend in the back of my mind that nothing important had changed."

"A lot of people tried to hold on to who we were," Carabali said. "Admiral, if I may be frank, please don't repeat your disappointment where others can hear. Too many would see it as criticism of who we've become."

"I didn't mean it to sound like disappointment in you or anyone else alive now," Geary said, already unhappy he'd spoken so candidly. "But I understand how it could be seen that way. Really, it's just . . . how much time I lost. Even if today were some utopian vision, I'd still be comparing it to the places I knew a century ago and missing what used to be."

"I see," Carabali said, mollified. "I can understand that. You know how it is for the military. We go away for years, and when we come back to our homes things have always changed. You've had to live with a much more extreme version of that." She gazed around carefully as the limo finally came to a halt. "Are you ready, Admiral?"

"Sure." He looked at all of the security again, wondering if anyone would actually try anything. But there had been that drone yesterday, so somebody already had.

Carabali opened the door and went out first, positioning herself to shield Geary as he got out. The waiting Marines had extended their lines slightly to meet the side of the limo, so unbroken ranks extended all of the way from the vehicle to the headquarters entry door.

As Geary straightened, his eyes by habit went over the nearest Marines, noting not just that their dress uniforms were immaculate but also that the hand weapons they were presenting in his honor were either charged if energy weapons or showing fully loaded magazines if solid-shot weapons.

He began walking along the roughly three-meter-wide aisle between the ranks of Marines, General Carabali staying by his side.

By the time he reached the halfway point to the door, he was feeling foolish that all of this security had been laid on for nothing.

There was no sound of a shot. He felt the wind of a solid round passing so close above his forehead from above and behind that it clipped a couple of stray hairs, followed by the whack of the bullet hitting the pavement ahead of him.

General Carabali staggered as another shot aimed at Geary hit her.

Men and women were shouting, the neat ranks of the Marines dissolving as they rushed to protect him and engage whoever was shooting.

This was nothing like an engagement between ships in space. In the next instant, Geary felt a line of fire clip one shoulder as a particle burst lanced across his skin, leaving a black streak in its wake. More than one person must be shooting at him. But where had that shot come from? He needed to know where it came from to know which way to dodge. Geary turned, searching, feeling as if the world had sped up around him and he was moving far too slowly.

FOUR

"GET down, you fool!" Instead of a bullet or energy burst, a body struck Geary, knocking him to the ground. He hit the pavement hard, followed by the weight of someone dropping on top of him, slamming into his back and forcing his body and head down onto the hard surface again.

He started to struggle, then caught sight of one arm of whoever had a firm position on his back. They were a Marine, and they were lying on him to physically shield him.

Another energy bolt scored the pavement about a meter from his face, followed by the rapid rattle of a short slug weapon burst shattering pieces of pavement just off to his left.

His view, on the pavement with someone heavy lying on him, was very restricted, but he saw more Marines appear close by, crouching or kneeling, using their own bodies to block any more shots from getting through to him.

He saw one Marine, bearing a long weapon Geary recognized as a sniper rifle, aiming carefully and firing. None of the other Marines around were shooting, though all had their weapons up and were searching for targets. He'd have to commend them for their excellent weapons discipline, Geary told himself, aware of how incongruous his thoughts were at this instant. In the distance, he heard more bangs, some cries of distress or pain, and the roar of police air cruisers zooming close to form a tight ring above the Marines around Geary.

A louder roar, and sudden shadow, told of one of the aerospace fighters dropping down to sit above the police cruisers. Twisting his head, Geary could make out the manta shape of the fighter slowly rotating as its sensors scanned the nearby buildings for any more shooters.

"Get him inside!" a woman shouted. Not Carabali. How badly had the general been hurt?

The weight on his back lifted, arms grabbed his arms, and Geary found himself being half carried and half running to a waiting door at headquarters, where more Marines crouched with their weapons aiming outward.

He felt helpless. And stupid. And, if he was honest, scared. This wasn't the sort of battle he knew how to fight. He'd used the command and control circuits to have virtual views from Marines engaging in combat, but that hadn't been the same. Not even close.

His escort finally came to a halt well inside the door, still holding on to his arms. "Were you hit, sir?" a Marine asked him, medical corpsman insignia on his collar.

"Just my shoulder," Geary said.

"Are you sure?" The corpsman went over him carefully, looking for other injuries, before telling the other Marines they could let go of Geary's arms. "Sometimes, in a fight, people don't notice they got hit, sir."

"No problem," Geary said as the corpsman carefully treated the shallow slash on his shoulder. "You're doing your job. Have I mentioned how much I like having Marines around when things get rough?" he added, getting grins from the nearest ones.

A major stepped forward, saluting. "The area has been secured, Admiral. Two known shooters dead. Local security and police are pursuing some other suspects."

A major. There should be someone else here. "Where's General Carabali?"

"Being loaded into an ambulance, Admiral. She took a round in the upper body that could've killed her but she got lucky. Now that she's in an emergency med pod the general should be out of danger."

"I want updates on her status," Geary said, straightening his uniform and trying to calm his pounding heart. "Your Marines did excellent work, Major."

"Thank you, Admiral. Captain Holmes wishes to speak with you."

"Captain Holmes?"

A Marine captain with a badly mussed-up dress uniform stepped forward and saluted. "I wish to apologize for using intemperate and inappropriate language toward the admiral."

Geary returned the salute, trying to remember any inappropriate language. "Are you the one who called me a fool?"

"Yes, sir," Holmes said, his expression impassive.

"And knocked me down and covered me with your own body to protect me?"

"Yes, sir."

Geary extended his hand. "Thank you. Your actions were in the highest traditions of your service."

Holmes glanced doubtfully at the hand, then took it.

"As for your words," Geary said, seeing a trace of alarm enter Holmes's eyes, "I've never known any admiral who didn't need to be called a fool at least once. And I've never met any admiral who didn't need people around willing to call them a fool when they deserved it. So, no worries on that count, Captain. But be careful about making a habit of calling your superiors fools."

Holmes's face split into a grin. "Thank you, sir. I won't make a habit of it, sir."

As the Marines reformed and headquarters security staff ran about in belated reaction to the attacks on him, Geary stood, feeling awkward and useless. He couldn't just walk off when he had no idea how headquarters was laid out.

A fleet captain hastened up, his eyes searching Geary as to assure himself that all was well. He saluted. "Good morning, Admiral. I'm Captain Romano. I've been assigned as your escort inside headquarters."

"Good morning, Captain." What else to say? How many people were listening and watching? This was one of those moments when he had to be Black Jack, projecting calm and confidence no matter how he really felt. "I've had better mornings, though."

"Uh . . . yes, sir." Captain Romano hesitated. "Are you prepared to go through with the scheduled meeting?"

"I've gotten a clean bill of health from a corpsman," Geary said, wishing he could sit down somewhere. He noticed the frantic security activity diminishing, glad that the mess was winding down.

The Marine major was back. "Admiral, I have a squad standing by to accompany you through headquarters."

He thought about the symbolism of that, and didn't like it. "That's all right, Major. Captain Romano, am I right in assuming there shouldn't be any danger inside this building?"

"It's a very large building, Admiral," Romano said. "But, no, there shouldn't be any danger. Everything and everyone going in and out is screened."

"I know I'm in no danger from the fleet or anyone working with it," Geary said. Had he managed to sound sincere enough? Because he knew how rattled he still was inside. But he couldn't let that show, because it might create the impression he didn't trust Alliance sailors or officers or civilians employed by the fleet. And there was no telling how many people were at this moment listening to every word he said. "Major, I'll be back here when my meetings are complete. Please commend all of your Marines on my behalf, and let them stand down when the situation permits." His experience might be poorly suited to being shot at by assassins, but it did give him the right words to say without having to think too much about them.

"Yes, sir," the major said, saluting again.

Geary noticed an odd sort of bubble around him. As the major went back to her Marines, only Captain Romano was close by. Everyone else was keeping their distance. "Why were you selected for the honor of being my escort?" Geary asked.

The question brought a small twist of Romano's lips that barely formed a smile. "I volunteered, Admiral. I don't know if Admiral Timbale ever mentioned me to you, but we've been close friends since serving together on a cruiser as junior officers. He's filled me in on what's happened at Varandal."

"Admiral Timbale is a fine officer," Geary said, trying to get some measure of Romano. "What's waiting for me in here, Captain?"

Romano hesitated, looking into the building. "Smiling faces, Admiral."

"I see." Everyone knew that expression. *Don't trust smiling faces.* It hadn't changed in a century. "Does headquarters know about my orders from the Senate?"

"I don't know if they officially know. But we've heard." Romano gave Geary a look from the corners of his eyes. "And they're trying to see what they can slip past those orders. I'm not supposed to know there's a shuttle on the way to your flagship with a new commanding officer aboard."

He should've expected that. "They want to relieve Captain Tanya Desjani? On what grounds?"

"Routine rotation of a commanding officer." Romano nodded toward the inner portions of the building. "Desjani's new assignment is to be at Fleet Headquarters."

"That's an interesting way of taking a hostage for my good behavior," Geary said. "But the new commanding officer is going to be disappointed. The Senate gave me authority over all personnel currently assigned to me."

"Headquarters knows that. They wanted to try to relieve her before she got word of your orders. Desjani already knows?"

Geary nodded. "She already knows. So does the commanding officer of *Mistral*. All right, Captain. Let's get this over with."

Romano hesitated. "Are you certain that you don't want to sit down for a while? It looked pretty wild out there."

"It wasn't anything I'd look forward to doing again." Geary leaned closer to Romano. "Captain, this is one of the times I don't get the luxury of being human. I have to be who these sailors need to see."

"I understand, sir." Romano smiled. "If you'll accompany me, then."

He led Geary toward the security stations controlling access to the inside of headquarters. Studying the many security personnel and the fortified security stations, Geary thought it seemed adequate to stand off an assault by at least a few hundred Syndicate Worlds special forces Vipers. But nothing like that kind of threat should have posed a danger on Unity. "This is quite a setup," he said to Romano as the captain led him through one of the security stations.

Romano cast an impassive glance around them. "No one wanted to be accused of failing to provide enough security for headquarters, so the security force and facilities just kept getting bigger and heavier as they kept worrying about bigger and bigger threats."

"It wouldn't have done much good if the Syndics had gotten to Unity," Geary said. "They just would've dropped rocks from orbit until this place was a crater."

"But we would've looked really secure right up until then," Romano said.

Geary decided he liked Captain Romano.

As they cleared the internal security barriers and entered headquarters, Geary was astounded to see the hallways and break rooms filled with personnel standing around or sitting, apparently doing nothing except talking about the recent excitement outside. The lack of activity didn't look like a reaction to the assault against him. Not that he wanted a fuss made of it, but it still felt odd. No one seemed nervous or worried, even those discussing the shooting, instead having the bearing of men and women who'd already spent time bored this early in the day. "What's going on? I know the fleet jokes about headquarters not actually doing any work, but . . ."

"You didn't hear?" Romano pointed down the hall. "It's been like this for a few days. No one can work. Everyone has been locked out of their systems and in most cases their work areas while special investigative teams go through everything looking for hidden files or information about government and fleet activities that weren't supposed to exist. They'll also root out malware and all of the other junk that gets uploaded, of course, but I understand mainly they're looking for anything pertaining to very highly classified programs."

"I know we had to have outside investigators come in to root out inside problems," Geary said. "But having everyone report for duty and stand around all day seems to have no purpose."

Romano nodded. "Those are our orders. Just in case someone is needed, they have to be here, even if all they end up doing is keeping a chair warm."

That shouldn't have been surprising, Geary thought. Mandatory things that had no purpose were pretty much a tradition in the fleet and the military as a whole. So was standing around waiting and doing nothing just in case someone should suddenly be needed.

He watched the sailors and officers they passed jerk with surprise when they saw his face, coming to attention with excited or awed expressions. He'd forgotten how hard it was to see people react like that to him, because those reactions reflected how much they expected of him.

Two people were arguing to one side of the hallway ahead, next to a firmly closed door. "There are people waiting on that paperwork!" an officer was saying. "For pay and medical benefits! How long—?"

"As long as it takes," the other person replied. She had the slightly distracted, slightly annoyed manner of a programmer having to interact with a difficult human being. "It's not my call."

The officer, frustrated, spotted Geary and took note of his rank insignia. "Admiral! Can you—?" His eyes widened in recognition and his voice cut off abruptly.

"I'm sorry," Geary said. "I'm sure you're working as fast as you can, right?" he said to the coder.

"Yes. Of course."

This seemed a good chance to address one of Desjani's concerns. "Are you also screening for enigma malware?" The enigmas, an alien race so named because they diligently worked to avoid letting any other species learn anything about them, had been spying on most of humanity long before most of humanity had realized the enigmas existed.

"Are you in coding?" she asked, startled. "How did you know about that malware?"

"One of my officers found it."

"One of your . . . ?" The coder looked at him more closely, then did an exaggerated double take that seemed totally real. "Oh. You're . . . that's you. Okay. Um . . . the existence of that malware is highly classified. Compartmented."

That shouldn't have been a surprise. But it still was. "How are people supposed to know what problems to look for if they aren't told that malware exists? Never mind. I know you didn't make the decision. But you can tell me if you're screening for it. Since I know all about it."

"Right." She gestured at the door behind her. "Yes, we are. We're using an upgraded version of the program developed by, um . . ."

"Captain Jaylen Cresida," Geary said, feeling a pang of loss as he said her name.

"Yes!" The woman gazed upward as if she could see through the intervening floors and into space. "Is she here? Did you bring her on your ship? I'd love to talk shop with her."

"I'm afraid that's impossible," Geary said. "Captain Cresida died soon after developing that program. Her ship was destroyed with all hands in combat."

"Oh." The woman's face fell. "What a waste." Her expression shifted to worry. "I'm sorry. That was impolite. I shouldn't—"

"No," he said. "It's all right, because you're right. It was an awful waste. Every person who dies in a war is a waste, because we'll never know what they might have done with their lives." He gestured to Romano to lead the way onward, feeling depressed and lonely despite the crowded hallway.

The emotions seemed to be reflected back at him from the sailors he passed. They were worried, unhappy, uncertain. His presence made them perk up, but outside that bubble of hope, gloom reigned in Fleet Headquarters.

They reached a bank of elevators, polished brass gleaming and the crowd before them parting to make room for Admiral Geary. Inside, one of the elevators was lined with expensive-looking wood and more brass. They got off on the highest floor, where Marines in full dress uniforms stood sentry. Highly polished floors reflected art lining the walls, every picture that of a spacecraft or ancient ships that sailed on water.

Captain Romano led him to a large door, which led to an anteroom where an aide waved them on, which led to an outer office where officers and sailors sitting with nothing to do in front of dead displays jumped to their feet as Geary entered. On the other side of that office, Romano opened another large door and gestured for Geary to enter while he remained outside.

Two admirals were waiting and came to their feet as Geary entered. One a man, the other a woman, both were smiling, bringing to mind Captain Romano's warning. This office was big and nicely appointed, with leather chairs and displays on the walls set to show the outside as if they were large windows. Oddly, though, instead of a single desk for the commander of Fleet Headquarters, there were two desks of equal size set on opposite sides of the room, the other furniture having been somewhat awkwardly shoved into a different configuration to accommodate the extra desk. The two admirals had been seated in chairs near the center of the room, their chairs facing a third, vacant chair.

"Geary! I'm Baxter!" one of the admirals said, extending a hand.

Geary shook it, then took the extended hand of the second admiral. "Rojo," she said by way of introduction.

"Have a seat!" Admiral Baxter said, gesturing broadly toward the third chair and still smiling as if this were a social call among old friends. "I heard you got nicked during that mess out front."

"It's nothing," Geary said, indicating the spot the corpsman had covered with wound tape. "Thanks to the Marines."

Admiral Rojo snorted. "If only the Marines were as good at behaving off the battlefield as on the battlefield. The liberty incidents we've had to deal with!"

"I've had experience with Marines on liberty," Geary said. "It's always an interesting time. But at the moment I'm particularly glad to have them around." He sat in the indicated chair, wondering which beast from which world settled by humanity had provided the leather covering it. Then, recalling some of the things he'd heard about Syndic practices, he wondered if this chair had concealed devices in it for monitoring whether he was telling the truth.

"Sad times," Admiral Rojo said, sitting down as well, her eyes sharp in contrast to her own smile. That smile slipped a bit as she studied him. "A senior fleet officer not safe on the streets of Unity. And a senior fleet officer causing considerable trouble for the fleet."

Geary kept his expression neutral. "I did my duty."

"You're not one to cross when it comes to duty, are you?" Admiral Baxter said, sitting down with careful precision. "Speaking of which, you'll probably be interested to hear that Captain Numos has finally been court-martialed."

So much had happened since he'd had Numos arrested that it almost seemed like something from another life. "What was the result?"

"Guilty, of course. Sentenced to death." Baxter kept smiling, his eyes on Geary. "As the officer who brought charges, you have the right to approve that penalty or demand the alternative."

That hadn't been something he was prepared to deal with. Which was probably why Baxter had brought it up, Geary realized. To throw him off balance. But it was a question he'd have to address. Did he want Numos dead? As bad as Numos had been? It was one thing to give orders that would kill someone in the heat of battle, but to do it in cold blood? "What are the alternatives?" Geary asked.

"Alternative," Admiral Rojo said. "There's only one. Dismissal from the service with loss of all benefits. We've had a lot of bad cases to deal with in a hundred years of war. Limiting options allowed the cases to be dealt with a lot quicker."

"How long do I have to decide?"

"We need your decision before you leave this star system."

"Not that you have to leave," Admiral Baxter said, his smile still firmly in place. "You've been through a lot. You deserve a rest. And we need someone to tackle the job of reorganizing the fleet and our entire training system. It's the sort of thing only you could do right." It was a clear attempt to consign Geary to a place in the depths of headquarters bureaucracy where he commanded nothing and could take no independent action, but Baxter made the offer sound like the sort of thing any officer would jump at.

Geary shook his head. "I'm sorry. I already have other orders. As you've probably heard."

"Oh?" Baxter looked at Rojo. "Did we receive orders?"

"We're locked out of all of our systems," Rojo said. "We can't officially receive anything."

"Well, damn! Geary, you know how it works. Until we officially receive any orders to the contrary, you're subject to our orders." Admiral Baxter actually managed to sound regretful as he said it. "And we really need you in that reorganization assignment."

Having prepared for any possibility, including that his orders might get "lost" at headquarters for an extended period, Geary held out his comm pad. "Here. There's a copy of my orders, authenticated as coming directly from the Senate. I was assured this meets all requirements for official transmission of the orders."

Admiral Baxter and Admiral Rojo didn't say anything as they read the order. "This is a bad precedent," Rojo finally said. "An officer going outside the chain of command like this."

"It wasn't my idea or initiative," Geary said.

"But it looks bad," Baxter said. "It's just not done, you know? That's not how the fleet operates."

"I had understood," Geary said, "based on existing records and his own statements, that command of the fleet that I inherited had previously been gained by an admiral going directly to the Senate Grand Council."

That floored both of the other admirals for a long moment. Rojo recovered first. "That was an exception. A nearly disastrous exception."

"Admiral Otropa also had a lot of political connections that he used to gain command," Geary said. "I could cite more. However, the important thing is that these orders exist, they take precedence over any orders from you, and you have officially received those orders. We should move on."

"We have responsibilities, too," Baxter said, still smiling.

Geary looked toward one of the fake windows, seeing a view over the city, white clouds on blue sky. It felt odd after so long seeing only space on outside displays, or the formless gray of jump space, or the nothing of hypernet travel. "Look, I've got these orders. I accepted them. This is an important assignment. It's the sort of thing the fleet used to do, before the war with the Syndicate Worlds. Since you two are here I'm assuming neither of you was involved in the Defender fleet mess. So why don't we play straight with each other? I don't want to run roughshod over you. But I have a job to do."

Baxter and Rojo looked at him as if considering their words. Finally, Admiral Baxter leaned forward a bit, his smile barely visible now. "Tell me something. Why aren't you sitting in this office? Why didn't you take over everything?"

"I have no desire to take over everything," Geary said, trying not to look aggravated. "I'm trying to do my job. The Senate obviously thinks that you can do the job of cleaning up problems here."

"You're not up to this job?" Rojo asked, her own smile completely vanished.

"Frankly," Geary said, "no, I'm not. I don't know enough people here, I don't know their histories, I wasn't part of the fleet for a long time. I'm still learning what that means. The incident outside reminded me forcefully that my skills and my experience are limited to certain areas. I can command a combat force in space. But cleaning up head-quarters requires different talents. I'm sure the Senate knows that better than I do. That's why you're in this office, not me." He'd been trying to figure out which one was in charge and which the second in command, but Rojo and Baxter kept giving conflicting clues to their relative status.

"Leaving you with command of most of the fleet's remaining fire-power, and now control of budgeting for your missions. The Senate aren't the only ones worried about how much potential power you have," Admiral Rojo said. "Believe it or not, I want the Alliance to survive."

"I believe it," Geary said. "Why won't you believe me?"

Baxter answered. "We don't have a lot of positive experiences with people who can do anything they want to."

"Have I abused my power yet?"

"From the perspective of Fleet Headquarters?" Admiral Baxter asked. "Hell, yes, you have. You're not just a loose cannon. You're a loose supernova."

"You've undermined Fleet Headquarters repeatedly," Admiral Rojo added.

"If we're being blunt," Geary said, trying not to get angry, "Fleet Headquarters has repeatedly tried to sabotage me by withdrawing ships, taking skilled personnel, and withholding necessary funding. I'm well aware that there was a faction here which didn't want me or my fleet returning from our exploration mission far beyond human-occupied space."

"Those are pretty serious charges," Rojo said.

"I can document them." He and Rojo held each other's eyes, daring the other to look away.

"Hold on," Admiral Baxter said, waving both hands and leaning back. "This won't get us anywhere. Cards on the table, Geary, we're going to try to rein you in. Not for our own personal advancement, but because you've got too much power. Even if you never use that power in negative ways, it still sets a very bad precedent."

"We?" Geary looked from Baxter to Rojo. "Which of you two is in charge?"

"Both of us," Rojo said. "Co-command."

"Because," Admiral Baxter said, "as you'd know if you'd been around the fleet for the last few decades instead of frozen in survival sleep, we hate each other. Have ever since we were ensigns. So the Senate decided we should command jointly, reasoning that if one of us tried to do something even remotely wrong, the other would happily turn them in."

"Which really wasn't bad thinking," Admiral Rojo conceded. "Neither one of us will let the other get away with anything that isn't by the book."

Surprised, Geary took a moment to respond. "I guess that supports my evaluation that I don't know enough about current leadership to clean up this place."

"Maybe it does," Rojo said. "I'd love to bust you, but I'd also love to bust this guy," she added, pointing at Baxter.

"Likewise," Baxter said, smiling at Rojo in a way that was now blatantly insincere. "One thing we agreed on was trying to neutralize you, but you've already outflanked us. We have to publicly support you, because you're that guy. Black Jack. But we'll be doing everything we can behind the scenes to limit your power and restrict your actions. Because we both believe it's not in the best interests of the Alliance for one officer to have as much influence as you do." His smile at Geary this time was oddly genuine.

"I'm not comfortable with the situation myself," Geary said. "I'll support your efforts to get headquarters cleaned up, and for making sure those who've been violating laws and regulations under cover of secrecy get called to account. But I'll also be doing everything I can do to carry out my orders from the Senate. Because that's my responsibility as an officer of the Alliance. And if either of you do anything to hinder that effort, including any measures that will harm the readiness and crews of my ships, or endanger my assigned mission, I will ensure that becomes known."

Rojo's smile had returned. "I have a vision of us offering aid to each other with one hand while holding a gun to each other's head with our other hand."

"As long as we understand each other," Geary said. "I'm curious how you're going to make co-command work if you both hate each other, though."

"You don't think we're professional enough?" Rojo asked, baring her teeth. "It's simple. If necessary things don't get done, we both get fired. If things go well, one of us gets promoted to being the only fleet commander. But we don't know which one."

Admiral Baxter nodded. "The Senate has informed us that the choice would be deliberately random to prevent us jockeying for credit for whatever goes right. So if we prevent the other from getting things done, no matter how we try to blame them, we get fired, too. But if we get things done, one of us might end up being the sole commander, and the other will be left in the dust."

"The only way to win is not to screw with each other," Rojo said, "and actually get the job done."

"They're not worried about a mutual suicide?" Geary said. "Where you each sacrifice yourself to take down the other as well?"

"Admiral Rojo isn't worth me sacrificing my career," Baxter said.

"And Admiral Baxter is worth even less to me," Rojo said. "They did choose us well. Perhaps the Senate should've intervened more in high-level fleet appointments over the last few decades."

"You're saying something good about the government?" Geary said, not bothering to hide his surprise.

Admiral Baxter made a face. "It feels nice to be able to blame someone else for your problems, but that's no way to fix things. As I believe a certain admiral told the public yesterday. It applies to the fleet as well. We have to face our own failures and address them from the inside."

"He does that to annoy me," Admiral Rojo said. "Saying things I happen to agree with so I can't tell him he's wrong. But, as long as we're being blunt with each other," she said, looking at Geary, "having you underfoot will make our efforts a lot harder. Just by existing here you constitute a challenge to our authority."

Baxter nodded. "If Black Jack gives an order, and we give an order, guess which one will be obeyed? And every order we give will be assumed to have been run by you for approval. That's not healthy."

"I agree with you," Geary said. "So does the Senate. You've seen that my orders will take me a very long ways from the Alliance for a while."

"The farther the better," Admiral Baxter said. "How soon can you leave Unity?"

"That's up to the Senate."

"True," Admiral Rojo said. "But once they release you, how long before you can depart Alliance space?"

"The ships I sent back to Varandal have a lot of combat damage to repair," Geary said, pausing to let that sink in and seeing both Baxter and Rojo look uncomfortable as a result. "And the crews deserve a break. I can't give you a firm departure date until I get back to Varandal and see the status of my ships and the ongoing repairs. I'm just as eager to leave Unity as you are to see me leave. But I have to finish with everything here, off-loading all of the people and materiel we brought from Unity Alternate to trusted agents appointed by the Senate. As soon as that's done I hope to take *Mistral* along with *Dauntless* and head back to Varandal." He saw not-quite-suppressed reactions from Rojo and Baxter. "You've already tried to redirect *Mistral* and the Marines aboard her, haven't you?"

"You inspire a lot of loyalty," Admiral Rojo said in a sour voice.

"Commander Young and Colonel Rico both know about the Senate's orders," Geary said.

Admiral Baxter leaned forward again, eyeing Geary. "These aliens. The Dancers. What do they want?"

"I don't know," Geary said. "They clearly see us as allies, but to what larger purpose remains uncertain. That's one of the reasons I'm being sent out there again, as you can see from my orders. We need a more permanent presence among the Dancers to try to get a better handle on how they think and what they expect from us."

"Then I'll wish you success on that errand, at least," Baxter said, his smile firmly in place. "Better that you deal with them than me having to get involved. How do you stand it?"

"Are you talking about their appearance?" Geary said, feeling as defensive as if someone had trash-talked a friend of his. "I think the key lies in seeing who the Dancers are, not what they look like."

"If you say so," Baxter said in the manner of someone not choosing to continue an argument rather than that of someone in agreement. "By the way, in terms of cleaning things up, some accountants here in headquarters want to go over your past expenditures."

Admiral Rojo nodded. "There're some questions about whether all of them were, um, handled appropriately."

Geary couldn't help smiling in return at the renewed oh-by-the-way attack. They'd apparently been honest when telling him one of the things leading to Rojo's and Baxter's willingness to cooperate was a mutual desire to trip him up. "I assure you, all expenditures were legal." He'd made sure of that, even while shuffling money around to provide enough funds for maintaining his ships. The trick had been to keep headquarters from figuring out how he was doing it so they wouldn't cut off those sources of funds before he'd pulled everything he could out of them. "I'll have Lieutenant Jamenson contact your accountants to discuss any questions they have." He hoped he'd have time to listen in to that discussion. Lieutenant Jamenson's unique skill, to render things as confusing as possible while still being technically correct, would face perhaps its greatest test at the hands of Fleet Headquarters' accountants. But having read (or tried to read) some of Jamenson's work, Geary had no doubt who would emerge victorious.

"A lieutenant?" Rojo asked, clearly skeptical. "Does this lieutenant have the experience necessary to answer every question the fleet accountants have?"

"I guarantee that she does," Geary said, trying not to smile at the joke neither Baxter nor Rojo yet understood. "I assure you that Lieutenant Jamenson is perfectly matched to the needs of this issue." Perfectly matched from his perspective, anyway.

"All right, then," Baxter said, standing. "Since we understand each other, I think it's time for some morale boosting."

Admiral Rojo stood as well, grimacing. "In case you didn't feel it on the way in," she said to Geary, "morale at headquarters is lower than the stomach of a chief passed out facedown in a deep ditch on liberty. The revelations from Unity Alternate hit everyone hard."

"They've been doing their jobs," Admiral Baxter said. "Thinking they were good guys helping to beat the enemies of the Alliance. Right now, they feel like people see them as enemies of the Alliance because they've been tarred by the actions of others."

Geary stood up, his guts tight with unhappiness. "I did feel it. They need to be told they are still seen as good guys."

"It has to come from you," Rojo said. "The guy who brought down the truth from the heavens. If you say it, they'll believe it."

"I'll have no problem saying it." Geary checked his uniform, wanting to look his best out of respect for the sailors they'd be talking to. He and the other two admirals left the office, Captain Romano joining them but staying a little behind as they walked, and a couple of other captains who must be aides to Baxter and Rojo joining the procession.

It took a long time, going through each floor of the vast building. They couldn't go everywhere, not in a single day, but with a lot of working spaces off-limits many of headquarters' personnel were gathered in large halls and conference rooms, which made it easier to see large groups all at once.

He'd done this before, reassuring worried and weary sailors that their efforts had been outstanding and that hope still lived. Geary repeated "I know you'll keep doing your best" and "the Alliance needs people like you" so many times he had to be careful to say each word rather than run them all together. Rojo and Baxter stayed only slightly back, clearly indicating they were with the great Black Jack and that he regarded them as with him as well. Despite his reservations about Admiral Rojo and Admiral Baxter, Geary knew how important it was for the sailors to have confidence in their leaders. In private, they could look daggers at each other and utter veiled threats. Here, in front of the men and women who looked to them for leadership, the three admirals did their best to look and act like a team with shared goals and beliefs.

In one way, it was exhausting. In other ways, being able to meet so many women and men who'd dedicated themselves to serving something bigger than themselves brought Geary the hope and energy that he was trying to give them.

One conference room had guards at the door. Inside was a group of officers who looked as if they were waiting for a firing squad to be assembled to carry out sentences on them.

"They were involved with Brass Prince," Rojo told Geary.

"We were told it was an authorized program!" one officer cried, her voice breaking. "We just shuffled money and personnel!"

"As far as we can tell," Admiral Baxter said, "those in here handled administrative matters and weren't aware of what Brass Prince was doing. But they're being specially screened to be certain of that. If they didn't have any way of knowing Brass Prince was an outlaw program engaged in actions contrary to Alliance law, they'll be all right," he added, raising his voice so everyone in the room could hear it.

"Did any of you ever encounter an officer named Paol Benan?" Geary asked.

The officers looked at each other, shaking their heads. All except for one, who frowned in thought. "I think I saw orders for someone of that name, sir. But that was a long time ago. Years."

"Have any of you heard of mind blocks? For security reasons?"

Blank faces looked back at him, except for two officers who looked appalled. "Those are illegal, Admiral. I would've reported that!"

"Good." He had no reason to think these officers had known what was being done under cover of layers of secrecy. They'd been pawns, told the program was legal but not enough about it to question whether it really was legal. And those who'd actually run the program, circumventing the law, would be happy if they could sacrifice these pawns to save themselves. "As Admiral Baxter says, this isn't about finding scapegoats. It's about finding those who knew the program was illegal, and bringing them to account. If you can assist with that in any way, please do so. If you did your duty and didn't know what else was going on through no fault of your own, you have nothing to fear."

There'd been skepticism when Baxter said it, but in response to Geary's words the mood in the room shifted dramatically and even a few smiles of relief appeared. They believed him. Like so many others, they believed in him. Sometimes he could almost forget the burden of that, but other times it felt crushing. Because he wasn't perfect, he couldn't do everything, he couldn't even be certain the words he just spoke would turn out to be true.

Once again, he had to hope that John Geary wouldn't let down the people who believed in Black Jack.

By the time he reached the entry area again, darkness had fallen outside. A ground forces general was waiting, not bothering to hide his relief when Geary appeared. "I'm to escort you back, Admiral. The surrounding area has been swept four times while you were inside, but we still have extensive security in place."

"Including Marines?" Admiral Baxter asked.

"Including Marines," the general said, sounding resigned to their presence rather than happy about it.

Outside, there were at least twice as many Marines as there had been this morning, forming solid walls that left only a one-meter-wide path between them. Anyone trying to get a shot at Geary would have a hard time even seeing him.

"May your actions honor your ancestors," Admiral Rojo said, offering her hand to Geary.

"As may yours," he said, shaking Rojo's hand and then Baxter's.

The general rushed Geary down the narrow path and into another armored limo, other armored limos before and behind it as escorts. After they were inside and the vehicle surged into motion, Geary focused on the general. "I didn't catch your name."

"Sorry. It's Wallach. I've got command of defense for this sector." He exhaled heavily. "A job which you've really complicated. No offense."

"None taken. How's morale in the ground forces?"

Wallach smiled crookedly. "It's been better, and it's been worse. Funny thing, the fleet officers behind those illegal programs and the politicians in the Senate backing them apparently didn't trust the ground forces to play in their super-secret sandbox. That means our hands are pretty clean. I guess interservice politics isn't always bad."

"I guess not," Geary said, seeing the irony in that. "Are there any updates on General Carabali?"

"She's out of danger," General Wallach said. "But she's in a med coma to speed healing, so you can't talk to her. I'm to get you back to the Senate building in one piece."

Geary slumped back, feeling totally worn out. "I was hoping I could take a shuttle back into orbit."

"Not yet, hero." Wallach grinned sympathetically. "But hopefully you will get a decent night's sleep."

A few hours later, General Wallach's prediction was rudely broken along with Geary's exhausted slumber by loud pounding on his door. Blinking sleep from his eyes and trying to clear his head, Geary checked the security screen and saw Senator Unruh outside.

He opened the door, knowing he looked like hell warmed over. "Am I right that it's 0200 here?"

"Close. It's 0204," Senator Unruh said. "This can't wait. Admiral, you need to get out of here."

"What? I'm being moved to another building?"

"You need to get off the planet, Admiral! As quickly as possible!"

FIVE

GEARY, surprised and still trying to get fully awake, looked past Senator Unruh, seeing an otherwise deserted hallway. "What happened?"

"Nothing has happened, yet. But support is building for a Senate vote requiring you to stay here at Unity until all matters pertaining to Unity Alternate are settled."

"All matters?"

"Every legal proceeding," Senator Unruh said.

Geary stared at her. "That'd be years."

"More likely decades. It's a safe vote, you see. Alliance law requires a defendant to be able to confront their accuser. So it seems very fair to have you here to personally testify."

He shook his head. "I'm not the accuser, am I?"

"No, you're not." Unruh clenched one fist and looked like she was ready to hit the door frame out of frustration. "All you did was bring the evidence here. The evidence is what forms the basis for accusations that will be brought by prosecutors. But keeping you here would keep attention focused on you, and on process rather than truth. It would also tempt you to overreach, and probably doom our plans for missions to both Midway and into Dancer space. We're going to stall, but you need to get yourself out of this star system. If you're gone when the vote is taken, it will have no force since the conditions specified in it no longer exist. Take your ship, and head back to Varandal. I promise I will send the other ship, and all your people aboard it, after you as soon as everything has been properly checked and off-loaded to ensure a clean chain of evidence."

"Won't the Senate just order me back here?" Geary protested.

"No." Unruh seemed absolutely certain. "Much of the support is being bought by knowing they can argue to the public that you're already here, so keeping you here is no hardship. If you're gone, to carry out missions for the Senate, then it'd be a matter of stopping those missions to recall you. That's a roadblock that should eliminate any chance of majority support for that vote. I've got a vehicle coming and my people are alerting the shuttle you came in. Get out of here."

He was in another armored limo, a rumpled and cross General Wallach sitting across from him, before Geary had time or leisure to think things through. "Won't this look like I'm running away in the night?"

"You?" Wallach said with a snort, followed by a yawn. "Excuse me. No, it'll look like you wanted to avoid any more danger to the good people of Unity caused by your presence. By leaving this way, having done everything you wanted to, you ensured no further attacks would mar the peace of the city."

"People will believe that?" Geary said.

"About you? Yeah. If I did it, I'd have rumors chasing me all the way back to Old Earth. But Black Jack? He's thinking of what's best for the Alliance."

It was hard to tell what Wallach felt about all that.

"Thank you for your efforts," Geary finally said. "I appreciate how difficult things have been the last couple of days."

"That's okay." Wallach actually smiled. "My kids couldn't believe I'd talked to Black Jack. In person! You've made me cool in the eyes of my teenage kids." He laughed. "Maybe you can do miracles!"

The limo passed through several extremely alert security check-points before gliding onto the landing field. It didn't stop until the door was right next to the lowered loading ramp of the shuttle. Geary paused before getting out. "Could you do me a favor, General? I'd like to get updates on General Carabali as long as my ship is still in this star system."

"No problem," Wallach said. He gazed steadily at Geary. "Look, I don't know what's myth and what's real when it comes to you, except that for most of their lives I expected my kids would end up fighting and maybe dying in the same war I fought and their grandparents fought. But you ended that war. What we've got now isn't a peaceful utopia, but it's a lot better than that. Thanks."

"You're welcome," Geary said, embarrassed. He nodded and got out, finding Gunny Orvis and Master Chief Gioninni waiting. Together, the three of them walked quickly up the ramp, the limo accelerating away from the shuttle.

The ramp came up almost on their heels. Geary had barely strapped into his seat before the shuttle lifted and soared toward the stars.

AS he walked off the shuttle onto *Dauntless* once more, Geary saw the hangar crew racing to fasten down the shuttle. Senior Chief Tarrani was waiting with a welcoming salute and a warning. "Better grab a handhold, Admiral," she warned. "The captain's in a hurry."

Geary felt thrusters firing and latched one hand onto the nearest hold. "I assume Senator Unruh spoke with Captain Desjani?"

"That's my understanding, sir," Tarrani said. "Hey, Gioninni, grab on, you dumb boot camp."

"Who you callin' boot camp?" Gioninni demanded as he gripped another hold. "I was sailing space while you were still learning to walk."

Tarrani's answer was forestalled as *Dauntless*'s main propulsion kicked in hard, hurling the battle cruiser out of orbit and on a vector toward the hypernet gate. Geary had to hold on tightly as inertial forces leaked past the dampers, which protested the rate of acceleration with high-pitched whines that filled the whole ship.

"I'm guessing Captain Desjani is at the helm?" Gunny Orvis asked Tarrani.

"You can tell, can't you?" Tarrani grinned. "Someone has to show these rear-area slackers how it's done right."

Moving his arm carefully against the acceleration, Geary reached up to touch a comm panel on the bulkhead near him. "Put me through to Commander Young on *Mistral*. Senior Chief, what's ship time?"

"It's 1400 for us, Admiral," Tarrani said.

Wonderful, Geary thought. He'd missed the rest of the night, skipping into the afternoon of the next day but not far enough to justify getting sleep anytime soon.

Commander Young's face appeared on the comm panel, looking startled. "You're leaving, sir?"

"I'll explain later," Geary said. "Urgent orders, no local danger. I've been assured that *Mistral* and all aboard her will follow to Varandal as soon as your off-load is complete."

That call finished, he tapped the command to speak to Desjani.

She was in her captain's seat on the bridge, of course. "Welcome aboard, Admiral."

"Thank you. I'm currently stuck in the hangar dock due to high acceleration forces."

"I was told to get you and *Dauntless* to the hypernet gate in an expeditious manner," Tanya said.

"I don't think the person who gave you those orders understood how you interpret the word 'expeditious,'" Geary said.

"It'll ease up in another twenty minutes." She gave him an intent look. "Nice to see you again. Alive."

"Likewise."

"How was headquarters?"

"Complicated," Geary said. "But I think it may be in good hands at the moment."

"Oh? Who's in charge? I had trouble getting a straight answer."

"As of yesterday, Admiral Baxter and Admiral Rojo. It's a co-command."

"Co-comm—?" She stared at him in shock. "Baxter and Rojo? Were they together in the same room?"

"I guess you've heard about their, um, feelings regarding each other?" Geary said.

"Are you kidding? Rumor has it when they were in command of ships, their ships were never assigned to the same force for fear they'd start shooting at each other instead of the enemy. You need to tell me about this."

"I will," Geary said. "As soon as the acceleration lets up."

"Which it will as soon as we're on vector," Desjani said, smiling.

He laughed, glad to be back aboard *Dauntless*.

IT took another hour before things had settled enough for Geary to get to his stateroom and collapse into his chair. Not five seconds later the alert on his hatch chimed. Groaning, he tabbed the open command.

Tanya Desjani entered, leaving the hatch open behind her, and giving him a disapproving look. "You're a fine-looking example for the sailors, Admiral. What's the expression horse people use? Rode hard and put away wet?"

"Thanks," Geary said, relaxing again. "I feel exactly like that. It's been a rough few days. I forgot to ask earlier. Did your relief show up?"

Desjani grinned. "He sure did. Commander William T. Door. I knew him when he was an ensign. He kept insisting his orders to take over command of *Dauntless* had precedence, and I kept pointing out that my orders had precedence. Since the crew only listened to me, Door had to get back in his shuttle and fly home."

"Good. Why didn't you warn me I'd encounter your godmother?"

Her eyebrows rose. "Nana Nakamura? Did she Old Family you?"

"What does that mean?" Geary asked.

Desjani shrugged. "A bit imperious, a bit condescending, a bit 'who are you again and why should I pay attention to you?'"

"Yeah, pretty much. I don't think she likes me."

"She doesn't really like anybody," Tanya said. "And you marrying into another Kosatkan family really dims her status by comparison, which I'm sure makes her particularly unhappy with you."

"Wonderful. Anyway, I've got another decision to make before we leave Unity," Geary said, rubbing his forehead. "Numos was finally court-martialed. And sentenced to death."

"Great! What's the problem?" Tanya asked, sitting down opposite him.

"I have to confirm the death sentence," Geary said.

"Great. What's the problem?" she repeated. Her puzzlement shifted to startlement. "Hold on. Are you seriously considering changing it to dismissal from the service?"

He sighed, thinking he knew the argument that was about to play out. "Why does that surprise you?"

"I didn't think you were that cold-blooded."

"What?" Geary dropped his hand, staring at her. "Changing his sentence to dismissal from the service would be cold-blooded compared to death?"

She stared back at him. "Yes. Of course. Ancestors save me, you don't get it? Dismissal from the service is a fate worse than death. He'll be totally dishonored, and that'll hang around his neck for however long the rest of his life is. His family and friends will disown him, no one will give him a job, so he'll have to live on basic welfare, and everyone he meets will treat him with contempt. It's a living hell."

"But . . ." Sometimes the future floored him. He'd thought he was past such moments. But, no.

Desjani sighed, looking up at the overhead. "You thought sparing his life would be merciful. Is that really how they thought a century ago? I don't know why you'd want to be merciful given what Numos did, of which desertion in the face of the enemy is just a small part, but if you do, then let him die and go to his ancestors."

"I hate this job," Geary muttered.

"Really?" She was angry now. "Numos's life means that much? If he'd done his duty, if he'd been a good officer, he'd have still been in command of *Orion* when *Orion* was destroyed. Instead, Shen died. His blood is on Numos's hands, along with that of a lot of other fleet sailors. And you're hesitating to punish Numos because his failures and misconduct meant he managed to survive where others died?"

He sat silently for a long moment, thoughts tumbling through his mind, aware of her anger radiating through the compartment. Two things finally stood out clearly. This was part of his responsibilities, and keeping faith with those who'd died meant holding accountable those who'd failed them. That didn't mean consigning someone to a living hell, though. "You're right," he finally said. "But you're okay with Numos being executed? You're not pushing for dismissal?"

Tanya looked back at him, her jaw still tight, but gradually relaxed. "No, I'm not pushing for dismissal. I don't think my ancestors would approve of me wanting to torment someone in the name of justice."

"All right. Thank you."

"Uh-huh. Right."

"I mean it." He nodded her way. "I needed to hear that."

"Okay." She looked away, plainly seeking to change the subject. "I heard Carabali got shot. How is she?"

"Out of danger," Geary said. "We should be getting updates on her status."

"Good." Desjani shifted her gaze to the starscape on one wall. "Are we really going out far into the dark again? Out to Dancer territory?"

"That's right. After our ships have had a chance to refit and repair."

She nodded. "I recommend, Admiral, that our refit and repair period be stretched out to around three months. That'll give the crews a chance to rotate through leave sections so they can all get home for a little while before we head out again. We'll probably need that much time for repairs anyway given how hard our ships have been used in the last several months."

"Good idea. Oh, one other thing. Lieutenant Jamenson needs to talk to the accountants at fleet staff."

"The accountants already called," Desjani said, unexpectedly smiling. "Apparently they wanted to ambush Jamenson. I listened in on some of it as Jamenson 'explained' things as only she can. I seriously thought my head was going to explode. Those accountants may have post-traumatic stress. I don't think they'll bother us again."

EVEN with *Dauntless* accelerating up to point three light speed to shave some time off the transit, the need to first accelerate and then brake velocity when approaching the hypernet gate meant it would take eighteen hours before the ship could leave this star system.

Eighteen hours could be a very long time.

Every high-priority message that arrived on *Dauntless* addressed to him (and every message for him was high priority) caused Geary to tense up until he checked who the message had originated from. Then, if it was directly from the Senate, he had to tense up some more until he read it.

But each of those messages were only updates. Senator Unruh had apparently decided that he needed frequent updates, which meant frequent alarming moments until he found out whether he'd be stuck at Unity for "more like decades."

However, each update only contained information on parliamentary maneuvers employed by one side of the debate to put off a vote, while the other pressed for a vote as soon as possible. Fortunately for Geary, his side seemed to be extremely good at preventing anything from being done. He had a suspicion that the other side probably was as well. It was a wonder that the Senate ever accomplished anything.

But then that had probably been the intent of the founders of the

Alliance, to prevent a too enthusiastic government from acting heedlessly, and prevent any one person from having enough power to act like a dictator.

With one hour to go until *Dauntless* reached the hypernet gate, the ship now stern-first toward the gate as the main propulsion units worked to slow her down, Geary went up to the bridge. His composure wasn't helped by knowing he had a responsibility to confirm Captain Numos's death sentence before *Dauntless* entered the hypernet gate. Well aware of how raw his nerves were, he tried to avoid snapping at anyone. The bridge watch standers (whose survival skills included being able to sense the moods of senior officers), were nonetheless very careful not to attract his attention.

Unity Star System normally had a lot of space traffic, much like other heavily populated places. But a surprising number of the ships here stood out for their speed. "I don't think I've ever seen that many ships boosting to point three light speed and above."

Tanya Desjani, in her command seat next to him, nodded. "Courier ships belonging to press organizations, trying to get the latest news from Unity out to the rest of the Alliance." She glanced at him. "The latest news being about you, of course."

"Great." With the hypernet still the quickest form of transport between the stars, followed by the jump drive, small and fast ships were the best way to get news around the Alliance as quickly as possible. Even that meant delays of weeks getting news to some star systems. He studied the fast-moving ships shown on his display, wondering exactly what news reports they were carrying. "I see a couple of small, fast ships just hanging around the hypernet gate."

"Sure," Tanya said. "That's normal. If some hot news comes out of Unity it gets sent to those ships at speed of light, faster than any ship can travel in normal space, and when they get the news, they enter the gate to be the first to carry it to important markets. I'm surprised there are still two ships there with all of the news you've been generating."

"I guess they had extras on hand," Geary said, shifting his attention back to the fast-moving ships. "There's a couple with diplomatic tags. Oh. Callas Republic and the Rift Federation."

"They're still associated with the Alliance," she said.

"I wonder what news the one from Callas is carrying back home?" Any mention of the Callas Republic brought up thoughts of Rione, who'd been a co-president of the republic as well as an Alliance senator before being voted out of office after the end of the war. "Are they rethinking their desire to leave the Alliance?"

"They're not technically part of the Alliance," Desjani said. "No matter how close they got while we were fighting the Syndics."

"I'm still getting routine status reports from Captain Hiyen," Geary said. He had ordered home the warships the Callas Republic had contributed to the fleet during the war, in great part to prevent mutinies by their crews over their long absence from their families even after the emergency of the war had ended. "Which means the republic hasn't detached them from the fleet yet."

"They're keeping their options open, I guess," she said, disdain at the machinations of politicians creeping into her voice.

"Options." He cast a glance her way. "The Callas Republic and the Rift Federation still have representatives in the Alliance Senate."

Tanya paused, thinking about that. "Meaning that ship may be bringing the republic news of your orders?"

"Right. As well as my account of how Rione died."

"Oh, that ought to go over well with the people who voted her out of office after the war." Tanya grinned. "That woman knew how to serve up revenge."

He gave her a surprised look. "That almost sounded like an admiring statement."

She shrugged. "It was something she did well. And something she could've done to you. Which is why I never trusted her."

His attempt to come up with a response ended as another message arrived. He bit off a curse before seeing it was from Fleet Headquarters. When had it become a relief instead of a major aggravation to get a message from Fleet Headquarters? He read the first lines, startled out of his grumpiness. "Captain Desjani, the death sentence for Captain Numos has been placed on indefinite suspension because he's begun fully cooperating with the investigations into corruption at high levels of fleet leadership."

Tanya glanced over at him. "Rats always turn on each other when the oxygen starts getting low."

"I guess facing death caused him to rethink his allegiances," Geary said.

She surprised him with a laugh. "You think that's what made him decide to cooperate? Death is easy, Admiral. We've lived with it most of our lives and seen it take a lot of our friends. No, I'll lay you odds that what changed Numos's mind was the possibility that you'd change his sentence to dismissal from the service. You said that you'd asked Baxter and Rojo about alternatives to a death sentence, right? Don't you think they found some opportunities to mention that to Numos, along with the chance he had to save himself from a fate literally worse than death?"

Once again, she'd thrown a curve at him. "Why would Numos believe that I'd do that? Choose to have him endure what you called a living hell?"

Tanya turned a look on him that combined tolerance with amusement. "You wouldn't understand that, would you? He'd believe that you'd do it, because that's what he'd do if your positions were reversed. You interacted enough with Numos to know that. He's the sort of malfunctioning widget who doesn't have enough imagination or empathy to realize that other people are different from him. Whereas you have so much empathy that you can even care about the fate of a broken switch like Numos."

"Oh." As faults go, too much empathy was probably better than most, he thought as he read on through the message. "General Carabali is doing fine and expected to make a full recovery and return to duty."

"More good news!" Desjani said. "Are you sure that message is from Fleet Headquarters?"

He frowned as he read the next part. *"Mistral's* departure from Unity has been delayed. Someone tried to smuggle a big EMP burster aboard her. If it had gone off inside the ship's shields, it would've fried every circuit on the ship and destroyed all the files of evidence we collected."

"You know what they say, if the evidence is against you, try to get rid of the evidence." Desjani shook her head, looking unhappy. "I hope your pals in the Senate can keep the pressure on."

"Me, too." Geary paused on the next section of the message.

"What is it?" she asked.

"They were able to arrest a few people using leads gathered from the ones who were killed trying to kill me." He read that portion again. "The security report says they identified a new group that poses a threat. They're people who are afraid of the Dancers."

She frowned at him. "Afraid enough of the Dancers to try to kill you? Why?"

"According to what Carabali told me, they think the Dancers are really hostile rather than friends." He sighed. "And they think I might be selling out humanity to them."

Tanya Desjani slapped both of her palms against her forehead. "Because the Dancers look scary, am I right?"

"From what I heard when I was down on Unity, yes." A warning ping announced the arrival of another high-priority message. "Damn. This one's from the Senate."

Desjani waited as he read.

"It's okay," Geary said, feeling his nerves subside a bit. "Senator Unruh says things were looking dicey if the vote was held for me to stay here until all legal proceedings were completed, but then Senator Sakai introduced a motion for a 'cooling-off period' and that passed. There can't be a vote now for at least eight hours after Sakai's motion passed."

"That message took about five hours to get here from the planet," Desjani said. "How long after the motion passed was the message sent?"

"Half an hour."

She smiled. "Meaning the next vote can't be for another two and a half hours, and we're forty-five minutes from the hypernet gate."

Geary felt himself smiling, too. "Which means we're sa—" He bit off the next word. "I didn't say it."

Desjani glared at him. "You were about to say it! Hypernet is probably the most reliable transportation system in existence, but tempting fate is always a mistake. If you dare the universe to mess with you, the universe will find a way, because that is what the universe does."

"Fortunately," Geary said, "I have you here to remind me of that."

"Yes, Admiral, you do." She turned her head to speak to the back of the bridge. "Lieutenant Yuon, give me a status check on the hypernet key."

"Hypernet key showing ready for gate entry," Lieutenant Yuon responded.

"Confirm destination gate shown as Varandal."

"Destination gate is Varandal," Yuon said.

"Lieutenant Castries," Desjani said. "Status."

"We're twenty-eight minutes from being close enough to the gate to enter," Castries said. "On vector, reducing velocity at projected rate to enter gate."

"Incoming message from *Audacious*," the communications watch reported.

"Direct it to me and the admiral," Desjani said, then grumbled in a much lower voice, "Zhao had better not try anything."

Geary checked the location of *Audacious*, seeing that the battleship was hanging in its patrol orbit a few light minutes away from the projected path of *Dauntless*. "He hasn't lit off his main propulsion."

A moment later, a window opened on his display, showing Captain Zhao on the bridge of *Audacious*. "Admiral Geary," Zhao said with a wide smile, "my orders are to ensure that nothing interferes with your expeditious departure from Unity. Please advise if you require any assistance. *Audacious* wishes you and *Dauntless* a safe voyage and success in your assigned missions. To the honor of our ancestors. Zhao, out."

Desjani, who'd seen and heard the same message, laughed. "Fleet Headquarters can't wait to get rid of you, can they?"

"Expeditious," Geary said, feeling mixed emotions at the eager send-off. "Somebody keeps using that word."

"Maybe it doesn't mean what you think it means," Tanya said.

"I think I know exactly what it means," he said. "I'm being politely run out of town before I cause any more trouble."

They were about fifteen minutes away from being able to enter the hypernet gate when alerts sounded.

"Captain," Lieutenant Yuon called out, "those two ships loitering near the hypernet gate are accelerating all out. They're exceeding safe acceleration limits."

"What the hell?" Desjani muttered, glaring at her display. "Lieutenant, confirm what I'm seeing. Are they both on intercept courses with us?"

"Yes, Captain," Yuon said, his voice betraying no hint of the worry he must be feeling. "Not just intercept, though. Maneuvering systems are predicting a seventy percent likelihood they are on collision courses. Update, Captain. Maneuvering systems now estimate seventy-eight percent probability both ships are accelerating onto collision courses with us."

"Captain," Lieutenant Castries said, "the identification being broadcast by both ships has changed. One now reports it is carrying children on an educational trip, and the other claims to be an Alliance military ship."

"Time to collision with both ships is six minutes, Captain. Systems now estimate ninety percent collision probability."

"Bring the ship to general quarters, full combat readiness, maximum airtight integrity." Desjani spared a moment to glance at Geary. "Looks like our friends aren't going to let you go that easily. Request permission to target both ships."

Geary brought a fist to his forehead, eyeing his own display where the tracks of both fast ships appeared as shallow curves ending where they intercepted the projected path of *Dauntless*. "Opening fire at Unity? Against ships broadcasting civilian and friendly identification?"

"That's not what they really are," she insisted.

"What if they are?" Geary asked, tightening his fist enough that it hurt his hand. "Wouldn't that be the perfect setup to discredit me and get me relieved of command? What are the chances of disabling them and not destroying both ships?"

Desjani rubbed her chin, eyeing her display. "Admiral, at the relative velocity we'll be moving at intercept, there won't be any chance of ensuring any shots are merely disabling. If we open fire, any hits are likely to be kills."

"Three minutes to collision," Lieutenant Yuon reported as the collision alarm came to life, blaring its warning to everyone aboard the ship.

SIX

"THOSE things have impressive thrust-to-mass ratios. Can you dodge them?" Geary asked.

Tanya raised her eyebrows at him as if surprised at the question. "They're very maneuverable. It'll take expert shiphandling."

"So you can do it?"

"If I can't, no one can. Lieutenant Castries, I'm assuming direct control of maneuvering."

"Understood, Captain. Two minutes to collision."

"Weapons request permission to power up hell lances and grapeshot projectors," Lieutenant Yuon said.

"Permission denied," Desjani said. "All hands brace for heavy maneuvering."

"All hands brace for heavy maneuvering!" Lieutenant Yuon said, his words being broadcast throughout the ship. "The captain has direct maneuvering control."

"Are you good with this?" Geary asked.

"Yes, Admiral," Captain Desjani said, not moving her eyes from her display.

Despite an urge to shout orders, to do something, Geary stopped talking, remaining silent.

"One minute to collision."

"Shut off the alarm," Desjani said, still not lifting her gaze from her display.

Lieutenant Castries moved her hand hastily to a control and the blare of the collision alarm halted, leaving a strange silence in its wake.

Geary could see one of Tanya's hands resting on the maneuvering controls built into her seat. Could see how lightly her fingers were suspended, slightly parted, each one poised above a specific control.

If those oncoming ships were trying to collide with *Dauntless*, something the ship's maneuvering systems now rated a one hundred percent probability, then they'd compensate for any movement *Dauntless* made to shift her vector. The changes Desjani made would have to be at the last possible moment, but not too late. Which also meant those changes would have to be big enough to ensure the suicidal attackers couldn't collide with the battle cruiser, but not so big the ship couldn't make the changes in time.

With only seconds left, Geary fixed his own gaze on his display, surprised to see how fast those two other ships were still accelerating. Their crews must be pinned down, suffering . . .

If they had crews.

He suddenly recognized something in the way those two ships had come onto their collision courses.

Tanya's fingers twitched on the controls.

Dauntless's main propulsion cut off, two sets of maneuvering thrusters firing to pitch her slightly down and to the right.

The two ships raced past, just ahead of the battle cruiser and just above her bow, close enough to cause Geary to flinch even though the ships were moving so fast he didn't really see the near miss that *Dauntless*'s sensors reported.

Captain Desjani's fingers were moving again, bringing *Dauntless* back onto the vector to enter the hypernet gate and cutting in main propulsion again to continue braking her velocity. "By the time they manage to come back around . . ." she started to say.

He knew why she stopped, as both small ships arced into impossibly tight turns to come back for another attempt at ramming *Dauntless*.

"They're AI-controlled ships!" Desjani snarled.

"Could a human crew have survived those turns?" Geary asked. "That amount of lateral g-forces as they shifted vectors that fast?"

"No, Admiral," Lieutenant Castries said, her fingers dancing over the controls before her. "Our maneuvering systems identify that amount of stress as fatal for any human occupants. The ships themselves shouldn't have been able to handle the stress."

As they steadied out to charge at *Dauntless* again, one of the small ships came apart, its hull shattering.

"One couldn't," Desjani said, her jaw tight.

"Estimate three minutes until remaining ship collides with us," Lieutenant Yuon said. "He's accelerating again."

"Give me an analysis of the wreckage of the one that came apart," Geary snapped. "See if it matches that of the wreckage from the dark ships."

"Ship's systems show a match," Lieutenant Castries said. "No signs of organic life in the wreckage, or of vented atmosphere or water."

"Kill the last one, Captain Desjani."

"My pleasure, Admiral. Power up hell lances. Report when ready to engage."

"Hell lances report they'll be ready in thirty seconds, Captain. One minute, forty seconds to collision."

"Target that ship. Weapons free once it's within the kill zone."

"Aye, Captain. Understand target the oncoming ship, weapons free when it's inside kill zone." Lieutenant Castries passed the information to the hell lances.

"Captain," the communications watch called, "we've received a message from *Audacious*. They want to know what's going on and whether we need assistance."

"Hold on that reply," Desjani said. "How are our engagement envelopes, Lieutenant Yuon?"

"We have three hell lance batteries that can bear on the oncoming ship," Yuon said.

"That should be enough." Desjani relaxed, sitting back, though her eyes stayed locked on her display.

Another fifteen seconds crawled by, the small ship accelerating all out toward its intercept with *Dauntless*, the fire control systems on *Dauntless* tracking the ship. "Whoever set this up was also part of the Defender fleet mess," Desjani said.

"Yes," Geary said. "Apparently they haven't all been shut down yet."

"They're already down one more ship, and in a moment they'll be down two."

The hell lances fired particle beams, streams of highly charged particles moving at tremendous speed. Shields of sufficient strength could deflect or absorb them, and the armor of battleships could sometimes stop them. Against anything else, they went through whatever was in their path.

The oncoming ship got close enough to *Dauntless* for the battle cruiser's hell lances to have a certainty of punching through the smaller ship's shields on every hit. Ship's power to critical systems was always kept as stable as possible, but less vital electronic items like overhead lights dimmed slightly as the hell lance batteries fired and immediately sucked up power in preparation for more shots as quickly as possible.

More shots weren't necessary.

Riddled by hell lance hits, the oncoming ship abruptly exploded as its already stressed power core blew up. A minor nudge to *Dauntless*'s vector ensured the very-fast-moving cloud of dust that had once been the attacking ship would miss the battle cruiser and continue on harmlessly into the vast space between stars.

Geary called up the message from *Audacious* and tapped reply. "No assistance is required. We were attacked by AI-controlled ships which attempted to ram. A full report on the engagement will be sent before we enter the hypernet. Be aware that other ships controlled by artificial intelligences may be in this star system, broadcasting false identities. To the honor of our ancestors. Geary, out."

Desjani sighed, stretching. "Stand down from general quarters. Return the ship to normal readiness. Well done to all hands."

Geary was already rapidly composing a report of the action. "I need an attachment with the ship's records of what happened."

"Lieutenant Castries."

"Aye, Captain," Castries said. "I'll have it to you within three minutes, Admiral."

"Somebody," Desjani said, "needs to dig into the construction records for the black ships and find out how many more might be wandering around."

"I'm certainly going to emphasize that," Geary said. "As well as the fact that this attack proves the threat from the black ships remains active, and that those responsible pose a physical danger to anyone trying to hold them accountable." He paused. "Of course. Now I get it."

"Get what?"

"Why people like Senator Costa and Senator Wilkes haven't already been arrested," Geary said. "As long as they and other senators involved in the illegal actions are in the same building as all of the other senators, they won't order something like blowing up the Senate building or dropping a rock on it from near orbit. They're hostages for the safety of the other senators, though they probably don't realize it."

"Wow," Tanya said. "The good politicians actually did something smart." She paused, looking startled. "I said 'good politicians.'"

"There are good people trying their best," Geary said, smiling despite the lingering tension inside him. "As well as rotten people. But we wouldn't want fleet officers all judged on the basis of Admiral Bloch, so we shouldn't judge all politicians on the basis of the worst of them."

"Stop being reasonable." She waved back toward the primary inhabited world. "You might advise those in power to make this public as fast as they can. Lots of people will see what happened when the light from these events reaches them. If they don't know the truth, the living stars alone know what else they might come up with to explain it."

"Good point," Geary said, rapidly adding that to his report.

The attachment from Lieutenant Castries popped up on his display just as he was finishing. Adding *Audacious* to the recipients of the message, Geary tried to speak calmly as he made his report. "How'd I sound?"

"Every centimeter an admiral," Desjani said. "An outstanding performance."

"Maybe I should redo it. Sound a little more concerned."

"With all due respect, Admiral, no. You need to come across as not rattled by this. Besides, we'll be at the hypernet gate in four minutes."

"I guess this is good enough, then." Geary touched the send command before closing his eyes and massaging his forehead with both hands. He wondered how Admiral Baxter and Admiral Rojo would react to this latest proof of ongoing problems. "Thanks for not saying 'I told you so' about the universe-messing-with-us thing."

"It never crossed my mind," Desjani said.

"The hell it didn't."

She laughed, in a good mood in the wake of the battle. "Request permission to enter the gate when we reach it."

"Permission granted."

Three minutes later, *Dauntless* entered the hypernet gate.

"I just realized something," Geary said to Desjani as their displays once again showed, literally, nothing outside the ship.

"What's that, Admiral?"

"I once knew some officers who were spending their careers trying to get promoted so they could someday make admiral and be stationed at Unity." He shook his head, thinking of those men and women, all long dead. "I didn't understand them then. And, now, having finally been to Unity, I understand them even less."

◇

BEING surrounded by nothing, being nowhere, meant nothing external could disturb the ship's routine. Service on a warship was never relaxing, but it was probably least stressful during transits between gates.

Which meant he could worry about other things than immediate problems.

The intelligence compartments aboard *Dauntless* were small in comparison to their importance. Geary tried to avoid going there often because the fuss surrounding his visits always seemed disruptive to the efforts of the intelligence specialists working for Lieutenant Iger. But he had a question that he didn't want overheard elsewhere.

Lieutenant Iger met him in the outer area, where the live plant (named Audrey according to ancient space-going tradition) was actually blooming, one of the flowers partially obscuring the "feed me" sign that was also a tradition. Normally reserved and quiet, Iger appeared to be even more so. Because he'd generally been both happier and more outgoing since his marriage to Lieutenant Jamenson, that caught Geary's attention. "Is there anything wrong, Lieutenant?"

Iger hesitated. "Nothing important, sir."

"Why don't you let me decide if it's important?"

Iger paused once more. "We should go into the inner office, sir."

The curious eyes of the intelligence analysts pretended not to watch as Geary followed Iger into the inner office.

"Now that we have privacy," Geary said as the door closed, "what's the problem?"

Iger looked unhappy. "While we were orbiting Unity, I received . . . guidance regarding my intelligence duties."

"Oh." Intelligence was a separate branch, supposedly answering to operational needs but independent enough to set its own priorities. "Are your bosses unhappy with your actions? Because in my reports I spoke very highly of you."

"Thank you, sir." Iger made a face. "Yes, sir. I was told that I shouldn't be making so many assessments in the field. I was getting out ahead of multisource single-interpretation policy."

"Which means what?"

Iger rubbed his neck as he thought through his response. "Basically, Admiral, it means everything we find and report is supposed to come into the central analysis department on Unity, which is then supposed to produce one result which everyone agrees on."

Geary nodded, trying not to let his feelings show. "Your bosses want everyone on the same page, even if that means I have to wait for months to get an interpretation of things we've encountered. And even if people many light years from the situation might not have the same grasp of it as those dealing with it."

"I did point out the operational urgencies we've been facing," Lieutenant Iger said.

"And?" Geary prompted.

"I was told I had to prioritize proper procedures," Iger said, his shoulders slumping in a helpless manner. "That's called Three-P management," he added.

"Three-P management." Geary shook his head. "You still work to support me, right? That's your job assignment."

"Yes, sir."

"So if I need assessments and interpretations right away, you'll continue to provide them, right?"

Iger paused, frowning. "Yes, sir."

"Which puts you between a meteor and the planet it's impacting."

"Yes, sir."

"What can I do to resolve the pressure on you?" Geary asked. "I need you focused on your job, not on wondering how somebody on Unity will react to you doing that job."

"Sir?" Iger appeared startled by the question, then his shoulders came up. "Admiral, I know this sounds odd, but the best thing you can do for me is put in your reports that I followed procedures even in, um, critical situations."

It made an odd, bureaucratic kind of sense. "If instead of saying you provided great support I say you always followed proper procedures they'll be happy?"

"If they see I've stuck by their rules they'll put me in for a medal," Iger said, looking apologetic. "Instead of counseling me for failing to set appropriate priorities."

"Then so be it," Geary said, smiling at the absurdity. You'd think he'd been in the fleet long enough to anticipate such things. "Now that we've resolved that, I need to ask you something sensitive."

"Sensitive?" Iger asked, immediately all-business. "If this is about the, uh, Defender fleet ships, I don't have any additional information. I don't know how many more of them might be out there."

"At least we know there are two less. No, I'm assuming all of their combatants are gone, and whatever is left is like the ships we encountered at the hypernet gate. Courier ships meant to carry information. It stands to reason some of those would have been away from Unity Alternate when we destroyed the AI-controlled ships there. No, my concern is with a different problem. I want to know if you've received any reports of a particular internal threat," Geary said. "At Unity, I discovered that there are people who fear the Dancers enough to resort to violence."

Iger nodded quickly. "Oh, yes. Internal security. That is sensitive. Some of those who tried to kill you were like that, motivated by fear of the Dancers. Were you told that?"

"I was. So you do have something on that?"

"Yes, Admiral. Normally, nothing I'm involved with should be aimed at Alliance citizens, but this is an exception."

"I'm glad," Geary said. "But why is it an exception?"

"Because of this," Iger continued as he pulled up a report on his display. "Right here. Men and women motivated by anti-Dancer feelings have been trying to join the fleet."

That was worse than he'd expected. Geary read the report, feeling grim. "They're joining to fight the Dancers. To protect humanity from the Dancers. At least we caught them during their enlistment screenings."

"Yes, Admiral," Lieutenant Iger said. "We caught some of them."

Geary turned a sharp look on the intelligence officer. "How many are we supposed to have missed?"

"We don't know, Admiral." Iger indicated the report. "That tells us how many were detected. But we have no way of knowing how many slipped past before new recruits began being specifically asked about the Dancers. If they weren't questioned about that, they wouldn't have betrayed their motivations."

"Are you telling me that any new personnel our ships receive as replacements might share that fear of the Dancers?" He looked over the report again. "This is mighty vague about their possible actions."

Iger nodded. "I believe, from my experience with such reports, that reflects a lot of uncertainty. You see where they say so far there only appear to be loose associations of those with anti-Dancer sentiments. 'Loose associations' means no clear doctrine, no leaders, or no patterns of action."

"Except for the one who tried to kill me." But then, one event didn't make a pattern. "Their reasons for distrusting or hating the Dancers also appear to be all over the map."

That brought another nod from Lieutenant Iger. "One of the things we were warned about in intelligence training was to avoid projecting our own fears or preconceptions into our analysis and conclusions. But that's exactly what the anti-Dancers seem to be doing. Their fears of the unknown, their fears of the Dancers', um, appearance, their fears of something truly different."

"That's a good point," Geary said. "They're looking at the Dancers and seeing their own fears. What can we do to screen our new arrivals for possible anti-Dancers? And can we do anything if we do find some? There's no law against disliking an alien species. Is there?" he added, once more aware that he hadn't caught up with all of the changes a century had wrought.

"No, sir," Iger said. "Not as long as dislike doesn't turn into actions contrary to orders or regulations. Admiral, all I can suggest is notifying the commanding officers in the fleet to be alert for anyone whose fears of the Dancers could constitute a security threat. Legal officers would have to be consulted on what else we can do. If it's just a political difference in opinion, I don't think we could do anything." He paused. "Or should do anything. There were some . . . incidents several decades ago, well into the war, where there were attempts to treat political dissent as if it were treason. You may not have heard of those, but it's one of the cautionary things we're taught about."

He shouldn't have been surprised, after the other excesses inspired by war that he'd heard of, but Geary was still saddened to hear it. "I'm amazed that the Alliance made it this far without turning into something unrecognizable, or falling apart."

Iger hesitated before speaking. "Whenever we most needed it, there have been some people willing to sacrifice themselves for doing the right thing. For following the law rather than expediency."

"Let's hope there are always enough people like that," Geary said, trying to deflect what might have been read as indirect praise for his own actions. "Is there anything else I should hear about?"

"Reports from Indras," Iger said. "And from our diplomatic contacts with the Syndics. Our diplomats were very unhappy that after denying any involvement with what happened at Indras, they learned it really was the work of the Defender fleet."

"That must have made their work harder."

"Oddly enough," Lieutenant Iger said, pointing to another report he'd brought up on a display, "it didn't. The Syndics always assume our diplomats are lying. They were happy to be able to point out proof, as if that somehow leveled the playing field, then continued arguing about what compensation the Alliance owes for that attack, along with veiled threats about retaliation."

"How much territory does the Syndicate Worlds now control?" Geary asked, leaning to look closer at the report. "Are they still losing star systems?"

"We . . . don't know," Iger said, calling up a star display that floated over the desk. Star systems in the space once controlled by the Syndicate Worlds were highlighted by various colored tabs to mark those still thought under Syndicate government control, those known to have rebelled and declared independence, those descending into civil war or anarchy, and those whose status was simply unknown. "There have always been time lags in our information. Some of this is months old. And reliability of the reporting varies a great deal as well. I've been tasked to find out as much as I could when we transited through Syndic space, because the picture remains very unclear."

Geary looked over the starscape, shaking his head. "How are the Syndic armed forces? Have they been able to replace their losses?"

Iger nodded unhappily. "All of the information we have indicates the Syndics appear to have never stood down from wartime production priorities. Their remaining shipyards are still turning out warships as fast as possible, and none of their ground forces have been demobilized. But we have data from many sources that Syndic losses have been staggering as they attempt to suppress every rebellious star system. It's very unlikely the Syndics would attempt a major engagement with us if a substantial Alliance fleet went through their territory, but they'll probably continue the sort of asymmetric attacks they attempted the last times we were in Syndic space."

The assessment could have been worse, but it also could have been a lot better. "How about the Syndic government?" Geary asked. "Has that stabilized?"

"That is also uncertain," Lieutenant Iger said. "The highest confidence estimate at this time is that a triumvirate is in charge of what remains of the Syndicate Worlds. But given how old our information is, even if that was true, it may no longer be."

"If I remember my history right," Geary said, "triumvirates tended to be unstable. Sooner or later the most powerful member got rid of the other two." He paused, looking over the display of the regions once ruled by the Syndicate Worlds. "What's our best guess for the future? Will it all fall apart?"

Iger shrugged apologetically. "There are too many variables, Admiral. People, especially. If someone with the right skills and charisma gets the right breaks, they could dramatically shift outcomes. Despite the vastness of space and the number of star systems and inhabited worlds, one person could make a big difference. And we simply don't know enough to predict if such a person might appear."

It didn't seem possible that one person could make such a difference, Geary thought. But what would've happened if the fleet hadn't found his damaged escape pod on the way to the Syndic ambush that nearly trapped and destroyed most of the Alliance's warships? What if he hadn't been there when the fleet was trapped and leaderless?

He didn't want to think he was special, or that important. He couldn't begin thinking that way.

Glancing at Iger, Geary could tell the lieutenant was thinking that, though. "I couldn't have accomplished what I have," Geary said, "without the support and assistance of a lot of good people. I'll grant that I made a difference, but alone I couldn't have done what was needed."

Iger grinned. "More variables. The more people involved, the more variables. Predicting what humans will do is a very inexact science."

He couldn't help smiling as well. "I won't argue with that. Speaking of things humans did that no one predicted, how are you and Lieutenant Jamenson getting on?"

"Very well, sir!" Iger cheered up instantly at the mention of Jamenson. "We're hoping for the chance of a brief honeymoon at Midway."

"Midway?" That sounded both perilous and odd, choosing a former Syndic star system for a vacation. Odd, until he thought about the fact that Iger had just spoken of dealing with his superiors in Intelligence. "You're not thinking of making that a working honeymoon, are you?"

Iger flinched, proving beyond any doubt that he wouldn't be very good at undercover work. "Only any open-source material available, or listening to conversations," he said.

"What about asking questions?" Geary said.

This time Iger hesitated. "Only if—"

"Never," Geary said. "Syndics watch for that, people asking the wrong kinds of questions. We knew that a century ago, and I haven't seen anything today that shows it's changed. Your superiors tasked you with doing this?"

"If feasible," Iger said, his eyes on the deck. "Sir, I wouldn't do anything that would risk any harm to Shamrock."

"Good." Geary took time to think through his initial reaction, reluctantly realizing that getting a firsthand perspective on attitudes at Midway would be a good thing. He didn't want Iger to endanger himself or Lieutenant Jamenson, but whom would he choose to send instead? "Are you good with doing it? Were you ordered to undertake that mission?"

"No, sir," Iger said, his head coming up, his eyes on Geary as he shook his head. "I was asked to see if it could be done. They were careful not to phrase it as an order."

"There are plenty of ways for superiors to make their wishes clear without giving a plain order," Geary said. "So I'm asking again. Do you feel that the asking if it could be done had the same effect as an order?"

"No, sir," Iger repeated, his voice firm. "The conversation was recorded, so they carefully avoided phrasing their wishes as something required of me." He smiled slightly. "We've been doing that for a long time in Intelligence, recording all conversations. Too many people got hung out to dry based on verbal orders and verbal assurances."

Geary nodded. "If the rest of the special agencies did that, the evidence should help ensure those responsible for the things we uncovered at Unity Alternate pay the price no matter how they try to blame underlings. Thank you, Lieutenant. I'll consider allowing you and Lieutenant Jamenson to, um, honeymoon at Midway. Ultimately, though, it's going to be up to Midway's own leaders whether you get that opportunity."

"Thank you, sir." Iger waved to another display. "We received an update on Atalia just before leaving Unity, sir."

"Atalia." The formerly Syndic star system, on the border facing Alliance space, had been badly battered many times during the long war, and then again recently by the AI-controlled ships of the Defender fleet running amok. "How bad off are they?"

Iger pointed to portions of the report as he spoke. "It's easier to list what hasn't been destroyed than try to list everything that's been torn up. The only thing keeping most of the population there is stubbornness. I've learned that they call it the Atalia Attitude, and take great pride in refusing to give up even when that's the only smart option."

"I have to respect refusing to give up," Geary said. "Though there's always a point where that stops being commendable and becomes insanity. They've asked the Alliance for help?"

"Yes, sir. But with all the demands on the Alliance government these days, there's not much available for aid to former Syndic star systems."

"Even though our ships were responsible for the last bout of unprovoked destruction there?"

"Out-of-control ships," Iger said, sounding apologetic. "There are legal arguments being mustered that the Alliance isn't accountable for what the dark ships did to foreign stars. Because the dark ships weren't authorized or funded following legal requirements."

"Alliance lawyers are arguing that because the dark ships were built by illegal methods the Alliance isn't responsible for what those ships did?" Geary shook his head. "How does that make sense?"

"I guess it makes sense to lawyers," Lieutenant Iger said. "Maybe we can run some human legal arguments through the translation software the Dancers gave us just to see how they come out."

"I'm not sure we want to know," Geary said. He wanted to ask about Varandal as well, whether everything was calm there and his fleet was getting the support it needed. But Iger wouldn't have the information. No one at Unity would have had it, either. Any ships carrying news from Varandal were probably on their way to Unity right now, "crossing paths" with *Dauntless* on its way to Varandal. "You and your people get as much rest as you can. There might be a lot of work waiting at

Varandal. I'm expecting to allow three months to prepare for the expedition to Midway and then Dancer space, so you should also work out a leave schedule to let all of your people get some time at home before we head out into the dark."

"Yes, sir," Iger said, smiling again. "That'll be very welcome news."

"And let me know if you and Lieutenant Jamenson want some time off for a real honeymoon," Geary added. "Eire is supposed to be a lovely world."

"We expect to have a lot of work awaiting us at Varandal—"

Geary held up his hand to stop Iger's words. "As valuable as you two are, I've never been the type who works valuable people to death because they're valuable. I think valuable people deserve breaks every once in a while."

As he headed back to his stateroom, though, he wondered when the universe would grant him, and Tanya Desjani, some time off.

DESPITE his recent experiences, Geary couldn't help but think of Varandal as he'd known it before the war. A century ago, the star system had held a single military orbiting facility capable of servicing at one time three destroyers, or two cruisers, or a single battleship or battle cruiser. Back then, that was enough to meet the needs of a smaller fleet that operated on a lean budget doled out by a government that had a lot of other priorities to deal with. The inhabited planet had been home to a decent and growing population, as well as a slowly developing industrial base.

So it was always a slight shock to him to see Varandal as it was now, with many more defenses, many more orbiting facilities, a score of massive shipyards, and hundreds of warships circling the star. All of those human-made objects in space had needed a lot more industry and population to support them, and the primary world's population and industry had expanded a great deal to meet those needs. Wartime spending had ballooned the Alliance's military spending, and even though that balloon had been rapidly deflating elsewhere since the end of the war, here at Varandal the cutbacks had so far only been minor in many places, reflecting the importance of what had become in effect the home star for the majority of the remaining fleet under Geary's command.

But some signs of the end of the war were visible on his display. Two massive ground forces bases that for decades had marshaled troops before offensives against Syndic star systems were now marked as decommissioned. Eventually, their buildings and their land would be used for some other purpose, but for now the places sat empty and silent where millions of men and women had made temporary homes before battle, temporary homes that in too many cases had turned out to be their last homes after they died on distant worlds.

Similarly, a huge orbiting base that had once housed squadrons of aerospace craft either defending the primary world or readying to be ferried to other stars had been shut down. Dark, cold, and still, it swung through space, awaiting new missions that would probably never come.

He shook off the mood, listening to the routine reports by the bridge watch standers as *Dauntless* dropped out of the hypernet and back into somewhere.

"Varandal is at routine readiness status four," Lieutenant Yuon reported. "No indications of unusual activity anywhere in the star system."

"Very well," Tanya Desjani said.

"Disappointed?" Geary asked.

"A little," she said. "I'm sort of used to crises when arriving at a star." She glanced at him. "It didn't used to be that way when arriving in Alliance star systems, but nowadays it's pretty much everywhere."

"You say that like it's my fault," Geary said.

"Did I?"

He smiled, glad Tanya had sensed his mood and lifted it a little. "I'd better send my status report out to everyone so they know that things are calm elsewhere."

The report had been crafted to both reassure and inform the rest of

the fleet. Everything was calm at Unity (sort of). A warning that some
courier ship–sized unarmed dark ships might still be active. About
three more months at Varandal to refit and repair, which also meant
three months to allow sailors to visit homes at other stars that they
might not have seen for some time. Then another mission, details to
be provided later. Unstated, but clear enough from the way he'd phrased
everything, was the news that the Alliance government had not (yet) collapsed, and that he had not (as some in the fleet still hoped) taken control of the government. "I am confident that those responsible for the
deaths of our comrades at Unity Alternate and other stars will be held
accountable for their crimes," Geary had told the rest of the fleet, regretting that he couldn't offer any examples as of yet.

He'd barely sent it off, and was preparing to send a specific greeting
to Admiral Timbale, grateful that he'd be able to depend on Timbale's
support, when Desjani made an angry noise. "What is it?" he asked.

"Did you send your message to Timbale yet?"

"I was about to. Why?"

"He's not in charge of Varandal anymore."

SEVEN

"WHAT?" She'd already highlighted a message for him. Dated only two days ago, it contained Timbale's official relinquishing of command, and the official assumption of the command at Varandal by Admiral Sharon Barnhorst. "Baxter and Rojo got the jump on me here. They must have decided Timbale was too willing to work with me. Do you know anything about Admiral Barnhorst?"

"Do you want to hear it?" Tanya asked.

"I need to hear it."

"Barricade Barnhorst has a reputation for being one hundred percent by the book. As in, she always follows procedures, step-by-step, and won't do anything that isn't plainly spelled out in regulations or orders. Her nickname refers to the way she prevents anything useful from happening."

"How'd she make admiral?" Geary asked, trying not to sound as upset as he was.

"She's masterful at managing upward. Her bosses think she's amazing. Her subordinates, not so much." Desjani grimaced. "Oh, hell."

He saw the message almost as soon as she had. "Barnhorst has put a hold on all repair activity pending review?" Geary tamped down his anger. "We'll see about that."

He'd have to wait until *Dauntless* reached Ambaru Station, the primary orbiting facility at Varandal, where first Admiral Timbale and now Admiral Barnhorst had their headquarters. But once he got close enough to shuttle over, he didn't intend to waste any time.

IN person, Admiral Barnhorst had the self-assurance of a large boulder blocking a road, oblivious to backed-up traffic and resisting any attempt to move her aside, depending on allies like mass and gravity to frustrate any attempt to get things moving. "I have responsibilities, Admiral Geary. I will carry them out."

It'd be so easy to get angry with her, to explode at the bland assurance. But he held his temper, knowing that was one of the approaches she expected him to take, instead pointing to his orders displayed on his comm pad. "I sent these on ahead. I'm presenting them to you now so you are officially in receipt of these orders just as I am. I am authorized to take all necessary actions to ensure the orders given to me are carried out, and my orders come from the Senate."

Barnhorst glanced at the orders, seemingly unimpressed. "I'll take a look at them."

"No, Admiral," Geary said. "You will read them right now. Because if you don't, these orders authorize me to relieve you of command as a hindrance to carrying out *my* responsibilities. Their wording is clear on that."

Admiral Barnhorst hesitated only a moment. "That's your interpretation of those orders. I don't agree with that interpretation of the wording."

"So you have read these orders." He made it a statement, not a question. He had learned a few things from Victoria Rione, including how to trick people into telling you things they didn't want you to know. "Admiral, since you have received and read these orders, if repair work on my ships has not recommenced within eight hours at every fleet shipyard in Varandal, I will send a courier ship to Unity requesting that you be immediately relieved of command and court-martialed for deliberately ignoring an order from the Alliance Senate."

"I'll consider your request," Admiral Barnhorst said in a cold voice.

"Eight hours, Admiral."

Geary sent some orders as the shuttle was carrying him back to *Dauntless*. By the time he disembarked onto *Dauntless*, a courier ship on standby had lit off propulsion and was headed for a position near the hypernet gate to await further orders. Once he was in his stateroom, he called Captain Smythe. "I gave Admiral Barnhorst eight hours to get repair work restarted. That was half an hour ago. Let me know if and when work starts again."

Smythe nodded, eyeing Geary. "If they prepare to get going again, we'll see signs of it hours before the work actually starts. I'll notify you of any indications like that. I have to warn you that I don't expect Barnhorst to move."

"Oh, she'll move," he said. "One way or another."

Captain Desjani had followed him to his stateroom, and shook her head as the call ended. "There are people who think you're a pushover, Admiral. Because you're not a hard-ass, or a screamer. I always warn them not to bet their career on that assumption."

He gave her a look. "You're hoping Barnhorst doesn't move, aren't you?"

"Yes, Admiral, I am. And if you want my honest assessment, she won't move."

As the last of the eight hours crawled by, Geary could tell that both Smythe's and Desjani's estimates had been correct. There wasn't any sign that work was about to start again. But he'd said eight hours, so he waited.

And at exactly eight hours he transmitted a message packet to the courier ship. It would take a few hours for the ship to receive that packet, but then it would enter the hypernet for Unity.

That left him with close to two weeks to wait for the courier to reach Unity, transmit its message packet to the primary world, wait for a response, and take the hypernet back. For a journey covering scores of light years, that was remarkably fast. But it still felt extremely slow.

He called Smythe in for a personal one-on-one, wanting to be sure work could restart quickly as soon as the courier returned from Unity.

"Repairs were going well," Captain Smythe said as he took a seat opposite Geary in the stateroom aboard *Dauntless*. The officer in charge of the fleet's repair ships rarely looked worried, instead usually appearing like a cat who knew a secret no one else was aware of. From what Geary had been able to learn, Smythe did in fact have more than a few secrets involving creative use of official funds. But he more than made up for that by being extremely good at meeting the fleet's needs. "The shipyards were grateful for the work," Smythe continued, "having heard their share of horror stories about downsizing afflicting other star systems that once heavily depended on military contracts. They are very much in your corner when it comes to wanting Barnhorst gone. But, even if that is achieved, the problem will be, as always, how to pay for the repairs. We're pretty much out of options. Well, legal options, that is."

"Money is on the way," Geary said.

"Admiral, with all due respect, I've heard that line many times." Smythe paused, looking thoughtful. "I've even used it myself on occasion."

"I can imagine," Geary said. "You've seen my orders from the Senate. This is the annex concerning funding."

"I can understand why you didn't send that to everyone in the fleet." Smythe read the annex, a smile growing. "I can do a lot with this."

Geary nodded, smiling as well. "You do realize that Lieutenant Jamenson will inform me of any . . . inappropriate draws on that funding?"

"Of course." Smythe sat back, his smile still in place. "I never should have told you about Jamenson. But a man can still dream!"

"Can we get all of the ships we need fully ready in three months?"

"Three months." Smythe rubbed his beard, thinking. "If Admiral Barnhorst is removed as an obstacle within another week or so, maybe. To give you a firm answer, I have to ask you a question. Which ships do we need to be fully ready in three months?"

Geary frowned, realizing that answering that question would require another meeting.

THE conference room could seem huge at times when the meeting software showed the table as big enough to hold hundreds of officers, their virtual presences not even rubbing elbows with each other. But this meeting was much smaller, small enough that everyone could be present in person.

Geary himself at the head of the table, Tanya Desjani seated to his left. On his right sat Captain Duellos. Occupying other seats were Captain Armus, Captain Badaya, Geary's grandniece Captain Jane Geary, Captain Smythe, Colonel Rico, and Master Chief Gioninni. The small group made far more obvious, and painful, the lack of Captain Tulev's presence.

"You all know what our orders are," Geary began. "What I want from you is advice on what we should take and any special concerns I need to be aware of. How big a force do we need to ensure the success of our mission?"

"How big a force can we take?" Duellos asked, leaning back casually. "How much needs to be left to defend the Alliance?"

"I was told to take as much as I needed," Geary said. "Other warships dispersed around the Alliance are supposed to handle any problems that come up while we're gone. Our priority is to ensure the emissary ship gets safely to Dancer space."

"In that case, we should take every battle cruiser," Captain Badaya said.

"Bluntly said, but accurate," Duellos agreed. "We'll need the maneuverability of the battle cruisers to deal with the enigmas when we travel through their space to get to the Dancers. We can't count on the Syndics and rebellious star systems in that region to have held the enigmas completely in check."

"The Syndics secretly fought the enigmas for decades without holding them in check," Badaya scoffed. "I doubt they're doing any better now. But those rebellious friends of ours at Midway are probably doing all right."

Captain Smythe seemed to be vying with Duellos for most relaxed posture. "If you're going out that far, Admiral, you should have four to six fast fleet auxiliaries, at a minimum."

"They're not exactly fast," Badaya grumbled.

"No, but they are necessary," Smythe said. "You have eight as of now. I'd advise taking them all."

Captain Armus, still as steady, slow-moving, and reliable as the drift of continents, nodded. "That means we need battleships. To protect the auxiliaries, as well as serving as mobile bastions for the rest of the fleet."

"At least four divisions of battleships," Jane Geary said.

"At least," Armus said.

"All of which will slow us down," Captain Badaya said, as tactless as ever.

A brief silence fell. It was the old dilemma. Battle cruisers were fast and agile, but couldn't take the punishment that battleships could, and didn't have firepower to match that of the battleships. But battleships were slower to accelerate or brake their velocity, moving ponderously compared to the battle cruisers. Both had important roles, but both came with trade-offs. And the auxiliaries, relatively slow, essentially unarmed, were immensely valuable for repairing battle damage and replenishing weapons, but a worrisome Achilles' heel in any battle.

Captain Smythe broke the silence. "This ship we're going to escort to Dancer space. It's a modified passenger liner?"

"Yes," Geary said. "That's about all I know about it."

"Unless they strap on a lot of extra propulsion," Smythe said, "that passenger liner is going to be about as maneuverable as one of the fast fleet auxiliaries. Liners aren't as slow as civilian freighters, but they're not built to handle like warships. And there's no choice about that ship coming along."

Jane Geary nodded quickly. "Yes. No matter what else, we'll have that ship along and need to protect it."

"That is battleship work," Duellos said. "And if we need to have battleships along to protect that ship, we might as well have the auxiliaries Captain Smythe recommends as well."

Captain Desjani looked at Geary. "This can't be a fast expeditionary force of cruisers and battle cruisers. We need a full, well-rounded fleet."

"If we're trying to avoid fighting the enigmas," Captain Jane Geary added, "having as many battleships as possible along with us is most likely to cause the enigmas to stay at arm's length rather than try closing with us to fight. Their advantages in maneuverability don't matter if we're not trying to force an engagement and they don't dare get too close to us."

"That might be true in Syndic space as well," Duellos said. "They won't force a fight if we've got a wall of battleships."

"The Syndics figured out how to destroy *Orion*," Desjani said, her voice harsh. "We can't count on them being overawed."

After a brief, uncomfortable pause, Duellos inclined his head apologetically toward Desjani. "An important event I should have taken into account."

"What about Marines?" Captain Badaya said, his social ineptness for once offering a welcome change of topic. "How many will we have? Just the colonel's unit?"

"I haven't received any information yet regarding Marine reinforcements," Colonel Rico said. "Given the mission, a large Marine force might be superfluous, though. There aren't supposed to be any planetary actions or major space boarding operations."

"True enough," Badaya said. "But it's a bad idea to base your force on what you expect to need when you don't know what to expect."

Desjani stared at Badaya, clearly surprised at hearing good advice from him. "Captain Badaya is right," she said, pausing afterwards as if shocked by her words. "We can put together warship groupings to handle various threats, but if it's something only Marines can handle we can't substitute sailors for them."

"That's usually not a good idea," Colonel Rico said with absolute seriousness. He seemed surprised when the others present laughed.

"General Carabali and the ground forces general I talked to at Unity seemed to think the Marines specially assigned there would be released before much longer," Geary said. "Hopefully we'll hear something about that soon. We have no idea what conditions will be like at some of the Syndic and former Syndic star systems we have to go through, or what's been happening at Midway. I'd prefer to have enough Marines along to handle anything we run into."

"Admiral," Master Chief Gioninni said, "there's something else we should be taking into consideration. A lot of enlistments are coming to an end. I think a healthy percentage of those sailors will reenlist, now that the odds of surviving an enlistment have improved quite a bit, and what with the job situations they're likely to find at home. But it's safe to say up to a third of the fleet's personnel may have to be replaced by new recruits or transfers from elsewhere in the Alliance."

Captain Armus made a face. "That's a very important point, Master Chief. We're going to be dealing with a lot of new sailors who'll need more training and lack experience."

"Not to mention the officers who may decide to leave," Desjani said.

She didn't look at Duellos, but he nodded to her as if those words had been addressed to him. "Officers may have other priorities to deal with as well," he said.

"Not you, surely?" Badaya asked Duellos.

Duellos shrugged. "I have a family."

"Oh. Of course."

"Speaking of families," Geary said, "we also need to factor getting everyone a chance at enough leave for a decent visit home."

"You still want us to work with up to one month authorized for each individual?" Armus asked. "That'll complicate preparations a lot."

"A lot of these sailors haven't had decent leave for a long time," Duellos said.

"I want each of you to also try to get some time home," Geary said.

"You should mention the Dancer thing," Desjani said.

"Right." He tried not to look as exasperated as he felt. "At Unity, and apparently elsewhere in Alliance space, there are fringe elements that think the Dancers are hostile. It's important we watch for that among our own crews and any new recruits coming in."

"Hostile?" Badaya asked. "In the name of my ancestors, why?"

"They're ugly," Desjani said.

It was a bit painful, Geary thought, to see the surprise created by Desjani's answer, and the understanding that appeared on everyone's faces as they realized what she meant. "It's stupid," he said. "But people are like that. And some people are willing to take serious measures to, um, defend us against the Dancers."

"One of them tried to kill the admiral while he was on the ground at Unity," Desjani said.

After a moment of shocked silence, Duellos shook his head. "That sort of thing shouldn't be a problem with our sailors. The crews of our ships have seen the Dancers fight alongside us. They know the Dancers may have made the difference between us winning or dying at Unity Alternate. To them, the looks of the Dancers don't count. What matters is their reliability when you need a tough ally." He paused, glancing at Colonel Rico. "It's similar to how sailors think about Marines, I suppose."

Rico flashed a very quick smile. "And how Marines feel about sailors. If ugly gets the job done, then ugly is what you want."

EIGHT days after that meeting, the shipyards still idle while Admiral Barnhorst continued her review, the courier ship returned from Unity.

Geary expected to receive a message from the courier as soon as light could carry it to where *Dauntless* orbited near Ambaru Station. What he didn't expect was to see Admiral Timbale delivering the message.

"Greetings, Admiral Geary," Timbale said. "I'd barely arrived at Unity for my new assignment when orders came for me to hustle to meet this courier ship and return to Varandal. I'm to immediately relieve Admiral Barnhorst and send her back to Unity. As soon as this message goes out I'm going to broadcast my orders to all units in Varandal, and get things going again. To the honor of our ancestors, Timbale, out."

Geary laughed with relief, then immediately called Captain Smythe. "You'll be hearing from Admiral Timbale any moment now. Get those shipyards going again as fast as you can."

Normally, he hated throwing his weight around. This time, though, it felt good. He hadn't dared hope that Timbale would be reassigned here, just asking for someone willing to get the job done.

Hopefully Timbale wasn't too unhappy about being yanked around.

THE weeks that followed were an unending string of days packed with inspections and reports and planning and preparations. His orders from the Senate gave him a lot of authority, but that meant he also bore a lot of responsibility. The staffs that operational admirals had once carried around with them, officers who'd handle much of the running of a command, had been pared down throughout the war to feed the insatiable maws of the war and Fleet Headquarters, replaced by automated assistants. Normally, the automated assistants could handle many of those functions fine. But this wasn't normal.

"We're staging an intervention," Captain Duellos informed Geary one afternoon during a meeting the senior fleet captains had requested. "You need help. Since you haven't listened to your flagship captain," he added with a nod toward Captain Desjani, "we'll try to get through to you."

"You can't do it all yourself," Captain Badaya said. "You've helped all of us, even *me*, learn some important things. Now it's time we helped you."

"We can handle some of these tasks," Captain Armus said. "Delegate. It's what admirals do."

"I have some lieutenants who are underemployed," Duellos said. "They'd be happy to pitch in."

"Really?" Geary said.

"I haven't actually asked them yet," Duellos admitted. "Asking for volunteers instead of assigning them just complicates things."

Jane Geary nodded. "And you need to know these responsibilities will be covered when you go on leave, Admiral."

"I'm willing to accept your proposals," Geary said, realizing how relieved he suddenly felt and wondering why he'd needed this to grasp the importance of delegating some of the preparations. "Thank you for working them up. But I'm not going on leave, so that aspect of things is already covered."

He saw the others glance at Tanya Desjani, but decided it would be wiser not to ask why.

COURIER ships arrived with regularity, bringing news and information. Senator Wilkes had been formally charged with treason. The head of one of the major Alliance intelligence organizations had been arrested. At least a half-dozen AI-controlled courier ships were unaccounted for, possibly destroyed at Unity Alternate, but possibly still moving about, mimicking other ships. Their fuel cells would run low at some point, but for now all security forces had been alerted.

The modifications to the emissary ship were proceeding on schedule. The ship should arrive at Varandal about two weeks before the projected departure date.

Accompanying the emissary ship would be General Carabali, her Marines, and the assault transports *Tsunami*, *Typhoon*, and *Haboob*.

The Senate had decided it was important to replace the Marines with ground forces normally stationed on Unity so that conditions would appear normal again despite the security risk that might still pose.

Sailors were leaving the fleet as their enlistments expired, and new recruits were coming in, just as Master Chief Gioninni had warned. Fortunately, the numbers appeared to be well less than one-third of the fleet's sailors. Unfortunately, they might end up being as high as one-quarter of the total number. Which required scheduling more training in the midst of everything else.

Geary was going through another batch of status reports, and trying to fight off a looming headache, when his hatch alert chimed. "Come in."

Tanya Desjani entered, glancing at his display. "That's no fun."

He gave her a sour look. "Since when are you concerned about fun? You run one of the tightest ships I've ever seen and you work longer hours than I do."

"But I do let my crew enjoy themselves when appropriate." She sat down opposite him, holding up her left hand so the ring was visible, their signal that the conversation would be about personal matters. "We need to talk."

"About?" Geary asked warily.

"You, me, honeymoon, Glenlyon Star System."

"What?" He waved a hand in denial. "I admit I'd enjoy a honeymoon—"

"Thanks."

"But Glenlyon is . . ."

"Your home." She let the words hang for several seconds.

He felt his shoulders hunching in defensive reaction. "Tanya, you know what'll happen if I go back to Glenlyon."

"Crowds. Adoration for their hero. Awkward moments. A few public appearances." She shook her head. "The same things you experienced at Unity."

"And which I did not enjoy at all!"

"Jack, your home world deserves a visit."

"Isn't my life hard enough without going through that?" he said.

"It's your duty."

Geary flinched. "Tanya, that's a low blow." Because she knew that was one button she could push that he had few defenses against.

"Am I right?" she asked.

"I also have a duty to ensure the fleet is ready to depart on time."

"Both Badaya and your niece Jane will be here while we're gone. Either one can handle things at Varandal for a few weeks. I'd prefer Jane Geary just because you never know what Badaya might decide is a good idea, but he's surprised me a lot in recent months. And since Admiral Timbale has settled in again we're not having any problems with the shipyards. Captain Smythe informed me he can handle anything that might come up."

"I know that, but I should—"

"Are you indispensible, Admiral Geary?"

He paused, realizing that was exactly what he'd been thinking without realizing it. "No. I shouldn't be. No one should be indispensible." He spent a few more moments trying to muster additional arguments, and failing.

"Jane has asked me about it," Tanya added.

He felt his last defenses crumbling. "Jane wants me to go back to Glenlyon?"

"She's wondering why you haven't." Tanya leaned forward. "It means a lot to her. She got the chance to meet the real man behind those heroic stories we were fed. She wants others close to the Gearys to have the same chance."

There were times when surrender was the only right course of action. "Three days."

"That's too short. One week. Not counting any time in transit or orbital transfers."

"When you add in travel time," he complained, "that'll have us gone more than three weeks even if we manage to get perfect scheduling from commercial passenger ships."

"It'll take twenty days," Tanya said. "I've talked to the other captains and my officers, and all agree we should take *Dauntless*. Arriving home in your flagship will show the proper respect for your ancestors."

"I can't just haul a battle cruiser to my home world so I can have some time off there!"

"Training, testing, and evaluation," Tanya said. "We've got new sailors to integrate into the crew, and some system work that requires operational testing. Both of which can be accomplished by a TT and E voyage within Alliance space. We have to go somewhere. Why not Glenlyon?"

"Your crew—"

"Will be treated like royalty by the good people of Glenlyon. It'll be their best liberty ever."

She'd planned and prepared the whole argument as if it were a campaign, covering every contingency. He had only one argument left. "If we take *Dauntless*, we'll be on duty the whole way there and back. That means no honeymoon while we're traveling."

She sighed. "Yeah. We'll have to make up for it while we're there." Seeing his reaction, she laughed. "I guess you like that idea."

Which was how he found himself riding *Dauntless* toward the hypernet gate, worrying during every second of the light hours the trip took that something would go wrong or not get done while he wasn't here.

Along the way, he realized how right Tanya Desjani had been to insist on this. Because no one should be indispensible, no single person should be critical to accomplishing a mission. But he'd talked himself into believing that he was even though his officers were experienced in repairing ships and preparing to carry out missions.

He still wasn't looking forward to Glenlyon, though. Aside from issues and memories that he'd tried to avoid confronting, he was certain there'd be a statue of him there. And who in their right mind would want to come face-to-face with a statue of themselves?

◇

A century was a long time in terms of human lives and the things they built. To a world, a century was the blink of an eye.

To the naked eye, from orbit, the planet named Glenlyon looked much as it had when he'd last left it. The primary orbital facility, though, had at least doubled in size.

He got up from his fleet command seat on the bridge, feeling disquieted at the idea of facing the changes a century had wrought on the surface, of directly confronting the ghosts of a past that still felt recent to him. "Have fun," he told the watch standers before leaving the bridge, listening to Tanya giving last-minute instructions to the officers who'd be in charge of each of *Dauntless*'s three watch sections. Each day, one watch section would be responsible for the ship, while the other two got to leave the ship for liberty. In order to even out the chances for every sailor to experience the same number of days off, Geary had agreed to extend the visit to the planet to nine days.

He went back to his stateroom, grabbed the satchel with his few small possessions in it, and then headed for the shuttle dock.

The sailors he passed looked and sounded happy, obviously looking forward to a few days as celebrities because of their status as part of the flagship's crew.

At the shuttle dock, some officers, several senior enlisted, and a lot of sailors were already lined up for the first liberty shuttle. Tanya arrived to the shout of "Captain's on deck!" from Master Chief Gioninni, all of the sailors coming to attention.

She walked to the nearest comm panel and activated the general announcing system so her voice could be heard throughout the ship. "All hands, this is the captain. I expect the sections on duty to be focused on their tasks and keep the ship safe. Those on liberty are authorized to have a good time. Remember while on the planet that you represent not just the Alliance fleet but also this ship, and Admiral

Geary himself. Conduct yourselves accordingly. Anyone who takes any action that blemishes the name of the fleet, this ship, and me will regret the day they were born. In case anyone is in doubt, excessive use of alcohol or other legal intoxicants is *not* an excuse for doing something stupid, illegal, or dangerous. Stay safe and stay smart." Desjani looked about her at the sailors within sight as if to assure herself that they were listening. "And now it is my pleasure to sound liberty call."

As she stepped away from the panel, cheers erupted throughout the ship.

Desjani turned to face the other ship's officers present, as well as the senior enlisted. Pointing at Gioninni, she moved her forefinger to one eye and then back at him in a clear gesture of warning to which the master chief responded with a look of surprised innocence.

Glenlyon had sent a special shuttle to rendezvous with *Dauntless.* Already uncomfortable, Geary was embarrassed to discover the shuttle was a VIP model decked out with every possible luxury. "I shouldn't be riding this down when the crew is using standard fleet shuttles."

"They won't begrudge you the experience," Desjani said as she took a seat and strapped in. "They know when food got short you ate Danaka Yoruk ration bars just like they did."

The drop through atmosphere was unusually smooth for someone used to the rougher rides of military shuttles, the view on the displays of the outside shading from the black of space to the twilight of the upper atmosphere and then to the blue of the sky on a world inhabitable by humans. The final landing took so long to come to a gentle rest that Geary found himself waiting impatiently. "Would it kill somebody important to feel a little bump on landing?"

"You never know," Tanya said. "Now stop complaining and get your happy face on."

"Sure," Geary muttered as he got up and turned toward the hatch.

"You can do it," Tanya assured him as the hatch cycled open.

He smoothed out his expression, and made sure they were walking side by side down the ramp from the hatch, not wanting to make it seem as if she counted less than he did. He had a confused impression of many people and the familiar scorched scent of a landing field as he tried not to trip on the way down the ramp.

At the foot of the ramp, an honor guard awaited, two lines of Marines in replicas of the original Glenlyon Marine uniform. The honor guard conjured up unpleasant memories of his visit to Fleet Headquarters on Unity, but otherwise there was nothing to cause concern. The vast crowds visible beyond the landing area held no sense of menace or tension, of being narrowly balanced against tipping into chaos, as the crowds at Unity had. Instead, their cheers sounded only jubilant.

He blinked against the light of the sun. A lot of people from a lot of other planets said the light of other stars never felt quite right, that only the light from the sun someone grew up under would feel like it had just the right cast. Maybe that was true, but at the moment the sun low in the sky just felt uncomfortably bright.

"Their hero has come home," Tanya murmured just loudly enough to be heard over the happy tumult.

Planetary VIPs waited at the end of the honor guard ranks, all of them beaming at the chance to greet Geary and get pictures with him. "Welcome back, child of Glenlyon," Council President Kennedy said as he embraced Geary. "And welcome to the new daughter of Glenlyon you've brought to the world that is now her home as well," he added, giving her the same quick official hug, arms exerting little pressure, upper bodies barely coming into contact.

Various council members gave their greetings one by one, followed by the heads of the local ground forces and star system defense offering salutes.

Geary found himself facing the watching crowds, a virtual microphone ready to broadcast his words to all of them, as well as to those watching from other locations on the planet and elsewhere in this star system. The speech he'd rehearsed in case it was needed vanished from his mind, leaving him groping for words. "I'm sorry it took me so long to get back to Glenlyon. I've been . . . busy with a number of things."

The laughter surprised him, but gave him a moment to collect his wits as well. "I hadn't realized how much I missed this world. So much . . . so much I knew probably isn't here anymore. The people I knew . . ." He had to pause, collecting himself, the watchers silent as they waited. "But much remains. All of you remain. Every battle we fight is both for the present, and for the future. And every battle honors those who fought for us in the past. Anything I've done is because of those who came before, and for those who stand here now. Please remember and honor all of those who could never come home, who gave all they had. They deserve more than I ever will, because they gave more than I ever have."

What else to say?

"I'm glad that I finally made it home," Geary said, stepping back to signal he was done speaking because he couldn't think of anything else to say. The thunderous applause surprised him, and it kept up as the VIPs of Glenlyon led him and Tanya to a caravan of official vehicles.

They were escorted into a limo also holding the two senior military officials, who seemed tongue-tied as the car began moving between lines of cheering citizens. The ground forces officer finally spoke up. "It's late afternoon at this location on the planet. We've only scheduled one event for the rest of the day so you can take time to adjust and rest."

The star system defense head nodded. "It's a buffet for veterans. We thought that should be the first thing."

"That was a good decision," Geary said. "How bad were Glenlyon's losses?"

The ground forces commander grimaced. "We never suffered direct attack. Like a lot of other worlds, Glenlyon sent out people. Some of them came back. A lot didn't. There's a memorial listing every single casualty from here over the last hundred years. It's sort of hard to handle, if you know what I mean. You're scheduled to present a wreath there two days from now."

"Good." That he didn't mind doing. The vehicle was already slowing in front of a very large building, one he didn't recognize, so it must have been built sometime in the last century.

"We're holding the buffet at the old, original veterans' service center," the ground forces commander said. "To sort of help you feel at home."

The old, original veterans' service center. Obviously it had been here for at least several decades, but he had no memory of this structure. It felt odd, again, to be reminded that what for him were memories a few years old from Glenlyon were actually memories of a century ago.

Inside, a vast hall was filled with tables that were piled with food, a large crowd of men and women waiting. Just from the way they stood and watched him he could have told they were all veterans.

All waiting to talk to him.

Feeling like he was about to be judged by his peers, Geary walked inside, Tanya beside him.

EIGHT

HE'D seen very old pictures of gatherings of other veterans. The difference between then and now was that the ancient pictures showed men and women lacking limbs, their bodies battered by their experiences, a visual testament to what they'd endured. These days just about any physical damage could be repaired, any limb regrown, even brain damage corrected. The physical scars were gone, all except those people chose to retain as marks of their service, but the invisible scars remained. In that way, gatherings of veterans remained the same as in ancient times.

He could do this. Geary walked slowly among the veterans, exchanging a few words with each, feeling uncomfortable that he was being singled out compared to them. Tanya disappeared briefly, returning with a plate so he could eat while he walked and talked, surprised to realize how happy it made him to taste some of the special foods Glenlyon took pride in.

"Admiral," one gruff man said, saluting even though he was in a civilian suit. He had weathered skin, and had retained a scar on his neck that cosmetic surgery could've removed. "Colonel Duncan. Two Hundred Fifth Ground Forces Division."

Geary returned the salute. "How are you doing?"

"Well enough. Could be worse." Colonel Duncan suddenly grinned. "I worried you might take over the government like they said, but you were smart enough not to. That's the last thing we need, right? The military has enough trouble trying to march and talk at the same time. It'd make an awful mess of trying to run the Alliance, wouldn't it?"

"That's what I thought," Geary said.

"I knew your nephew when I was a lot younger. Michael's boy. And his daughters. Fine people, all of them."

"Thank you." How long had it been since his brother's children had died? Best not to dwell on that.

He felt a nudge and saw Tanya gesturing toward an elderly woman sitting against one wall, a younger woman beside her. To show that many signs of age, to need to use a mobile chair, the woman must be near the end of her life.

Why was she by herself?

He began walking toward her, Tanya following. Colonel Duncan followed as well, speaking to Geary. "Do you know about her? No? One of the uglier episodes of an ugly war, while I was still a boy. She was part of a ground forces unit dropped onto a Syndic planet without enough support. They were twelve hundred strong when they went in. Only fifty were evac'd alive afterwards. She's the last of that fifty still living, the sole survivor of the few who survived. She's not very sociable, but no one begrudges her that."

The younger woman saw them coming and stepped forward to meet them. "Can I talk to her?" Geary asked.

"I think she'd like that," the woman said.

"Is she your mother?"

"My great-aunt." The woman looked back at the aged veteran in her mobile chair. "She was a sergeant. All of the officers died. She was one of the two sergeants who lived and got the others to the evacuation point before they were wiped out. I learned that from other people. She's never talked about it."

"Damn," Tanya muttered.

Geary walked up to the old woman, extending his hand. "Sergeant? I wanted to meet you."

The aged veteran looked up at him, her eyes searching his face. "You're Black Jack?" Her voice was as thin and weak as her body, but still held traces of the power it had once projected. "Why does an admiral want to meet an old grunt like me?"

"Because I know how it feels. I'm the last survivor of the crew of *Merlon*. I tried to save as many as I could. It wasn't enough. The rest died a long time ago."

She gazed at him for a long moment, then reached up to grasp his hand. "I should've saved more of them," she whispered. "I see them every day."

"Yes," Geary said. "But you saved as many as you could. Sometimes that's all we can do. Thank you."

The old sergeant nodded, her eyes meeting his, exchanging a message of understanding that couldn't be put into words. Finally she looked at Tanya, her eyes going over her uniform. "Alliance Cross," she said. "How'd a space squid earn that?"

"A boarding action," Tanya said.

"A bad one?"

"Very bad."

"There aren't any good ones," the sergeant muttered. "Glad to know girls these days can still get the job done." She closed her eyes, breathing slowly, worn out by the conversation.

Geary spent some time afterwards walking through the hall and talking to other veterans, but the image of the old sergeant stuck with him. He realized that if that single meeting had been the only reason he'd come back to Glenlyon, it would've been all the reason he needed.

It was getting dark when he and Tanya left, getting into the official limo. "We'll be staying at the Geary place," he told the ground forces commander, who like the other VIPs was still accompanying them. Jane Geary had insisted he stay there, and he hadn't really fought against the idea.

"That's what we expected," the general said.

"I remember a lot of open fields around the house," Geary said, staring at the buildings lining the road as the limo hummed along, the other limos with the other important people ahead of and behind it. "And a lot of trees. The first generation of Gearys on the planet, Robert and Lyn, built their place a ways out from the city. The capital still hadn't grown enough to reach the place the last time I was here." More than a century. Would he recognize anything? But Jane had told him the place hadn't changed much except for a wall around the property to keep out people wanting to barge into the home of the great Black Jack.

"It's a stand-alone house?" Tanya asked.

"Yeah. They'd come from a crowded Old Colony, and lot of people from those places when they had a whole new world to live on wanted a little bit of that land for their own. Robert and Lyn lived on the orbital facility for a while, they had jobs there, before settling down here on the surface. It's sort of an old style of house, I guess."

But then the buildings on the right side of the road fell away, leaving a section of land fenced in by a wall high enough and sturdy enough to keep out even the most determined. Looking at it, at the effort made to make the wall look decorative from the outside, he could tell the government must have built it. The tops of trees could be seen rising over the wall.

Their vehicle paused before the gate, a human guard coming forward to check their IDs and barely able to restrain her delight at seeing Geary.

Once inside the gate he felt himself smiling as he saw the house. From the outside, it seemed little changed. It didn't seem large enough to be any family's ancestral home, but that was what it was. Not big and grand, but low and sprawling. And it was fitting, he thought, that it wasn't an ostentatious building that boasted of the wealth and influence of the family that lived there. Because the Gearys had never been a family of great wealth or influence, and even if they were, wouldn't have enjoyed living in a place like that.

"We'll leave you here," Council President Kennedy said. He and the other dignitaries said their farewells, got back in their limos, and the vehicles retreated out the gate, which closed to block off the sight if not the sound of the masses craning for a look at the hero who'd at last come home.

A woman was waiting at the front door, smiling and blinking away tears. "Jane hired me to look after the place while she was gone. It's all ready for you. The kitchen is stocked. I can get anything else you need."

"Thank you," Geary said. "I'm sure we'll be fine." He looked at the security panel to one side of the door, wondering. Walking to stand before it, he pressed his palm against the outline of a hand.

"Welcome back, John," the house's voice responded. Supposedly the voice was that of Lyn.

"You're still in the system," Tanya said, bemused.

"He was supposed to come back someday," the housekeeper offered. "That's what the legends said."

Which made a strange kind of sense. Geary walked the housekeeper to the gate, then came back to Tanya. "Ready?"

The door opened for him, and he stepped inside, feeling as if he'd also stepped back in time a hundred years. "It's hardly changed at all."

"I'm glad," Tanya said. "This place is only one story but it's bigger than it looks, isn't it?"

"Sort of. As the family grew they added rooms here and there so the house sprawled a bit. There were six bedrooms when I left last."

"How much land is inside this wall?"

"It's two and a half acres," he said. "I guess land was pretty cheap when the planet was first settled. Though there's a family story that the land actually was given to Robert and Lyn Geary by the government to reward their services in the early years when the planet was threatened."

He looked around him, realizing there was one place he had to go first. He walked through the great room and into a smaller room to one side. The family shrine. One wall was dominated by pictures, some larger, some smaller, of all the Gearys who'd died in the many years since the home was built. Beneath them on top of a low chest were the same sort of partly burned-down candles that he'd grown up seeing here.

He focused on the central picture, a family portrait that had always been there. The first Gearys. Robert in the uniform of Glenlyon's small navy before it had completely merged with others to form the Alliance fleet, Lyn wearing a large pin showing lines of code, their eldest daughter in Marine uniform, and two younger boys gazing eagerly outward as if poised to follow their own lives into space. "We grew up here, and then we left, and sometimes we came back," Geary said, looking at the image. "Sometimes we didn't." He looked at another picture, that of his mother and father, standing with young him and his brother Michael, who'd all believed him dead at Grendel, and he wished he'd done a better job of saying goodbye to them the last time he'd been here.

"Jane told me she hasn't been back since Michael was declared missing in action." Tanya gazed at all of the pictures. "She said because of the losses during the war, and after her parents died in combat, she and Michael were the last two Gearys left of the family. I understand now why she said the house felt way too big for them, and why she didn't want to come here alone."

"My fault," Geary said, feeling the pain of that. "They had to follow the example of Black Jack. Try to be heroes for the Alliance."

"That was *not* your fault. You didn't create that Black Jack legend, and you didn't demand that your relatives be forced to try to live up to it." Tanya gestured toward the wall of images with one hand, grasping his hand with her other. "Do you feel anger toward you from them? Resentment? They know you did the best you could, and they tried to do the same. Do you know what I feel? How proud your ancestors are of you. Standing here, I can feel it. Oh."

"What?" He followed her gaze. And saw his own picture, from when he'd assumed command of *Merlon*. He remembered sending that to his parents. "I guess we should take that one down." Feeling awkward, Geary looked for another picture and didn't see it. "There's no photo of my great-nephew Michael."

Tanya nodded. "Jane doesn't think he's dead."

"Did she tell you *they* hated me, growing up, for that legend locking them into careers in the fleet? For being constantly measured against that impossible standard. But they still did their best. Like, sure we're Gearys, so we'll do what we have to do, but you can't make us happy about it."

"I know someone else like that," Tanya said. "And now that Jane knows who you really are, she doesn't hate you. Who's this?" she added, pointing to an old, small photo of a woman that seemed to have been taken for an ID card. "That's not a formal picture."

"Lieutenant Martel. She was on Robert Geary's ship. Family lore says she died far from home with no family, so the Gearys adopted her spirit as part of our family."

He reached down to the chest, wondering if it would be as he remembered, pulling open what should be the correct drawer and seeing the matches inside. Sparking one to life, he used it to light one of the candles, then handed the match to Tanya. She took it and lit another candle next to his. And in that moment, standing before the images of his ancestors, and of the Gearys who'd come after him but died before he'd been found and revived, he realized how very right this was and how much he'd needed to do it. To stand here looking at them, thinking of them, thanking them, while holding Tanya's hand and formally presenting her to them as a new member of the family. "Thank you," he said in a low voice.

They stood there before the pictures for he didn't know how long, the candles burning, memories tumbling through his mind. But no clear images came, no clear messages or feelings. Finally he reached to put out his candle, and Tanya did the same. "Thank you," he said again, this time to Tanya. "You were right. I needed to come here."

"I'm always right," she said, smiling.

"I keep forgetting."

"I know. I'll keep reminding you."

"Are you hungry?"

"After that buffet?" she said. "No."

He pointed down a hallway. "I only came to visit occasionally, but they had extra room, so they left my old room for me. It's probably been changed since then, of course."

"Why don't we find out?" she said.

The hall felt both eerily familiar and oddly strange, the same hall, pretty much the same furnishings, but some new pictures added to the old ones, along with some new plaques and other items nestled among those he'd often looked at a century before. At least one of the new plaques was about Black Jack's Last Stand, but he refused to look directly at it and read it.

He nerved himself before opening the door to the room, his room, not knowing just what it was that worried him.

Inside, he stopped to stare around him.

"Are you okay?" Tanya asked.

"I'm not sure." He studied the room, trying to spot details. "As far as I can tell, it's exactly as it was when I last left here. Obviously it's been kept clean, but I don't think anything has been moved or replaced."

"They didn't change anything over the last century? Does that feel welcoming, or creepy?"

"A bit of both."

She looked about her, spotting something tossed onto the top of the desk. "Concert tickets?"

He laughed. "They even left those sitting there? Yeah. Printed tickets to frustrate counterfeiting. Jump Space Riot was a really popular group on Glenlyon back then."

"There's two tickets here," Tanya observed. "Who'd you go with?"

"Uh . . . a friend." Why did he feel awkward about that? About a woman he'd known a century ago?

She gave him a skeptical look.

"Really," he protested. "Aileen just liked me as a friend."

"I notice you're not saying how you felt about her." Tanya touched the tickets gently. "Don't look guilty. Friends are important. I hope she found the person she was looking for."

"I didn't want to look it up," Geary said. "Her, or others I knew. It was bad enough finding out what had happened to the surviving members of my cruiser at Grendel."

"I understand." Tanya looked around again, then brought out a small device, examining it. "The only bugs in this room are some commercial gimmicks. Standard home security stuff." She touched the device a couple of times. "The ones in this room have now been deactivated, and anything I couldn't spot is being jammed."

"Good." He took another look at the device she held. "That looks familiar."

"It was a bequest to me from a mutual friend, along with instructions on how to use it." Tanya turned the device in her hand as if studying it. "I don't know where that woman got gear like this, but she must have known some very interesting people."

"Victoria Rione gave you that?" he asked, astounded.

"I told you it was a bequest." She shrugged. "Yes, I was startled. Apparently that woman thought I'd need to have it. It's a very handy little item. I let Senior Chief Tarrani take a look at it and she was extremely impressed." Tanya looked at him. "I assume we're sleeping in this room."

"Yes," he said, feeling his heart beating a little stronger at the thought as he looked back at her.

She grinned at him, reaching up one hand to touch his face. "Then let's check the bedding. If it's the same bedding you last used a century ago, we're going to change the sheets."

HE woke up in the late, late hours of the night, at that time when everything felt hushed. Gazing at the ceiling through the dimness, he tried to grasp the memory of a dream that was fading so quickly he was left with no recollection of the dream itself. All he still knew was the feeling it left in its wake.

"What's the matter?" Tanya, next to him.

He reached to hold her close. "I'm sorry I woke you."

"I'm a ship's captain," she said, her voice low, her breath warm against his face. "I have hair-trigger wake-up reflexes. What's wrong?"

"Nothing. I had a dream."

"About what?"

"I don't remember." He looked into the darkness. "I was happy. No. Comforted. It was all right. Everything was all right. That's all I can remember. That feeling. It was just a dream."

"Just a dream?" She sighed, her body moving against him.

How many times did he dream about that when they were aboard the ship and couldn't even touch?

"Jack, it wasn't just a dream." Tanya sounded as confident as always. "You're home. It welcomed you. This is where your ancestors' spirits gather. They welcomed you. Of course you felt comforted."

"I hope you're right."

"I'm always right."

He laughed and kissed her, and she kissed him back. "Are you thinking what I'm thinking?" he asked.

"That it'd be a shame to just go back to sleep?" she murmured.

THE next morning, before heading out to fulfill his many public obligations, Geary took Tanya to a narrow section of wall in one room. He ran his fingers across the molding next to it, found the catch, and pressed it.

The section swung open, revealing steps leading down.

"What the hell is this?" Tanya asked, looking down the stairs.

"A secret passage," he said, grinning.

"You got to grow up in a house with a secret passage?"

"Sure did." He reached in to turn on the lights. "Family legend says Lyn insisted on having a secret passage in the house when it was built."

"She was a serious code monkey, right? Because that sounds like something a programmer would do," Tanya said.

He led the way down, noting that the stairs showed signs of not having been cleaned for a few years, but only a few. "It looks like my brother Michael passed on the secret to his kids, and they passed it on to his grandkids." The stairs ended in a large room, with sturdy furniture of timeless design, and walls lined with real books as well as entertainment and other computer gear, some of it old enough to be original with the house but other pieces much newer. Geary went to an open section of wall, smiling as he looked at it despite the ache it brought inside him. "Another tradition. We all signed our names here when we were let in on the secret. Generation after generation. There's mine. And there's where my brother signed."

"This is so cool," Tanya said. "You have a secret passage leading to a secret underground . . . what is this? Just one room?"

"No, there are other rooms. A kitchen, a bathroom, a storeroom. And another passage that comes out a ways outside the house."

"Does all of this gear still work?" she asked, waving around the room.

"It did when I lived here," Geary said. "Oh, if you link into the home network, you never know when some hidden subroutine planted by Lyn will activate and mess with you. Those all still worked when I lived here, too."

"Your great-whatever-grandmother turned herself into a cyber-poltergeist who's still haunting the home network?" Tanya said. "We are going to live on this planet. In this house. This is where our kids get to grow up. Not in a high-rise on Kosatka where the only hidden passages are maintenance shafts and all the computer problems are caused by bad programming."

"I'm good with that." He picked up the pen resting at the bottom of the wall. Was it the same one he'd used? Unlikely, given how long it'd been. "Are you going to sign?"

"I get to sign?" Tanya grabbed the pen and carefully wrote her name next to where his had been placed well over a century ago. "This wall is like a totally disorganized family tree, isn't it?"

"I guess so. You've now been officially let in on the family secrets."

"I guess that means you're stuck with me," she said.

"Lucky me."

OUTSIDE, the sun shone brightly down on the crowds waiting to catch a glimpse of him. They cheered. He smiled and waved. The police holding back the crowds smiled and waved. Council President Kennedy, standing next to a limo, smiled and waved.

Smiling faces, Geary couldn't help thinking. But, in this case, the smiles were very likely all real.

"Good morning, Admiral," Kennedy said. "And good morning, um . . ."

"Captain," Tanya said. "Captain Tanya Desjani."

"Captain! Yes. I wasn't certain how you preferred to be addressed." Ushering them into the limo and then following, Kennedy relaxed in his seat as the vehicle surged into motion.

Geary, better rested than the day before, examined the limo's interior, seeing indications that it was only lightly armored. Real windows of thick material showed the outside world and the many people waving as the limo went by. He realized they could see him, and raised his hand to wave back.

"You need to do what they call the royal wave," Council President Kennedy advised, raising his own hand and moving it gently a little ways back and forth. "Otherwise you get tired out really fast. Captain, you already seem to know how to do it."

Tanya nodded, her raised hand moving slightly. "Old Family on Kosatka," she explained. "We got to visit with the royal family. One of the princesses showed me the trick when we were kids."

"Desjani!" Kennedy said. "Of course! I should have made the connection. What do you think of Glenlyon?"

"It's lovely," she said.

"We've decided to retire here someday," Geary added, knowing that was what Kennedy wanted to know.

"Praise our ancestors," Kennedy said, looking relieved. "It's . . . well, it's important to everyone here. With the house empty these last few years, people worried. There's always been Gearys on Glenlyon. Legend says the first person to set foot on the planet was your ancestor, Admiral."

"Really?" Geary laughed. "That's a new one on me."

"Legends tend to acquire details as time goes on," Kennedy said. "History forgets details, and legends acquire more of them. People are like that." He gave Geary a sharp look. "These aliens you've met. Are they like people?"

"Yes and no," he said. "Figuring out how they think is the biggest challenge. But they seem to have characteristics we can identify with."

"Any chance you'll be able to bring some here? Those cute ones, the, uh . . ."

"The Kicks?" Tanya said, startled.

"No," Kennedy said, hauling out his personal pad to check. "The Ursataurians. They look like they'd be good neighbors to humanity."

"Like little bear-cows?" Tanya asked. "When did the Kicks start getting called Ursataurians?"

"It's something combining the scientific names for bears and cows," Kennedy said. "What does Kicks mean?"

Tanya gave him a look. Geary cleared his throat. "It's a slang term the fleet has used," he said, not wanting to explain it was a phonetic for Crazy Killer Cows. "There's no chance of any of them coming here. They're extremely hostile, very dangerous. They refused all attempts at communication."

"And did their very best to kill us on sight," Tanya added cheerfully. "They kill everything that isn't part of their herd, or used by their herd. I think 'fanatical' is the right word, isn't it, Admiral?"

"Yes," Geary said, unhappy to learn the idea that the Kicks were friendly because they were cute was this widespread. "We did our best to speak to them, and they didn't want any part of it."

"Oh," Council President Kennedy said. "Well, perhaps when diplomats contact them they'll have better luck."

Geary sighed. "That's unlikely. As Captain Desjani said, they refused to talk to us, and just kept attacking. We managed to capture a few alive, and they immediately committed suicide. Believe me, we wanted to talk to them. We didn't want to fight. But to them we're predators, not part of their herd. It's going to be very difficult to establish any relations with them."

"The aliens who've proven friendly," Tanya said, "are the Dancers."

Geary gave her a did-you-have-to look. "Yes. Natural engineers, and they seem to share common values with us."

"Dancers?" Kennedy asked. "Wait, are those the spiders?"

"They're not spiders."

"They're more like a cross between spiders and wolves," Tanya said, clearly enjoying herself.

"They have common values with us? Really?" Kennedy said.

"Really," Geary said. "As far as we can tell. They've provided valuable assistance to us in battle, fighting alongside us. And they're willing to talk to us."

"Maybe they want our technology."

"No," Geary said. "All indications are that their technology is superior to ours." If he was going to turn around appearance prejudices, he'd have to start with each person he talked to. That was probably why Tanya had goaded him into doing this. "I know how they look is jarring. But inside they're the closest to us of any alien species we've yet encountered."

Council President Kennedy frowned in thought. "You know a lot more than I do, of course. Still . . ." He laughed. "You know, given what people have done to each other, maybe saying they're like us isn't the best recommendation!"

"You've got a point there," Geary said.

"We're still looking for something better than us," Tanya said. "Maybe intelligent life is inherently complicated."

"That I would believe," Kennedy said. "It's a little difficult to think something that looks like the . . . the Dancers is friendly, but my best friend would never be called handsome and there's no one I can count on more. So, that's two alien species. There's a third, right?"

"Yes," Geary said. "We call them the enigmas, because they are obsessed with not letting anyone learn anything about them, and we still know very little. We've tried reaching out to them without success so far."

"They're afraid of us because we're curious," Tanya said. "That's what we think. They don't want other species knowing anything about them, and we're a species that always wants to learn things."

"That's a tough one," Council President Kennedy said. "And yet it's so amazing you actually found three intelligent alien species! Do you think there are more out there beyond where humanity has gone?"

"I wouldn't be surprised," Geary said.

"Here I am talking about aliens when you're finally home," Kennedy said. "I hope we haven't overscheduled you, Admiral. There are so many people in so many places that want to see you."

"I understand," Geary said, trying not to show how little he was looking forward to all of that.

Tanya leaned close to murmur in his ear. "Be strong."

IT wasn't until the day after that an event he'd particularly dreaded took place. Glenlyon had indeed built a statue of him. He wouldn't have gone anywhere near it except that he had been scheduled to lay a wreath at the site in honor of those from Glenlyon who'd died during the war. Even if he could have wriggled out of that he wouldn't have. It was the least he could do.

But it took all of his self-control to keep his expression properly respectful as he walked past the statue. It was larger than life, and so taller than he really was. The statue portrayed Black Jack standing, shoulders back, head tilted upward to gaze toward space. One arm was raised, the hand clenched into a defiant fist. The other arm extended out a little, forever frozen in a dramatic sweeping gesture. The face of the statue was set in lines of heroic determination.

It also didn't look all that much like his face, he thought.

Tanya must have felt the same way. "I guess that Black Jack was a really handsome fellow."

"Too bad you didn't end up with him," Geary muttered.

"I wouldn't have wanted him," Tanya said. "He's not human."

She had a point, he thought as he solemnly placed the wreath. In their zeal to portray Black Jack as the greatest hero of all time, the creators of the statue had robbed him of humanity.

He dropped all thought of the statue as he adjusted the position of the wreath and then stepped back, turning to face those watching. In his mind, he didn't see the crowd, but rather all of those he'd known who he would never meet again in this life, from those who'd died aboard *Merlon* to those lost at Unity Alternate a hundred years later. "May their sacrifices always be remembered, their memories always honored," he said, trying not to choke up.

But his feelings could be heard in his voice, and the applause that followed told him that these people approved of a hero who rather than being perfect felt the same emotions they did.

PUBLIC encounters over the next few days became a blur of old places he'd remembered and new places built over the last century, and of a seemingly endless number of meetings with people who claimed some connection to him. It felt as if most of the population of the planet had grandparents or granduncles or grandaunts who'd claimed to have gone to school with him. "You must have attended some really huge schools," Tanya commented after another such encounter.

"I don't remember so many people wanting to claim association with me," Geary said. "Especially not in high school."

They'd finally gotten home after another long day of public appearances and another excruciatingly long formal dinner. He was sitting in the main room in what looked like a familiar chair, which meant it must have been reupholstered at least once since he'd last sat in it. Tanya stood by one window, looking out from the back of the house at the grass and trees there. "What was it like when you left this planet the last time?" she asked.

He paused, trying to remember that day a century past. "I was on my way to assume command of *Merlon*, the heavy cruiser I lost at Grendel."

"I wish you wouldn't put it like that. You always make it sound like a defeat."

"I guess because it felt that way at the time," he said. "Anyway, I had a couple of weeks to come home and see my parents and my brother."

"And Aileen," she teased.

"I saw her one time," he said. "The day I left . . ." He hesitated, surprised by how vivid the memories suddenly became. "I got up really early because the shuttle I needed to catch was lifting about sunrise. Mom and Dad got up to see me off. I thought I'd see them again in another couple of years, but that'd be a while, so we made sure we said our farewells. It was still dark when I left here. I remember how quiet the street was when the ride came. It took me to the launch field, the same field my ancestors had used, and my parents before me. The sun was just coming up when I walked up the ramp into the shuttle. It was beautiful. There was a cold wind, though."

She turned her head to look back at him. "No one was there to see you off?"

"No. Hardly anyone was there at all. The only other passengers on the shuttle were contract employees commuting to work on the orbital facility. I was the only person in uniform."

"That's weird," Tanya said. "All of my life there've been a lot of people in uniform around. Forgive my saying so, but it sounds like you were lonely."

"I was." Geary shrugged. "At the time the military wasn't a, uh, high-prestige way of making a living. It wasn't any way to get rich, that's for sure. And I knew how much demand on my life being commanding officer of *Merlon* would require, so I didn't think it was fair to expect any partner to put up with that."

She laughed. "Instead you ended up marrying a ship's captain. I admit you're a lot of work sometimes, but you're worth making time for. So there wasn't anyone special you left behind? I mean, outside of family?"

"No." He inhaled deeply, thinking about it. "That would've made it so much harder. Even if there'd been a close girlfriend. Imagine if I'd had a wife and children. Knowing they'd grown old and died while I was locked in survival sleep. That would've been . . . very hard to live with. So I guess I was lucky that I was lonely at the time."

"You know how I feel about that." She walked over and sat down next to him. "You and I were meant to be together. We were born at the wrong times, though. So that had to be fixed. I'm sorry the burden of that fell on you."

"I doubt that the living stars cared so much about my happiness," Geary said. "I do wish my parents could've met you."

"We met the first night I was here," she said, absolutely serious. "Couldn't you feel it?"

"Maybe," he said. "You really want our kids to grow up here?"

"Where they can be haunted by the cyber-ghost of their ancestor? Hell, yes. Two or three, I think. Does that sound good?"

"It sounds great. When are we going to start?"

"Not until we get back from this latest mission," Tanya said. "At the earliest. Is it okay to admit I miss my ship?"

"You missed that ship the moment you stepped off her deck," he said.

"Yes. So?"

"So, in a couple of more days you'll be back with your first love."

"*Dauntless* is not my first love, but go ahead and keep believing that."

He studied her, thinking about the future. "What will you do when the command of *Dauntless* passes to someone else?"

"That's when I'll leave the fleet," Tanya said in a matter-of-fact way. "It would've been different if the war was still going on, but now I can do that with a clean conscience. I can't think of any other job in the fleet that I wouldn't feel was a step down after having commanded *Dauntless*. So I'll put in my resignation and move on." She smiled. "Or rather, move here, I guess. Not alone, I hope."

"When you leave the fleet, so do I," Geary said. "We'll be here together, carrying on the family tree." Unexpectedly, the conversation reminded him of something. A thing that had happened while growing up. He stood up. "There's something out back I need to check."

She tilted her head slightly as she looked at him, having apparently picked up something in his voice. "Can I come with?"

"Sure." Outside, vision of the area beyond the yard blocked by trees and fences, only the sound filtering past telling them bystanders were still gathered and police still in place, Geary led the way toward a particular spot, glad that enough daylight remained to see.

"They should be here." He stopped, looking at one old tree, rising into the sky, its leaves thick. "There should be two trees. We planted them here. My brother Michael and I. It was a tradition. The Geary children always planted a tree." He looked around again, knowing it was absurd, but not willing to accept that there was only one tree here. "I guess . . . one of the trees died."

She watched him, staying silent.

He reached out and touched the old bark, pressing his hand against it, trying to feel something. "I bet this is Mike's tree. I think his is the one that survived."

"Yeah," Tanya said. "That must be his tree."

"Because we each planted one," Geary said, realizing he was repeating himself and not able to stop. "And whenever I was back on this planet Michael would come by, too, and we'd stand here and look at them and how tall they were getting." His voice broke. The things he tried not to think about filled him, all that had been lost in the century he was frozen in survival sleep, the deaths of everyone he'd ever known, all summed up in this old tree that was left to stand alone, and for a moment he couldn't speak at all.

Tanya's arms came around him, holding tight. She said nothing, just holding him as the light faded and darkness settled on the yard.

After a while, he moved a bit and she let go. "Thanks," Geary said. "I know you've lost a lot of people, too."

"Doesn't make it any easier," she said.

"No. It never does, I guess." They walked back inside.

The kitchen had been stocked with more than just food. "We have beer," Geary said.

"They know how to keep sailors happy, don't they?" Tanya said, taking a bottle and eyeing the label. "Martin Page's India Pale Ale. Is he a local celebrity?"

"A legendary brewer on Glenlyon over a century ago," Geary said. "This is top shelf. Martin Page was also reputedly the finest knife fighter on two worlds in his prime."

"Knife fighter? The same Page our boarding party instructors kept quoting?"

"That's the guy."

"Then here's to him." She took a drink. "It's good all right. I have to admire anyone who masters two such socially significant areas of expertise."

They sat down, he still brooding over the tree, she apparently not certain what to say. Finally, Tanya touched the remote. "Do you mind if I check the local news? I want to see if my crew is behaving."

"Be my guest," he said.

"Crew, liberty, *Dauntless*," Tanya said as the room's main display lit up. A moment later scenes appeared of sailors partying amid crowds of Glenlyon natives. "That's a relief. I was afraid the first link those words brought up would be about arrests."

Geary noticed that just about every sailor had at least one similarly aged companion from planetside. "I wonder how many members of your crew will fall in love before we leave Glenlyon?"

"There are always at least a few sailors who think they've found their soul mate on liberty," Tanya said. "Even in a rotten port. Great liberty like this ought to produce a lot of spur-of-the-moment engagements."

Geary smiled, glad to have something else, something pleasant, to focus on. "I remember after one great liberty almost half of my division was ready to get married then and there."

"That must have been a really great liberty," she said, taking another drink of the ale. "Do you remember where it was?"

"Kosatka," he said, smiling at her reaction. "Remember me telling you my ship was there for a royal wedding? I was a lieutenant back then."

"Oh, yeah." She grinned. "That's why my world created a royal family. To serve as a nonpolitical symbol of the planet for everybody on Kosatka, and to be a reason to hold big parties whenever one of them was crowned, or got married, or had a kid, or whatever. The whole planet gets to let its hair down."

"I don't know about the whole planet. We had liberty in Lodz, the capital."

"My hometown." Tanya turned an arch look on him. "How about you? Did you meet any girls in Lodz?"

"No." He hesitated as the memories came back. "Well, yes. One of the times I was on the surface I'd wandered away from the parties and ended up in a museum."

"You haven't changed much, have you? And you found a nice girl in the museum?"

"She was interested in history, too," Geary said. "We ended up talking for hours." Should he say the rest? Best to get it all out so it wouldn't slip out later and cause problems. "I had to leave, to get back to the ship for duty. She gave me her contact info for the next day I was supposed to have free, but as it turned out a critical piece of equipment broke on the ship and I had to stay aboard to oversee the repairs. Then we left. So I never saw her again."

Tanya smiled, drinking more beer. "I told you we were fated to be together. What was her name?"

"Ummm . . . Sonia."

Tanya, in the middle of another drink of beer, nearly choked. She managed to swallow her drink, looking at Geary with wide eyes. "Sonia?" she asked in a hoarse voice. "Sonia was my grandmother's name."

He stared back at her, his mind momentarily blank. When it started working again, he shook his head. "No. She was not your grandmother."

"What was her last name?"

"I don't remember."

"Did you make out with her?"

"No!" He glared at Tanya. "This is getting weird."

"*You* think this is weird? When I'm the one who just found out my husband could've been my grandfather?" Tanya sat back with a groan. "The last several times I've communed with my ancestors I've felt like Bobcha Sonia was irritated with me. Now I know why! I need to apologize to Granmama the next time I speak with her. So do you."

"Why do I need to apologize to your grandmother's spirit?"

"For standing her up!"

There were times when the only right strategy involved surrender. This was one of those times. "Okay."

NINE

HE'D feared that each day on Glenlyon would drag, that he'd welcome the chance to finally leave again and be a little less deluged by the idolization of Black Jack, but on the last morning at home Geary found himself saddened at the thought of leaving. "Tanya, there's something I never told you."

"There's just one thing you never told me?" she asked, sitting in the main room drinking coffee.

"Well . . . I'll get around to everything someday." He hesitated, looking about him. "One of the reasons I didn't want to come home was because as long as I didn't, I could pretend in my head that everything was still the same. That Mom and Dad were still here. Coming here meant confronting reality. Meant visiting their memorial."

"Are you okay?" Tanya asked.

"Yeah. I think I am. Because now I realize holding on to them, keeping them here, wasn't fair to them. And because I couldn't move on with my life as long as I couldn't accept what had already happened."

She sighed, standing up and coming over to him. "You moved on enough to marry me, but I'm glad this is closing the circle for you. Hold me tight, will you? In a few hours we'll be back on board and not even able to give each other meaningful glances."

"That's one of the reasons I'm reluctant to leave," he admitted.

"As long as we're confessing," Tanya said, her voice low as she held him close, "I should tell you that I needed this. I was starting to wonder if we could be a real couple. If the whole captain-and-admiral thing was all we were, keeping each other at arm's length. And I know we still did a lot of that here whenever we were in public, but in this house we were able to be close and I'm grateful for that."

They stood there a little longer before he sighed and moved away. "I need to make sure I've packed everything I want to take."

Tanya frowned. "You're not thinking of taking some of those century-old civilian clothes that were still stored in your room, are you?"

"I think those are a little outdated."

"Yeah, maybe just a little."

An hour later they left the house. As he locked it with his palm on the security plate, Lyn's voice wished him a safe trip.

Waiting at the gate was the usual limo, this time once more part of a procession for the farewell events. More crowds, more waving, another speech, this time saying he couldn't wait until he could return and meaning every word of it, then into the VIP shuttle and up through atmosphere.

As the shuttle approached *Dauntless*'s dock, Tanya leaned close and kissed him, holding it until the shuttle reached the ship.

The shuttle docked, the ramp lowered, and they walked off onto the decks of the battle cruiser once more, Geary in the lead in accordance with military etiquette and Desjani following. "Admiral, Alliance fleet, arriving, *Dauntless* arriving," the all-hands circuit told everyone on the ship as the ship's bell was sounded six times to mark Geary's rank, then four times for Desjani's.

They both returned salutes from the officer of the watch. "I'll be on the bridge preparing the ship for departure, Admiral," Desjani said to him.

"Thank you, Captain," he said. "I'm going by my stateroom before joining you on the bridge. I want to be on the bridge when we leave orbit."

"Understood. I'll see you there."

Everything was the same as before, and nothing would ever be the same.

But they still had the same job to do back at Varandal.

GEARY had gotten more and more restless on the trip back. No longer distracted by worries about visiting Glenlyon or looking forward to time with Tanya off the ship, he could only focus on the preparations for the upcoming mission, painfully aware that his information was already more than two weeks old. A lot could happen in two or three weeks.

Dauntless's crew, though, seemed to have exceptionally high morale. It appeared none of them had paid for a single drink or a meal while on the surface at Glenlyon. And as predicted a fair number of requests had been submitted for extra leave justified by either an impending engagement or impending marriage. Those requests, in turn, generated the only negative moments on the trip back to Varandal, as senior enlisted and officers counseled smitten sailors (with varying degrees of success) on the necessity of thinking about how enduring love born of a few days of planetside liberty might turn out to be.

Geary nerved himself for the worst as he sat on the bridge, awaiting the exit from the hypernet. In just a few moments he'd learn what had happened while he was away from Varandal.

"Exiting hypernet in three . . . two . . . one."

The first thing he noticed was the absence of alarms that would've been triggered by any nearby threat. The second thing was that nothing seemed amiss as the ship's sensors updated his display with all the information that could be seen. Some of it was hours time delayed because of how long it took light to cover the distance, of course, but it was still reassuring to see no sign of problems.

There was something off, though. Something unexpected. What was it?

"We have a new battleship," Tanya remarked.

That was it. An extra battleship. Sort of a ridiculous thing not to key on immediately. "*Audacious*?" Geary wondered. "No, it's . . . *Reprisal*. And she's broadcasting ID as part of the fleet." *Reprisal*, and the other warships the Callas Republic had once contributed to the Alliance fleet, had been sent home by Geary after the war to prevent their crews from mutinying at being forced to remain far from their families. "Why'd they send *Reprisal* back?"

"It looks like the Callas Republic wants in on whatever the fleet does next," Desjani said. "Remember that diplomatic courier ship we saw racing to leave Unity? They found out what your mission is and they want a piece of it. So much for them reasserting their independence."

"If that's the only unexpected thing that took place while we were gone, I'm grateful," Geary said. "It looks like everything else is fine."

"Are you disappointed, Admiral?"

He laughed. "As someone reminded me, I shouldn't be indispensible."

It took close to two days for *Dauntless* to reach Ambaru Station, giving him time to get up to date on everything. "Nothing untoward to report," Captain Badaya said (a bit smugly) in a welcoming message. "Except that I assume you've seen *Reprisal* showed up, along with four destroyers from the Callas Republic. Captain Hiyen and I agreed he should wait until you returned to make a formal visit with the fleet commander since I was only acting commander."

Once *Dauntless* was close enough to Ambaru Station and the rest of the fleet, *Reprisal* sent a shuttle over. Captain Hiyen looked much the same as he had when the battleship had left, though he definitely seemed under a lot less strain. He exited his shuttle to a full compliment of honors before accompanying Geary back to his stateroom. "Welcome back to Varandal," Geary said, waving Hiyen to a seat. "I admit I wasn't expecting to see you or any Callas Republic warships again."

Hiyen sat down carefully, and then spoke with the same care, as if choosing each word. "The Callas Republic has not forgotten how many sacrifices the Alliance made during the recently ended war. We want to continue to contribute to Alliance efforts."

"Exactly how are you supposed to contribute?" Geary asked, also taking a seat. "Do you have specific instructions?"

"The warships under my command are to accompany you, Admiral, as part of the Alliance fleet. Just as before."

"What if I want your ships to stay here and assist in the defense of the Alliance?" Geary pressed, already suspecting the answer.

"My ships are to accompany you, Admiral," Hiyen repeated.

Geary leaned back, sighing. "In other words, the Callas Republic wants to be represented when I take a force to Midway Star System again, and when we go back to Dancer-controlled space."

Captain Hiyen spread his hands. "I have my orders, Admiral. I don't disagree with them. I'm . . . grateful that my government has seen fit to renew our cooperation with the Alliance. You know me. No Alliance commander I've served under has ever had any complaints about my performance." He paused, a shadow crossing over his expression. "I also carry the republic's condolences on the sacrifice of former co-president Victoria Rione. Her death was a great loss for both the Callas Republic and the Alliance."

"She spoke highly of you," Geary said. "I think you know how difficult it was to gain Co-President Rione's approval. Are there any diplomatic representatives of the republic's government aboard your ship?"

"Yes," Hiyen said without trying to deflect the question. "To meet with the Dancers. I've been told arrangements have already been made for his accommodations aboard the Alliance emissary ship when it arrives here."

"There shouldn't be any problems, then," Geary said, wishing he had Rione at hand to tell him about whoever this Callas Republic representative was. "Captain, I don't see any problem with including your ships in the mission to Dancer space. The Callas Republic does realize there are substantial hazards in this mission, correct? That you could suffer combat losses?"

"Yes," Captain Hiyen said. "That is understood." He frowned, gazing at the star display on one wall. "There's something else that you should know. Officially, I'm not telling you this. It regards the Rift Federation."

"Oh?" The Rift Federation was even smaller than the Callas Republic, and had also been distancing itself once more from the Alliance in the wake of the war.

"They also want a presence in Dancer space," Captain Hiyen said. "But not as part of an Alliance fleet. They're going to send their own ships independently."

"Independently?" Geary let his alarm show. "How big a force do they have?"

"According to my information, one heavy cruiser, a couple of light cruisers, and five destroyers."

Geary made a fist, bringing it down on one arm of his seat. "The odds of a force that small making it to Midway aren't good. But making it past there, through enigma space to Dancer space? They won't have a chance. The enigmas will wipe them out."

Hiyen nodded slowly, his unhappiness clear. "I understand the commander of the Rift Federation force advised her superiors of that, and was told to go regardless. It's Captain Kapelka, on the *Passguard*."

At least that was also someone he knew, though not very well. Geary shook his head. "Do you know what route they plan on taking?"

"Doubtless the route they know from having accompanied your fleet before." Hiyen leaned forward, his eyes intent. "Admiral, in the aftermath of the war, both my republic and Kapelka's federation wanted to reassert their independence from the Alliance. But both have discov-

ered that during the war they integrated their economies and regulations very closely with the Alliance. Disentangling all of that is proving
far more difficult than expected. That leaves the leaders of the republic
with the need to demonstrate their independence despite remaining so
closely tied to the Alliance. I think the Rift Federation's leaders face the
same problem. You see? Independent diplomatic outreach to another
intelligent species offers a means to do that."

"But Kapelka knows what'll happen if she tries to reach Dancer
space with that small a force," Geary said.

"She does," Hiyen said. "But she can't travel as part of an Alliance
fleet, either. The Rift Federation believes it is on the verge of being absorbed by the Alliance, and while many of the federation's people
would welcome that, others are fiercely opposed. Captain Kapelka has
always tried to be discreet about her political leanings, but from my
knowledge of her I believe she is one of those determined to reassert
the independence of the Rift Federation."

"Normally that shouldn't be any concern of mine," Geary said. "The
Rift Federation is independent. I don't dispute that." Hiyen was telling
him this for a reason, though, and the reason must involve the impending mission. Geary thought about it, his own gaze going to the star
display. "Kapelka's going to follow the same route this fleet used before?"

"That is my understanding," Hiyen said.

"Which would mean entering former Syndic space at Atalia Star
System. Do you know if she's planning to jump from Varandal?"

Hiyen nodded, his expression somber. "I believe so."

"When?"

"I don't know. But I think their aim is to get a jump on the Alliance."

"They want to leave before we do?" There it was. Geary felt his jaw
tighten and made an effort to relax it. "And alert everyone and every
place along the way just before we get there. That'll substantially increase the risk to my force. I can't allow that." But could he stop it?

Captain Hiyen nodded somberly. "Admiral, Captain Kapelka and her crews fought well alongside us during the war. If there's any way they can be convinced to accompany your force, I will do all I can to assist."

"What will Captain Kapelka do if I tell her not to leave Varandal before we do?"

That made Hiyen hesitate. "I do not know."

AS if wanting to ensure his worries weren't allowed to settle, the universe arranged for Lieutenant Iger to visit that afternoon. "Admiral, I wanted to be certain that you'd seen my report about the anti-Dancer sentiments among the new recruits."

"Yes," Geary said, rubbing his forehead as he tried to recall details. "Nothing serious, and the veteran crews are working to turn around anyone who thinks the Dancers are enemies."

"Yes, sir," Iger said. "But I wanted to tell you in person something that couldn't go in the report because it's pure speculation."

Geary dropped his hand and looked straight at Iger. "What?"

"There's something missing," Iger said, looking stubborn. "Something we should be seeing and aren't."

"And something that clearly worries you," Geary said.

"Why haven't any of the new recruits, even in private conversations that have been reported to us, expressed serious reservations about the Dancers? There hasn't been even one case reported like that," Iger added, clearly frustrated.

"And you think we should have seen some?"

"Admiral, we know people with those serious anti-Dancer sentiments exist. We know some were caught during screening of recruits. But we haven't seen one such person at Varandal."

Geary sighed heavily, leaning forward. "What's the official line on that?"

"Officially," Iger said, "the lack of serious anti-Dancer sentiment detected among new recruits we've received is because our screening process caught everyone. But that assumes no one was deceitful during screening, or that anyone practicing deception about their feelings would be caught. And that's if every new recruit was asked about that."

"What do you think?" Geary asked.

"Admiral, the total lack of detections of serious anti-Dancer sentiment means either no one arriving has such sentiments, or that they're keeping quiet about them. I don't believe that we should ignore the second possibility."

He didn't want to have this additional complication to deal with. And it was, as Iger said, pure speculation. But he'd learned when his initial reaction was to reject something that he should examine his reasons for doing that. And right now all of his reasons had nothing to do with the possibility that Iger was right, or that Iger had had the guts to personally bring up the problem to him rather than keep it to himself. "'Absence of evidence is not evidence of absence,'" Geary said. "Somebody said that a long time ago. You might be right, Lieutenant. What can we do?"

Iger hesitated, looking startled that his argument had been accepted. "Notify the senior enlisted and senior officers, Admiral. There's not much else we can do. But just being aware that we need to be alert for it could make all the difference in spotting it. If it's out there."

"Draft me up a message to send to the captains in the fleet on what to watch for," Geary said.

"Yes, sir." Iger hesitated again. "Thank you, sir."

"Lieutenant, I've learned to trust your assessments. I'm not going to disregard a warning from you just because I don't want it to be true."

As if to emphasize Iger's suspicions, the next day another courier ship arrived at the hypernet gate. Accelerating toward the fleet's ships light hours distant, it broadcast a message that it had highly classified information to be passed directly to Admiral Geary. Over the next day and a half it responded to requests for more information with variations on the same message.

If it hadn't been for the attacks at the hypernet gate at Unity, no one would've been alarmed at the unusual actions of the courier ship. But they were unusual enough to draw notice at a time when everyone was keyed up.

As the courier ship neared *Dauntless*, Geary waited on the bridge along with Captain Desjani. The other battle cruisers of the Fourth Division were orbiting nearby, *Daring*, *Victorious*, and *Intemperate* all at full battle readiness.

"Talk to me, Lieutenant Castries," Desjani said.

"Still no indications the courier ship is a dark ship," Castries said. "Its performance profiles and exterior appearance still match standard courier ship models."

"Am I set up for my message to relay?" Geary asked.

"Yes, sir. It'll go to *Daring*, and then be sent from *Daring* to the courier ship as if you're aboard *Daring*."

Geary tapped his message controls. "Fleet Courier Ship 793G, this is Admiral Geary. You are ordered to immediately begin braking your velocity to point zero zero one light speed."

The courier ship was close enough by this time that the reply came with only a tiny delay. Unlike earlier messages, this one showed a visual, a lieutenant who displayed no apparent tension. "We have urgent materials for direct delivery to Admiral Geary by order of Fleet Headquarters. Proceeding to delivery."

"The courier ship is firing maneuvering thrusters," Lieutenant Yuon reported. "His main propulsion has lit off. Captain, he's not swinging around to brake velocity. He's accelerating and steadied on a new vector aimed at *Daring*. One minute to collision."

Desjani looked at Geary.

He nodded.

"All hell lance batteries engage the target," Desjani said at the same time as she hit her comm controls. "All ships in Fourth Division, weapons free to engage the approaching ship."

Hell lances speared out from all four battle cruisers to meet the oncoming ship at the same time as *Daring*'s main propulsion lit off at full power to shove her out of the path of the courier ship still accelerating toward her.

The courier ship tried to alter vector to match *Daring*'s movements, but disintegrated as dozens of hell lances tore through it.

"Captain?" Lieutenant Castries said, her voice higher pitched than usual. "We're picking up organics in the wreckage as well as traces of atmosphere."

"What?" Desjani inhaled deeply, glancing at Geary.

Had they destroyed a real courier ship, with a real crew aboard it? Before he could reply, a call came to the bridge. Senior Chief Tarrani, her expression somber. "Captain, last night I was talking with Master Chief Gioninni about how we'd sneak one of those dark ships through. He said he'd stuff a frozen human cadaver inside it so we'd get the right organic signature."

"Is there any way to tell if what we're picking up is from a recently dead human or a cadaver?" Desjani asked.

"Gioninni suggested checking acid levels in the remnants of the organic material. The moment a person dies, he said, pH levels start dropping as acidity increases."

"Lieutenant Castries—"

"Already on it, Captain." Castries's hands paused after she'd entered the search parameters. "Chemical analysis shows higher-than-normal levels of acid."

Geary let out a breath he'd been holding. "Get those readings to Dr. Nasr. I want his call on whether they're consistent with a human who'd just died, or a cadaver." He gave Desjani a sharp look. "Just how did Master Chief Gioninni know that?"

"There are some questions that are better not asked," she said. "Let alone answered."

Dr. Nasr called in, looking troubled. "Admiral, it's impossible to make a definite call, but those acidity levels in the organics are higher than would be seen in a living person."

"Take time to take a good look at everything," Geary said. "I'll report any analysis at this point is preliminary. Doctor, how hard would it be for someone to get their hands on a human cadaver?"

"If they could forge authorizations?" Dr. Nasr said. "It would be quite simple. A lot of people die every day, and all too many of those people die without family or friends to look after their remains. DNA identification cannot overcome that problem. Someone posing as such a relative would have no trouble getting what they wanted."

"But couldn't DNA testing rule out someone as a relative?"

"No. If it was too difficult to falsify the DNA test results, the person could simply claim to have married into the family and present documents apparently proving the relationship." The doctor shook his head in disapproval. "Too many die alone. It is a challenge we still have not conquered." His frown deepened as he paused in thought. "Those acidic levels. If someone died alone, and was not discovered for several hours or a day before the body was transferred to a cold environment, the pH levels we're seeing would be consistent with that."

"Thank you, Doctor." Geary put together a quick report and sent it off to Admiral Timbale and the rest of the ships in the star system. Then he called Lieutenant Iger. "How many more of those things might be out there?"

Iger didn't have to look it up. "The best estimates we've received in the last month show a maximum of six AI-controlled courier ships that cannot be confirmed as having been destroyed."

"So there are five left."

"Yes, Admiral. A maximum of five. There might be fewer."

"Is there any chance someone could still be building more of them somewhere?"

"No, Admiral," Iger said. "The shipyards and workers involved in that were all identified and shut down. No one in Alliance space could be building more."

That should have been reassuring. It wasn't. "What about outside Alliance space?" Iger stared at him, momentarily wordless. "Is there any chance the Syndics got their hands on the plans for those things?" Geary pressed.

"I haven't seen anything indicating that," Iger said, speaking slowly. "But I don't know if that's because we've looked and haven't found anything, or because we haven't looked. Perhaps the Alliance should be looking for signs of that."

"Perhaps it should," Geary said.

One more thing to worry about.

FOUR ships arrived at Varandal's hypernet gate a couple of days shy of two weeks until planned departure. Three were well-known, the assault transports *Tsunami*, *Typhoon*, and *Haboob*, carrying General Carabali and the Marines she'd taken to Unity. Aside from being a reassurance that his mission was still on, the return of the Marines also meant the government was feeling less concerned about its own security.

The fourth ship was big. It broadcast its identity as *Boundless*, an Emissary-class ship.

"What the hell is an Emissary-class ship?" Desjani said.

"That, apparently," Geary said. "And here's an incoming message from *Boundless* for me."

He didn't recognize the woman whose image appeared. She wore a civilian suit and an air of authority that both seemed well fitted to her. "Admiral Geary, this is Ambassador Rycerz. I look forward to meeting you in person as soon as possible. We have much to discuss."

"Are you worried about that last line?" Desjani asked. "Because I am."

"She doesn't look evil," Geary said.

"Neither do the Kicks."

It would be a few days before the *Boundless* reached the orbit of Varandal station and positioned itself near *Dauntless*. Plenty of time for him to worry over what Rycerz wanted to talk about, especially since she would have authority over him in nonsecurity matters.

◇

THE *Boundless* had once been a large passenger ship, capable of carrying thousands of people in varying degrees of comfort and luxury depending on how much money they could pay. Sometimes the passengers had been immigrants heading for new homes around unfamiliar stars. Other times they'd been tourists, gazing at the changing views of the heavens as the ship had jumped from star to star, the constellations themselves altering when viewed from places light years apart.

During the war, the *Boundless* had been converted to carry military personnel from training camps at distant stars to their units near the front, up to ten thousand at a time, crammed together as new recruits fed the insatiable maw of the endless war.

Now, her interior rebuilt, her systems replaced with the newest equipment, *Boundless* carried a new set of passengers, totaling only about five hundred in a ship originally designed to carry several times that number in comfort.

"The crew totals about three hundred," Captain Matson told Geary as he led him on a tour of the ship. General Carabali walked with them, several other of *Boundless*'s officers following behind. The crew wore uniforms that attempted to look professional without looking military, since *Boundless*'s new assignment was as a platform for civil tasks.

"That's pretty large for a civilian ship, isn't it?" Geary asked.

"It is," Matson agreed, indicating the other ship's officers with the group. "We need to have enough skilled people with us to operate and maintain the ship, and care for our passengers, for an extended period. If something breaks out there, we have to be able to fix it ourselves."

He pointed aft. "A lot of the former passenger space has been converted into storage for extra food stocks, water tanks, and fuel cell reserves. We can go a long time without running out of food. There are also a couple of compact manufacturing shops. In case of emergency, we can even fabricate new fuel cells if we can get the right raw materials."

"That's pretty impressive," Geary said. "How many people are you carrying total?"

"About five hundred." Matson began walking the group toward the bow. "The biggest group among our passengers are the diplomatic corps and their support staff, including the military honor guard. One hundred of them in all, directly answering to Ambassador Rycerz just as I do. Then there's a group of roughly sixty that makes up the engineers and scientists. Their overall supervisor is Dr. Kottur. The smallest group is the one everyone is calling the Ollies."

"Ollies?" Carabali asked.

Captain Matson smiled. "Specialists in biology, sociology, anthropology, zoology, neurology, psychology, and a bunch of other -ologies. They're supposed to learn more about the Dancers. I'm sure you've already heard from them so they could find out what you've learned so far."

"No," Geary said. "I haven't had any contact from them."

"Oh." Matson's smile went away. "Their leader is a man named Macadams. He's . . . well, I don't want to prejudice you."

Which, Geary thought, is what someone says when the only other things they can think to say are very prejudicial. Since Matson had already impressed him as being professional and capable, that didn't bode well for what Macadams might be like.

They'd reached the forward parts of the ship, which had been rebuilt into the diplomatic section, with conference rooms and offices in addition to living quarters. The other ship's officers stopped in a break room while Captain Matson led the way to the ambassador's office, gesturing for Geary and Carabali to enter while he stayed outside.

The large office had clearly been designed to impress without boasting, the walls lined with displays of art and other human achievements, the furnishings sturdy and elegant without being luxurious. Enough open space had been left to accommodate seating designed for Dancers once it was learned what kind of seating they used. At the far end of the office from the entry was the ambassador's desk, with several seats positioned facing it.

Ambassador Rycerz stood up from her place behind the desk as the group entered, as did a ground forces colonel, who'd been seated facing her. Out of habit, Geary ran his eyes over the ground forces officer first, seeing an immaculate uniform oddly lacking in medals, ribbons, or specialist insignia for someone so senior.

This was his first chance to study Ambassador Rycerz up close and in person. He saw sharp eyes that took in everything around her, and posh but not ostentatious clothes that projected an air of authority tempered by humility. Given how much was riding on the success of this mission, he hoped that snap assessment was accurate.

"Please sit down," Ambassador Rycerz said. She relaxed into her own chair, looking at Geary. "It's a pleasure to meet you, Admiral. This is a risky mission with a lot of unknowns, so I'm happy to have you commanding the security aspect of this expedition."

"I'm happy to be of assistance," Geary said. "I know the Alliance's diplomats face serious hazards sometimes to do their jobs. We'll do all we can to protect you and hopefully establish better relations with the Dancers."

"We all owe a great debt to the women and men of the fleet," Rycerz said. "I'll do my best to minimize any danger to them. I do want to make it clear how important I consider the fleet's contribution to this mission. I'm glad that you'll be able to speak directly to the Dancers whenever any security issues arise."

"Thank you," Geary said, wondering why Rycerz had specifically mentioned him talking to Dancers directly.

"This is Colonel Webb," Rycerz said, indicating the ground forces officer. "He's both the military attaché for this mission, and the head of the ceremonial honor guard."

"This is General Carabali," Geary said. "Commander of the Marines attached to my forces." Carabali was fully recovered from her injury on Unity, the only reminder of it an additional star on her combat wounded badge.

"Just how large is your ceremonial honor guard?" Carabali asked. Geary noticed that she kept her eyes on Webb as she asked the question.

"Twenty," Webb said, smiling politely. "Twenty-one, counting myself."

"Perhaps we can get together another time and discuss experiences during the war," Carabali said.

Geary, wondering why Carabali was extending a social invitation so quickly, saw Colonel Webb smile again. "I didn't really do much worth talking about," Webb said.

Carabali glanced at Geary in what seemed a request for permission, so he nodded.

"Elite special forces don't say much about their past work, do they?" General Carabali said.

TEN

COLONEL Webb gave Ambassador Rycerz a sidelong look but didn't say anything.

"Twenty-one is the number of personnel in a reinforced special forces squad," Carabali continued. "Isn't it?"

Ambassador Rycerz sighed. "Tell them, Colonel. The general has obviously figured it out already."

Colonel Webb nodded, the polite smile gone. "That's correct, General. I am the military attaché for the ambassador, and my force will carry out honor guard duties. But we're capable of handling other tasks if required."

"You're insurance?" Geary said. "But against what?"

"We'll be traversing some dangerous regions of space," Colonel Webb said. "It's a given that your forces will be doing all they can to prevent any hostile actors from boarding this ship. But, if one does get aboard, they will regret it." He leaned forward slightly, eyes curious. "I haven't seen anything in official reports about the aliens as far as their ground combat capabilities."

"Which aliens?" General Carabali asked.

"The, um, Dancers."

"That's because we haven't seen them demonstrate their ground combat capabilities," Carabali said. "But, based on how they use their ships, I'd assume they operate in close coordination, a number of individuals working as a single unit."

Webb shrugged. "That's what we do."

"We also fly spacecraft," Carabali said. "Have you seen vids of the Dancers maneuvering their ships?"

The colonel paused. "I see your point. We'd have to be on the top of our game." He noticed the reactions from the others. "I'm not saying we're going in to fight them. I just have to consider what we'd do if one of them did try something. Humans go rogue and act on their own, as the admiral found out firsthand at Unity. Aliens might be the same. And then there's that other species. The enigmas. Definitely hostile, and we don't seem to have anything on their ground capabilities, either."

Geary shook his head. "The people at Midway may have some knowledge of that. We don't."

"The people at Midway? You mean the Syndics?" It wasn't hard to tell how Colonel Webb felt about that.

"Former Syndics," Geary said. "They've played straight with us, and seem to be trying to build a better system than the one they revolted against."

Ambassador Rycerz nodded. "Perhaps former Captain Bradamont can offer a candid assessment."

"Former captain?" Geary said, startled.

"Yes, she—" Rycerz spread her hands in apology. "The courier ship reached Unity long after you'd left and not long before we departed. It had been sent to Midway with orders for Captain Bradamont to return."

"Orders?" Geary asked. "Whose orders? I assigned her to a critical task at Midway."

Rycerz shook her head, sitting back slightly. "Given the time required for the round trip, it must've been someone in a high position at Fleet Headquarters perhaps six months ago."

Not Baxter and Rojo, then. "But you said former captain."

"Yes. The courier ship reported that rather than return, Captain Bradamont had resigned her commission and taken service with the Midway Star System." Rycerz studied Geary. "Do you know why she did that? I'd also like a better understanding of why you assigned her in particular to stay at Midway."

He decided the best course of action would be total honesty. "She was in a position to be compromised by people working in Alliance Intelligence. Hopefully some of the same people exposed by the evidence found at Unity Alternate, but I don't know."

Ambassador Rycerz sat forward, her attention focused on Geary. "Compromised?"

"Captain Bradamont was captured by the Syndics," Geary said. "While a POW, there was a serious accident on a ship transporting them to a Syndic labor camp. The senior Syndic ground forces officer aboard the ship violated orders to let the Alliance POWs assist in saving the ship. He was punished by being given command of the labor camp. Since Bradamont was the senior Alliance officer present, she and the Syndic came to know each other and mutual respect developed, becoming . . . something more."

"You're joking," Colonel Webb said, looking appalled.

"No," Geary said, turning a stern look on Webb. "Neither one of them broke any of the rules governing their relationship. But Syndic intel found out, and instead of executing the Syndic officer decided to try to use Bradamont's feelings for him to turn her. They put her on another transport, and arranged for the Alliance to learn where it would be so the Alliance could take the ship and free the POWs. Bradamont was supposed to begin passing intelligence to the Syndic officer. Rogero, that's his name. She reported everything to our own intel when she was debriefed, and they decided to use her to try to turn Rogero. Our intel services gave Bradamont outdated or bad information to pass to Rogero. It turned out the Syndic intel services were doing the same thing with Rogero, passing us bad info."

"How did that compromise Bradamont?" Rycerz asked. "She was following orders, wasn't she?"

"Her orders were part of a special secure program," Geary said. "In the months before our forces reached Midway, Captain Bradamont had received anonymous threats that if she didn't agree to take actions against me, her passing of information to the Syndics would be leaked to the media."

Ambassador Rycerz grimaced. "And if the special secure program wasn't declassified, she wouldn't have been able to defend herself by proving she'd been acting under orders. That's a nasty dilemma."

"Emissary Victoria Rione suggested we assign Captain Bradamont to Midway to keep her safe from those threats, and to provide expert assistance to Midway's forces to help keep that star system from being reconquered by the Syndicate Worlds," Geary said. It felt odd to use Rione as a way of proving the action had been in the best interests of the Alliance, given how askance she'd long been regarded, but her heroic death for the Alliance had made that possible. "I still think that was a wise move. Captain Bradamont represented . . ." How should he say it?

Rycerz smiled knowingly. "Your own independent diplomatic actions."

"I had to make decisions based on the situation at hand," Geary said, feeling both guilty and defiant. "With the best interests of the Alliance foremost. I'm sure you're aware that the residents of both Syndic and former Syndic star systems regard the Alliance in the same way people of the Alliance regard the Syndicate Worlds."

"*We* didn't start the war," Colonel Webb interceded in the tone of someone ready to give a lecture to the uninformed.

"I know," Geary said, not happy to be interrupted. "I was there."

Apparently unprepared for that comeback concerning a battle fought a century ago, Webb subsided.

"I'm not here to argue whether former Syndics are justified in their feelings," Geary said. "But those feelings exist, and we need to deal with them."

Ambassador Rycerz, her elbows resting on her desk, her hands supporting her chin as she gazed at Geary, nodded. "Whereas you personally, Admiral, are . . . what's the phrase they use? For the people?"

"I've heard that," Geary admitted.

"A perception which allowed Captain Bradamont, one of your officers, to be seen not as a representative of the Alliance, but as representing your personal backing for the new regime at Midway."

"That was part of the intent," Geary said.

"You walked a fine line on that one, Admiral," Ambassador Rycerz said. "But given the circumstances, it was an action the Alliance was willing to stand behind. You do understand that with me along to represent the government, independent diplomatic actions by you are no longer an option?"

"Of course I understand that," Geary said. "But I hope it's understood at Unity that my actions then were not independent. I had a representative of the government with me."

"Victoria Rione," Rycerz said. "Who was not authorized to approve such measures."

"I was not aware of that," Geary said. "The government didn't share the content of her orders with me."

Ambassador Rycerz sighed. "Everyone was trying to be too clever. No one trusted anyone. I hope, Admiral, that you and I can trust each other."

"I have no reason to believe we can't," Geary said.

"Excellent. Admiral, there's something I need to discuss with you, just the two of us. Colonel Webb, will you wait outside for a few moments?"

General Carabali was already on her feet as Webb stood up. They left the ambassador's office, walking side by side yet somehow clearly not walking together.

Rycerz sat watching Geary for several seconds, saying nothing. "I need to be sure of something," she finally said. "Will you follow my directions?"

"I'm responsible for getting you to Dancer space," Geary said. "Dealing with threats to the safety of you and the force as a whole."

"That leaves some gray areas," Rycerz said. "If we encounter Syndicate Worlds warships, do you expect to take the lead in dealing with them?"

Geary frowned, thinking. "I guess that would depend on how they act. I'd have to respond if they attacked. But if they're just in the same star system, there's no reason I'd have to be the one negotiating with the Syndic CEO."

"All right. That's reasonable. I deal with handling Syndic authorities to try to prevent us having to fight our way through. Will your fleet accept that?"

"Yes," Geary said. "They don't trust the Syndics, but they trust me."

"I've been instructed to take the lead when we get to Midway," Rycerz added. "Do you think the leaders there will accept that?"

"They may. President Iceni and General Drakon realize the Alliance works differently than the Syndicate Worlds does."

"What about Bradamont? Will she act against us? Can we trust whatever she tells us?"

He didn't have to think about the answer to that. "She won't act against us. She won't lie to us. Captain Bradamont's honor is beyond question."

"But she's willingly taking orders from Syndics," Rycerz said.

"Former Syndics," Geary said. "Don't assume President Iceni and General Drakon are like average Syndicate Worlds CEOs. They're tough and they're tricky, but they're also smart, and seem to really care about the welfare of their people."

Rycerz sat back, sighing. "I've seen your reports on them. It's still hard to believe, though."

"When the enigmas were attacking," Geary said, "and the primary world at Midway was being evacuated, Iceni stayed on the planet overseeing the evacuation."

"Instead of getting on the first ship out, carrying every bit of wealth

she could with her?" Rycerz shrugged. "That's definitely not normal
Syndic CEO behavior. All right, I've asked my questions. Do you have
any for me? This is your chance, the moment where Black Jack exercises
his vast, under-the-desk authority over anything that happens."

"Sorry to let you down, but no," Geary said, somehow glad that
Rycerz had brought that out into the open so he could dispose of the
idea. "I'm aware of the . . . popular authority I wield. But I grew up and
was trained at a time when the military was far less prominent in the
Alliance. I'm uncomfortable with too much military influence on the
government."

"We're in agreement on that," Rycerz said.

"There is a matter you should be aware of regarding the Rift Federation."

"Oh?" Rycerz eyed Geary warily. "I know they were invited to take
part in this diplomatic mission and turned it down."

"They're sending their own delegation accompanied by their own
ships," Geary said. He explained what Captain Hiyen had told him,
then waited while the ambassador took in the information.

"They want to do it on their own," Rycerz finally said. "What are the
odds of them making it to Dancer space?"

"Zero," Geary said. "Their force is too small. If some of the Rift
Federation's ships somehow make it to Midway, they'll surely be annihilated by the enigmas before reaching Dancer space."

"You've told me this for a reason. What is it?"

"Because I don't want to let them head for Midway before we leave.
They'll set on high alert every star system we're planning to pass
through, as well as the Syndicate government."

Rycerz tilted her head back, staring at the ceiling. "The Syndicate
Worlds has probably already heard of our plans, but I can easily understand why giving them a heads-up that we're coming to certain places
would be a big problem. What do you suggest we do?"

"I want to help them in a way that the commander of their force can
accept," Geary said. "The crews of those Rift Federation ships fought

alongside our own during the war. No one in the fleet wants to see them wiped out on what amounts to a suicide mission."

"Nor do I," Ambassador Rycerz said. "How can you help them if their orders require them to operate independently of the Alliance?"

"My proposal is that I offer Captain Kapelka an unwritten agreement that her ships will travel along with ours, not formally part of the Alliance fleet forces, but protected by our nearby presence."

Rycerz rested her chin on her hands as she thought. "Why should we do this, Admiral? Set aside humanitarian reasons. How does it advantage the Alliance?"

Did the ambassador really think in such mercenary terms, or was she asking for arguments to use with her own superiors? "I don't think the Alliance wants the Rift Federation weakened by the loss of those warships and their trained crews."

"That's a military argument," she said. "I know you can think in larger terms, Admiral. What's in it for the Alliance? You're asking me to agree to facilitating the travel of a different diplomatic delegation along with that of the Alliance. That's certain to produce complications when negotiating with the Dancers."

He paused to think, remembering his last encounter with the Dancers. Complications of one form or another seemed to be routine when it came to communicating with alien species. "Don't we need to know as much as we can about what those complications will be?"

Her gaze on him sharpened. "What do you mean?"

"The Dancers have already demonstrated the ability to jump from deep inside Alliance-occupied space back to their own region, or close to it," Geary said. "That means they can, on their own, make contact with human star systems in Alliance space, or anywhere in space controlled by or once controlled by the Syndicate Worlds. Now that contact has been established, the Dancers can and probably will deal with other humans. We can't blockade them in their own space even if we make it difficult for other humans to reach them."

Rycerz slowly nodded, her eyes going distant with thought. "There will be other human factions the Dancers deal with. We need to know how the Dancers will deal with them. Being able to observe their reactions and interactions with the Rift Federation delegation could provide extremely valuable information for us." Her eyes regained her focus as she looked at Geary again, smiling. "Now there's a good argument. We need to know what the Dancers will do when approached by other human governments or groups. How they see the Alliance relative to other humans. And the only way we can learn that is if we can watch what happens when they have us and the Rift Federation's representatives to deal with at the same time."

She nodded again. "Yet the federation is so much smaller than the Alliance that they couldn't seriously threaten any deals we could make with the Dancers. Yes. I think your idea will benefit us a great deal, as well as saving the lives of the sailors on those Rift Federation ships. But I can't make that decision without informing my superiors. Here's what I'll do. I'll submit the proposal to offer unofficial protection to the Rift Federation delegation so we can learn how the Dancers react to dealing with different human entities. But I'll do it under my name to avoid having anyone think this is another Black Jack plot."

"*Another* Black Jack plot?" Geary asked, knowing Rycerz was right about needing to keep his name off the proposal, but also feeling a bit annoyed that he couldn't take credit for something that he'd thought of.

"Sorry," Ambassador Rycerz said with a smile. "To certain fans of conspiracies, your hand is everywhere. When Captain Kapelka arrives at this star system, make your offer to her. Put nothing in writing or on the official record. She'll probably insist on that anyway to protect herself from charges that she disregarded her orders to get to Dancer space on her own. Let me know whether she agrees. And then I'll pretend not to notice that those ships are staying with us as we travel to Midway and then Dancer space."

"All right," Geary said. "Although what you just told me also isn't in writing."

Rycerz made a face. "You have every right to be wary of entrapment.

When I send my message to Unity asking for approval, I'll make my message UOD. Unless Otherwise Directed. If Unity doesn't get contrary orders here before we depart, you and I will both be legally covered."

"There's another problem," Geary said. "There's a possibility that the Rift Federation ships will refuse to comply with instructions not to jump before we do. As I said, that could create serious problems for us."

"Is there any way to stop them from doing that?"

"I can station warships near the jump point and threaten to fire if the Rift Federation ships approach. But that means I'd have to be willing to fire if they kept coming regardless."

The ambassador's eyes widened. "You want permission to fire on ships of the Rift Federation?" It was hard to tell if she was primarily shocked or horrified.

"No," Geary said. "That's the last thing I want to do."

"Good. Because I'd never approve it!" Rycerz sat back with a stunned expression. "Using force against the Rift Federation would lend credence to all the conspiracy theories that the Alliance is preparing to annex the federation's star systems and then those of the Callas Republic as well. It'd produce catastrophic results. Why did you even mention it?"

"To let you know that if the Rift Federation ships insist on going ahead of us, I don't have any good way to stop them," Geary said.

Rycerz closed her eyes and shook her head. "If they insist on doing it, we have to let them." She opened her eyes, focusing intently on him. "Are you going to blame me for your not being able to stop those ships?"

"No," Geary said. "I take responsibility for my own decisions. But I will notify you if the Rift Federation ships insist on going ahead. If you can get them to change their minds, I'd be grateful."

"I'll try if it comes to that." The ambassador grimaced. "The Rift Federation knows we can't stop them without precipitating a crisis that would rock the entire Alliance. I wouldn't be surprised if some elements in the Rift Federation are hoping for that, willing to martyr some of their ships and crews to bring about a complete rupture in relations."

"If they get martyred, it won't be at the hands of the Alliance fleet," Geary said.

"Good." Ambassador Rycerz locked a somber gaze on him. "This mission is bigger than you or me, Admiral. I won't do anything that might compromise it."

"Nor will I," Geary said. Rycerz was saying all the right things. Did she mean them? "I guess we should keep this private meeting short to try to prevent feeding the conspiracy theorists."

Colonel Webb accompanied Geary and Carabali on the way back to the shuttle dock to return them to *Dauntless*. "Would you tell me something, Colonel?" Geary asked. "Why would you and those in your unit volunteer to spend five years away from home?"

Webb frowned. "There are plenty of people who were happy when the war ended. And there were plenty of people who were happy to have the chance to be something other than whatever they did in the military. But what about us who take pride in that identity? I didn't want to move on, to some civilian job sitting at a desk somewhere, dreaming of the past, or being a mercenary for some company that wants to protect its precious assets. I'm special forces and I'm proud of it. But there's downsizing going on. The war's over. The Alliance can't afford to maintain the same size of military to deal with the problems that remain."

Webb turned an unyielding look on Geary. "That's why I volunteered, and why my people volunteered. It meant a guarantee that for at least the next five years we could still be the thing we trained to be, the thing we took pride in being. One of my sergeants, an outstanding special forces operator, couldn't wait to get out. He was tired of the killing, tired of losing friends, tired of wondering when his luck would run out. I wished him the best of luck and I meant it. But I also knew that wasn't what I wanted."

"I understand," Geary said. "We're on the same side here. You work directly for the ambassador. But your mission, and mine, will have greater chances of success if we work together."

Colonel Webb nodded. "I understand, Admiral. And I agree." As they reached the shuttle he stopped walking and saluted in farewell. "I'm sure we'll be speaking more in the future."

As Geary and Carabali strapped into their seats on the shuttle, he looked over at her. Carabali had a distant look, her brow furrowed slightly. "What are you thinking, General?"

Carabali gave him a glance from the corners of her eyes. "That anti-Dancer sentiment we're worried about. The same sentiments that earned me a new star for my combat wounded badge. I'm thinking that if I wanted to sabotage a mission like that, I'd want to use someone already trained and experienced in how to sabotage equipment and kill people. Someone on the inside who'd be in a position to learn the entire security setup."

It took him a moment to understand. "You think one of the special forces in the honor guard could be a threat? I'd think they were very heavily screened before being accepted as volunteers."

"There are ways to mislead even the strictest screens," Carabali said. "Among those most well trained in how to do so are . . ."

"Elite special forces," Geary finished. "How good do you think these guys are?"

"I think they're Wendigos."

"Wendigos?" Geary said, not liking the sound of that.

Carabali twisted her mouth in disapproval. "Special forces that are officially not known to even the rest of the special forces. That officially don't even exist. But there are stories about them. Enough stories with enough reality to them to convince me they're real."

"You don't seem to like them."

"They do the jobs too tough, or too ugly, for regular special forces. The sort of thing the Alliance doesn't want to admit it ever does." Carabali glanced at him. "Some rumors claim they've done political assassinations. I don't believe those. But I don't like units that operate outside the chain of command. Whose actions aren't allowed to see the light of day. We've had recent experience with where that can lead."

Rumors didn't add up to reality, no matter how many there were. But Carabali wasn't the sort to give credence to something she didn't have good reasons to believe. And, as she said, excessive secrecy had already been proven to create serious problems. "What are your recommendations?"

"With your permission, I'll have my own force recon people and senior enlisted reach out to the honor guard. Coordination meetings, social gatherings to get to know each other, all routine things. But that'll give my people a chance to see if any of the special forces types don't feel quite right."

"Permission granted," Geary said as the shuttle's thrusters pitched it over for the final approach to *Dauntless*. "I hope you're wrong."

"I hope I'm wrong, too," Carabali said. "But Colonel Webb displayed some odd priorities. He asked questions about the Dancers, seemed to regard them as a primary security concern, but didn't even mention the internal security issues you and I have been alerted to."

Which did seem a bit odd now that Carabali had brought it up. Geary nodded to her. "Keep me informed."

Captain Desjani was waiting at the shuttle dock. "How'd it go?" she asked as they walked toward his stateroom.

"Not bad," he said.

"Really?" Desjani shook her head, pausing to acknowledge a greeting from a petty officer going the other way down the passageway.

He could easily hear the skepticism she hadn't directly voiced. "Before Grendel," Geary said, "before the war, I used to admire diplomats. A lot of people did. Not the political hacks who bought themselves choice postings, but the professionals. The people who worked for the Alliance government, and went to places where no one else wanted to go, and tried their best to make things better."

Desjani shrugged. "There wasn't much call for diplomacy for the last century. The Syndics would demand we surrender, we'd refuse, and the war would keep going on."

"But we needed people like that," he said. "And we need them now."

"They didn't prevent the war from starting," she pointed out. "And they couldn't end it."

Which was certainly true. "Tanya, I didn't live through decades of the war like you did. But I believed in dedicated diplomats before the battle at Grendel, and I believe in them now. I guess in some ways I have to believe that people trying their best can make a difference."

She stopped as they reached the hatch to his stateroom. "You'll believe that until the day you greet your ancestors, won't you?"

He paused as well, looking at her. "It's why I do this."

"And it's why people follow you."

"Have you ever heard of Alliance special forces called Wendigos?"

"Everybody's heard of them. I don't know if they're real, though."

"Carabali thinks they are."

Desjani studied him closely. "Why are you bringing this up?"

"There may be some aboard *Boundless*. That's just between you and me."

"Great." Desjani shrugged. "Another fine day in the fleet. I can't wait until the Rift Federation ships get here and add another problem to the pile."

CAPTAIN Desjani's wish was granted a couple of days later, when a heavy cruiser, two light cruisers, and four destroyers popped out of the hypernet gate. That was one destroyer less than Captain Hiyen had predicted. Knowing the limited resources the Rift Federation had, Geary couldn't help wondering if the fifth destroyer had been deliberately cut from the force or if it had been in too bad a shape to make the journey.

Proceeding at a sedate (for warships) point one light speed, the Rift Federation force had quickly steadied out on a vector for the jump point to Atalia. With six light hours to cover, it would require sixty hours, or two and a half days, before the Rift Federation ships could reach the jump point.

If they'd sent their arrival report upon exiting the hypernet, it should show up at any moment, right after the light showing their arrival. As the minutes went past, he became increasingly impatient.

He'd played this game himself. Take as long as possible to send a message, depend on light speed limits to require hours for it to be received, and then gain additional hours before the reply could get to him. The Rift Federation ships could be halfway across the star system before initial greetings had been exchanged.

Not this time. He decided to send his own message immediately. It would still take hours to reach the Rift warships, but that was the best he could do. "Rift Federation warships, welcome to Varandal. This is Admiral Geary. Please proceed to an orbit near Ambaru Station for critical discussions. I also request that you review the proposal attached to this message as I believe it would greatly benefit both your mission and my own. To the honor of our ancestors, Geary, out."

He wasn't certain whether to be grateful for the impending meetings that would keep him occupied while waiting to hear from the Rift Federation ships. Among his responsibilities was the need to coordinate with both the technical and the scientific teams aboard *Boundless*. Which meant meeting with both teams.

In what he later realized was an ominous portent, at the insistence of the science team leader Dr. Macadams the meeting with his team was by virtual conference instead of face to face.

Geary sat at one of the long sides of a table in one of *Dauntless*'s secure conference rooms. Since the focus of the scientific team was the Dancers, Geary had General Charban beside him. On the other side of Charban, Lieutenant Iger and Lieutenant Jamenson also sat. With Victoria Rione dead, those three were the ones most experienced with dealing directly with the Dancers.

Facing them along the other side of the table were the virtual presences of Dr. Macadams and his senior assistants. They'd finally shown up ten minutes after the scheduled time of the meeting, arriving without any apology for the delay. But even though Geary was annoyed, he kept his bearing and his voice polite. "Dr. Macadams, welcome to Varandal. I understand that you're in charge of the people who will be trying to gain more knowledge about the Dancers."

Macadams didn't answer immediately. Instead his forehead crinkled into a frown with glacial slowness, the expression finally coming to rest on his brow like a whale washed onto a beach by the incoming tide. "The sapient aliens should not be referred to using a flippant and insulting term."

Surprised that the doctor was opening the meeting in that fashion, Geary glanced at Charban. "Dancers is neither flippant nor insulting," he said. "It's a name given out of respect for the aliens by our sailors."

"What our *sailors* think scarcely matters," Macadams said. "What matters is how the sapient aliens feel about it."

General Charban smiled as if Dr. Macadams had just said something nice. "I've talked with the Dancers about the name. Once I explained what dance meant to humans, the Dancers seemed to be very pleased. Their word for dance appears to be the same as their word for work, as both involve using learned, repeating patterns. I believe they see the name as human praise for how well they do their tasks, which is indeed why the sailors gave them that name."

Geary nodded. "The ease and gracefulness with which the Dancers maneuver their ships. That's impressed everyone who's seen it."

Macadams turned his frown on Charban. "Given your lack of qualifications, your interpretation of how the sapient aliens feel about the word is irrelevant," the doctor said, giving no sign that he was aware he'd just flipped his prior argument on its head.

"Excuse me," Geary said, his instincts to defend those working for him kicking in. "General Charban is the most qualified person in human space to interpret the feelings of the aliens because of his practical experience dealing with them."

After a long pause in which Macadams gave no sign of having heard Geary, the leader of the science team spoke again. "That word is no longer to be used to describe them out of respect for the sapient aliens."

Resigned to having to work with the doctor, and knowing the limits of his own authority, Geary made a slight, ambiguous gesture with one hand. "What term do you want used in official correspondence?"

Dr. Macadams's expression shifted to annoyance. "What do they call themselves? That's what we should call them."

Charban was no longer trying to smile, but he kept his voice neutral. "I've asked the . . . them many times, and the answer is always 'we call ourselves we' or 'we call ourselves us.' I'm not sure whether they don't understand the question or are deliberately withholding it out of cultural considerations."

One of Macadams's assistants nodded, his expression thoughtful. "It might be they consider their name for their own species to be some sort of taboo item not to be shared with outsiders. But they also might not categorize themselves in the same ways humans do."

Dr. Macadams twisted his head enough to bend a withering look at the unfortunate assistant who had dared to comment. The assistant fell silent, staring at the table. "More likely, your translation device is not up to the challenge of dealing with communications."

"It's not *our* translation device," Charban said. "The Dancers sent us the software for it, which when loaded into an isolated device adapted itself to our hardware so the Dancers' software could function. Our coders still don't know how the Dancers did that." Charban had apparently made up his mind to repeat the word "Dancers" as often as possible.

"Operator error," Macadams said, dismissing Charban's words. "My assistants will go over it and get it working properly as soon as you send it to this ship."

Another brief pause followed before Geary interceded. "We will send *Boundless* a copy of the software sent to us so you can load it into your own device. But we will not give up our own means of communication with the . . . aliens."

"No," Dr. Macadams said. "All communications with the sapient aliens will henceforth come only from my assistants. No one else will attempt to contact them. Multiple points of contact with unqualified individuals would only confuse the sapient aliens and make my own task more difficult."

So that was why Ambassador Rycerz had emphasized Geary's ability to speak directly with the Dancers. She'd been telling him that she'd support him against Macadams. Geary shook his head, not bothering to look regretful. "That's unacceptable. My flagship will retain the means to independently communicate with the Dancers on matters of security and any other issue the Dancers choose to speak with us about. My responsibilities do not permit surrendering that capability."

Dr. Macadams let his frown slowly flow down his forehead once more. "My instructions to you regarding the translation device were not a request."

"They weren't an order, either," Geary said, wishing that Victoria Rione were here to help pin Macadams's ears back. "Because you can't give me orders, Doctor. The sooner we establish a relationship based on mutual respect and understanding, the better we'll be able to forge a relationship with the Dancers based on mutual respect and understanding."

Dr. Macadams reached toward a control in his conference room. His virtual presence vanished, along with those of his assistants.

After a moment of silence, General Charban slapped his forehead. "How did that dolt get put in charge of such an important part of the mission to the Dancers?"

"You mean the sapient aliens?" Geary asked. "I'm guessing it was a political payoff to win someone's support for voting for the mission. Lieutenant Iger, try to find out anything you can on Macadams. No illegal collection against an Alliance citizen. Just public record material."

"I can do that, Admiral," Iger said.

"You should register a formal complaint," Charban told Geary. "Try to get Macadams fired. He's obviously unsuited for his role."

"I'll find out what my options are," Geary said. "But since Ambassador Rycerz hasn't been able to fire him, we may be stuck with Macadams. I want our hands to be clean on this, so we will cooperate our best with all reasonable requests from Macadams."

"I'm looking forward to hearing a reasonable request from Macadams," Charban said. "It would be a nice change of pace."

"General?" Lieutenant Jamenson asked. "They didn't ask for any information about how we've communicated with the Dancers."

"You're not PhDs," Charban said. "Neither am I. There's a class of people who think anyone without a doctorate isn't worth listening to. We have to hope some of his assistants are more open to hearing about our experience than Macadams is. In any event, your experience will still be valuable for any discussions with the Dancers from this ship." He stood up. "At least it was a short meeting."

"Which is good, since I have another meeting coming up," Geary said.

"I pity you, sir." Charban stretched. "At least you can be fairly certain the next meeting won't be as bad as this one was."

"I've learned never to assume things can't get worse."

ELEVEN

AN hour later, Geary sat in the same conference room, this time with Tanya Desjani beside him, facing another set of people from the *Boundless*. He felt cautious optimism over the fact that this group wanted to meet in person.

Their leader, a tired-eyed man whose age wasn't otherwise obvious, smiled at Geary. "I'm Dr. Kottur. It's a *great* pleasure to meet you."

The others with Kottur all nodded in agreement, smiling, except for one woman at the far end who seemed either bored or unamused. Geary found his eyes drawn to her not for that reason, but because of a nagging sense that she resembled someone he knew. "We're happy to help make this happen," he said to Dr. Kottur.

"This is quite an opportunity, Admiral," Kottur said. "If we can successfully link the hypernet gate at Midway to the Alliance hypernet, it'll be a huge scientific and technical breakthrough."

"We'll have to convince Midway's leaders to let us try, Dr. Kottur," Geary said. "They're bound to be concerned, and they don't entirely trust the Alliance."

"But I understand they trust you?"

"I think so," Geary said.

"Well," Kottur said, "you'll be able to tell them that we've got some of the best minds in the Alliance with us when it comes to hypernet theory and engineering. Allow me to introduce Dr. Ken Bron, and Dr. Talisen Rajput, and Dr. Jasmine Cresida—"

"Cresida?" Geary looked at the woman he'd noticed earlier, realizing who it was she resembled. "Are you related to Jaylen Cresida?"

Dr. Cresida gave Geary a cold look. "I was. She was my sister."

Tanya Desjani was also gazing at Dr. Cresida in surprise. "Jaylen's personal record listed her parents as her only next of kin."

"We had a falling-out," Dr. Cresida said, her voice somehow even frostier. "I thought she was risking too much by entering military service, that her talents would be far better put to use working in theory with me. I didn't want her mind, her potential, thrown away in some senseless battle. Unfortunately, I was right."

Geary spoke into the silence that followed Jasmine Cresida's words. "Jaylen played a major role in saving the fleet by analyzing the danger of the hypernet gates. She also figured out the nature of the malware used by the enigmas. Her loss was a terrible blow, but she made invaluable contributions before then."

Dr. Cresida didn't look at him as she replied. "So you sent her to her death. What a fine reward."

Dr. Kottur finally recovered from his shock. "Let's not—I mean, we have an important purpose. I don't want any . . . unprofessional behavior."

"I can do my job," Cresida said. "I don't have to pretend to like who I'm working with."

Captain Desjani gave her a thin smile. "Likewise."

Geary exchanged a hapless look with Dr. Kottur. Together, he and Kottur got the meeting back on track. The science and engineering team's questions mostly revolved around *Dauntless*'s sensor records of the hypernet gate at Midway, and the best means of convincing the leaders of Midway to buy in to the proposal. For his part, Geary wanted to know as much as possible about any risks or uncertainties associated with the project, since he'd have to sell the idea to those at Midway. Through it all, Dr. Cresida sat in icy isolation, only occasionally responding briefly to one of her comrades.

The meeting ended with mutual promises of cooperation and high expectations, which made it a nice contrast to the fiasco of the meeting with Dr. Macadams's team. The others left the conference room with Captain Desjani as she escorted them back to the shuttle dock, Dr. Jasmine Cresida walking as if every step she took on the deckplates was distasteful.

Geary watched them go, then stood alone, thinking about Jaylen Cresida. Wondering if he could've given slightly different orders during the fight with the Syndics at Varandal, whether anything he could have done would have made a difference. The same thoughts he had about every battle, about every officer and sailor who'd died under his command. Senator Costa had tried to trip him up at Unity, tried to back him into a corner by asking if he'd like having his decisions and actions second-guessed. What Costa hadn't understood, and perhaps couldn't understand, was that Geary himself was his own harshest critic when it came to wondering if he could have done things differently, done them better, saved at least a few lives among those who'd been lost.

"You should congratulate me," Desjani said as she walked back into the conference room.

"Well done," Geary said. "What am I congratulating you for?"

"I let that so-called sister of Jaylen's walk up the ramp onto the shuttle without giving in to the temptation to wind up and kick her butt so hard she would've flown to her seat."

Trust Tanya to give him a reason to smile even at such a time. "That wouldn't have offered a very good example for your crew."

"They would've applauded," Desjani said. "Sailors can tell when someone thinks they're a low order of life." She sat down, one hand over her face to avoid looking at the spot where Jasmine Cresida had sat. "At least we don't have to waste any time wondering why Jaylen never mentioned her sister."

He sat down again as well. "With any luck we won't have to interact with her again."

"If she had any idea how much the fleet's losses haunt you she wouldn't have been so high and mighty about it."

"Maybe her experience is with commanders like Falco," Geary said. Why was he defending Jasmine Cresida? "Tanya, I know exactly how you feel. But I don't need the added work of nursing a grudge against Jaylen's sister. I'm going to do my best not to think of it."

"I don't like seeing you thought of that way." She frowned and inhaled deeply. "You're not Falco. He wouldn't have cared what Jaylen's sister thought of him. But she'll never know that. Smart people can be really stupid. Unfortunately, I do think we're going to end up dealing with her again. From what the others said, Dr. Cresida is their primary theory person."

"At least Dr. Kottur is easy to work with," Geary said.

"He's sort of the antimatter version of Macadams, isn't he?" She frowned. "Kottur is too nice, really. What's he after?"

"Maybe," Geary said, "he wants to do his best to make sure the hypernet gate project is successful."

"Maybe," Desjani conceded with another frown.

Geary checked his comm pad after an alert sounded. "We've received the arrival message from the Rift Federation ships."

"Time flies when you're having fun."

"Yeah." He called up the message, feeling a frown of his own forming as he read it.

The message provided required information and nothing more. "This is Captain Kapelka of the Rift Federation Navy. We are transiting through the star system en route to the jump point for Atalia. Kapelka, out."

"What's the matter?" Desjani's jaw tightened as she listened to the message. "The bare minimum that they had to tell us, no formal greeting, and an unceremonious sign-off. I've had more courteous messages from Syndics. You've already told her to alter track to come to Ambaru, right?"

"Yes. They should've received my message about twenty minutes ago. How's their track?"

Desjani checked the nearest display. "Our information is hours time late, of course, but there's no sign yet that they changed their vectors. They're still tracking right for the jump point to Atalia. If they did change vector when they got your message, we won't see it for another . . . three hours." She looked at him. "They're not going to change vector."

"I know."

"What are we going to do?"

"There's nothing we can do," Geary said. "I can't make threats that I wouldn't be able to act on. If those ships are determined to jump for Atalia ahead of us, the only way to stop them would be with force, and I can't do that."

"Because of the ambassador being here?" Desjani asked.

"No. I'd have reached the same decision regardless," he said. "I can't order the Alliance fleet to fire on Rift Federation warships. Not without causing an immense amount of damage to the Alliance."

She considered his words before finally nodding with visible reluctance. "And those Rift Federation ships know that, so they're going to push on."

He rubbed his eyes, wishing he were as powerful as popular imagination thought he was. Maybe then he'd be able to fix this. "I appealed to Captain Kapelka's conscience. It doesn't take a military genius to know she can't get to Dancer space with a force that size. They'll be destroyed along the way. If they'll agree to accompany our force without any formal deal being made, she can save her ships and their crews."

Captain Desjani shook her head as she looked away from him. "Conscience is a weak opponent against pride," she said. "I saw enough of her when they were attached to this fleet to know that Kapelka won't want to admit the Rift Federation needs the Alliance's help to do the job."

"Captain Hiyen thought the same thing. He's also appealing to Kapelka."

"Yeah, well, don't get your hopes up, Admiral."

WITH hours to wait to see what the Rift Federation ships would do, and feeling sick at the idea that pride was carrying them to needless destruction, Geary tried to distract himself by dealing with another problem.

He called Ambassador Rycerz from his stateroom, seeing her virtual presence appear before him just as his virtual image would be facing her aboard *Boundless*.

"Ambassador, I've held preliminary meetings with both groups of specialists traveling on *Boundless*."

Rycerz sighed, looking resigned to an unpleasant conversation. "And you want to talk about Macadams."

"No, I'd honestly prefer never to have to talk about or deal with him again," Geary said.

"You and me both." Rycerz sat back, running one hand through her hair. "He's a political appointee. I could go over all the debates and arguments over who should head the academic side of the mission, but what it all came down to was just about every candidate was seen by some of the senators as either too sympathetic to the Dancers or too hostile. Macadams, on the other hand, is hostile to every form of life in the universe, so he couldn't be accused of being particularly biased against the Dancers one way or the other. That and he knew the right people, and could pull the right strings. Buying support for this mission from enough senators involved some . . . unfortunate selling and trading."

"How can we afford to let politics as usual screw this up?" Geary swept one arm out in an angry, frustrated gesture. "Something this important and we're letting it be controlled by someone totally unsuited for the job?"

"Let me be clear about something," Rycerz said, her usual calm being replaced by a hard set to her mouth and eyes. "If I believed that Macadams could sabotage this mission, I would've resigned rather than lead it. But Macadams is the sort who sabotages himself. I already have alternate contacts among his staff who are upset by their inability to work freely even among themselves."

Geary shook his head. "Assuming you can manage away an awful leader by bypassing them doesn't always work out if you leave them with the same responsibilities."

"Granted. Admiral, I have to play nice with regards to Macadams until we reach Midway and get the hypernet gate part of the job done. Once we leave there, heading for Dancer space, Macadams won't have any means of communicating with his backers except through me or you approving any messages he wants to send on your ships." Rycerz smiled in a way that set off alarms in Geary's instincts. This was not a woman who'd simply accept conditions forced on her. "At that point, Dr. Macadams is going to find his responsibilities redefined in ways that effectively sideline him so the other specialists can actually try to do their jobs."

"What if Macadams refuses to accept that?" Geary said.

"Don't you have jails on your fleet ships? What do they call them?"

"Brigs?" Geary stared at the ambassador. "You'll want me to arrest Macadams and throw him in the brig?"

"Tell me you don't already like the idea." Ambassador Rycerz grinned. "That's only if we have to, of course."

"Of course."

"Ummm . . ." The ambassador paused. "That bread and water thing. Is that still an option? If we jail him?"

"Yes," Geary said. "Brig time with only bread and water is still a legal punishment in the fleet."

"That's good to know."

After the call ended, Geary spent a while gazing at the nearest bulkhead, wondering if Ambassador Rycerz would really want Macadams thrown into the brig.

He already did like the idea, though. Especially the bread and water part.

CAPTAIN Kapelka's eventual reply to his message didn't start off in a promising way. Kapelka had recorded the message while standing rigidly in her stateroom as if conversing with an officer personally unknown to her. Her voice was as unyielding as her posture. "The warships of the Rift Federation under my command do not choose to alter vector to suit the desires of an Alliance officer. You may be unaware that the Rift Federation has formally notified the Alliance that the military assistance agreements between our two governments no longer have force."

That was news, though not entirely unexpected. As Captain Hiyen had warned, the Rift Federation was intent on trying to break the ties that war had forged with the Alliance.

"Your suggestion," Captain Kapelka continued, "that we delay our mission to allow Alliance forces to proceed along with us is impossible to agree to." She made it sound as if it were the Alliance forces seeking protection from the few Rift Federation ships. "My orders are to reach my objectives without delay. We are not servants of the Alliance. Nor are we in need of your protection. Kapelka, out."

Pride seemed too small a word to describe the attitude of the Rift Federation's commander, Geary thought as he called Captain Hiyen.

Hiyen looked stubborn and angry. "I was sent a copy of Captain Kapelka's reply to you, Admiral, probably because I'd sent my own message to her urging Kapelka to agree to your proposed course of action. I deeply regret that my suggestions led to you being treated in such an insulting manner."

"It sounds like you got the same treatment," Geary said. "Do you have any suggestions?"

"I wish I could offer some advice, Admiral, but clearly this is seen as a matter of even greater importance to the Rift Federation than I thought. They will march to their deaths rather than admit the task is too large and their resources too small."

"Thank you, Captain," Geary said. "I still appreciate the advice you gave me. It was the best option for all of us, but if the Rift Federation refuses to dance along, we can't make them."

Next came another call to Ambassador Rycerz. "She told you the Rift Federation has canceled its military assistance agreements with the Alliance? That's the first I've heard of it. It's not really a surprise, though." Rycerz looked to one side of her desk, apparently viewing a display there. "If they've canceled those agreements, Rift Federation warships no longer have free right of passage through Alliance space. That's probably why they had this Captain Kapelka tell us of it at a point where we couldn't physically enforce a denial of passage."

"We still couldn't use force, could we?" Geary asked. "The same problems would still flow from that."

"Yes. You said that Captain Hiyen made a personal appeal to Kapelka?"

"That's right," Geary said. "Invoking his status as someone who'd fought alongside her, and as a representative of another smaller entity also concerned about asserting independence."

"How far ahead of us are those Rift Federation warships going to be?"

"About a week and a half," Geary said. "If they run into trouble, all we'll be able to do is search for any survivors. I doubt any fighting would still be going on."

"Admiral, we no longer have legal grounds to assist them by military means if they run into trouble," Ambassador Rycerz pointed out. "If we see them being attacked by a Syndic force, it will be an incident involving two foreign powers."

"Are you saying we'd have to let them fight on their own?" Geary demanded, appalled.

"That's exactly what I'm saying, because canceling the military assistance agreements with the Alliance means the Rift Federation is on its own and that's how the Rift wants it." Rycerz rapped one fist against her forehead, but suddenly paused. "What about the aliens? The enigmas? What's the legal status of us assisting the Rift Federation ships against them?"

"You don't know?" Geary asked.

"Hell, no." This time the ambassador rapped both fists against her forehead. "And there's not enough time to send a courier ship to Unity and for it to return with guidance. Admiral, is there some . . . fleet thing that would guide our actions?"

"Fleet thing?" He paused, thinking. "There's an old rule that whenever a ship encounters another ship in trouble, or survivors from a wreck, that ship is supposed to offer aid and rescue. It's an obligation. That's a rule older than space when it comes to ships. Older than the Alliance or the Syndicate Worlds or the Rift Federation."

Rycerz gazed at him, her eyes intent. "That might have to do, Admiral. This rule came from Old Earth?"

"That's my understanding, yes. I haven't really thought about it in legal terms, but that's why the Alliance fleet defended Midway against the enigmas," Geary said. "They were people, and they needed help. They were being attacked, so we helped defend them."

"Which gives us precedent, as well as a rule established by our ancestors." She nodded as much to herself as to him. "The ancestors who came from Old Earth, meaning the ancestors of every human. We can't very well ignore the wishes of those ancestors. The only question will be whether the Rift Federation will allow us to save them if it comes to that."

He wanted to say that wasn't something they should worry about, that of course the Rift warships would accept help, but thinking about the posture and the attitude of Captain Kapelka in her last message he realized Ambassador Rycerz was right to be concerned about that.

THEY could only watch over the next couple of days as the Rift Federation ships swung through space to reach the jump point, then vanished into jump space.

"If I lose one sailor because of those idiot Rifters alerting everyone we're coming I'll personally take it out of Kapelka's hide," Captain Desjani vowed.

The sentiment was widespread in the fleet, Geary found. Nor could he blame everyone for feeling that way. He felt the same anger whenever he thought about the possible consequences of the Rift Federation stirring up trouble just before his own ships arrived.

Luckily, he was too busy with the last-minute preparations to depart to spend much time brooding over the actions of the Rift Federation.

In the midst of those preparations he got a text message from Desjani. "You need to talk to Roberto Duellos."

Groaning at the interruption, but knowing she wouldn't have sent that unless it was important, he called Captain Duellos on the *Inspire*. "How are you doing?"

Duellos used his lips to sketch a brief smile that didn't reach as far as his eyes. "I've been worse."

Frowning, Geary took another look at him. "You look like hell. What happened? Didn't you get back from leave just a day ago?"

"Yes," Duellos said. "I put it off to ensure my ship was ready before I took leave."

"Tanya said you put it off because you didn't know what would await you at home."

Duellos smiled again, this time the expression lasting a little longer. "Tanya Desjani always speaks the truth, even when it's uncomfortable. Well, as commander of the fleet, you deserve to know of matters that might degrade the performance of your senior officers." The smile faded, leaving a look of weary despair. "My wife and I have officially separated. She wanted her husband back. But I couldn't bear the idea of spending the rest of my life in an office somewhere, dreaming of a past when I was doing things that mattered. We still might have hung on, but . . . there's a new ensign assigned to *Warspite*."

The abrupt shift in topic startled him out of the condolences he'd been about to offer. "*Warspite* got a couple of them," he said, calling up the data with one hand while he was speaking. "Ensign Dimitri Gamal and Ensign . . . Arwen Duellos." Geary focused on his friend. "Your daughter?"

Duellos nodded. "Following in her father's footsteps. Or, to my wife, placing herself in unnecessary peril far, far from her home and family because of the poor example provided by her father."

"I'm sorry."

"I know you mean that. Thank you. I assure you that I will continue to carry out my duties to the best of my abilities."

"You know that's not what I'm worried about."

That earned him another small smile. "Indeed." Duellos grimaced, looking away. "The hell of it is she's right. She deserves a spouse who's there, who puts her above everything else. But when push came to shove I couldn't. I loved space more than I loved her. I guess that's the hardest part. I hate that I didn't love her more. I should've. But I didn't. I failed her."

There were times when no words seemed adequate or right. Times when only silence felt appropriate. As much as Geary wanted to say something, anything, that would make things better, he could think of nothing.

Finally, Duellos looked back at him. "I won't fail anyone else. Not my crew, not my commander, and not my daughter. No matter what it takes. You don't need to worry about me, Admiral."

"I will worry about you, because I care about you. Promise me that you'll speak with me or with Tanya if you need to."

"A promise easily given," Duellos said. "Fear not, Admiral, I have a role model to look to in my loss. A man who lost every person he'd ever known or loved, and still managed to keep going. I hear he even saved the Alliance."

Geary felt a twisted smile form on his own lips. "He's not much of a role model. He makes a lot of mistakes."

"I don't think anyone wants or needs a role model who's perfect," Duellos said. "How could any aspire to match such a person? But a flawed, human individual, that's someone useful to look to. It's not perfection that makes someone great. It's what they achieve despite their many imperfections."

"That applies to you as well," Geary said.

"It does. I'll be all right, Admiral. Thank you for your concern. At least Arwen is on a battleship rather than a destroyer. There's something comforting about knowing my daughter is behind that much armor and is that well armed." Duellos looked exasperated. "She told me she's putting in for a transfer to a battle cruiser."

At least he could help with this. "I'd have to approve that, and regardless of who the ensign is I don't want to move around people just as our crews are getting settled again. It's not special treatment to tell you I won't be approving any transfers among ships for some time."

"That is a relief." Duellos nodded to him, gathering himself to look more like his usual nature. "I should get back to work."

"Me, too," Geary said. "Be well, my friend."

EIGHT days later the Alliance force finally began moving, the various warships sliding into their assigned positions as the entire mass of ships began accelerating toward the jump point for Atalia.

He'd wrestled with the right formation to adopt, wanting something that looked too powerful for anyone to want to mess with but also wanting to avoid looking as if the Alliance force was arrayed for attack.

The result was a formation of boxes positioned around a cylinder.

The leading box, and that at the rear, each held a division of battle cruisers. Due to losses that hadn't been replaced, Geary had reorganized the remaining battle cruisers into only three divisions. In the lead was the new division commanded by Captain Badaya on *Illustrious*, also including *Incredible*, and *Valiant*. Guarding the rear was Captain Duellos on *Inspire*, accompanied by *Formidable*, *Dragon*, and *Steadfast*. "Above" the cylinder was the last battle cruiser division, led by Captain Desjani on *Dauntless*, along with *Daring*, *Victorious*, and *Intemperate*. Each group of battle cruisers was accompanied by a division of heavy cruisers, as well as squadrons of light cruisers and destroyers.

The walls of the cylinder itself were made up of battleships, forming a fearsome barrier against any attack. The battleships had taken fewer losses than the fleet's battle cruisers, but their numbers had still been whittled down, so they had been regrouped into five divisions. The first held *Gallant*, *Indomitable*, *Glorious*, and *Magnificent*. The second consisted of *Dreadnaught*, *Fearless*, *Dependable*, and *Conqueror*. The third was made up of *Warspite*, *Vengeance*, *Guardian*, and *Resolution*. In the fourth division were *Colossus*, *Encroach*, *Redoubtable*, and *Spartan*, while the fifth included *Relentless*, *Superb*, *Splendid*, and the newly rejoined *Reprisal* from the Callas Republic. The fleet's remaining heavy cruisers, light cruisers, and destroyers roamed around the battleships.

Inside the front portion of the cylinder were the four assault transports (*Tsunami*, *Typhoon*, *Mistral*, and *Haboob*) carrying General Carabali's Marines. Inside the back part of the cylinder were the eight fast fleet auxiliaries, boxier and slower than warships, but able to fabricate any new parts or weapons or fuel cells needed by the fleet. Without ships like *Titan*, *Tanuki*, *Kupua*, *Domovoi*, *Witch*, *Jinn*, *Alchemist*, and *Cyclops*, Geary never would've been able to get the fleet back home after it had been trapped deep in Syndicate Worlds space.

Finally, in the center of the cylinder was *Boundless*. The ship carrying Ambassador Rycerz and the scientific teams had the least defenses on it but was in the most well-protected position. Anyone trying to reach *Boundless* from any angle would have to fight their way through walls of defenders.

The damage inflicted at Unity Alternate and other battles had been repaired, in some cases (such as with *Incredible*) so many repairs that the crews joked they were new ships. Every ship held as many supplies, as much food and weapons, and as many fuel cells as they could safely carry, and the crews were close to full strength. That last was a bit of an illusion, since as Master Chief Gioninni had predicted roughly a quarter of the sailors in the fleet were new, with too little experience in their jobs. Others were veterans, rescued survivors whose original ships had been destroyed. But in a sense almost everyone in the fleet (Geary himself included) fit into that category. Tanya had never told him how many ships she'd had blown out from under her since she'd joined the fleet as an ensign, but he knew there'd been at least three.

The fleet accelerated as one, every ship just where it was supposed to be. It formed a magnificent sight, even though Geary kept seeing the ships that weren't there, having been lost in earlier battles. But it should still be powerful enough to get through Syndicate Worlds space unscathed, and hopefully to deter the enigmas from attacking. That was assuming everyone behaved rationally, though. He had enough experience with both people and aliens to have little expectation of that.

As a matter of fact, he'd already had an example with the Rift Federation ships.

He wondered how far they'd get.

It took a while to get up to speed, because the "fast" fleet auxiliaries and *Boundless* couldn't match the acceleration of warships. But eventually the main propulsion units on every ship cut off as the fleet reached point one light speed.

"All ships on station, on vector for Atalia jump point," Lieutenant Yuon reported.

Geary stood up from his seat on the bridge of *Dauntless*. It would be a couple of days before the fleet reached the jump point, leaving him with a sense of anticlimax. He looked around the bridge, trying to recapture some of the excitement of beginning the mission. "I see you kept your lieutenants, Captain Desjani."

"They all came back," Desjani replied. "I let them go and they came back."

Lieutenant Yuon grinned. "There's nothing I'd rather be doing, Captain."

Lieutenant Castries nodded. "This mission is historic, Captain. Why would I want to miss it?"

Desjani gave them a skeptical look. "You two are agreeing on something? That's pretty historic in and of itself."

"It won't happen again, Captain," Lieutenant Castries promised.

"Good." Desjani looked at Geary. "Admiral, there's something we have to discuss."

He followed her off the bridge, through passageways, all the way to the secure conference room that was usually used for meetings. Gunnery Sergeant Orvis was waiting there.

Desjani sealed the hatch, activated the security measures in the compartment, and then held out her hand to Orvis. The Marine handed her a small box. "We've got a problem," she said to Geary, opening the box.

He looked inside, seeing a black speck. "What is it?"

"A sophisticated, state-of-the-art bug called a tick. It's tiny, it can move on its own, or it can latch onto someone and get carried to other places."

"Someone bugged this room?" Geary said. "How? Why didn't the security measures detect it?"

"It has some new passive concealment features," Gunny Orvis said. "The good news, Admiral, is that when the security features in this compartment are active, that bug couldn't transmit out. The bad news is it was in here, so it could've sent information about what people in here were saying before security features were activated for a meeting, and it has a limited storage capability that would've allowed it to save some of what was said during a secure meeting and transmit it later."

"How'd we find it?" Geary asked, trying not to get angry at whoever had done this. Anger would only cloud his mind when he needed it clear.

Desjani held out the device she'd been bequeathed by Victoria Rione. "Handy gadget, like I said."

"Do we have any clues who planted it?"

"It seems to be Alliance manufacture, Admiral," Gunny Orvis said. "But that doesn't mean anything. There aren't any indications of who put it here."

"We can't even narrow it down to people who attended meetings," Desjani said. "Someone else could've planted this on one of them, and when it got here it would've dropped off."

"Who knows about this?" Geary asked, staring grimly at the black speck.

"You, me, Gunny, and his hack-and-crack specialist," Desjani said.

"All right. I'm going to notify Ambassador Rycerz and General Carabali. Gunny, I want you to deliver that tick to Lieutenant Iger and tell him what you know about it. No, wait. Is it still working?"

"No, Admiral. My hack and crack disabled it," Orvis said.

"Good. Then go ahead and get it to Lieutenant Iger. Tell him he's authorized to share any information he gets from it with General Carabali."

"I'm on it, Admiral."

After the gunnery sergeant left, Desjani stopped Geary from following. "Are you thinking this might involve the special operators on *Boundless* who are pretending to be spit-and-polish peacocks?"

He raised both palms out in surrender. "Yes. The ones Carabali thinks might be Wendigos. We have to make sure the rest of the fleet doesn't suspect who they are."

"The entire fleet already knows who they are. At least that they're special operations types. You can dress knuckle-draggers up in pretty uniforms but everyone can still tell they're knuckle-draggers." She eyed him warily. "Do you really think they might be the ones who bugged this room?"

"Maybe," he said.

"If it was them, then they messed with my ship," Captain Desjani said, her eyes growing hard. "That's a serious line to cross."

"I'll make sure the ambassador knows that."

"I'm not joking, Admiral."

"I know."

"Why do you think this ambassador isn't behind it?"

Tanya rarely expressed anti-government sentiment, but like the rest of the Alliance military she'd been affected by the long, terrible war. The military couldn't blame itself for the failure to end the war, not when its men and women were dying in the effort. But the failure hadn't been only the government's fault, Geary knew. Both the Syndicate Worlds and the Alliance had access to vast amounts of resources and people, so neither side could overwhelm the other. His own final victory owed at least as much to the impending collapse of the over-stressed Syndicate Worlds as it did to the efforts of his fleet. The Alliance itself had been trembling on the edge of failure due to the stress of the war as well. But while the Syndicate Worlds was falling apart, racked by rebellion, the Alliance had held together. And its military officers had never raised their hands against the Alliance government.

"She's in overall command of this mission," he said. "Tanya, diplomats like Ambassador Rycerz risk their lives to try to keep the military from having to risk military lives."

"There you go getting all idealistic again." She waved off his words. "All right, Admiral. But please keep me informed."

"I will."

Ambassador Rycerz wasn't happy at the news, calling in Colonel Webb immediately, who in turn disavowed any knowledge of the tick but requested to have it turned over to him so he could try to learn the source. Geary only agreed to grant him access to scans of the tick. "We will, naturally, be keeping a close eye out for similar incidents," he said.

"Believe me, Admiral, so will I," Colonel Webb said. If Webb wasn't angry, he was doing a great job of pretending. "If one of my people was behind this, they'll find out how little I like rogue operators."

Geary sat in his stateroom after the call, thinking that he seemed to be dealing with a lot of rogue operators. Before it had been those involved in the black programs that had culminated in the Defender fleet. Now it was the Rift Federation warships, already doubtless creating problems ahead of the Alliance fleet. And Colonel Webb's people. And Dr. Macadams. It might be a nice change of pace to deal with external problems again, such as the Syndicate Worlds and the enigmas.

But that brought up thoughts of Atalia. The last time he'd seen Atalia Star System, it had been getting ravaged by out-of-control dark ships. And beyond that, haunted Kalixa. Past Kalixa was Indras Star System, still firmly controlled by the Syndicate Worlds. The last time an Alliance military force had been at Indras it had been the black ships of the Defender fleet, carrying out a "secret" retaliatory attack for Syndic provocations. The Syndics wouldn't be happy to see Alliance warships showing up again, might have prepared traps, and would've been alerted by the Rift Federation ships.

When the fleet finally jumped for Atalia a day and a half later, Geary's worries were focused on what lay ahead.

TWELVE

AN alert sounded aboard *Dauntless* as the fleet dropped out of jump space with the familiar but always painful and momentarily disorienting lurch that caused in human minds. Everyone took precious moments to clear the haze from their minds as the alert warned of possible danger.

"It's an Alliance courier ship," Lieutenant Castries reported on the heels of *Dauntless*'s sensors tagging the contact on their displays.

What would normally be a reassuring assessment was more than a bit unnerving after their recent experiences.

"Two light seconds distant," Captain Desjani said, frowning. "He's not maneuvering."

"Sensors do not identify it as a likely dark ship," Lieutenant Yuon said.

"It's about where the courier ship stationed at Atalia should be orbiting," Geary said. "I—damn!" Alerts began proliferating on his display as dozens of warships nearest to the courier ship locked their weapons onto it as a target. Nervous from the earlier attacks, they might open fire on a friendly ship. His hand hit the necessary comm circuit without having to look. "All units, this is Admiral Geary! Hold fire! I repeat, no ship is to open fire unless I directly order it to do so!"

For a few seconds, as the fleet swept closer, the fate of the Alliance courier ship hung on a knife-edge.

A message came in, highest priority, the expression of the courier ship's commanding officer a mix of confusion and terror. "Why are we being targeted? Urgently request that you confirm your identities."

"He's worried we're more dark ships," Desjani said.

"If we were, he'd already be dead," Geary said, his tense gaze on his display. "If anyone has an itchy trigger finger, he might still end up dead." This was one of the consequences of the dark ship fiasco, that Alliance ships feared other Alliance ships and might open fire on them. One more unintended consequence the minds behind the dark ship program hadn't thought about when coming up with the idea.

The fleet that had existed when he inherited the command contained any number of ships that would have already opened fire out of excessive zeal or simply poor discipline. But he'd managed to train his captains to think, and earned their trust, two things that paid off now. "All units, this is Admiral Geary," he said, trying not to sound or look breathless. "The courier ship here has been confirmed as a crewed Alliance vessel. Repeat, the ship is friendly. Geary, out."

He tapped the command to reply to the courier ship. "I regret the confusion that led to you being momentarily targeted. We've encountered more than one surviving dark ship courier vessel which has attempted to ram. Be aware that given current threats it's critically important to quickly establish your identification as a crewed vessel whenever encountering other Alliance ships. Request you forward to me a status report on recent events in Atalia."

He rubbed his eyes, trying to relax. Destroying a friendly ship by accident would have been an awful way to start this mission. Geary lowered his hands and focused on his display, taking in the picture it presented of this star system.

They'd last seen Atalia reeling from devastation caused by the Defender fleet. A frontline star system in the war while Atalia was part of the Syndicate Worlds, it had been devastated over and over again, each time the human towns and cities and defenses rebuilt by the Syndicate Worlds, all of them repopulated with new settlers from deeper in Syndicate space. Because the Syndicate Worlds didn't want the Alliance to have even the symbolic victory of an abandoned star system. It might have seemed a uniquely insane policy, except that the Alliance had done the same thing with its frontline star systems. The treasure and lives expended to keep resurrecting those star systems were the price of maintaining the illusion by both sides that the war wasn't being lost.

Now, having been battered again, Atalia seemed to be a sea of wreckage on the surface of its primary world and in space. "I can't believe the population is still hanging on here instead of evacuating," Geary said. "It's not like there aren't a lot of other worlds out there with plenty of room on them."

"That'd mean admitting they'd lost," Desjani said. "People don't like to do that."

"I don't like admitting the Alliance is responsible for the latest round of destruction here, either, but I have to accept that."

"We're actually responsible for *all* of the destruction here," Desjani said. "All of the rest was during the war, though."

Which made it legal, if not all right. "I'm glad *Boundless* is with us."

"Why?" she asked. "So the ambassador can see this?"

"No," he said. "Because if Ambassador Rycerz wasn't here, I'd have to answer the messages Atalia's people are going to be sending asking for help. But she is here, so that'll be her job. Not every lousy job gets shipped downhill."

Desjani leaned back in her captain's seat and gave him a look from the corners of her eyes. "But you'll still feel guilty that we can't help them."

"Of course I will."

In the back of his mind had been a vague hope that the Rift Federation ships would've had an attack of common sense and waited here to accompany the Alliance ships the rest of the way. But there was no sign of them.

The update from the courier ship soon confirmed that the Rift formation had arrived at Atalia, cruised across the star system without sending or acknowledging any messages, and then jumped for Indras. Since the Rift Federation ships hadn't identified themselves as no longer part of the Alliance fleet, the people of Atalia had interpreted that as a deliberate snub of their suffering by the Alliance, as well as an insult to their own fragile independence.

"I'm beginning to wish I'd let you open fire on them," Ambassador Rycerz told Geary after dealing with another set of messages from the leaders of Atalia. "They certainly complicated an already difficult task for me. Do you have any insight into why the Rift Federation ships acted the way they did here?"

"No," Geary said. "I asked Captain Hiyen and he couldn't guess why they refused to communicate."

"You don't have anyone else with a good insight in Rift Federation thinking?"

"I had Victoria Rione," Geary said. "She was so good at it that I never tried to develop an alternate source."

Rycerz closed her eyes and nodded. "The biggest problem with someone who does their job really well is that they make it too easy not to think much about their job. Until they're not around to fill it anymore. Have you learned anything else about whoever bugged that secure conference room aboard *Dauntless*?"

"We've analyzed the bug as best we can," Geary said. "I'm sure you won't be surprised to hear it contains no clues to its origin, except that Lieutenant Iger believes it came from a civilian source and not a military source."

"What does Colonel Webb think?"

"He hasn't been informed of those findings yet."

"Please do so." She spotted his hesitation, her gaze on him sharpening. "Is there some reason you don't want to let Colonel Webb in on everything you find out?"

He could deny his reasons, avoid any confrontation or the possibility of word getting back to Webb, but Geary didn't like the feel of that. He looked back at Rycerz, thinking that he'd want her to be candid with him. But he couldn't expect that of her if he didn't do the same. "There's some concern regarding Colonel Webb's feelings about this mission."

"I see." Rycerz sat back, her eyes hooded. "Is that concern based on concrete actions or statements?"

"No," Geary said. "It's based on the impression he created with me and others. I freely admit there's no solid evidence that gives reason not to trust him specifically."

"Because you haven't been able to tie the bug you found to anyone. I'm going to make what may seem like a radical suggestion, Admiral. If you want a better feel for Colonel Webb, share that information and see how he reacts. Discuss it with him. See what he says and what he doesn't say."

He considered the idea, finally nodding. "That's the only way to learn more about him, isn't it? How candid do you think he'll be?"

"I've found Colonel Webb to be very straightforward," Rycerz said. "In some areas, that is."

"How does he feel about the Dancers?"

Rycerz smiled. "He distrusts them. Colonel Webb distrusts every potential threat. That's how he sees the universe and that's one reason he got the job he has. Part of my job is to make sure he doesn't go overboard with his concerns about security, but part of his job is to be a bit paranoid about whatever we might encounter."

"And I failed to consider that was part of his job," Geary said, realizing he'd looked at Webb from only one angle. Had Carabali done the same? He did need to size up Webb in a longer encounter. "All right. I'll contact the colonel and set up a meeting."

Rycerz raised both of her eyebrows as she gave Geary a look of surprise. "Are you always so reasonable, Admiral?"

"No," he said. "But I do try to listen to people before I make up my mind."

The ambassador didn't reply for a moment, seeming preoccupied with thoughts she didn't disclose. Finally, she spoke again. "Atalia's representatives are also worried about the Syndics, which is understandable. They say they've been threatened repeatedly."

"According to the courier ship monitoring the star system," Geary said, "Syndic warships have been popping out of the jump point from Kalixa at random intervals. It's clearly meant as intimidation, letting the people here know that the Syndicate Worlds could hit them again anytime they want to."

"Why haven't they, then?" Rycerz asked. "There's nothing here that could stop even a small Syndicate Worlds force from taking over again."

"I think," Geary said, "the Syndics are letting Atalia remain a buffer between them and the Alliance. Maybe because Atalia is so badly beaten up that occupying it would impose more costs than benefits on the Syndicate Worlds. But they're making it clear to Atalia that its independence is entirely at the sufferance of the Syndicate Worlds."

"Will we encounter Syndic warships at Kalixa?"

"We might. If not there, we're guaranteed to encounter some at Indras."

"What will they do?"

"Threaten us. Tell us to leave Syndicate Worlds space. Invoke the peace treaty they've broken repeatedly. Technically, an Alliance fleet entering Syndicate Worlds space without prior approval is an act of war."

"But we've done it before," Rycerz pointed out.

"Because they couldn't stop us," Geary said. "And because a prior peace agreement granted me leeway to transit Syndic space. But once their threats don't work, they may attack. I don't expect a direct attack, but rather the sort of low-level, deniable actions we encountered last time."

"How dangerous will those be?"

"One time they cost us a battleship. They could've cost us a lot more. They can't be disregarded."

The ambassador looked even less happy than before. "I was led to believe the transit of Syndicate Worlds space would not be a major problem. I thought most of this force was to deter attacks by the enigmas once we left human space."

"The enigmas will be a greater threat," Geary said, wondering why the ambassador hadn't asked questions at this level of detail before leaving Varandal. "But the Syndics have never stopped trying to attack us. I don't know who told you that part of the transit would be without risk, but they were wrong. And this time the Syndics might use the attack of the black ships on Indras, an attack by the Alliance, as justification to be even more aggressive."

"But we won't respond to their provocations," the ambassador said, in a way that sounded more like an order than a suggestion.

"My ships are authorized to defend themselves," Geary said, not willing to give ground on that. "We won't seek out a fight, but if a fight comes to us we'll stop it."

Ambassador Rycerz twisted her mouth, looking down at her desk. Finally, she looked up at him again. "We are not authorized to restart the war with the Syndicate Worlds."

"Ambassador," Geary said, deliberately using her formal title, "I'm not interested in restarting the war. But I am specifically authorized to take any necessary measures to protect my ships, including *Boundless*."

"Our actions may decide whether there is renewed war." She had her eyes on him now, her expression set in firm lines, clearly wanting to establish dominance on this topic.

He kept his eyes on hers as he answered, wondering why the mood of this meeting had shifted so suddenly. "Our actions didn't start the war the first time. If the Syndics want war, our choice will be the same now as then."

"The situation then, a century ago, was more complex than you imply."

"I recall the situation then very clearly," Geary said. "It was only a few years ago for me."

Rycerz stopped her initial response, pausing to rethink her words. "I'm not in a position to lecture you on the situation when the war began. Fine. I don't want any shots fired unless I approve it first. In each and every case."

"I can't agree to that," Geary said.

"I didn't ask for agreement. That is how we will deal with the Syndics if they appear to be attempting aggression. They may well want us to fire first, which is why I will not approve that."

What was happening? Why was he suddenly being given specific directions on how to do his job after being promised full authority? Geary spoke slowly. "My orders give me the responsibility for the protection of this force."

"I've told you how we'll handle this," the ambassador said.

"I do not agree. This falls under my authority."

Ambassador Rycerz shook her head, her voice steady. "You don't have the final say, Admiral. My orders give me authority to relieve you of command if necessary to ensure the success of this mission. I'm sure that provision won't have to be invoked, though."

There it was, laid out in clear language. The sort of do-this-or-else that was supposed to put him in a position where he had to agree. Sprung on him without warning, despite assurances to the contrary.

He was supposed to give in on this, bend to higher authority, which as it turned out hadn't been candid about the reach of his own orders.

But he'd already given more than enough. And he wasn't going to give on an issue that could literally mean life and death for those over whom he had responsibility. Especially since the ambassador's authority to relieve him had not been disclosed prior to this.

If they wanted someone else, let them get someone else. "Go ahead," Geary said, his voice flat. "Relieve me of command. Or we can make it simple. You can give me an order that my ships can't fire without your authorization, and I can give you my resignation."

Ambassador Rycerz stared at him for several seconds, not speaking. "That's not a bluff, is it?" she finally said.

"No, it's not."

"We're already outside Alliance space. You can't simply walk away from this mission. Everyone in the fleet is counting on you."

Which explained why the ambassador hadn't tried to assert this authority before they left Varandal. They'd wanted to box him in at a point where he'd feel compelled to go along. Where his sense of responsibility would force him to comply.

This had been planned, perhaps from the moment he received his orders at Unity. A way to make him unquestionably submit to a civilian superior, even though he'd made clear over and over that he respected the fact that he worked for the government and would obey its orders. Yet instead of being up-front about their concerns, they'd tried to pin him between his sense of responsibility and his personal honor.

"I can walk away and I will," Geary said, surprised at how emotionless his voice sounded.

"You can't—" Rycerz glared at him, plainly thrown off by his refusal to go along. "That's it? You'd surrender everything you have? Surrender all of your responsibilities and your standing?"

"My standing? Do you think being fleet commander matters to me?" Geary said. "Do you think I love the status and the rank? That's never why I served."

"What about all the men and women in the fleet? What will happen to them if you walk away?"

He felt his own face stiffening at her words, anger threatening to loose his tongue. But in that moment what came to his mind was his brief meeting with the old sergeant on Glenlyon. The sole survivor of the survivors. Officers in the chain of command must have known that unit was being dropped into an impossible situation, that the attack was sure to result in disaster. But had anyone spoken up? Had anyone sacrificed their career in an attempt to save those soldiers? Maybe some had, and hadn't been listened to. That had happened far too often in military history, and history as a whole. Cassandra had been right, even though her fellow Trojans blamed the gods for their own failure to believe her. But, as also happened far too often, others had surely gone along with what they knew was a mistake, convincing themselves that staying in their position was best in the long run.

And over a thousand soldiers, over a thousand men and women, had died, to no purpose.

He knew what he owed that old sergeant. And what he owed those now in the fleet.

Geary kept his voice calm. "I'm not irreplaceable. I will not buy one minute longer in command of the fleet if the cost of that minute is one life that could've been saved if I'd been listened to. This isn't my choice. It's yours. If you disagree with my orders, you can appoint another commander. And any repercussions of that decision will rest on your shoulders, not mine."

Rycerz sat back again, her expression as hard as his own must be. "You know I can't accept your resignation. I don't like being black-mailed."

"Neither do I," Geary said.

Another period of silence for several seconds was broken by the ambassador. "Perhaps a cool-down period would be wise."

"I agree," Geary said. "Until I get a formal order from you to the contrary, my ships will continue to follow the self-defense guidelines I have authorized."

"Understood," Ambassador Rycerz said, ending the call.

That hadn't gone very well.

He was still going over the conversation in his mind, trying to figure out where it'd gone off the rails and concluding that the ambassador had badly misjudged how he'd react to coercion, when General Charban called.

"Is this a bad time?" Charban asked, eyeing Geary's expression.

"Yes," Geary said, "but I need to get past it. What do you need?"

"Dr. Macadams has issued another demand that we turn over all of our equipment to him." Charban made an apologetic gesture. "I don't have the authority to deny his, um, request."

"I do," Geary said. "Tell Dr. Macadams—" No. He couldn't give in to that temptation. "Don't answer him. Don't do what he wants, but don't bother replying to him. He knows he's supposed to submit any requests for support through me."

"No matter how many times he's told he can't tell us what to do, I don't think Dr. Macadams views his demands as requests," General Charban said.

"That's not my problem," Geary said. "It's not yours, either."

"All right, Admiral." Charban paused. "Is there anything . . . ?"

"Nothing you should concern yourself with," Geary said, immediately feeling that sounded too much like he was dismissing Charban as well as his worries. "The ambassador and I have been discussing policy."

"Oh. Is there anything I can help with?"

"It involves the Syndics, not the Dancers."

"Then good luck," Charban said. "Would you like some good news? Dr. Kottur has been speaking with us. He's trying to learn as much as possible about the Dancers."

"The Dancers?" Geary frowned. "Why is Dr. Kottur interested in them? His team is supposed to do their work at Midway. If it works, if they manage to link Midway's gate to the Alliance hypernet, they can all go straight home from there and never encounter the Dancers."

"Perhaps Dr. Kottur can take over for Macadams," Charban suggested.

"I won't get my hopes up," Geary said. Dr. Kottur was so easy to work with. Always smiling and friendly.

Smiling faces.

Damn. Between the ambassador's surprise demands and the problems with Macadams, he was becoming paranoid.

ANOTHER meeting to not look forward to. But an important meeting nonetheless. And one Geary felt he had to honor in order to show Ambassador Rycerz that he had meant what he said about listening to people before making up his mind. Plus he wanted to see how Colonel Webb acted toward him, whether the ambassador had shared any unhappiness with Geary with the colonel.

Lieutenant Iger was waiting in the secure conference room when Geary arrived, coming to attention. "Colonel Webb is standing by, sir."

"Let's get going, then." Geary took a seat while Iger activated the room's security systems, then established the link with *Boundless*.

The virtual image of Colonel Webb appeared, standing at attention.

"Please take a seat, Colonel," Geary said.

Webb sat down in a seat aboard the other ship, the conferencing software making him appear to sit at the table opposite Geary and Iger.

Lieutenant Iger remained standing. He took a deep breath. "Here's what we've been able to determine on the bug found earlier in this compartment," he said before calling up screens full of technical data.

Colonel Webb looked over the screens, which were mimicked on the table he was sitting at on *Boundless*. Geary listened, saying nothing, as Webb and Iger discussed the data, throwing around terms that Geary didn't fully understand.

He waited, though, to see if Webb would try to bully Iger, to try to dress him down for things Iger hadn't been able to determine.

That didn't happen. After a good half an hour of back-and-forth, Webb let out a deep breath of exasperation. "Lieutenant, you seem to have done all of your homework on this. What I'm seeing agrees that even though we can't identify with any certainty the origin of the tick, it shows a couple of indications of not being of military origin."

"Yes, sir," Lieutenant Iger said. "If I had to make a call, I would say it's from a civilian manufacturing source."

"Which doesn't mean whoever planted it is a civilian," Webb said unhappily. He looked at Geary. "Admiral, if someone in the military, one of my people for example, planted that tick they'd probably try to get a tick that didn't come from a military source."

He understood that. "To divert suspicion from themselves."

"Exactly." Webb glared at the technical screens as if they were an enemy. "It tells us nothing. It doesn't rule out anybody."

"You're certain it wasn't any of your people?" Geary asked.

"As certain as I can be. They've been asked directly if they pulled this stunt. Sometimes operators do that," Webb explained. "For fun. And if they get caught they say it was a training exercise, and congratulations you did a great job catching them. None of my people would dare try that, though."

"How can you be so sure?" Geary asked, once again wondering if Webb himself might've been involved.

Webb's face went rigid for a moment before relaxing a little in an obvious effort. "You wouldn't be aware of this, sir. When I was a junior officer, a friend of mine who was also a junior officer died when his team leader decided to launch an unauthorized mission. The team leader was afraid if he asked for permission it'd be denied. And for good reason. It was a stupid mission. But my friend and the rest of the team didn't know that. They died." Colonel Webb inhaled slowly. "No one plays games in my units, Admiral. If anyone does something unauthorized, I will make them pay the maximum price I can exact. My people know that."

That put a new spin on things. Geary nodded slowly to give himself time to think. "I'm sorry for the loss of your friend."

"We all lost a lot of friends," Webb said in the manner of someone who didn't want to dwell on it. "I don't want to lose any more. Which is why this bothers me. We've got someone with access to this place, or access to someone with access to the compartment that you're in, who wanted to know what was being discussed here. But we have no idea who they are or their motives."

"Admiral Geary has been concerned about anti-Dancer sentiment," Lieutenant Iger said, not realizing that he was sharing something Geary didn't want Webb to know.

But Webb didn't act defensively, instead frowning in thought. "That doesn't narrow things down, though. If we're talking about people who wouldn't want this mission to succeed, it includes a lot of possibilities. The Syndics, former Syndics, Alliance personnel with anti-alien sentiment, and those personally opposed to the admiral here, among others."

Lieutenant Iger paused. "Sir, I hate to direct attention at a civilian, but . . ."

"Macadams?" Colonel Webb asked. "He certainly seems determined to sabotage the mission, doesn't he? He's being watched. Which unfortunately means he'd have had trouble doing this, I think."

This seemed as good an opportunity as any to learn more about Colonel Webb's feelings toward the Dancers. "Lieutenant Iger has been one of the leads on communicating with the Dancers. If you have questions about them, he's one of the best qualified to answer."

"Iger. Yes," Webb said. "I read the report compiled by General Charban with your assistance. I did have a few questions. This pattern thing. How well does it help predict their actions?"

"Not very well," Iger said. "The problem is their actions seem to be governed by how they perceive humanity fitting into some larger pattern, but we don't know what that pattern is. It's like trying to predict which way a ground vehicle will go when you don't have a road map. The vehicle is going to follow the roads, but we don't know where they are."

"Huh." Webb chewed that over for a few seconds. "They seemed to know about the Defender fleet."

"Yes, sir. They sent help for us against it."

"Any idea how they knew?"

"No," Geary said. "I've talked this over with everyone. Either the Dancers have some ability to tap into what the Alliance was doing, or they somehow picked up some other indications."

"Sir," Lieutenant Iger said, "I've wondered about something regarding that. Do you suppose we're not the only intelligent species to have built something like the Defender fleet? Maybe others have, including maybe the Dancers themselves. That would have told them what to look for, and might be why they knew we'd need help."

This time both Geary and Webb fell silent while considering that idea. "It's certainly possible," Geary finally said.

Webb fixed Iger and then Geary with an intent look. "In your opinion, have these aliens been eager to help us?"

"Eager?" Geary sat back, thinking. "I'm not sure that's the right word."

"Usually it's more like willing to help," Iger said. "That's how I'd characterize it. Like when we were trying to communicate with them, they could've told us they needed patterns in the words of our messages, but they didn't. It's like they were waiting until we figured it out."

"They didn't establish contact with us," Geary said, "even though they could have. They waited until we reached them."

"Interesting."

"Why did you ask that?" Geary said.

"In my experience, Admiral, when people are very eager to help they either need something from you very badly, or are trying to lure you into some trap. That doesn't mean the aliens would operate the same way as humans, but it might've been something to consider." Webb shrugged. "But that's not an issue here. I'm intrigued. I've spent a long time trying to anticipate the most likely actions of people. Trying to do the same with these aliens will be a real challenge. Speaking of different ways of thinking, though, how confident are we about the actions and intentions of the people running Midway Star System?"

"They seem to be sincere in wanting to build something stable," Lieutenant Iger offered. "The times we've been at Midway we've picked up a lot of traffic indicating overhauls of the justice system, for example. Not just changes to the surface appearance, but fundamental shifts."

"I've been able to work with them," Geary said. "And they've proven reliable enough that I thought assistance to them was a good idea."

"Do you mean assigning Captain Bradamont to stay at Midway? If she—" Colonel Webb, usually able to maintain a poker face, showed a flash of understanding. "Ah. Certainly. Lieutenant Iger, thank you. You did a first-class job analyzing that bug. Keep me informed—I'm sorry. I keep forgetting I'm not in the military chain of command here. Admiral, can Lieutenant Iger keep me informed of any new developments or findings regarding that bug?"

"Of course," Geary said.

"Thank you. Admiral, may I speak privately to you for just a moment?"

"Yes," Geary said, wondering what this latest thing was about.

After Lieutenant Iger had left, Colonel Webb turned an openly admiring look on Geary. "Admiral, I admit I got taken in by the Bradamont thing."

Not sure what Webb meant, Geary confined his reply to a small smile that hopefully looked like he knew what was being discussed.

"You needed a mole with access to the highest level of the leadership at Midway," Webb continued. "She needed your help. You gave her an out, gaining her gratitude, and you've still got leverage over her. And because of the Syndic connection she's been accepted by them. That's just brilliant tradecraft, sir."

"It seemed like the best way to handle things," Geary said, deciding that contradicting Webb wouldn't serve any purpose.

"Admiral, you've got an amazing ability to cause opponents to underestimate you," Webb said. "No wonder you've won so many fights. I'm looking forward to continuing to work with you. I'll see if I can find any new leads on that bug, and let you know if I do. By your leave, sir. To the honor of our ancestors." Webb ended the link.

Geary sat still, trying to decide whether Colonel Webb's last statements had been compliments or not. Finally, he got up, thinking that he wished he were half as clever as other people seemed to think he was.

Lieutenant Iger was waiting just outside. "Admiral, I wanted to let you know Dr. Kottur contacted me again for more information on the situation at Midway Star System. He was particularly interested in the Syndic software for preventing a catastrophic collapse of their hypernet gate."

"Do we have a copy of that software?"

"No, sir. Just some older versions of the standard Syndicate Worlds anti-collapse system. It's certain that Midway has made some local modifications to prevent the Syndicate Worlds from using back doors and vulnerabilities that exist in the standard system."

"I guess Dr. Kottur and his team want to get a head start on their work at Midway," Geary said. "But they'll have to wait until we get there."

THE rest of the transit through Atalia had been gratifyingly quiet, though in a star system littered with so much wreckage of human works, and the remains of humans who had died among them, the quiet could seem eerie at times. Sailors on the Alliance warships muttered prayers to their ancestors and, as sailors had always done, waited out the time until their crossing of this forlorn region should be over. The distance between the jump point where they'd arrived from Varandal and the jump point that would take them to Kalixa was four light hours, or roughly four billion three hundred million kilometers. Even at point one light speed, or about thirty thousand kilometers per second, covering that distance took forty hours.

Like the sailors, Geary had waited, too. Waited to hear from Ambassador Rycerz. But nothing had come from her since the meeting that had ended so badly.

He sat on the bridge of *Dauntless*, standing by until he could order the fleet to jump. Tension tightened his muscles in expectation that he'd receive a last-moment order from the ambassador, an order that might require him to delay the jump until a new fleet commander could be appointed.

"She won't do it," Captain Desjani murmured just loud enough for him to hear. "They need you too badly."

He'd confided in Tanya, of course. She'd instantly seen something was wrong, and he'd needed someone to hash over the matter with, to see if his own perceptions of what had happened were amiss. "That's good," he muttered in reply. "And bad."

"We're about to jump," she reminded him.

Which meant there was a message he needed to send. "All units, this is Admiral Geary. Prepare to jump for Kalixa. We don't know what we'll encounter there, so be prepared for anything when we arrive. Self-defense measures are authorized, but make sure you know what you're shooting at before you fire, and make sure you have no alternative." That was a tough set of conditions to set for his ship commanders, but then being a ship commander meant being expected to handle such things, and make the right decisions even when only a few seconds were allowed to decide them. "We expect to jump in five minutes. Geary, out."

"Find out anything more about the bug?" Desjani asked.

"No. Except that Colonel Webb seems far less likely a suspect. Even General Carabali agreed with that, though she's still suspicious of him and his unit."

"Some special forces types are real loose cannons," she said. "They make regular forces wary of them all. Marines, now, you have to always worry about what they're going to do if you don't keep your eye on them. But I understand the average soldier doesn't need to be watched as closely."

"I've heard differently," Geary said.

"I wonder if they can get into as much trouble as sailors?" Desjani wondered.

"That would be a challenge."

"Approaching jump point," Lieutenant Yuon said. "One minute to jump."

The last minute counted down, Geary feeling more relaxed after talking to Desjani. "All units, this is Admiral Geary. Jump now."

The universe vanished, replaced by the endless, formless gray of jump space.

Geary began to stand up, determined to try to get some rest after long days waiting for the worst to happen. But he halted in mid-motion as the ship's displays lit with sudden bursts of light. He watched them flare and die, feeling a shiver run down his back at the sight. Seeing occasional mysterious lights appear in jump space had become common, but seeing three of them so quickly wasn't.

"Three of them," Lieutenant Castries said, her voice awed. "One right after another."

Desjani gazed at her display, where the mysterious lights had quickly faded and vanished, leaving no trace they'd ever existed, and no clue as to what had created them. All anyone knew was that initial human trips through jump space had seen none of the strange lights, but they'd been seen more and more often over the centuries as more and more human ships traversed jump. "Do you think the Dancers know what the lights are?"

"General Charban has asked about that. The Dancers haven't replied," Geary said, aware that everyone on the bridge was being careful not to look at him. He knew people linked his presence to odd behaviors by the baffling lights of jump space, and even though he discounted the idea he had no way to disprove it.

"It's a good omen," Desjani said.

"I hope so," Geary replied.

THIRTEEN

IF Atalia had been uncomfortable because of the amount of devastation there, Kalixa was a nightmare that familiarity made no easier to experience.

A hypernet gate had collapsed at Kalixa, a gate without the safe-collapse system installed, creating a nova-level pulse of energy that had torn through the star system, devastating the inhabited world that had once orbited the star, and leaving the star itself unstable.

"There's only one Syndic warship here," Desjani said, gazing at her display. "A single Hunter-Killer near the jump point for Indras. In a few hours when he sees that we've arrived he'll probably jump to give Indras warning that we're coming."

"Odd that we didn't catch any other Syndic warships here," Geary said, "given that they've been popping out at Atalia often enough to intimidate the people there."

"They know we're coming," she said. "Thanks to our former friends in the Rift Federation. That HuK on picket duty is to let them know exactly when we'll get there."

"Which means they will have something waiting for us," he said.

"Not a straight-up fight, if our intelligence assessments of Syndic fleet strength are anywhere near accurate. But something designed to hinder or hurt us."

"Which they will end up regretting," Desjani said.

He didn't reply, wondering if the ambassador would call with that order while they were at Kalixa.

Ambassador Rycerz finally called Geary a few hours after they'd arrived at Kalixa. He braced himself for the worst, but she said nothing about rules of engagement with Syndic threats. "The enigmas did this?" she asked, looking ill.

"We're pretty sure they did, yes," Geary said. "They wanted the Alliance and the Syndicate Worlds to start deliberately collapsing each other's hypernet gates, wiping out the human presence in every star system with a gate. We think the enigmas are the ones who leaked hypernet technology to both the Alliance and the Syndicate Worlds at about the same time, both to keep the war among humanity going and to trick us into building unimaginably huge mines in as many star systems as possible."

"Why didn't it work?"

"It almost did. After what happened here at Kalixa, which the Syndics blamed on us, we narrowly stopped a Syndic retaliatory attempt to collapse the gate at Varandal. If they'd succeeded in that, there would've been pressure for the Alliance to respond in kind. Fortunately, Captain Cresida had already developed safe-collapse software for the gates, so we got that distributed as quickly as possible."

"To Alliance hypernet gates, and Syndicate Worlds hypernet gates," the ambassador said, gazing at him. "I'm aware that the safe-collapse software was 'accidentally' leaked to the Syndics," she added, giving an extra twist to the word "accidentally."

"Ummm . . . yes," Geary said, not wanting to contradict the official version of how the Syndics had gotten their hands on the software. Only Victoria Rione and he had known the truth, and she could no longer reveal her role in that event. But there'd been plenty of suspicion over how that particular "accident" had happened. "That did ensure the gates couldn't be used as weapons by either side."

"I'd heard of this, but seeing it in person is . . . horrible." She looked at him with a steady gaze. "We're fortunate that things happened the way they did. That people made the decisions they did. I understand Captain Cresida was the sister of Dr. Cresida aboard *Boundless*?"

"That's correct," he said.

"I'll have to pass on to Dr. Cresida my appreciation for her sister's work. Thank you, Admiral."

He spent a few minutes looking at his display after the call ended. It looked as if the ambassador had chosen to let the matter of who would decide when to fire continue to rest with him. It was very strange to think that the devastation here at Kalixa might have contributed to that decision.

The Syndic HuK did indeed jump within a few minutes of when it would've seen the light showing the arrival of the Alliance fleet. After that, the Alliance ships were alone in the star system as they transited to the jump point for Indras, something that only served to emphasize the way death had laid its hand here. Lines of sailors formed outside the small worship rooms located deep inside the ship as men and women sought comfort by communing with their ancestors, and every display that didn't have to show space outside the ships was set for images of other places.

Geary held a meeting of all the fleet's captains, the sort of thing he'd dreaded since assuming command when the fleet was on the verge of being annihilated. But the meetings had grown less contentious, and he wanted to ensure everyone understood what to do.

The conference room appeared to be huge thanks to the virtual meeting software, the table stretching far enough to accommodate every captain in the fleet from those commanding immense battleships to those in much smaller destroyers. Captain Matson of the *Boundless* sat among them. If Geary focused on any one of the captains, their image would appear close, and when anyone spoke, their words came as

clearly as if they were sitting next to you. As software went, it was remarkably seamless and easy to employ.

General Carabali and her senior colonels were there as well.

So was Ambassador Rycerz, who had opted for an observer seat,
away from the table but able to watch and hear all that was being discussed.

"We don't know exactly what the Syndics will have waiting at Indras," Geary began, "but we do know they'll lie to us and try to trick
us. An open assault is unlikely since they don't have the numbers of
ships to give them any chance against us, but they may try some deniable attacks on us. I want everyone to understand that firing in self-
defense is only authorized if there is no alternative. If you can dodge an
attack, do so. The exceptions to that are the auxiliaries and *Boundless*.
If something aims at them, it will not be allowed to get past the battleship screen. If something tries to maneuver to avoid the battleships, the
battle cruisers will move to block it." Even a small, fast courier ship
couldn't outmaneuver a battle cruiser.

"Our job is to get through Indras, to the hypernet gate there," Geary
continued, "without suffering any damage or losing any people, and
without engaging in any combat that isn't absolutely necessary. We
don't want to fall for any Syndic trick or trap that's waiting for us, and
we don't want to give them any cause to believe or to claim that we
intend attacking them."

"They're going to try something," Captain Badaya said, resting his
chin on one hand. "They know we're coming thanks to that picket ship.
How do we keep from losing another battleship if we can't fire until the
last moment?"

Captain Armus smiled. "We have an idea. With your permission,
Admiral. The battleships carry large bombardment munitions. If
something is on a collision course with us, and we fire such a weapon
at it, the impact will turn the attacker to dust, leaving no wreckage
continuing down the original vector to endanger our ships. But if the
attacker dodges at the last moment to avoid the munition, it will pass

close by us, and can be totally destroyed using our normal anti-ship weapons."

"We've gamed it," Captain Jane Geary said. "It's the perfect counter to an attempt to ram by anything up to a heavy cruiser in size. Even a civilian freighter loaded with rocks would be blown into tiny fragments on different vectors. And it allows us to let the attacker get closer before we fire, so there won't be any doubt we acted in self-defense."

"We're talking about using a BFR against an attempted ramming?" General Carabali asked, using Marine slang for the large bombardment projectiles. "What if they're coming after one of the assault transports? Can one of those launched by a battleship stop the attack?"

Jane Geary nodded. "It's simple physics. Whichever battleship has the best firing angle can launch to intercept anything approaching another ship."

Commander Young of the *Mistral* spoke up. "What if they dodge off the track for their initial target and aim for another of our ships?"

"We time the shot," Captain Armus said, "so the attacker will maybe have just enough time to dodge the incoming bombardment round. But, velocity and momentum will not allow enough time for a large enough vector change to aim for another target."

"The same for the auxiliaries?" Captain Smythe asked. "You can cover all of them?"

"In this formation," Armus said, "easily."

Captain Matson of the *Boundless* looked around the apparently vast conference table. "These bombardment projectiles. They're what I've heard called rocks?"

"That's right," Captain Jane Geary said. "No warhead of any kind, just a solid chunk of matter that depends on kinetic energy to destroy whatever it hits. The large ones are heavy enough to take out the entire center of a city." She paused, casting a quick glance at her granduncle. Everyone in the fleet knew how Black Jack had reacted when he learned that the Alliance fleet had adopted the tactic of indiscriminate bombing of cities in another futile attempt to win the war. "We . . . don't have much use for them now, but the battleships still carry them."

"What about smaller bombardment projectiles?" Captain Desjani asked, as if there hadn't been any moment of awkwardness. "The sizes the battle cruisers carry?"

"It depends on the mass of the attacker," Captain Armus said. "For most of them, a medium bombardment projectile will do the job. They either dodge, or they die. And if they dodge, they die another way."

"I like this option," Captain Duellos said. He seemed once again his usual self, aside from a slight haunted look at the back of his eyes that only someone who knew him well could spot. "It lets us refrain from firing until there is no doubt of the attacker's intent, but ensures our ships will be successfully defended."

"That's to be our primary option if any ships approach with apparent attempt to ram," Geary said. "Battleships will take the lead on engaging with bombardment munitions, unless something comes in from a vector where they're best engaged by battle cruisers or heavy cruisers. Good job coming up with this option."

"Captain Geary suggested it first," Captain Armus said, nodding toward Jane. "You know those Gearys. Always coming up with ideas." He smiled at his own joke.

But it wasn't a bad joke, Geary thought, unable to resist a smile himself. "Sometimes the ideas are good ones," he said. "Sometimes. Are there any questions? I don't want anyone to have any doubts about when they're allowed to shoot, and when they should not. The Syndics want us to look like the aggressors. We won't give them that."

The conference ended, the ship captains all came to attention and then began vanishing as the virtual presences left the compartment. The seemingly immense table shrank along with the dwindling number of attendees, until only Geary and Desjani were left.

He turned to look back to the virtual observer's seat where Ambassador Rycerz had been watching the meeting. But she, too, had left, leaving him wondering whether she'd been reassured that he wasn't out to start a fight.

"I'm worried about Roberto Duellos," Desjani said. "Did you see him?"

"He's better," Geary said.

"He looks better, if you don't look too close. I've invited him to a virtual dinner, captain to captain, but he says he's too busy."

"That doesn't sound like Duellos," Geary said, even more worried for his friend.

"However," Tanya said, "if the admiral invited him to a dinner, along with his daughter on *Warspite*, Captain Duellos could not refuse the invitation."

"What about the captain of *Dauntless*?" he asked. "Could she attend as well, seeing as this dinner will be aboard her ship?"

She paused to think. "Yes. That'd be expected, really. Anything else might seem like a snub."

"It'll have to be dinner today," Geary said. "We'll be jumping for Indras early tomorrow. I'll get the invitation sent."

Which is how he found himself, a couple of hours later, seated in his stateroom, where he rarely ate, preferring to share meals with the officers and crew. But getting a meal delivered to his stateroom had been easy. He and Desjani were there in person, of course, seated on two sides of a small table. Occupying the other two sides were the virtual presences of Captain Duellos and his daughter Ensign Duellos. Geary hadn't thought about the menu, but the cooks had, arranging with their counterparts aboard *Inspire* and *Warspite* to ensure everyone had the exact same meal.

Captain Duellos hadn't been exactly thrilled at the invitation, but he had accepted readily enough. His daughter Arwen, in a uniform that still looked painfully new, sat rigidly, unsuccessfully attempting not to look nervous at dining with the admiral.

Geary almost asked how things were back on Catan, fortunately realizing how tone deaf that would be before he could speak.

"How's life on *Warspite*?" Desjani asked Arwen.

"It's very demanding and very rewarding, Captain," Ensign Duellos answered.

That rote response got a smile out of her father. "Quite the professional, isn't she?"

"She didn't get that from you," Desjani said.

"I'll have you know I can be extremely professional when I want to," Captain Duellos said.

"What's training like these days?" Geary asked Ensign Duellos, thinking that would be a neutral topic.

"They've revamped some things, Admiral," she said. "We spent a lot of time studying Bla—I mean, studying your victories."

That was sort of good, as long as they were studying the tactics. "My victories?" He smiled and shook his head. "I couldn't have accomplished anything without the skills, dedication, and courage of the officers and sailors of the fleet. Officers like Captain Duellos here. He's one of the finest officers I've ever served with. I'm afraid living up to his example will be a very difficult task for you."

Ensign Duellos's professional facade cracked as she turned a loving gaze on her father. "I'm going to do my best, Admiral."

"You're a lucky man, aren't you?" Desjani murmured to Captain Duellos.

He nodded, smiling. "I suppose I am." The smile slipped. "I wasn't there enough for her when she was growing up. I was out here."

"You were always with me," his daughter said in a rush. "Every day. I saved every message you sent. I knew why you were gone, what you were doing, and why, and how hard it was. That's why I want to—" She stopped speaking, looking embarrassed.

"That's about the best performance appraisal I've ever heard," Geary said, raising his glass of water in a toast.

Captain Duellos smiled again, joining in the toast to himself.

Afterwards, Geary reflected on the odd fact that the meal formed a bright spot in his memories even though it had taken place at Kalixa.

◇

DESPITE the worries about what might await at Indras, everyone felt relieved when they jumped from Kalixa the next morning. It wasn't morning by any planetary standard of course. Ships kept their own time, all of them supposedly linked to the same "universal" source that had originated at Old Earth. Supposedly, if a ship from the farthest reaches of human expansion into the galaxy visited Old Earth, the time aboard that ship would still match that along the prime meridian on the ancestral planet. The one time Geary had actually visited that part of Old Earth he'd completely forgotten to check that, though.

Spending too long in jump space made humans uncomfortable, most people describing it as a growing feeling that their skin didn't fit right. But the jump from Kalixa to Indras only required a few days, not long enough for the sensation to become really noticeable, let alone serious. What did become more difficult were the worries about what the Syndics might have waiting for them at Indras. The picket ship had alerted the Syndics to when they'd arrive, and the Rift Federation warships had already reached Indras more than a week earlier. What had happened to them?

As the fleet left jump space, all ships were at full alert, ready for the worst.

THE Syndics were indeed waiting at Indras.

A Syndic flotilla was orbiting about ten light minutes from the jump point. Close enough to need watching, but not close enough to be an immediate threat. Four battleships, three battle cruisers, four heavy cruisers, and eleven Hunter-Killers. Outmatched by Geary's force, the flotilla was nonetheless strong enough to testify to the ability of the Syndicate Worlds to still churn out warships.

"No sign of the Rift Federation force or any recent wreckage that might correlate to those ships," Lieutenant Yuon said, gazing at his display.

"How do you suppose they got past that Syndic flotilla?" Desjani wondered.

"Maybe the Syndics will tell us." Geary looked at his display, where the projected track from the jump point to the hypernet gate at Indras formed a sweeping curve through space. "Six . . . no, seven merchant freighters traveling from the gate to the jump point we just left."

Desjani nodded, her own eyes studying the track, a frown slowly growing. "Those freighters will pass close by us," she said. "Why are seven freighters heading for the jump point to Kalixa?"

"What did we learn at Atalia about their current level of trade with the Syndics?"

"Sporadic," Desjani said. "Atalia has high demand but little ability to pay. One freighter possibly en route to Atalia would make sense. But seven?"

"Maybe an invasion force disguised as peaceful trade?" Geary suggested. "Midway told us the Syndics are using modified freighters to carry soldiers."

"Maybe." Desjani looked toward the back of the bridge. "I want a close watch kept on those merchant ships. If there's anything the least bit odd about them, I want to know it."

"Yes, Captain," the watch standers chorused in reply.

It was nearly half an hour after their arrival at Indras, the fleet steadied out on its vector for the hypernet gate, before the first message arrived from the local CEO. The fact that it had arrived so quickly meant the CEO must be aboard one of the warships ten light minutes away.

The CEO was a man, not the woman they'd last seen when at Indras berating them for the attack by the black ships. That wasn't surprising, given the unsettled state of Syndicate Worlds politics. CEOs were probably rising rapidly as political factions jousted for power and falling just as quickly when they lost.

It also wasn't surprising, given past events, that the CEO's message was sent to Geary on his flagship. Of course they expected him to be in overall command of this force.

The new CEO looked like a typical Syndic CEO. Perfectly tailored suit, perfectly coifed hair, and perfectly superior attitude. What former CEO and current General Drakon on Midway had referred to disdainfully as a CEO uniform. But this one also looked competent in a dangerous way. If Ambassador Rycerz had an evil fraternal twin, that twin might've resembled this CEO.

"To the Alliance force conducting an unprovoked and unlawful invasion of space controlled by the people of the Syndicate Worlds," the CEO began. "This is CEO Paulson of the New Enduring Syndicate Directorate. You are required, in accordance with the peace treaty between us, and in the name of the people and in the interests of the peace we all desire, to immediately alter vector so as to jump back for Kalixa Star System and thence out of Syndicate Worlds space.

"I'm sure you are disappointed to learn that we did not fall for your simplistic trap," CEO Paulson continued with a smug smile. "Sending ahead of you a weak advance force was an obvious lure. An advance force that tried to incite attack by refusing to respond to communications. You expected us to destroy that force, giving you every excuse needed to carry on your war of unprovoked and unlawful aggression against the peace-loving people of the Syndicate Worlds. As your sensors tell you, there is no wreckage of that advance force here. In keeping with the Syndicate Worlds desire for peace and concern for the lives of all people, those ships were allowed to cross this star system and enter the hypernet. This clearly demonstrates our interests in avoiding any more senseless conflict. However, those warships also refused to pay standard transit fees for the use of *our* hypernet. You will of course make good on their debt.

"The people of Indras cannot be responsible for any mishaps that may befall if your warships continue an unauthorized and illegal transit of Syndicate Worlds space. I urge you, in the name of the peace dear to us all, to abandon your aggression and return to the Alliance immediately. For the people, Paulson, out."

The Rift Federation's strategy finally became clear. "That's why they're not communicating," Captain Desjani said, her words distorted slightly by the angry tightness of her jaw. "They know everyone in Syndic space will assume they're still part of the Alliance fleet, so they can benefit from our protection even when we're not in the same star system, and at the same time pretend they're doing this all on their own. All they have to do is not talk to anyone, which would require them to either lie about their status with the Alliance or admit they're no longer under our umbrella."

"They also stuck us with the bill for their Syndic hypernet use," Geary said. "Captain Kapelka is a lot more clever than we gave her credit for."

"The next time I meet Captain Kapelka I'm going to give her something a lot more painful than credit."

"I need to speak with Ambassador Rycerz." With no immediate dangers looming, he left the bridge, wanting the privacy of his stateroom for a talk with the ambassador.

Rycerz looked annoyed. "I assume you're not planning on responding to the Syndicate Worlds CEO?"

"They're used to me being in charge of the entire force," Geary said. "They'll be surprised to hear from you. But, no, I had no plans to deal directly with the CEO. I'll leave that to you."

"Do you know anything about this New Enduring Syndicate Directorate that CEO claimed to be part of?"

"I've never heard of it," Geary said. "I assume they're the latest group to gain control of the central government. For all we know they've already lost control and a replacement for CEO Paulson is on the way."

"The Rift Federation's strategy was better thought through than we realized," Rycerz said. "Will it get them through Midway's star system?"

"It might," Geary said. "If they're posing no obvious threat and seem to be part of the Alliance fleet, Iceni and Drakon will probably not attack them. But the enigmas won't care whether those Rift ships are part of the Alliance fleet. They won't make it to Dancer space."

"It doesn't look like the Syndics are going to try to attack," Rycerz said, eyeing Geary.

"No. As long as they don't, we'll be fine. We'll keep a close eye on some freighters whose paths will cross ours, but so far they appear to just be normal freighters."

"You're not worried about them ramming one of our ships?"

Geary shook his head. "No. Freighters are slow and clumsy. Even our auxiliaries can dodge a charge by a freighter. The Syndics know that. If they try anything with those freighters, it won't be ramming."

Rycerz sat silent for a moment, watching him. "All right," she finally said. "I'll talk with CEO Paulson. I'll probably have to pay whatever transit fee I can negotiate with them, and that for the Rift Federation warships. I want us to get to that gate without any fighting."

"So do I," Geary said. It was obvious that Rycerz hadn't given up the battle over who had dominance when it came to defending the fleet, but she wasn't going to push it. He had to be satisfied with that.

IT felt odd not to be verbally sparring with the local Syndicate CEO, but it was also a relief. Rycerz sent him information copies of the messages she exchanged as the ambassador and the CEO debated how large the transit fees should be and whether the Alliance fleet had any right to be here and why was the Alliance trying to start another war against the peaceful Syndicate Worlds who never attacked anyone except in self-defense. He did have the satisfaction of watching Ambassador Rycerz parry another claim that the Alliance was trying to once again start a war by telling CEO Paulson that "we do have Admiral Geary with us, who was present at the start of the first war. If you like I can have him tell you how that war began based on his personal experiences."

The Syndic CEO issued more warnings denying any responsibility for any problems the Alliance fleet encountered if it remained in Syndicate Worlds space. But in terms of active Syndic measures to stop the Alliance fleet, nothing could be detected. And that worried him. Routine scans for minefields had shown none of the anomalies that should be apparent in careful examination of small regions of space.

Six hours after the fleet had arrived at Indras and steadied on a vector for the hypernet gate, Geary walked with Desjani down one of the passageways of *Dauntless*. Late in the ship's day, there wasn't much other traffic in the passageways, giving them room to walk and think. Their feet could only carry them in circles around the ship, of course, and their thoughts seemed to be confined to circular paths as well.

"May I speak to you, Captain?" Master Chief Gioninni came hustling down the passageway, moving more quickly than his usual casual pace.

Desjani stopped and turned to face him, as did Geary. "What is it, Master Chief?" Desjani asked.

"Captain, I was talking with Senior Chief Tarrani," Gioninni began. "And she was saying how easy it'd be to target those Syndic freighters heading for the jump point to Kalixa, because they're all coming down the same track."

"That's right," Desjani said. "They're all coming from the same gate and heading for the same jump point."

"But wouldn't there be more variations in their tracks?" Gioninni asked. "The gate and the jump point and everything else in space move, and civilian ships are lousy at accelerating in close coordination. One always goes a little faster and another a little slower, which puts them on different vectors. We learned that doing convoy operations."

"True, now that you point it out," Desjani said, her eyes narrowing. She walked to a nearby display and called up a view of the tracks of the Syndicate freighters. "Yes. The later ships are following vectors that match the path through space of the earlier ships even though those vectors are less efficient for them."

"Like they were threading the eyes of cosmic needles we couldn't see," Gioninni said. "That's not natural."

"Why are they doing that? We've been watching those freighters very closely. There's no sign they're anything but freighters. And we've scanned for minefields in those areas and seen nothing."

"Well, Captain," Gioninni said, "one thing people learn when they're trying to fool people, which I'd never do—"

"Of course not."

"Is what's called misdirection. That is, you make people look at one thing while you're doing something else. They don't see what's happening because they're looking at what you want them to look at."

"Misdirection." Desjani inhaled sharply. "They want our attention focused on those freighters."

"I think so, Captain," Gioninni said. "Which means there's something else they don't want us looking at too closely. Probably something else in those parts of space where those freighters are being careful to go through the same way. Something we might spot if we really carefully look not at the freighters, but at the space they're transiting."

Desjani looked at Geary, who was nodding as he realized that Gioninni was right. Trust a scam artist to figure out what the Syndics were trying to do. "The freighters caused us to scan those regions first," he said, "and discount that threat because we didn't see mines. What if the Syndics have made new mines that are harder to spot?"

"Thank you, Master Chief," Desjani said. "I was going to ask you about a vacuum still in one of the voids, but as long as that still is destroyed in the very near future we won't have to talk about it."

"A still?" Master Chief Gioninni reacted with outraged surprise that seemed oddly genuine.

"It's not yours?"

"No, Captain!" Gioninni paused before remembering to add, "Of course not! I guarantee you that still will be gone within the hour."

"Good," Desjani said. "Here's the void number," she added, calling it up on her display. As Gioninni hustled away, she looked at Geary. "I wondered if that still was the Master Chief's work. He knows what boundaries not to cross and he doesn't want any rivals operating on his ship. So he'll shut that still down and find out who was behind it. It's probably one of the new sailors who thinks they're smarter than the old hands, and is about to learn the hard way not to underestimate old-timers."

"He's right about the freighters, isn't he?" Geary said. "There's something we're not supposed to be noticing. We'd better start looking harder."

"Focusing again along the tracks of those freighters, and not on the freighters themselves?"

"Right."

He didn't have to depend solely on the sensors aboard *Dauntless* for the study of space. Every sensor on every ship in the fleet could be and usually was linked seamlessly, integrating their observations and allowing multiple perspectives on the same things or places. The normal rule was that it was very hard to hide anything in space. To human ingenuity that was not an immutable fact, but rather a challenge.

It was nearly four hours later, both Geary and Desjani on the bridge again, when they finally got some answers.

"Anomalies," Lieutenant Castries announced as Geary watched warning markers appearing on his display.

"Minefields," Desjani said. "They are there. Why didn't we spot the anomalies earlier?"

"The readings are more subtle," Castries said. "Chief Yusef thought the anomalies might be so weak they were being filtered out as system noise. We tweaked the sensor algorithms and found them once we got close enough. Fleet sensors are rescanning all regions of space using the new detection criteria. These must be next-generation Syndic mines with improved stealth."

"And what better place to test them than at Indras where the Alliance fleet would be coming through," Desjani said. "How the hell did the Rift Federation ships avoid them?"

The answer to that seemed obvious to Geary. "The Syndics didn't want to tip us off by having those Rift ships, an apparent advance force, hit the mines. They must have deactivated the mines while the Rift Federation formation went through the minefields."

"I'll bet those mines are active now," Desjani said.

"Me, too. And the Syndics have been warning us not to travel to the gate so they can try to claim it's all our fault." He jerked in surprise and worry as another cluster of anomalies appeared on his display, much closer ahead on the vector the fleet was traveling. Way too close ahead. His hand hit the comm controls. "All units, this is Admiral Geary. Immediate execute, all units turn up three zero degrees, turn port zero four zero degrees. I say again, immediate execute, turn up three zero degrees, turn port zero four zero degrees. Execute. Geary, out."

The maneuver, ordered without warning, was slightly ragged as ships immediately began the vector changes, maneuvering thrusters tilting them "up" as measured against the plane of the star system and to "port" away from the star, then their main propulsion cutting in to bend their paths into new arcs leading away from the burst of anomalies. The more maneuverable ships such as destroyers and battle cruisers curved swiftly onto the new vector, while the less agile ships such as battleships and the auxiliaries lumbered through wider arcs.

The entire massive cylinder of the Alliance formation distorted a bit, like a 3-D jigsaw puzzle suddenly developing gaps, as every ship swung onto the new vector at different rates of turn.

He'd called the maneuver by instinct, knowing it would be enough to get his ships clear of the field of anomalies that were very likely mines. Geary watched the movement of his ships, seeing that he'd called it right. Every ship should avoid—

"Captain!" Lieutenant Castries called.

Geary had already seen the new anomalies appearing, a wide field of them.

And thanks to his evasive maneuver to dodge the initial mines, the Alliance fleet was heading straight into that new minefield.

FOURTEEN

"THEY assumed we'd evade when the lead ships hit mines!" Desjani said.

Which meant he still had a little room to play with. His fleet had begun turning before it was fully into the trap the Syndics had created. But it was very little room indeed.

"All units, this is Admiral Geary. Immediate execute, all units turn up nine zero degrees, turn port zero six zero degrees. I say again, immediate execute, turn up nine zero degrees, turn port zero six zero degrees! Execute. Geary, out."

Momentum could be an ally, but it was often an enemy, dragging ships to their doom. Having done all that he could, nothing was left for Geary to do but watch, hoping no new anomalies would appear beyond the ones already seen, hoping that all of his ships could get turned in time, swinging the entire fleet way up and turning so the star was behind them, trying to get so far off the track from the jump point to the hypernet gate that they'd be clear of potential minefields.

His captains knew when emergency commands went out to obey first and ask why later. Ambassador Rycerz had no such limits and the authority to override any barriers to her message immediately being received. "Admiral," she said, her image appearing in a window in his display, "what is happening? We're turning so hard people can't keep their balance."

He didn't have time for this. "We're trying to avoid minefields," Geary said, perhaps louder and harsher than he should have. "I'll brief you when we're clear!" He hit his own override, hoping it would disconnect the ambassador and remove a distraction he didn't need at this moment.

To his relief, it worked, the ambassador's image vanishing, leaving him free to watch with growing tension to see if his ships would all be able to turn in time, the arcs of their movement through space bending with what seemed like glacial speed.

If he'd placed the clumsy auxiliaries near the front of the cylinder, they wouldn't have made it. As it was, the more agile fast transports carrying the Marines seemed like they would barely clear the field of anomalies, which was itself only a vague depiction of where the Syndic mines were located.

Except for *Tsunami*, the arc of whose movement was sliding far too close to the danger area.

The battleships leading the cylinder formation were swinging around slowly as well, but *Gallant* abruptly altered her swing, going wider. *Gallant*'s status didn't show any problems with thrusters or propulsion, so the maneuver must be deliberate. Geary's hand went to his comm controls to demand the reason, but paused as he realized what was happening.

"She's protecting *Tsunami*," Desjani said, having grasped it in the same instant he had.

The massive, heavily armored bulk of *Gallant* plowed through space ahead of the track *Tsunami* was taking, deliberately risking the mines to ensure the transport wouldn't get hit.

Less than a minute later the existence of minefields was confirmed as an explosion detonated ahead and just to one side of *Gallant*. Loaded with the ball bearings known as grapeshot, the mine hurled a tight field of metal balls toward the oncoming battleship. Moments later two more mines went off, both also firing swarms of ball bearings at *Gallant*.

"Each of those mines threw off as much grapeshot as a battle cruiser could unleash," Desjani said, her voice filled with anger and concern.

The first mine's payload struck *Gallant*'s shields, the ball bearings instantly converting their kinetic energy into a brilliant display of explosions that sparkled against the battleship's powerful shields. On the heels of that blow, the grapeshot from the other two mines hit. *Gallant*'s shields facing the attack, already weakened, flared in a final effort to stop the oncoming projectiles before collapsing.

Gallant's shields had stopped most of the grapeshot, but the rest hurtled into contact with the hull.

Tsunami would've been destroyed. Even *Dauntless* would've taken significant damage.

But battleships were designed to endure an immense amount of damage and keep fighting. Bursts of light flared along *Gallant*'s armor as grapeshot hit, trying to hammer through into the guts of the warship. Trying, and failing. Her armor bearing new craters still glowing with heat, *Gallant* sailed onward, as if contemptuous of the attempt to destroy her.

The rest of the fleet turned, clearing the field of anomalies now outlined with scarlet warning markers on their displays, heading away from the star Indras.

Geary let out a long breath. "*Gallant*, this is Admiral Geary. Well done. Your ship deserves the name she bears, and so do all of your officers and crew."

Captain Pelleas of *Gallant* replied, smiling. "It's what battleships do, Admiral. We were happy to offer ourselves in protection of our comrades on other ships."

"That was quick thinking and brilliant maneuvering, Captain," Geary said. "Above and beyond what's expected of anyone."

Another image appeared on Geary's display, that of Commander Kahale, captain of *Tsunami*. "*Gallant* has our gratitude as well. Next port call, *Tsunami*'s crew will be buying the drinks for any sailor off of *Gallant*."

Those calls ended, Geary sat back, trying to relax the tension in him. Space was immense, so even the Syndics couldn't plant enough mines to cover more than small segments of it. No new anomalies had appeared along the fleet's current track. Unfortunately, that track was leading nowhere except deep space. "I want a recommended track to the hypernet gate, along with a full analysis of every place where we spot anomalies and every place minefields might have been laid to hit ships transiting from the Kalixa jump point to the gate. We want to leave as large a margin as possible between those areas and our new track."

"Get it done," Desjani told her watch standers. "Admiral, if the Syndics planted mines right in front of the hypernet gate, there won't be any way to avoid them and use the gate."

"That'd be extraordinarily risky, wouldn't it? If we couldn't avoid the mines going in, any ship coming out couldn't avoid them, either. And the Syndics here at Indras have no way of knowing when new ships are arriving, so they wouldn't know when to deactivate their mines."

"I didn't say it wouldn't be stupid," Desjani said. "But sometimes enemies do stupid things. Though those minefields were way too smart."

"Way too smart," Geary agreed. Realizing he couldn't put it off, he called Ambassador Rycerz back.

Ambassador Rycerz had a wide-eyed look to her. "Is that ship all right? The one that got hit?"

"*Gallant*? Yes, she's all right. Damage to her armor that might be a problem in a future fight, but nothing beyond that. No personnel casualties."

"I've seen such things in videos, but never live, as it was happening not so far from me." Rycerz shook her head. "How bad could that have been?"

"It depends how many mines were planted by the Syndics. The fields might not be very deep since they apparently tried to cover some wide areas. But it could've been bad. Those mines are new, and they've got a powerful punch. Any destroyer or light cruiser that encountered one would be destroyed."

Rycerz nodded, her eyes pensive. "We're in Syndic territory, without permission. We had no right to be in that region, and we were warned not to go there, so we can't claim that we were attacked. I understand your position expressed at Atalia much better now, Admiral. If you'd had to ask permission before dodging those mines it would've ended badly. We'll continue the current command arrangement. Can we reach the hypernet gate safely?"

"We're working on a safe path now," Geary said, trying not to think about what could've happened.

The call over, he focused back on his display, seeing the outlines of warning areas fluctuating slightly as the fleet's sensors updated their evaluations of danger areas.

"I really want to hurt them," Desjani said, still angry. "Do you know how many ships we might've lost? How many of our people might've died?"

"I know." He rubbed his eyes. "Vengeance might be nice. But Indras got badly shot up by the dark ships, remember? We could call that pre-vengeance, I guess."

"Yeah." Desjani's face brightened as she remembered the damage inflicted at Indras by the AI-controlled warships. "The Syndics here did get their butts kicked at that time, didn't they?"

"Those new mines of theirs are nasty pieces of work."

"The characteristics are part of the fleet database now. We'll spot them earlier in the future as long as we look in the right places." She grinned. "Damn. I owe Gioninni one."

"Me, too. When are we going to learn that con men are best at seeing through the tricks of CEOs?"

WORKING up a new, safe route to the hypernet gate took a while. The sensor search for anomalies had been out of necessity set at such a sensitive state that it also identified system noise as potential minefields. Each such apparent detection had to be analyzed carefully to see if it was real or noise. Further complicating matters, the freighters that had been sedately proceeding toward the jump point for Kalixa one by one turned and braked their velocity, assuming steady orbits wherever they ended up.

"What the hell is that about?" Geary complained, glaring at his display as if it could be intimidated into producing answers.

"No telling," Desjani said. "Look at this. Unless these detections are bad, the Syndics do have another minefield near the hypernet gate."

"Ten light seconds away," Geary said, studying the image. "That leaves enough room to get by them."

"If we come in slow, at a high angle," Desjani agreed. "That'll increase our vulnerability to attack, but unless the Syndics have invisible ships, that shouldn't be a problem. We'll have to watch those freighters and see if they reposition, though."

"Let's get going." The fleet's navigation systems had no trouble at all coming up with a recommended track, looping wide of any direct path between the hypernet gate and the jump point for Kalixa, approaching the gate from nearly directly "over" it, and then diving down to position the fleet for entering the gate. It wouldn't pass any test for most efficient path to the gate, but it was as safe as seemed possible.

Syndic CEO Paulson hadn't contacted them again after the nearmiss with the minefields, and Ambassador Rycerz, knowing how flimsy the Alliance's legal arguments were, hadn't tried sending messages to the CEO complaining about the trap.

The otherwise normal message traffic being sent around the star system continued as if nothing were out of the ordinary, lending an air of unreality to the dangers facing the Alliance force. But the mines had impressed on everyone that those dangers were real.

Despite the lengthened time required by the new vector, though, no other dangerous activity by the Syndics could be detected. The freighters continued to orbit, traveling around the star but otherwise going nowhere. And the Syndicate Worlds warships remained orbiting near the jump point for Kalixa.

What were they not seeing this time?

A nerve-racking two days later, the fleet finally reached the area "above" the hypernet gate, slowing to almost a stop relative to the gate before turning to dive down until the fleet neared lining up with the front of the gate where it could enter the Syndic hypernet.

But as the fleet prepared to enter the gate, Lieutenant Yuon called out. "Captain, the hypernet key is showing no access."

"Reboot it," Desjani said, looking at Geary.

"I already tried, Captain. The key is not showing any destinations available through this gate."

"The Syndics blocked their hypernet again," Desjani said.

"Looks like it," Geary said, disappointment welling up inside him. They'd feared the Syndics would do this again, but he'd hoped the Syndic leadership would want to avoid shutting down their entire hypernet given the costs that would inflict on their efforts to regain control of rebellious star systems. "All units, this is Admiral Geary, brake velocity to match movement of the hypernet gate. Assume fixed orbit."

His next call went to Ambassador Rycerz. "We can't enter the Syndic hypernet. The fleet is braking velocity and matching the orbit of the hypernet gate, so we'll be sitting here just outside it. But unless we come up with another workable option, we can't get to Midway."

Rycerz nodded, her expression grim. "Fortunately, we have another option. Aboard this ship is a team of the best hypernet theorists and technicians the Alliance can muster. Maybe they can find an answer. I'm calling a meeting with Dr. Kottur's group."

"I'll get down to the conference room and link in." Geary looked at Desjani. "The ambassador and I are going to check with Dr. Kottur's team to find out if anything can be done. Keep an eye on things for me."

"Yes, Admiral," she said. "Good luck."

It didn't take long to reach the conference room, activate the security protection, and link to Ambassador Rycerz's conference room. Moments after Geary arrived in virtual form, Dr. Kottur came into the room where the ambassador waited.

Ambassador Rycerz looked beyond Kottur as if searching. "Where are the rest of your team?"

"We don't need them for this," Dr. Kottur said. For the first time in Geary's experience, Kottur seemed deflated. Sitting down, Dr. Kottur spread his hands in an age-old gesture of helplessness. "There's nothing we can do."

"Shouldn't we still consult the others?" Rycerz demanded.

"We'd get the same answer. I've wanted this mission to succeed as much as anyone, but impossible is still impossible."

Geary sat, watching and listening with growing unhappiness, as Ambassador Rycerz kept probing for possible solutions and Dr. Kottur kept deflecting all of them.

"I don't want to accept failure," Rycerz said, her voice bitter, "but you've always been helpful up to this point, Doctor. If you believe there are no—" She stopped speaking, looking up in surprise.

As the meeting software updated, Geary saw several members of Dr. Kottur's team entering the room on *Boundless*, Dr. Cresida among them. Dr. Rajput spoke up first. "We think we have some possible solutions."

Dr. Kottur frowned. "How can you—"

"It's not a hardware modification," Dr. Cresida broke in. "We know that because it affected the gate at Midway to which the Syndicate Worlds does not have access. That means it's an operating system modification. And that means we can try to work around it."

The frown on Dr. Kottur deepened. "Messing with the operating system on a hypernet gate is very risky."

"Isn't that what we were going to do at Midway?" Ambassador Rycerz asked. "If your team thinks it's possible, we should give them a shot at it."

"Just a moment," Geary said as the security features in his conference room relaxed for a moment to let in Tanya. "Captain Desjani?"

"I needed to inform you we have a time limit, Admiral," she said. "The Syndic flotilla near the jump point from Kalixa has accelerated onto a vector aimed at intercepting us in our current orbit."

Ambassador Rycerz had the look of someone wondering what else would go wrong. "They aren't that much of a threat, are they? We outnumber them by a large margin."

Geary shook his head. "If they hit us while we're in a fixed orbit it will give them a substantial advantage. We don't want that to happen. How long do we have until they reach us, Captain Desjani?"

"Thirty-seven hours," she said. "They don't have to dodge their own minefields on the way here."

Dr. Bron, who'd just sat down, stood up again. "Then we need to get going on this. Let's hit it." The other new arrivals followed him out.

Dr. Kottur spread his hands again. "I don't have high hopes for this."

"We're damned well going to try before we give up," Ambassador Rycerz responded.

The meeting ended, Geary cut the link. "It's a good thing the other scientists showed up. Dr. Kottur was ready to throw in the towel." He noticed something about Tanya. "Did you have anything to do with that?"

"Me?" Desjani asked in mock surprise. "Maybe. I didn't have anything else to do so I decided to call Dr. Cresida to discuss a couple of personal effects of her sister's, and I may have mentioned that a meeting was going on."

"You didn't have anything else to do." Coming from a ship's commanding officer, that statement ranked about as impossible as anything anyone could say. "What made you think Dr. Cresida and the others wouldn't be at this meeting?"

"I can monitor activity in this compartment from another secure location," she reminded him. "I'm the ship's captain, you know. And you did tell me to keep an eye on things."

"So I did." He stood up, thinking. "Why do you suppose Dr. Kottur didn't even want to try? He's been extremely enthusiastic about this mission."

"He's been asking a lot of questions," Desjani agreed, but left it at that.

Something else occurred to him. "Dr. Cresida talked to you?"

"She kept her responses as monosyllabic as possible," Desjani said. "But we talked long enough for me to get my message across, and then she was happy to have an excuse to end it."

"I don't want to dislike Jaylen Cresida's sister," Geary said.

"Jaylen Cresida's sister makes it real hard not to dislike her," Tanya replied.

THIRTY-SEVEN hours.

He called another conference of the ship commanders in the fleet to bring everyone up to date.

"There's no chance the gate will collapse and destroy us all?" Captain Parr from the battle cruiser *Incredible* asked.

"The safe-collapse system was definitely active on it before the gate shut off," Captain Desjani said. "I don't trust Syndics any more than you guys do, but they know what'll happen to this star system and everyone in it if they caused a destructive collapse of their own gate. Kalixa is right next door."

"That'd take a special kind of crazy," Parr agreed. "And I guess if they planned on doing that, their flotilla wouldn't be coming this way.

It would've stayed near the jump point so it could jump to safety after sending the collapse command."

"So all we can do is wait?" Captain Badaya asked. "What will we do if the code monkeys can't come up with a work-around and get the gate working?"

"These are top-level scientists and technicians," Geary pointed out. "They're not exactly code monkeys."

"Too bad," Captain Duellos said. "It sounds like what we really need are hackers."

"I've offered them assistance from my Marine hack and cracks," General Carabali said. "Apparently this problem is at another level from what we usually deal with. Captain Hiyen, you're good at hypernet theory, aren't you? Can you assist the scientists?"

Hiyen shook his head firmly. "They're operating at a different level than my knowledge, which hasn't kept up with many developments while I've been serving as a combat officer. I'm good compared to the average person, but I'd just be in the way of these people."

"So," Badaya said, "back to the question. How long do we sit here?"

"I'll make a decision when the Syndicate flotilla is ten light minutes from us," Geary said. "That'll leave enough time for all ships to get up speed and onto the vector we want."

"Do we know where all the minefields are now?" Captain Armus asked.

"We're pretty confident," Captain Desjani said. "But we're going to keep looking. Now that we know exactly what to look for, we should be able to spot the mines before we're in danger of running into them." She paused, listening to something coming in on a personal circuit to her. "Three of the Syndic freighters that were sitting in fixed orbits have lit off propulsion. Initial estimates are they're moving onto vectors toward this gate."

"They're planning something else," Badaya insisted.

"I agree," Geary said. "One way or another, we won't be here when they arrive to spring their latest surprise."

"I heard one of the scientists is Captain Cresida's sister," Captain Jane Geary said.

"That's right," Desjani replied.

Captain Badaya and most of the other officers visibly perked up at that news. "If her sister is half as brilliant as Jaylen," Badaya said, "she'll solve whatever tricks the Syndics have played with this gate."

"We just have to give the scientists time," Geary said. "Let them work without interruption." He had to leave it at that, unsatisfactory though it was. No one liked waiting for the Syndics to do something. No one liked reacting to the Syndics instead of forcing them to react to whatever moves the Alliance fleet made. But that was the best option at the moment, because this wasn't a problem that could be solved with firepower or tactics. It required the special knowledge and insight that he hoped Dr. Kottur's team possessed.

BY the time twenty-four hours had passed, patience was wearing thin on all sides. Geary could almost feel the pressure from his ship commanders for updates on the work of the scientists, but the only way to get such updates would be by breaking into their work. "Have they given you any hints of progress?" he asked Ambassador Rycerz.

"No," Rycerz said, looking as if she hadn't slept for some time. "They just keeping inhaling coffee and other stimulants and continue working. Except for Dr. Kottur, who keeps advising me to abandon the mission and get all of our ships home before someone gets hurt. He seems to have been seriously spooked by the minefields we encountered."

"Once the Syndic flotilla gets within ten light minutes of us, I'm going to have to break fixed orbit next to the gate. That doesn't mean we can't come back to it, but it will make it a lot more difficult."

"I understand, Admiral. I'll call you as soon as— What?" The ambassador looked to one side in surprise. "You've got something you want to try?"

"That's Dr. Kottur?" Geary asked.

"No. Dr. Rajput and Dr. Cresida. Is what you want to try dangerous? No? Then proceed. On my authority. I don't want this held up while Dr. Kottur reviews your work." Rycerz looked back at Geary, hope appearing in her eyes. "Pray to your ancestors, Admiral."

"How long until they know if it works?"

"Dr. Cresida said it'd take hours."

Which wouldn't leave any room for a retry if whatever it was failed. "All right," Geary said. "I'll prepare for the worst and hope for the best. They're sure it's not dangerous?"

"You haven't dealt with these scientists much, have you?"

Which was apparently as good an answer as he'd get because Ambassador Rycerz signed off quickly.

He hadn't slept much recently, either. Geary looked at the starscape decorating one wall of his stateroom, trying to decide whether he should notify the fleet that the scientists were trying something that would take hours to determine if it worked and might or might not be dangerous. This seemed more like an ignorance-is-bliss situation, since the little he knew wouldn't reassure anyone.

With one hour left before the oncoming Syndic flotilla was ten light minutes distant, Geary went back to the bridge. Captain Desjani was there, of course, monitoring everything.

He sat down, looking at what was by now an all-too-familiar picture on his display. The fleet orbiting in sync with the hypernet gate, the Syndic flotilla still on an intercept vector and still moving at point one five light speed, five freighters now also accelerating toward the gate. What the freighters would do once they got here remained a puzzle since they'd betrayed no sign of being anything except what they appeared to be. The best guess was that they were packed with explosives or fuel cells and would "accidentally" detonate inside the Alliance formation. But there was no way he'd allow them to get that close, and the blundering freighters couldn't catch any of the Alliance ships unless the Alliance cooperated.

"We've got some vectors worked up," Desjani said.

Geary saw three proposed tracks if the fleet accelerated away from the hypernet gate. He didn't like any of them. It didn't take much inner contemplation to realize he didn't like them because each one represented a failure to enter the Syndic hypernet and get to Midway Star System.

But he had to pick one. As the time left kept diminishing with remorseless speed, Geary chose a vector that would dive the fleet "below" the gate and then in a wide arc back in the general direction of the jump point to Kalixa. That would require the oncoming Syndic flotilla to remain in a stern chase if it pursued the Alliance fleet, and leave all of the approaching freighters completely out of position to do anything.

"I know it sucks," Desjani said. "But we can't risk sitting here until the Syndics arrive."

"I know." Geary checked the time again. "Ten minutes until we leave."

With eight minutes left a call came in from Ambassador Rycerz. "They want another twenty minutes, Admiral."

"The scientists?" he asked. "They don't have another twenty minutes. We have to get moving in eight minutes."

"Admiral, I'm not demanding, I'm asking. Can we give them twenty minutes?"

He looked at Desjani, whose face was tight with concentration as she adjusted data on her maneuvering display, checking options. She paused, rubbing her chin, then shrugged. "It's possible, Admiral. It's shaving it real close, though. If the Syndics accelerate on their final approach the auxiliaries will be in trouble."

There were times when he hated being the one who had to make such decisions. A lot of times, really. Geary clenched one fist, inhaling slowly. Looking back at Ambassador Rycerz, he nodded. "Twenty minutes. Not one second longer."

"I'll tell them."

As the ambassador's image vanished, Geary called the fleet. "All units, this is Admiral Geary. Stand by to maneuver in twenty minutes.

Auxiliaries, we're going to need everything you've got when we start moving. Geary, out."

"Lieutenant Castries," Desjani called.

"Yes, Captain?"

"If there's an undetected minefield along our proposed vector I'm going to be very upset with you."

"I understand, Captain. I'll be very upset with me as well."

"The admiral will also be very upset," Desjani said. "We want to avoid that."

"I understand, Captain," Lieutenant Castries said again.

Geary gave Desjani a look. "Part of you loves this, don't you? Waiting to see whether all hell will break loose."

"I've always wanted to see if hell could beat me in a stand-up fight," she said, smiling. "Or if I could tame it. We've got twelve more minutes to kill before we get this fleet moving."

Seven minutes were left when Lieutenant Yuon let out a yelp. "Captain! The hypernet key shows the gate active, Midway Star System set as the destination."

"I'll be damned," Geary said. "They did it." He hit his comm controls. "All units accelerate along current heading. Prepare to enter hypernet in . . ."

"Thirty seconds," Lieutenant Yuon said.

"Thirty seconds," Geary repeated.

In the midst of his relief, he thought about the Syndic flotilla approaching, CEO Paulson ready for whatever his latest plan was, and how they'd feel about nine minutes from now when they saw the Alliance fleet had vanished. "Icing on the cake," he murmured.

"Ready to enter hypernet," Lieutenant Yuon said.

"Enter hypernet," Geary ordered.

His display abruptly went blank, everything in Indras Star System vanishing along with the star system and the universe around it, as *Dauntless* and the rest of the fleet once again entered the nowhere that existed between one gate and the next.

Tanya Desjani laughed softly. "I guess Dr. Cresida might be half as smart as Jaylen was," she said. "Now I have to be nice to her." She touched her own controls. "All hands, this is Captain Desjani. Well done during recent operations. Go to transit condition two. Everybody get some rest. It might be our last chance at it for a while."

Geary stood up. "I think I may try to get some rest as well. Too bad there's no way to communicate inside the hypernet. I'd like to know how the scientists got the Syndic hypernet unlocked, and whether it was a onetime thing or a permanent fix."

"Odds are we wouldn't understand the answer," Desjani said. "Maybe when we come back to Alliance space we shouldn't come through Indras again."

"Maybe," Geary said. "But we know what's at Indras. Any other place we wouldn't know what we were running into. And the Syndics are probably also thinking we'll choose another star system close to Alliance space next time. Going back to Indras might surprise them."

"You're not exactly predictable," Desjani agreed. "Doing the same thing again probably will throw off the Syndics. How do you think our sort-of friends at Midway will react to us showing up?"

"Hopefully with open arms," Geary said. "I hope Bradamont is all right."

"I hope she doesn't insist on us calling her Kommodor."

HE might know what lay behind at Indras, but arriving at Midway was always tense, wondering if the Syndicate Worlds or the enigmas had managed to defeat the tough but brittle defenders of what they called their "free and independent" star system.

So he was alert for anything when *Dauntless* and the rest of the Alliance fleet left the Syndicate Worlds hypernet at Midway, on the far side of Syndic-occupied space and as far as humanity had expanded in this direction before running into space controlled by the enigma race.

"Looks like everyone is home," Captain Desjani said as their displays updated.

A single battleship, a battle cruiser, four heavy cruisers, and a gaggle of light cruisers and Hunter-Killers. A small fleet by comparison with the forces under Geary's command, but impressive out here in the former hinterlands of the Syndicate Worlds, and doubly impressive since Midway had gained that fleet by hook and by crook. Every one of the warships had been "acquired" by various means from the Syndicate Worlds.

Midway's warships were in an orbit that placed them ready to react to anyone arriving at the hypernet gate or through some of the many jump points Midway boasted, and which had earned the star system its name. "It looks like they've been in another big fight since we saw them last," Desjani commented as the fleet's sensors reported new damage visible on most of Midway's ships.

Geary ordered his own fleet into an orbit near the hypernet gate, aware that proceeding deeper into the star system without approval might seriously anger the people here. His fleet could just as easily be an invasion force, after all.

It felt odd not to be sending out the message accompanying his arrival in the star system. But now that role properly rested with Ambassador Rycerz.

Still, it wasn't a surprise when the response several hours later was addressed to him. "Welcome back to Midway Star System, Admiral Geary," President Iceni said. "I would prefer to deal directly with you when discussing this 'adjustment' to our hypernet gate that your emissary is proposing. I also desire an explanation for the Alliance force that came through this star system earlier, and jumped for Pele without responding to any communications. Your flagship is authorized to proceed to orbit about our primary world so we can conduct negotiations without unneeded delays. For the people, Iceni, out."

On the heels of that message came a call from Ambassador Rycerz.

"Why did President Iceni call me your emissary when I clearly identified myself as the senior Alliance official?"

"Because she believes I am running everything," Geary said. "It doesn't matter what I say. They think that's all part of the game where I pretend not to be in control."

"You must tell them again," Rycerz insisted. "And tell them *Boundless* also has to go to their primary world."

"I'll be happy to," Geary said. "But based on experience they won't believe me when I say I'm not in charge."

He made sure his uniform looked good, and sat straight to send his response. "Thank you for your greeting, President Iceni. As you have heard, the senior Alliance official with this force is Ambassador Rycerz. She and her staff are aboard the *Boundless*, the large former passenger ship in the center of our formation. *Boundless* carries no offensive weapons. With your permission, we would like both *Dauntless* and *Boundless* to proceed to orbit about your primary world. To the honor of our ancestors, Geary, out."

He was prepared for a wait of several hours for the reply and was surprised when another message arrived soon after. But the new message wasn't from Iceni. "This is Kommodor Bradamont for Admiral Geary. Sir, I have received permission to speak with you directly and bring you up to date. Both President Iceni and General Drakon are eager to speak with you. We recently repulsed an enigma attempt to establish a base at Iwa. That star system should have been out of reach of the enigma jump drives, but they've obviously managed to extend their range. That was apparently what the Dancers meant when warning us to watch different stars. Naturally, Midway feels its defense of human space should be supported in material ways by those who benefit from it. We can offer you in exchange some more information on the enigmas. Colonel Rogero captured some of their weapons during an action on the surface of a planet orbiting Iwa.

"You also need to be aware that stars within reach of Iwa are now controlled by a woman named Granaile Imallye. She's ruthless and smart, and for the moment is working in concert with Midway's association of star systems to defend against both the enigmas and further Syndicate attacks. Her primary star system is Moorea."

Bradamont paused. "President Iceni and General Drakon have married. Their government is stable and continuing to implement reforms. It is my personal and professional recommendation that all possible support be given to them.

"Admiral, I . . . I didn't want to leave the Alliance fleet. I hope you've heard under what circumstances I had to make that decision. But the people here deserve everything I can give them.

"To the honor of our ancestors, Bradamont, out."

He called in Desjani to view the message. "What do you think?"

Desjani shrugged. "She's sincere. If she was being coerced to say those things she would've sent some signal."

"If the enigmas can reach Iwa, there are other human-controlled stars that may be within their reach."

"Yeah. That sucks. How does our ambassador feel about you being sent this message instead of her?"

"I haven't told her yet," Geary admitted.

"It's a military-to-military contact, so it's not out of line, is it?" Desjani studied the image of Bradamont for a moment. "It's strange seeing her in a different uniform than Alliance fleet. It's not bad looking. Of course, Honore Bradamont is the sort of officer who'd manage to make a sack look sharp if she was wearing it."

"I'll forward this to Ambassador Rycerz and discuss it with her," Geary said. "This expansion of the enigma threat will probably complicate our negotiations here."

"They're going to want to talk to you," Desjani said. "You've got to convince the ambassador to let you be in the room, too, or they'll walk."

"I know. I know." He suddenly saw the humor in that. "I'm supposed to be all-powerful, but I can't even guarantee my presence during the negotiations."

Desjani grinned. "I've never known an admiral who didn't benefit from realizing the limits of his real power."

He forwarded the message. There were questions he'd been worried about for some time. Would Midway agree to the proposed experiment with their hypernet gate? And what would Midway demand in return for any agreement? Soon enough he'd finally get some answers.

FIFTEEN

AMBASSADOR Rycerz gave Geary a not particularly welcome look. "It's nice to see you in person again, Admiral."

Not being thrilled himself to have to transfer to *Boundless* for the first formal talks with Midway's leaders, Geary only nodded in reply. It wasn't like he *wanted* to be trapped in political negotiations. The fact that Rycerz clearly suspected he did want that only added insult to injury.

The meeting was to be in Rycerz's office, at a large, formal table to one side of the room. Geary took a seat next to Rycerz, glancing at the third seat along their side of the table. "That's for Dr. Kottur?"

"Yes."

Great. Monosyllabic answers. This was going to be a wonderful meeting. "I've meant to ask, whatever they did at Indras to make the Syndic hypernet accessible, is that a long-term fix we can use?"

"That's what I understand," Rycerz said, unbending a little. "Dr. Kottur has expressed some worry about it, but the others on his team are confident their work-around will not be easily blocked by the Syndics. Apparently the hypernet operating system is a marvel of robust simplicity."

"Why did it take us so long to realize it had been coded by aliens?" Geary wondered.

That actually earned him a smile from the ambassador. "It doesn't sound like a human-coded operating system, does it? Ah, here's—"

Geary looked as another person entered, seeing not Dr. Kottur but Dr. Jasmine Cresida.

"Where is Dr. Kottur?" Ambassador Rycerz asked, looking as surprised as Geary and not very happy.

"Dr. Kottur is ill," Cresida said. "He asked me to fill in since I know everything that needs to be discussed."

Rycerz paused as if trying to both suppress her anger and to ensure her next words were diplomatic. "This meeting is not only about scientific and technical matters, but also very political. We have to convince these people to let us conduct our experiment on their hypernet gate. That will require careful wording during our discussion."

"I'm acquainted with politics," Dr. Cresida said. "I've spent decades dealing with academic peers and with the requirements for gaining funding and support for my own research." She gave Geary a single quick look before sitting down in the third chair, on the opposite side of the ambassador from him.

"Office security functions activated," a voice said from the air around them. "Establishing link to surface."

Geary stood up, as did Ambassador Rycerz, followed a moment later by Dr. Cresida, who was obviously annoyed at having to get up again right after sitting down, in a reaction that didn't bode well for her professed diplomatic skills.

Three virtual presences appeared, standing on the other side of the table. A moment of silence followed until Geary realized he should make introductions during this first meeting. "This is President Gwen Iceni and General Artur Drakon, and Cap—Kommodor Honore Bradamont. And on this side is Ambassador Rycerz of the Alliance, myself, and Dr. Jasmine Cresida."

Iceni nodded in greeting, then sat down at the table on the surface of the planet, the actions being mimicked here on *Boundless*. Drakon sat on one side of her, and Bradamont on the other. "I understand you have a proposal for us," Iceni said, her attitude that of someone not ready to easily give in to any offer.

"This is a great opportunity for Midway," Ambassador Rycerz said, smiling.

"General Drakon and I will decide if it is a great opportunity," Iceni said. "It involves our hypernet gate?"

"Yes, Madam President." Rycerz paused briefly for drama before continuing. "We have a means to link your hypernet gate directly to the Alliance hypernet."

Whatever they'd been expecting, it wasn't that. Iceni looked at Drakon before responding, her voice wary. "You would delink us from the Syndicate hypernet?"

"No," Rycerz said. "It would allow your gate to access either hypernet. I know you're concerned about self-defense. If this was done, if ships could transit directly from the Alliance to Midway, it would allow us to station ships here to assist in your defense."

Drakon narrowed his eyes. "I wasn't aware that we'd asked you to station ships here."

Geary finally spoke up again. "You did want my commitment to your defense."

"Yes. But that's not the same as saying we want you to take over defending us." The words "take over" seemed to have special resonance, hanging in the air long after they'd been spoken.

Ambassador Rycerz smiled reassuringly. "There's no intent for the Alliance to exercise any authority in your star system."

"Why such a large flotilla, then?" President Iceni asked. "You brought quite an armada, Admiral. But then you usually do."

"Once our task is completed at Midway," Geary said, "we're going to proceed to Dancer space, where *Boundless* will remain as an embassy. The force we brought is to ensure we can cross enigma-controlled space safely."

Bradamont started with surprise, looked to Iceni for permission to speak, and then addressed Geary directly. "Admiral, why did you send that small advance force ahead of you? They jumped for Pele about two weeks before you arrived."

"Those weren't Alliance ships," Geary said, seeing immediate skepticism rise in the eyes of Iceni and Drakon. "They're from the Rift Federation, a small grouping of star systems that formed ties with the Alliance during the war. They operated with the Alliance fleet then. But the Rift Federation has cut ties with the Alliance. I have no control over those ships."

"It wasn't a test probe of enigma space?" Drakon demanded in disbelief. "They seriously mean to challenge the enigmas with that small a flotilla?"

"Yes," Geary said, letting his tone carry his opinion of the Rift Federation's actions.

"Couldn't you have stopped them, sir?" Bradamont asked.

Iceni smiled knowingly. "Kommodor, you must learn to think at a higher level. These Rift Federation ships were no longer acknowledging orders from the admiral. Wild cards of a sort. But the enigmas will remove that problem very effectively, and the admiral will no longer have to deal with them, as well as having an object lesson of what happens to those who stray from his umbrella."

What was she saying? Geary tried to adjust his thinking to match President Iceni's, that of someone brought up on Syndicate Worlds methods. Wait. She thought he'd let the Rift ships go as a means of getting rid of a problem? "Madam President . . ." Geary began.

She held up a hand. "It need not be discussed further. Though it serves to remind us of the subtlety with which you weave your stratagems, Admiral. We will not underestimate you."

"But you see that we do understand you," General Drakon said. "Let's proceed on that basis."

Ambassador Rycerz, having finally figured out what the leaders of

Midway were implying, was staring at Geary as if trying to figure out if they were right.

Bradamont, after a surprised glance at Iceni, made a quick gesture to Geary that clearly urged him to move on to some other topic.

"Uh . . ." Geary tried to reorder his thoughts. "Ambassador Rycerz has the lead on the negotiations, but I assure you this isn't about the Alliance trying to extend its control."

"We'd much rather know that we had reliable and firm allies," Rycerz began.

"Associates," Drakon interrupted with a sour look. "We don't use any words that smack of Alliance. That's poison out here, unless your name happens to be Black Jack."

"Associates," the ambassador corrected herself, her smile a little forced. "In this region."

"And you want to mess around with our hypernet gate?" Drakon said.

Dr. Cresida interjected herself into the conversation. "Our purpose is not to 'mess around' with the hypernet gate. We have a carefully thought-out protocol with step-by-step adjustments that should result in the gate here becoming entangled with the Alliance hypernet just as it is with the Syndicate Worlds hypernet."

"Entangled." General Drakon didn't seem to like the taste of the word. "A word which implies being trapped. Ensnared."

"Yes," Dr. Cresida said as if unaware of any sinister implications to what Drakon had said. "When particles are entangled in quantum mechanics it means they can no longer be evaluated independently of each other. Their quantum states have to be described in reference to the particle they are entangled with. Hypernet gates make use of quantum entanglement to link the gates, every gate in a hypernet being entangled with the other gates."

"It's just a scientific term chosen without regard for any emotional connotations the word might evoke?"

"Of course," Dr. Cresida said. "When Dr. Schrödinger discovered entanglement back in the twentieth century I doubt he was thinking of any . . . political aspects of the word. It simply describes the state of the particles."

President Iceni gave Cresida a long, evaluating look. "And this process you are proposing is a certainty? One hundred percent safe and reliable? No chance of damage to the gate? No chance it could be rendered inoperative or collapse?"

Dr. Cresida shook her head. "There's no such thing as one hundred percent certainty," she said, apparently unaware of how her words caused Ambassador Rycerz to clench her jaw. "We have a high probability of success based on numerous evaluations and run-throughs of possible complications or events. We've gone through every conceivable possibility."

"What about the inconceivable possibilities?" General Drakon asked.

Cresida stared at him as if uncertain how to react, finally settling on an authoritative frown. "Perhaps you don't understand what 'inconceivable' means."

Geary knew his flinch would be visible to the others, but this time Ambassador Rycerz's only outward reaction was a twitch to her mouth before she began speaking hastily. "I'm sure the doctor doesn't mean any, um . . ."

"Insult?" Drakon asked, smiling slightly, his expression reminding Geary of a lion looking at potential prey. "I've heard worse. Perhaps your scientist should look up the meaning of 'inconceivable.' It literally refers to something you haven't or can't think of. I've found that the things people haven't thought of are often far more dangerous than those they've given thought to."

Dr. Cresida stared at Drakon in surprise as if he were himself some impossible thing. "That is very insightful," she finally said.

"Thank you," General Drakon replied, appearing amused. "So what's the answer?"

"We used multiple teams," Dr. Cresida said. "Each took their own approach, and each attempted to find any possible problem with the other teams' approaches. We wanted the different teams to think of things the other teams hadn't, both in terms of success and in terms of possible hazards or problems. So, you see, we did seek to conceive of the inconceivable."

Geary spared a sidelong glance at Dr. Cresida, surprised to hear her sounding as if she liked General Drakon.

For his part, Drakon nodded. "Thank you. That does indeed address my question. But I have another. Would you do this on a hypernet gate in an Alliance star system?"

"We tested it on a gate in Alliance space," Dr. Cresida said. "Though we halted just short of actually establishing a link to the Syndicate hypernet."

"How short was just short?"

"Five milliseconds."

That earned another nod from Drakon. "That's short."

"Explain, in clear terms, what will happen if you succeed," Iceni said. "What will be the practical impact on those using our hypernet gate?"

Dr. Cresida took a moment to answer, her brow furrowed as she thought. "Are you familiar with the quantum cat? Schrödinger's?"

Iceni shook her head. "Enlighten me."

"It's an ancient thought experiment to help understand how the quantum world works," Cresida said. "Imagine there's a cat in a box, along with a canister of poison, and a device that has exactly a fifty percent chance of releasing that poison. In our macro world, we would open the box and find that the cat had either died or lived, and all we would do would be confirming what had already happened. On the quantum level, until we opened the box, the cat would be neither alive nor dead, but in an indeterminate state. The universe would not decide what its fate had been until we opened the box to look."

Geary noticed that both Drakon and Iceni had expressions of mild interest on their faces, the sort of thing that might imply boredom or lack of understanding, but their eyes were intent, sharply focused on Cresida. The apparent barely listening expressions were just camouflage, designed to hide their interest and comprehension.

From the way she plowed on with her explanation, Dr. Cresida had seen their expressions but apparently not noticed their eyes. "That is what we will do to the hypernet gate's quantum links. It will have the potential to link to either the Syndicate Worlds hypernet, or the Alliance hypernet, but until someone approaches the gate with a hypernet key, it will be in an indeterminate state. Only when a key is activated within range of the gate will the gate 'decide' which hypernet it is linked to." She waved one hand in a casting-away motion. "If it decides to link to the wrong hypernet for that key, it will appear to be inactive. In which case the key just has to be reactivated, causing the gate to once again decide what its link is. Each time, you'll have a fifty percent chance of getting the link that matches the hypernet key."

"That's all?" Bradamont asked in disbelief. "It's that simple?"

"It's extremely complex," Dr. Cresida said. "My explanation was simple."

"Ancestors help me, you really are Jaylen Cresida's sister!" Bradamont said, smiling.

"Who is Jaylen?" Iceni asked, watching Dr. Cresida trying to decide how to react to the comparison.

"A captain in the Alliance fleet," Bradamont said. "She was the first to work out the danger posed by the collapse of a hypernet gate. She was also the one who found the quantum-coded malware worms the enigmas had planted in human computer systems."

"She died in battle," Geary added.

"My condolences, Dr. Cresida," President Iceni said. "What you offer, then, is a virtually guaranteed route directly from Midway to the Alliance? I see. Naturally, as part of any agreement we make for this you will provide us with Alliance hypernet keys in exchange."

Geary felt the silence on his side of the table. He glanced at Ambassador Rycerz, who seemed to be rapidly thinking through options. "Why would that be part of the agreement?" the ambassador finally asked.

"So we can make use of the gate to reach Alliance space. Just as you will be able to," Iceni said.

Ambassador Rycerz once again took a while to respond, while Iceni waited with an expectant look. "President Iceni, the Alliance has agreed to support the freedom of Midway and allied star systems—"

"Associated star systems," Drakon broke in.

"*Associated* star systems," Rycerz said. "As I said, the Alliance will agree to continue to guarantee the freedom of this star system. There won't be any need for you to possess a key."

Iceni laughed as if Rycerz had just told a joke. "Certainly! You get the gate, and make a promise, and we're supposed to take those words as payment for the risks we run and for the advantages you gain. What a deal you're offering!"

"President Iceni," Ambassador Rycerz said, her voice still composed, "the Alliance honors its commitments. The deal contains great advantages for Midway and its people."

"Your honor has no value to us," Iceni said, as General Drakon nodded slowly in agreement. "Your commitments are only as good as the intent of your leaders to follow them. We cannot risk our own welfare on your promises." She sat back, her posture casual, but her words suddenly as hard as stone. "Here is the deal you will agree to. We will receive two Alliance hypernet keys. That will allow us to run trade convoys each way between here and Alliance space, vastly increasing the value of our gate and the income we receive from the ships using it. It will also allow us independent use of the Alliance hypernet, without having to request your permission."

"I can't agree to that," Ambassador Rycerz said. "The Alliance can't allow you free use of our hypernet just as if you were a member star system."

General Drakon spoke up. "Isn't that how you currently make use of the Syndicate hypernet?"

"The Syndicate Worlds did not voluntarily provide that key," Rycerz said.

"So, despite your talk of trust and honor," Drakon said, "you don't trust us, and don't want to give us any means to control *your* use of *our* gate. You're thinking of our gate in terms of spoils of war, just as you do that Syndicate hypernet key."

It was, Geary had to admit, a brutally direct summing-up of the Alliance's position. And Iceni and Drakon were playing very well off of each other, their teamwork creating arguments that boxed Ambassador Rycerz into a corner.

Rycerz spoke in heavy tones. "I was sent with instructions to implement the agreement I've described."

President Iceni's frown combined disappointment with curiosity. She gave Geary a glance even as she continued to address the ambassador. "The Alliance sent an envoy without the authority to negotiate a deal?"

"I have an approved agreement in hand—" Rycerz began.

"That 'agreement' was approved only by the Alliance," Iceni said, her tone once again unyielding. "Which makes it not an agreement, not a deal, but extortion. Do you think we owe you tribute? Do you think you can dictate our actions and force us to accept whatever one-sided deal the Alliance wants to further its own aims? I don't see any grounds for continuing this discussion."

President Iceni stood up, looked at Bradamont with a tilt of her head toward the Alliance side of the table, and vanished as she broke the virtual link to her.

General Drakon also stood, and without a word also vanished.

Ambassador Rycerz, her jaw tight, stared at the surface of the table.

Geary looked at Bradamont, the only virtual presence remaining on her side. "Were you given some sort of instruction?"

Bradamont nodded, looking pained. "I'm supposed to help you understand Midway's position. They can't agree to the deal you're offering. It's too one-sided."

Ambassador Rycerz looked up, her voice under tight control. "We're committing to the defense of this star system! We've already done that."

"That means *nothing* to them," Bradamont said. "What means do they have to ensure you keep that commitment? What tangible returns does Midway get for agreeing to let you do something that will bring immense benefit to the Alliance? I'm not a diplomat, but even I can see how the Alliance is gaining a lot from the proposal and giving very little."

"It's a difference of perspective," Geary said. "Among other things. To them, a solemn vow from the Alliance doesn't mean anything."

"That's the system they were raised in," Bradamont said. "Syndicate CEOs lie for advantage and break deals all the time. If you lacked enough power, you had no choice but to accept deals you knew wouldn't be honored. The only deals that really mattered were those between equals, because each offered the other something tangible, making it in the interests of both sides to keep the agreement."

Ambassador Rycerz blew out an angry breath. "And what we just offered sounded as if we thought they lacked power and had to agree to whatever we proposed."

"Exactly," Bradamont said. "They expect, they need, to feel they are being treated as equals. And that means they need something tangible, something they gain, from a deal."

"Are you talking bribes?" Rycerz asked.

Bradamont clenched her teeth and took a moment to relax before replying. "With some raised in the Syndicate that would be appropriate. Not here. Iceni and Drakon have all the power and wealth they need. They're worried about the survival of Midway as an independent star system. That takes money. The hypernet gate is their primary source of income from outside sources, but trade in this region has been badly impacted by the collapse of Syndicate authority and Syndicate counterattacks."

Ambassador Rycerz listened closely. "But if they can offer a trade route direct to Alliance markets, and from Alliance markets to this part of space, they could earn substantial sums from transit fees."

"And it would build stability in the region by improving the economies of every star system involved," Bradamont said.

"Where did you pick up all this?" Rycerz asked. "Were you given these topics to deliver to us?"

Bradamont sat back, her expression fixed. "No. I'm no one's puppet. I discussed these issues with others, but I reached my own conclusions. They couldn't necessarily explain how they feel in terms you'd interpret the same way they would."

"Kommodor," Geary said, deliberately using her Midway rank. "As one of the ranking fleet officers for Midway, you're involved with discussions about the size of the fleet and defense expenditures, aren't you?"

"Yes, sir," Bradamont said, once more relaxing a bit. "And that's something we talk about a lot. Midway needs strong enough defenses to deal with Syndicate attacks, and with attacks from the enigmas. That's expensive. We've been able to make use of Syndicate legacy supplies and funds to keep things going, but the bottom line is that Midway's current economy cannot support the military it needs. I know why the Alliance framed the proposed agreement the way it did. But I also know the people of this star system won't accept that agreement. They have good reasons to demand more, and those reasons also work to the long-term benefit of the Alliance."

"You can understand the positions of both sides," Geary said, "because you've worked closely with both sides."

"And because I have friends on both sides," Bradamont said, her tone growing more forceful. "Friends and . . . leaders I admire," she added, nodding toward Geary.

Ambassador Rycerz studied Bradamont. "Are you still loyal to the Alliance?"

"I've taken an oath to defend Midway," Bradamont said. "But I will not betray the Alliance. That would dishonor my ancestors. I don't think those positions need to be in conflict."

Rycerz leaned back, her fingers steepled in front of her, thinking. "The Alliance does gain substantial benefit from having a government at Midway that's willing to deal with us."

"And which holds the line against the enigmas," Geary pointed out.

"Yes." Rycerz paused, her eyes hooded. "But the Alliance is struggling to fund the postwar military it needs. There wouldn't be any appetite for subsidies to Midway to help it defend itself."

"They wouldn't take subsidies from the Alliance," Bradamont said.

"Because they'd look like bribes?"

"No." Bradamont shook her head, looking sad. "That wouldn't bother anyone. Bribes were just the way things were done in the Syndicate. But if the money came from the Alliance, it would be tainted in the eyes of everyone here. President Iceni and General Drakon would be accused of having sold out this star system to the Alliance. Even if their government survived the popular uprising that would cause, other star systems currently working with Midway would pull back and break existing commitments."

"They hate us that much?" Rycerz asked.

"Yes," Bradamont said. "As the Alliance. You heard General Drakon. They can't even use a word like 'allied' because it evokes the Alliance and implies some sort of similarity. But they'll work with individuals, because that's also how the Syndicate worked. Personal relationships that allowed deals to be made. But to them the Alliance is . . ." She sighed. "What the Alliance sees the Syndics as."

"As Admiral Geary told me before we left. And you're an individual who has personal relationships on both sides," Rycerz said. "So you've gained their trust, enough to be given a high position in their military."

"Yes," Bradamont said. "The fact that Colonel Rogero vouched for me helped a great deal, as he is personally highly respected. There are still plenty of people here who are leery of me, but Iceni and Drakon have given me their trust." She shook her head. "No, that's not right. They don't really trust anyone. But they accept me as a rational player whose decisions will support them. And they're willing to deal with you, Ambassador, because they think you're Admiral Geary's sock puppet, if you will forgive my bluntness. They know their people will not be angered by an agreement with Black Jack, because he gained a reputation for caring about the people even while fighting a war to defeat the Syndicate."

Rycerz sat silently for a few moments before looking at Geary. "What do you think?"

He nodded toward Bradamont. "Everything she says is consistent with what I've learned from working with Syndics. And I still consider her word of honor to be good. Kommodor Bradamont wouldn't lie to us, even if ordered to do so."

"Thank you, Admiral," Bradamont said.

"But agreeing to give them Alliance hypernet keys . . ." Ambassador Rycerz's voice trailed off as she gazed into the distance. "That would be a huge decision to make. I don't think it would be received happily at Unity."

"If you can't agree to it," Geary said, "we're at an impasse, aren't we?"

Rycerz glanced at him, smiling slightly. "I told them I was instructed to present the agreement I outlined. I never said I lacked the authority to negotiate a different agreement if necessary." She switched her gaze to Bradamont. "I said that in front of you for a reason. I also have to make a deal that will pass muster with the people of the Alliance. It has to be framed properly, and it can't be perceived as a blank check to Midway's rulers. Even one Alliance hypernet key would be seen as a huge giveaway. Perhaps there are things Midway can offer to sweeten the deal."

"Perhaps," Bradamont said cautiously. "I know of one thing that might be of great value. And perhaps others."

"Of course," Rycerz added, "any agreement differing from what I was sent with will be subject to ratification by the Alliance Senate."

"President Iceni will insist on having the hypernet keys in her hands before she agrees to let you begin work on the gate," Bradamont said. "She will not give in on that. Again, that's because of experience with the way the Syndicate does things. Verbal and written commitments mean nothing and can be easily violated without physical commitments to guarantee the agreement."

Rycerz nodded, unhappy. "Why did it take us so long to defeat a government that worked like that?"

Bradamont kept her eyes on Rycerz as she answered. "Because there are always people who figure out how to get things done despite the way things work, and because the Alliance had its own shortcomings."

"You indeed have a perspective that most of us lack," the ambassador said. "I'm going to have to discuss options with my staff, as well as how we can sell such an agreement to the Senate. Please inform President Iceni and General Drakon that we do wish to continue negotiations, and that we now have a better grasp of their position."

"Certainly," Bradamont said.

"Dr. Cresida," Rycerz continued. "I would appreciate it if you did not divulge any details of this conference. Please limit your report to Dr. Kottur and your other colleagues to saying that negotiations are continuing."

Cresida shrugged, then nodded. "If that's what's necessary to get clearance for the work."

"Dr. Cresida," Bradamont said. "Your sister was a good friend of mine. A good friend and a fine officer. I offer my sincerest condolences on the loss to your family. I am certain that she has a place of honor among your ancestors."

Dr. Cresida eyed Bradamont silently for a few seconds before responding in an almost emotionless voice. "Thank you."

After polite farewells, Kommodor Bradamont's image vanished.

"Are we once more secure in here?" Ambassador Rycerz asked Geary.

He checked the security panel. "Everything's green. We can talk freely."

"Good. Dr. Cresida." Rycerz's voice was polite but businesslike. "Please ensure that you give Dr. Kottur and your other fellow scientists only a vague report of the discussions here."

Dr. Cresida eyed the ambassador. "Why are you repeating the same request to me?"

"Because I need to emphasize the importance of it. You want a deal so you can mess with that hypernet gate," Ambassador Rycerz said, stepping closer to Cresida. "If too much of what was said here gets out too early, that deal might become impossible. To get what you want, you need to listen to what I want."

"Diplomacy," Dr. Cresida said, as if speaking of some form of the dark arts. "I understand."

After Cresida had left, Ambassador Rycerz looked at Geary. "Dr. Kottur has developed an unfortunate tendency to not show up for important meetings."

"Was he that badly shaken up by seeing the mine strikes on *Gallant*?" Geary asked.

"He hasn't been acting as if he were dwelling on that particular issue. Day-to-day interactions are, as always, pleasant and smiling. Something is certainly worrying him, though. He's spending a lot of time alone in his office, letting the others handle getting work done."

"At least he's not getting in the way," Geary said. "Should I talk with him?"

"It wouldn't hurt." Rycerz sighed. "Speaking of scientists who are in the way, I've already started the measures to isolate Dr. Macadams. As for you, Admiral, I need to know something about the industrial capabilities in this star system. Can you get me the answer?"

"What do you need to know?"

"Can Midway duplicate a hypernet key?"

DR. Kottur's office held a pleasantly disorganized air, with everything from personal items to scientific materials scattered about. It never would have passed a military inspection, but it offered a glimpse into the mind of the occupant. "Yes, Admiral?" Dr. Kottur asked. He was sitting at his desk, a variety of displays open before him and a virtual starscape floating beyond them. A quick glance told Geary the stars shown were probably those in Dancer space, though he couldn't be certain.

The doctor didn't show any signs of being ill, though, his eyes clear as he gazed at Geary.

"I was concerned about you," Geary said, which was true enough. There wasn't any need to say that Ambassador Rycerz had urged this visit on him. "You missed our conference with the leaders of Midway, and Dr. Cresida said you weren't feeling well."

Dr. Kottur seemed troubled for a moment. "Facing certain things can be difficult."

"If you're still concerned about the mines we encountered at Indras—"

"No, no!" Dr. Kottur laughed and waved away Geary's words. "It's a matter of putting a face to the abstract."

What did that mean? "So you're all right?"

"Hmmm. What does 'all right' mean? Is it defined by circumstances or state of mind?" Dr. Kottur leaned back, his gaze upward and outward as if he were seeing through the hull of *Boundless* and into the infinite beyond. "We are much the same, Admiral. Sailors and scientists, I mean. We try to find our ways to places no one else has ever been. We always want to know what lies over the horizon. We want to see what no one else has ever before seen."

He sighed. "Sometimes we wish we hadn't found what we did, though. Not every discovery is welcome."

Geary watched him. "But we can't know if the discovery will be welcome until we find it. If we stopped looking, we'd never find all of the things we are glad we found."

"Does it make us happier, though?" Dr. Kottur was still gazing outward. "Were our ancestors wise to leave Old Earth, to go exploring the mysteries of the galaxy? What if they had stayed in their home, using their minds to explore? What might we have learned if not distracted by the colonization of new worlds, the wars, the political disputes, the research that only found more and deadlier weapons?"

"I don't think that would've been possible," Geary said. "You said it yourself, comparing scientists to sailors. Humans are restless and curious. We can't look at the horizon without wondering what lies beyond it. I have to admit the enigmas have reason to be frightened of humanity. We don't just wonder about things, we try to go there, and learn more. That's who we are."

"But is that what we should be?" Dr. Kottur asked, his eyes still on infinity.

"I'm afraid the answer to that still eludes humanity," Geary said. "I certainly don't know the answer. All I do know is that when humans see a wall, we want to go over it."

Dr. Kottur smiled. "Yes. There you have it. A wall must be a fearsome thing to stop us. No ordinary barrier would suffice."

"Are we still talking about what humans are like?" Geary asked.

"Of course." Dr. Kottur looked at him, still smiling. "I've been dealing with some scientific issues. I've probably let them overstress me. Sometimes the true answers are difficult, don't you agree?"

"I suppose," Geary said. "You'll be at the next meeting with the representatives from Midway?"

"Why wouldn't I be?"

It wasn't until much later that Geary realized he should have pressed for an answer to Dr. Kottur's question in response to his own.

AMBASSADOR Rycerz, expecting another meeting with the leaders of Midway soon, had asked him to stay aboard *Boundless* for the night. The former passenger liner had plenty of spare rooms, as well as food better than the fleet's, but Geary still felt unhappy to be spending the night off of *Dauntless*. In some ways the battle cruiser had come to represent home to him. Which was absurd. An admiral couldn't afford to develop such tight ties to a single ship. But there it was.

He checked in with Captain Desjani, learning that the situation appeared to be quiet. A single freighter had arrived at Midway at the jump point from Kane Star System, but nothing else had changed.

After a very nice meal in a "cafeteria" that felt more like a high-end restaurant, Geary felt restless. With the whole ship open to his access, he began wandering through it, curious to see how *Boundless* differed from the warships he was familiar with.

A lot of the differences were cosmetic. Where warships left pipes and conduits and wiring exposed for easy access, the *Boundless* had ceilings blocking views of the ship's mechanical and electrical veins and arteries and the true overhead. Bulkheads were mostly smooth as well, adorned with displays that shifted among images of worlds. The deck was covered by what appeared to be a smooth surfacing that was slightly resilient but also offered a decent grip to someone walking. It all felt a little luxurious to someone used to the spare efficiency of a warship. He also found himself getting a bit upset and realized it was because he couldn't see vital systems and didn't know how he'd access them in an emergency.

But that wasn't his job on this ship.

His wandering took him to a place labeled the Star Gallery. Looking inside, Geary saw a long compartment set up as if it were a wide balcony. The far side was composed of a single seamless display from deck to overhead, portraying a view of the outside as if the compartment were actually open to space on that entire side. A waist-high railing just in front of the display added to the illusion that someone here was really, impossibly gazing directly at space.

His instincts found the compartment extremely disturbing, wanting to pull himself back from the vacuum of space that loomed before him, to seal this door, sound an emergency alarm . . .

As much because of that fear as anything else, Geary forced himself to step into the Star Gallery. Wouldn't it be nice to just be able to enjoy the awesome sight, and not have his experience in space screaming warnings in the back of his head?

He'd taken several steps inside, slow stubborn steps driven by his need to confront his fears, when he realized that he wasn't alone in the gallery.

Dr. Jasmine Cresida stood with her back to him, gazing out at the heavens, countless stars glittering against infinite space. "What brings you here, Admiral?" she asked without looking.

Not sure how to answer that, he settled on the easiest reply, one inspired by his earlier discussion with Dr. Kottur. "Curiosity. What about you, Dr. Cresida?"

"I come here to think. People look at the large things, the stars and the dust clouds and the movements of galaxies, and they feel awe. But those things are too easily seen and understood. The fundamental structure of the universe is a beautiful and mysterious thing. It withholds some of its secrets from us and refuses to bend to the rules we want to impose on it. Humanity doesn't only want to understand; we want to use that understanding to control. And the basic foundations of the universe mock our ambitions and our pride. They refuse to let us know everything. They change when we try to observe them. They let us play around the margins, as with the hypernet system, but only if we do not stray from the paths they allow."

She paused, but Geary sensed she had more to say, and so remained silent himself, wondering why she was confiding in him.

"I could forgive my sister for joining the military," Dr. Cresida said, abruptly changing the subject. "She told me that she was willing to give up some of her freedoms to defend the freedoms of all of us. Jaylen was always the practical one in the family, seeing herself as the part of the equation that balanced the whole. But I can never forgive her for perverting her skills to deliberately craft the means to turn hypernet gates into weapons. That went against everything our family believed, everything she said she believed. It was a crime against not just humanity, but against the universe itself."

Surprised to learn that Dr. Jasmine Cresida was driven not by human politics or scientific rigidity, but by an almost romantic form of idealism, it took him a moment to reply. "Dr. Cresida," Geary said, "I don't know where you heard that version of things, but I swear to you that your sister did not set out to find a means to weaponize hypernet gates. Her intentions, her goals, were the opposite of that."

Dr. Cresida's voice held rigid control as she answered. "How can you know that?"

"Because I discussed it with her," Geary said. "The fleet was on its way to a Syndic star system with a hypernet gate. Because we had a Syndic hypernet key, we could use that gate to get much closer to home much faster. But we realized the Syndics might destroy the gate to prevent us from using it, and our people who had knowledge of the theory behind the hypernet, of which the foremost was your sister, were concerned about the theoretical possibility that the gate would emit an energy pulse when it collapsed. She went to work, with my agreement, to try to figure out how to collapse a hypernet gate in such a way that any energy output would be minimized. That way if the Syndics started to break their gate, we could control the collapse to prevent harm to our ships and everything and everyone else in the star system."

He paused, remembering those days that seemed so long ago already, even though they hadn't been that far in the past. Remembering the ways in which Captain Jaylen Cresida had been like and unlike her sister. "But Jaylen discovered that figuring out how to control the collapse to minimize the energy output could be easily run in the other direction, instead maximizing the output and turning hypernet gates into nova-scale bombs menacing the star systems they were built to serve. She was horrified at the possibility that the gates could be used that way. I swear on my honor that is how she felt. Horrified. But she also knew if she could work out the way to do that, so could someone else. So she gave me the only copy of the means to maximize the destructive potential of the gates, so we could use it to develop programs that would ensure gates couldn't collapse in ways that made them weapons.

"Even before we made it back to Alliance space, safe-collapse programs had been created so they could eventually be installed in every hypernet gate. I won't deny that some people suggested using the gates as weapons, but most were just as appalled at the idea as your sister had been."

He took a deep breath. "Your sister didn't set out to weaponize the gates. She discovered the means to do that while trying to ensure their collapse didn't cause harm. And when she did find out how it could be done, her thoughts were about how to prevent it from ever happening."

The stars looked on as Dr. Cresida stayed silent for a long time, her back still to Geary, before finally speaking, a ragged edge to her voice. "Why haven't you told people this?"

"I did," Geary said. "It was in my official report, and I've spoken of it to those I worked with on the matter. But of course I couldn't make public statements about it because officially the danger of hypernet gate collapse remains classified."

She laughed, a single brief, pained sound. "Information distribution systems are like hypernet gates in that respect. If you know how to use them to accomplish one end, a safe collapse of the gate or the effective distribution of information, you also know how to use them for the opposite purpose. There's nothing better at filtering out information than a system designed to very efficiently preserve and deliver information."

He felt uncomfortable, knowing how Dr. Cresida must be feeling. "I'm sorry you weren't made aware of the truth a long time ago. But that truth is that your sister didn't betray your family's ideals. Jaylen Cresida did her best to uphold them."

Another long period of silence before Jasmine Cresida spoke again. "I can never forgive you for ordering my sister to her death. But . . . I am very grateful for the knowledge that she didn't want the gates to be used as weapons, and strove to prevent that. Th . . . ank . . . you." The last two words came out as if they were being physically pulled from her resisting throat.

Feeling that any words would be inadequate, Geary turned to go.

"Admiral."

He paused.

"How do you do it?" She still had her back to him, gazing into forever. "How do you give orders knowing that those who must obey them will die?" The question didn't sound hostile, but rather both curious and sad.

"I don't know," Geary said. "I don't know how I can. Maybe I can because of why I do it. I don't choose battles or wars. But if they come, do I accept a role and responsibility, or do I leave that to others? Others who may care less about those who die. Others who may not have my experience. It nearly broke me when I woke up from survival sleep and learned that everyone I'd ever known had died while I slept, that a war begun during my first battle was still going on, and that it had changed my own people in ways I had trouble dealing with. But they needed me. Well, they needed Black Jack. So I had to do my best to be him, in the way that he should be. But people still die. I still give orders that, even if everything goes perfectly, end with deaths of some of those entrusted to me. And I carry every death with me. Not just your sister's, but all of them. That's my responsibility, too. To remember each and every one of them, and to try to ensure their sacrifices mean something."

"I understand responsibility for our actions," Dr. Cresida said. "Dr. Kottur seems to want to avoid it. He won't even meet with those from Midway, as if unwilling to face them. But we have to think of others as just as human as ourselves. Otherwise we avoid accepting our responsibility for whatever happens to them."

"Do you think Dr. Kottur will try to prevent the modifications to the gate?"

"He seems eager to proceed with doing that. I don't know why the contradiction exists. Dr. Kottur is our own Schrödinger case," Dr. Cresida added. "He seems to exist simultaneously in a state of reluctance to proceed and of zeal to go forward."

"Do you trust him?"

"I don't trust anyone, Admiral. People are even less predictable than quantum particles, and like those particles, we can never know all there is to know about them."

He waited, but she said nothing else, so Geary left, wondering as he did why he'd also confided in Jasmine Cresida. But she was Jaylen's sister, so he'd owed her that much on those grounds alone.

TO his surprise, Geary was roused early for another meeting with Midway's leaders. Wondering at the urgency, he hastened to Ambassador Rycerz's office.

President Iceni and General Drakon both had a wary insistence about them, as if they were in a card game with their Alliance counterparts and about to demand that everyone show their hands. "You doubtless noticed the recent arrival of a freighter at the jump point from Kane," Iceni began without any polite exchange of greetings. "The freighter brought word that a Syndicate invasion force is attacking Kane."

Drakon picked up the story. "Before it jumped out of Kane, the freighter saw one Syndicate battle cruiser, two heavy cruisers, and seven Hunter-Killers, along with a dozen troop transports or freighters modified to carry people instead of cargo."

"We are still concerned about another Syndicate strike here," Iceni said, "as well as a retaliatory strike by the enigmas after our repulse of their attack at Iwa. Our mobile forces are also still repairing damage sustained during the fighting there."

"You committed to the defense of Midway and our associated star systems," Drakon said, looking at Geary. "Can we count on that, Admiral?"

Geary glanced at Rycerz before replying. "You're asking us to send ships to defend Kane against the Syndicate Worlds?"

"In keeping with your commitment," Iceni said.

Ambassador Rycerz looked stunned, her eyes going to Geary. This could be a make-or-break decision for whether Midway would agree to the hypernet gate modification. But it would also drastically expand the Alliance's role in the fighting on this side of Syndicate Worlds space.

Any decision they made would potentially be a bad one, but the attitudes of President Iceni and General Drakon made it clear that not making any decision—and not making it right now—wasn't an option.

SIXTEEN

AMBASSADOR Rycerz made an attempt to dodge the issue anyway. "The Alliance Senate confirmed the commitment made by Admiral Geary to Midway Star System. But the defense of . . . associated star systems was not specifically covered by that commitment."

"If you don't send warships," President Iceni said, still addressing Geary, "we'll have to, and that will weaken our defenses. It will also cause us to doubt current and future promises made to us, and re-evaluate current discussions."

"May we speak privately for a moment?" Rycerz asked. After Iceni and Drakon nodded gruffly, Rycerz touched the control to "mute" the virtual presences of the two leaders of Midway. "This isn't a cut-and-dried issue. I could refuse their request based on the literal wording of the commitment you made, but I could also agree to it based on a reasonable interpretation of that commitment."

"This may be a make-or-break matter for them," Geary said. "On whether they should reach any other agreements with us. I think it'll decide how they respond to the hypernet gate offer."

"They made it fairly clear this will impact their decision on that," the ambassador said. "And getting that gate linked to the Alliance hypernet is the critical issue here for us. How much would we need to send to Kane?"

"To ensure defeat of the Syndicate Worlds invasion? We'd need something to take out the Syndic warships, and some Marines to help deal with any action on the surface, and something to protect the Marine troop transports as well as bombard Syndic positions on the surface," Geary said. "And there's a possibility the Syndic forces the freighter saw have been reinforced since it left. I'd suggest a division of battle cruisers, all four of our troop transports and the Marines on them, and a division of battleships to protect the transports and conduct surface bombardment. Plus an appropriate number of cruisers and destroyers."

"What is that? About a quarter of our strength here?"

"Roughly," Geary said. "The forces remaining at Midway would be well able to handle anything that might show up. Captain Duellos would be well suited to command the expedition to Kane."

Ambassador Rycerz shook her head, frowning. "There's one other reason that I'm leaning toward approving sending military assistance to Kane."

"What's that?" Geary asked.

She gave him a frustrated glare. "No matter how many times we tell them I'm in charge, and no matter how many times you openly defer to me in front of them, they're still talking to you. You say Duellos could command the expedition to Kane. Is he qualified to command what remains at Midway while you command the forces sent to Kane?"

The question took him aback, requiring Geary to think for a moment. But he understood the ambassador's reasoning. And such an open endorsement of his confidence in Duellos would be good, since as fleet commander he had to worry about something happening to him and who would assume command afterward. "Yes. Captain Duellos would be suited to command the forces left at Midway."

"Are you willing to do this, Admiral?" Rycerz pressed. "Take those forces to Kane, either defeat the Syndicate Worlds invasion force or require it to withdraw, and leave me here as the unquestioned leader of the Alliance mission in your absence?"

"Yes," Geary said.

"Good. I'll continue to conduct negotiations. You get going as soon as you can. We want to show them that their concerns matter to us."

"WE'RE what?" Captain Desjani said as she stood in his stateroom aboard *Dauntless*. He'd taken a shuttle back to the battle cruiser immediately after the meeting with the leaders of Midway ended, working up a rough plan in his head on the way.

"Taking the Second Battle Cruiser Division, the Fifth Battleship Division, the assault transports, and Carabali's Marines to Kane to kick out a Syndic invasion force," Geary said.

"I love you." Tanya flinched. "I'm sorry. That was extremely inappropriate, Admiral. I was overcome for a moment by your news. How soon do we get to leave to kick Syndic butt?"

"As soon as we get things sorted out," Geary said. "I'm going to notify Duellos he'll be in command in my absence. Oh, we're going to have company. Since we're leaving a strong force here to defend Midway, Midway is sending their battle cruiser along with us, agreeing to have it operate under my control."

"Their battle cruiser?" Desjani said. "A Syndic battle cruiser?"

"A Midway battle cruiser. The *Pele*. Their Kommodor Marphissa will be aboard that ship as well, and their Colonel Rogero will accompany the Marines to provide the latest inside information on Syndicate ground forces."

"Sure. Why not." Desjani grinned. "I was getting bored."

Since the entire Alliance fleet was already in a high state of readiness, it took only a few hours to sort out the necessary arrangements. More detailed planning could be done while the ships transited to the jump point for Kane. "Keep an eye on things here," Geary told Duellos.

"Yes, sir," Captain Duellos replied. "And thank you for the vote of confidence."

"My confidence in you has never wavered," Geary said. "I'm happy this offers me a way to make my confidence clear to everyone. I don't think Ambassador Rycerz will try to railroad you on anything important. Remember that she is the ultimate Alliance authority in this star system. We answer to her."

Every ship participating had indicated its readiness to go, the responses usually taking only moments. Geary had the impression of a pack of hounds straining at the leash, eager to be set loose. He'd already transmitted to them the formation for the transit to Kane. And he was on the bridge of *Dauntless* along with Captain Desjani. All that was left to do was give the command to go.

"All units in Task Force Kane," he sent on the special communications circuit set up for them, "this is Admiral Geary. Immediate execute Formation Zebra."

The designated ships swung out of the fixed orbit they'd been in with the rest of the fleet, converging together, the battle cruisers *Dauntless*, *Daring*, *Victorious*, and *Intemperate* arranged in a box in the lead, followed by the assault transports *Tsunami*, *Typhoon*, *Mistral*, and *Haboob*, the four battleships *Relentless*, *Reprisal*, *Superb*, and *Splendid* bringing up the rear. Two divisions of heavy cruisers ranged alongside the transports, as well as two squadrons of light cruisers and six squadrons of destroyers.

"Good hunting!" Duellos sent as the task force accelerated toward the jump point for Kane.

"You know," Geary commented to Desjani, "this task force is about the same size as the entire Alliance fleet before the war."

"Do you think we'll get down that small again?" she asked, looking disturbed at the prospect.

"No. I don't think at any time in the near future the Alliance will have the luxury of such a small fleet. Even if we weren't dealing with the Syndics and the chaos of their collapsing empire, there'd still be the alien species to worry about. Plus those idiots on the far side of Sol," Geary added, remembering their encounter with the representatives of those humans who had gone farther out along the galactic arm to settle new worlds, instead of inward toward the center of the galaxy as those who founded the Alliance and the Syndicate Worlds had.

"Battle cruiser *Pele* is on intercept with us," Lieutenant Yuon reported. "They should join up in five hours."

"What about the ship bringing Colonel Rogero to *Typhoon*?" Desjani asked.

"The, uh, heavy cruiser *Gryphon* said they'll meet us one hour from the jump point. *Typhoon* has reported the *Gryphon* requested one of *Typhoon*'s shuttles transfer Colonel Rogero and intends to grant that request."

"Very well." Desjani turned an arched eyebrow on Geary. "When that Syndic—ex-Syndic battle cruiser gets here, where are you putting it in the formation?"

He pointed to the center of the box formed by the Alliance battle cruisers. "Here, a little ahead of the rest of us."

"Really? You're going to use them as a mine detector?"

"No," Geary said. "I'm going to let them feel like they are leading the way to Kane to save an allied . . . excuse me, associated star system. I think the symbolism of that is important to both the people of Midway and the people at Kane."

"It's your task force, Admiral," she replied.

ONCE *Pele* had joined up with the fleet, the battle cruiser bearing the scars of fighting at Iwa and other stars proudly taking the lead in the formation, Kommodor Marphissa asked for a virtual meeting with Geary and the senior officers in the task force.

Kommodor Marphissa had a very professional bearing to her, as if determined to show what she thought a senior officer should look and act like. There was something about her eyes, though, that made it clear

Marphissa wasn't all show. Something in her eyes, Geary thought, that made a smart person careful about crossing Marphissa. From what he'd learned about Syndicate Worlds practices, he wondered whether Kommodor Marphissa had personally killed any rivals. Certainly the former Syndic commanders of the warships now part of Midway's fleet had apparently all come to rather abrupt ends.

But whenever President Iceni's name came up, a trace of almost fanatical loyalty also shone in the Kommodor's eyes. Marphissa certainly wasn't going to be leading another rebellion as long as Iceni was in charge.

"We can expect the Syndicate flotilla at Kane to follow doctrine. That's all they know. It's likely the Syndicate warships are lacking in training and undercrewed," Marphissa told Geary, Captain Desjani, Captain Hiyen of *Reprisal*, and General Carabali, all but Geary and Desjani participating in the meeting in virtual form. "The Syndicate long since ran low on volunteers, and is shunting every volunteer it still gets into the ranks of internal security service agents, people we call snakes, to terrorize the new conscripts and veterans into obeying orders."

"Haven't Syndic ships always been run that way?" Desjani asked.

"To some extent," Marphissa said, showing no sign of offense at the question. "But there'd be one snake on most ships, with some of the crew secretly working for the snake to spy on the others, and maybe three or four on the large ships. Now there are dozens of snakes on the ships, because the Syndicate knows one or four snakes can no longer intimidate a crew into remaining loyal."

"So you had a 'snake' on your ship when you revolted?" Captain Hiyen said. "What happened to them?"

"They died," Marphissa said. "Of course."

"Is it the same with the Syndic ground forces now?" General Carabali asked. "A lot more of these snakes watching everyone for any sign of disloyalty?"

"Colonel Rogero can speak better to that than I can, but yes. At Iwa, the Syndicate had brought in not only ground forces, but also the families of those ground forces workers to serve as nearby hostages. That way the workers knew any failure could result in instant retaliation against their families."

"What is wrong with such people?" Captain Hiyen said, dismayed. "Why would anyone agree to be one of those snakes, knowing what they would be expected to do?"

Kommodor Marphissa gave him a look that held steel. "Don't fool yourself. There are always those willing to follow orders, no matter what the orders are. I know such people are in the Alliance. We fought them, and saw what they'd done."

An uncomfortable silence fell, the Alliance officers looking down, not able to meet the Kommodor's eyes. All except for Desjani, who kept her gaze defiantly on Marphissa. Finally, Geary broke the uneasy quiet. "War is too easily used to excuse acts we'd never consider otherwise. I assure you, Kommodor, the Alliance no longer permits actions like that."

"Of course," Marphissa said. "And both President Iceni and General Drakon have made it clear such Syndicate practices are no longer permitted in our free and independent star system. Forgive my bluntness, Admiral. We all know you are for the people. And now Kane will benefit from that as Midway has."

After the meeting ended, the virtual attendees vanished, Desjani stood up with a scowl. "That's some nerve. A Syndic lecturing us on war atrocities."

"She didn't pretend the Syndics hadn't done such things," Geary said. "Kommodor Marphissa didn't offer excuses for them."

"It still sits badly with me." Tanya looked away as if composing herself. "If Kostya Tulev had been here, that meeting might've gone very badly. He would've told her what the Syndics did to his home world." She paused as if recalling something before looking at him again. "Yes, I remember telling you we were also bombarding cities from orbit, and seeing how shocked you looked. I wondered why."

"You understand why I was shocked," he said.

"Yeah. Now I do. But you can never know what it was like, decade after decade, more and more dying, just endless." Desjani sighed. "I can't forgive the Syndics. But people who revolted against the Syndics I'll give some benefit of the doubt to. They know what they're fighting."

"Colonel Rogero is going to report in to me when he gets to *Typhoon*," Geary said. "Do you want to be present for that?"

"Why would—oh. Bradamont's husband." Desjani straightened, rubbing the back of her neck. "Yeah, I do want to check him out. He's got to be a decent person. Honore Bradamont wouldn't have looked twice at him otherwise. A few years ago I would've dropped a rock on him without a moment's hesitation, though. And I bet he would've expected me to do that, because we were on opposite sides. Did he know he was fighting for the bad guys?"

"We can ask him," Geary said.

"Maybe when we get to know him better," Desjani said.

A call came in. "Captain? The Midway battle cruiser wants to re-initiate the secure link."

Desjani tapped the nearest comm panel. "All right. Make it happen."

A moment later the virtual image of Kommodor Marphissa reappeared. "I have a request, Admiral, on behalf of President Iceni."

"What's that?"

"I request that I be permitted to physically transfer to your flagship and accompany it through the jump and whatever occurs at Kane."

Desjani hit the mute control. "No way."

"Tanya . . ." Geary pointed to the image of Kommodor Marphissa, waiting patiently. "Shouldn't we find out why?"

"Sabotage? Spying? Assassination? Do we really need to know exactly why?"

"She's not a Syndic."

"Did you see the look in her eyes when she talked about that snake on her ship?" Desjani demanded. "'They died.' Are you going to bet me who killed them?"

"I want to know why she wants to come to this ship," Geary said. "And I want a chance to get a better feel for her as a commander."

"Ancestors save me!" Desjani shook her head, composed her expression, and unmuted the link.

"Why do you want to ride this ship?" Geary asked.

Marphissa had obviously been expecting the question. "I was directed to be open with you, and I will be. President Iceni wishes me to observe the operation of your ship. The way the crew and the officers interact. Your organization. Your discipline. We have learned a great deal from Kommodor Bradamont, but that is no substitute for first-hand observation."

"Aren't you worried about being aboard this ship and leaving the *Pele* without your command presence?"

She shook her head. "Kapitan Kontos is extremely competent. His crew is loyal. President Iceni also thought you would welcome the chance to learn more about myself and the ways in which we are trying to operate our ships."

President Iceni had obviously foreseen Geary's reaction to the proposal. A glance at Desjani showed her revealing nothing of her feelings. She noticed him looking and with a put-upon sigh nodded slightly. "How would you get over here, Kommodor?"

"We have a shuttle on *Pele*. Or I could use one of yours if you would prefer."

"We would prefer," Captain Desjani said. "Let us know when you want to transfer. I'll make preparations."

After the Kommodor's image had vanished again, she shook her head at Geary. "Okay. This will be a good opportunity to see what she's like and maybe learn more about these people. But I will have her escorted everywhere she goes. And you will have two Marines on guard at the door to your stateroom the entire time she's aboard."

"Fine." He knew better than to argue, especially since those were common-sense precautions.

Two hours later *Dauntless*'s shuttle returned from the *Pele*. Kommodor Marphissa came down the ramp, followed by Gunnery Sergeant Orvis, who'd been sent to escort her, resplendent in his dress uniform.

At the bottom of the shuttle ramp, Marphissa paused for just a moment to study the dock and the honor guard drawn up for her arrival. Walking up to Geary, she saluted in the Syndic fashion, bringing her right fist to her left shoulder. "Thank you for this opportunity, Admiral." Turning to Desjani, she repeated the salute. "Thank you for your hospitality, Captain."

"My pleasure," Desjani said, returning Marphissa's gesture with an Alliance salute. "While you're aboard, Gunnery Sergeant Orvis will accompany you at all times when you are outside your stateroom to ensure your safety."

"Oh?" Kommodor Marphissa turned to look Orvis up and down. "An Alliance Marine as my escort? These are strange times."

"I was thinking the same thing," Desjani said.

THE heavy cruiser *Gryphon* swung in close enough to transfer Colonel Rogero to *Typhoon*, then broke off as the task force approached the jump point for Kane.

"He's brought some valuable things with him," General Carabali reported just before jump. "Malware customized for the latest Syndic ground forces armor operating systems that they encountered at Iwa. Our hack and cracks were impressed by the coding work on that malware. Midway has some sharp coders."

"They gave you malware that could also be used against them?" Geary asked, surprised. "Don't General Drakon's soldiers still use Syndic armor?"

General Carabali nodded. "They do, but they've deliberately been modifying their own systems to have less commonality with the Syndic ground forces. They don't want the Syndics to be able to drop malware on them, either."

"These guys are smart," Geary said.

Carabali nodded again, her expression reflecting respect. "I hope we don't end up fighting them. Drakon has built a real professional force. They'd be tougher than any regular Syndics we've ever encountered."

"I hope we don't end up fighting them, too," Geary said. "They're an anchor of stability in a region that otherwise might fall into anarchy as the Syndicate Worlds lose their grip on it. I'll be interested to hear your opinion of Colonel Rogero."

"I'll get to know him while we're in jump and picking his brains," Carabali said. "He said he needs to report in to you before jump, though. Is it okay to link him?"

"Yes, go ahead."

The image of Colonel Rogero appeared. He saluted in the Syndic fashion. Not a salute in crisp parade-ground style, but the firm gesture of a veteran who did it right without even thinking. "I wish to report my arrival with your force, Admiral."

"We're glad to have you, Colonel," Geary said. "Please assist my Marines to the best of your ability."

Rogero saluted again, and the link ended.

"That was it?" Desjani said. They were seated on *Dauntless*'s bridge, waiting for the jump. Kommodor Marphissa occupied the observer seat at the back of the bridge that had once been the usual place for Victoria Rione. "That was your arrival interview?"

"We didn't have a lot of time," Geary said.

As if to emphasize his words, Lieutenant Yuon called out, "Five minutes to jump for Kane."

Geary reached for the controls to speak to his entire force, but paused. "*Pele* has been linked in, right?"

"They're part of the comm net," Captain Desjani said. "They can't link with the full net because of system incompatibilities, but we've got a basic data exchange work-around in place."

"Kapitan Kontos is satisfied with the current arrangement," Kommodor Marphissa said.

"Good." Geary touched his communications controls. "All units in Task Force Kane, we know the Syndics have warships at that star. Be at full combat readiness when we exit jump just in case they've posted a sentry or guard force at the jump point. Do not initiate hostilities, but if they fire you are authorized to immediately respond. Detailed plans of action will be formed when we see the situation at Kane, but we have to assume Syndic ground forces are on the surface of the primary world. We're going to make sure they don't remain there. To the honor of our ancestors, Geary, out."

A couple of minutes later he sent one more command. "All units in Task Force Kane, jump."

IT did feel odd to have even a former Syndic officer walking around the ship. The fact that her uniform was no longer Syndic made her more an object of curiosity than of hostility, and in any case the intimidating presence of Gunnery Sergeant Orvis kept anyone from openly express-ing negative opinions.

"What's she up to?" Geary asked Lieutenant Iger.

"She's observing things, Admiral," Iger said. "The interactions of the officers and the enlisted seem to be of particular interest to her, but she also wants to observe drills to see how we do things. She was taking notes on an epad, so I asked to see it, and she turned it over without hesitating. I scanned it and there wasn't anything on it except a basic operating system and her notes."

"I'd think if they'd send malware or some other espionage tool with her it'd be a bit better concealed than placing it in an epad," Geary said.

"There's no indication the Kommodor has anything like that," Lieu-tenant Iger said. "Captain Bradamont sent me a message telling me that Kommodor Marphissa was a potential friend to us and asking me to treat her right."

"I got the same message," Geary said. "She's still eating all of her meals in the crew areas?"

"Yes, sir. Observing. And she says we have good food." Lieutenant Iger smiled. "Better than the Syndics provide to junior officers and sailors, anyway. I sat next to her during a meal, asking her questions. She didn't seem to mind at all once she realized I wasn't anything like the Syndicate Worlds security people. Admiral, maybe this Kommodor is the greatest actor ever, but when I asked about her feelings about the Syndicate Worlds it was like a nova had gone off. The heat and intensity of her hate were off the scale. She said most of the people at Midway feel that way."

"From what I know of the Syndicate Worlds I can believe that," Geary said. "Did you learn anything else?"

"She said she'd been watching a lot of vids," Iger said. "Entertainment. Because she wanted to see what people were allowed to show and do and say in our entertainment. I never thought about it that way, but the Kommodor said in the Syndicate Worlds there were things you could never do. A CEO could never be a villain. Internal security agents were always right and concerned for the people. The system was always right and anyone rebelling against it was evil and heartless. There couldn't be any shortages or poorly made items, unless it was because workers were ignoring their responsibilities."

"Huh," Geary said. "And she wanted to see what rules existed for entertainment in the Alliance."

"Yes, sir. She said there didn't seem to be any rules except that Syndics were always bad guys. But the Kommodor thought that was understandable. She was impressed that we showed problems. In the Syndicate Worlds, she said, no one was supposed to admit problems existed, even though people were often disciplined because of problems."

"Keep an eye on her," Geary said. "Gunny Orvis hasn't reported any difficulties?"

"No, sir." Iger smiled. "He said Kommodor Marphissa told him the Syndicate Worlds claimed Alliance Marines were genetically modified monsters. Everyone knew it wasn't true because they'd captured some Marines, but the official story never changed."

"How did Gunny Orvis take that?" Geary asked.

"He . . . thought it was funny, Admiral. Marines have a slightly odd sense of humor, don't they?"

"That's one way of describing it," Geary said.

THE jump to Kane was only six days. Enough time to get bored with jump space, but not long enough for jump space to get on the nerves of everyone.

Geary sat on the bridge of *Dauntless*, Captain Desjani in her seat nearby, Kommodor Marphissa at the back of the bridge.

"Shields at maximum, all weapons ready," Lieutenant Castries reported. The lieutenants had been particularly wary around Kommodor Marphissa, but at the moment they were too caught up in their duties to make much note of her presence. "If we're fired upon, fire control systems are set to automatically return fire."

"They can't have planted much in the way of mines," Geary said to Desjani, worried that he'd placed *Pele* in the lead. If they did come out facing a minefield, it would've been far better to have the battleships leading the formation. "They haven't had the time or the resources here."

"Admiral, the Syndicate didn't expect Midway to be able to respond to this attack," Kommodor Marphissa said. "They thought our mobile forces would have been wiped out or at the least suffered serious losses in the trap laid at Iwa."

"Do you think Kane is still holding out?" Geary asked.

"The ones left alive on Kane are tough," Marphissa said. "I think there's a good chance they're still fighting."

"We'll know in a couple of minutes," Desjani said.

The drop out of jump space delivered the usual jolt to their brains, creating a few seconds in which they strove to recover and be able to think and act again. As Geary fought through that, he was relieved to realize that no alarms were sounding on the ship as they would have been if Syndic warships were nearby.

His head finally clear, Geary watched his display update. The information from the primary world was hours old, of course, but it offered a reassuring picture.

"One battle cruiser, two heavy cruisers, seven Hunter-Killers in orbit about the primary world," Lieutenant Castries reported. "Also two troop transports and ten modified freighters. Judging from what we can see there was still fighting underway on the surface of the primary world as of when these images originated."

"Can you tell how heavy the fighting is?" Geary asked.

"That'll require more message analysis, sir. There's another battle cruiser coming in toward the primary world. It must've arrived at the jump point from Kukai and is more than a day out from joining up with the rest of the Syndic warships."

"It's still great odds for us," Captain Desjani remarked.

"We're only allowed to fight if we have to," Geary said. "Do I look okay?"

"Yes, sir." But she leaned over far enough to straighten one side of his uniform. "Circuit six will broadcast to the star system."

"Thanks." He took a deep breath, then activated circuit six. "This is Admiral Geary. I am in command of a task force sent to Kane to protect its independence as part of an agreement to defend star systems associated with the free and independent star system of Midway." He'd chosen those words carefully, wanting to be sure they'd pass muster with the people from Midway as well as with the people from Kane. "All foreign forces attacking Kane, ground forces as well as warships and transports, must depart immediately. If they do not, we will take all necessary actions to defend Kane. To the honor of our ancestors, Geary, out."

"Do we have to let them run?" Desjani grumbled. "We could catch them before they reach that other jump point."

"We have to give them the chance."

"The CEO in command of the mobile forces won't run," Kommodor Marphissa said. "They know if they run without a fight, if they don't even fire a shot, then their life will be worth nothing. The Syndicate will not forgive them. Their only chance is to try to engage this force, do some damage, and then retire having proven their eagerness to carry out the Syndicate's commands."

"They have two battle cruisers to our four," Desjani said. "And we outnumber them in cruisers a lot more than that. I hope they do come at us."

"As do I," Marphissa said. "But we have five battle cruisers, do we not?"

Desjani paused, then smiled. "Yes, we do. How good is the commander of your ship?"

"Kapitan Kontos is young but gifted. His skills are astounding, as if his battle cruiser was an extension of his own body and can be directed with the same finesse and accuracy."

"Damn," Desjani said. "I wish I was going up against him."

"Four to one?"

"No. One on one." Desjani looked back at Marphissa and actually smiled. "But he's on our side. I'm looking forward to seeing him in action."

Geary looked to the back of the bridge as well. "Kommodor, do you think you should send a separate message to Kane? They'll see my broadcast, but maybe seeing you would reassure them that we really are here to assist Midway and not to lay claim to Kane ourselves."

"That is a good idea, Admiral."

"Give her a circuit," Desjani ordered. "Directional toward the primary world."

"Yes, Captain. Circuit four, Kommodor."

Marphissa looked down at her controls, brow furrowing as she chose the right one. Tapping it, she looked forward as she transmitted. "People of Kane, this is Kommodor Marphissa of the free and independent star system Midway. I accompany this relief force, as does the

Midway battle cruiser *Pele*. We are here to protect your freedom. The Syndicate's forces will withdraw, surrender, or be destroyed. Hold on a little longer. Help will be there soon. For the people, Marphissa, out."

Geary altered the vector of the task force, bending it onto a course aimed at intercepting the primary world in its orbit. After thinking a bit more and viewing the situation, he decided to do one more thing, calling *Reprisal*. "Captain Hiyen, I'm going to detach the battle cruisers to swing wide where they can intercept those Syndic warships before they can get near our transports. They will be Formation Zebra One, along with the Fourth Heavy Cruiser Division and the Seventh and Twelfth Destroyer Squadrons. The battleships and all other remaining warships will remain in close escort of the transports as Formation Zebra Two. You have local command of the forces remaining with the transports."

Hiyen looked back at Geary in surprise. "Admiral, I am Callas Republic, not an officer of the Alliance."

"The Callas Republic is still working with the Alliance," Geary said. "Which makes you an Alliance officer."

Captain Hiyen rendered a sharp salute. "Thank you, Admiral. No harm will come to the transports."

"Captain Desjani," Geary said, "maneuver your battle cruisers independently to cover the transports from a distance of at least ten light minutes."

She grinned. "Thank you, Admiral. All units in Formation Zebra One, accelerate to point two light speed, come port zero three zero degrees."

The formations separated, the battle cruisers, heavy cruisers, and destroyers under Captain Desjani's control swinging out from the others and accelerating away at an angle that would place the force between any move by the Syndic warships and the transports.

After that, they could only wait. The messages sent would take hours to be received, and the reactions and any replies the same number of hours to be seen or received.

"One of the transports and all of the freighters broke orbit around the planet soon after they saw us," Lieutenant Castries reported when the light from that event finally reached them.

"That's normal for the Syndics," Desjani said. "Their transports never risk themselves to extricate ground forces."

Geary looked back to see Kommodor Marphissa's reaction to the event and to Desjani's words, and saw her nodding.

"Equipment is expensive, people are cheap. Ships are hard to replace, but you can always get more people to replace the ones 'expended,'" Marphissa said. "That's the way the Syndicate thinks."

Desjani uttered a short laugh. "I've met some people in the Alliance who think the same way."

"Then the problem is not the Syndicate? The problem is people?"

"The problem is always people," Desjani said. "But the solutions are always people."

"I see." Marphissa nodded slowly, her eyes on Desjani.

"Are you really giving her pointers?" Geary asked Desjani in a low voice.

"I thought you wanted me to do that," Desjani said.

"Yeah, but I didn't think you would."

"I didn't think I would, either," she admitted.

"Captain, a shuttle came up from the surface . . . no, three shuttles and several aerospace craft. They rendezvoused with the remaining transport in orbit. It also broke orbit after that. All of the transports and freighters are on vectors to the jump point for Kukai."

"We could stop them," Desjani said, giving Geary a look from the corners of her eyes.

He shook his head. "Not if they're leaving."

"What about *Pele*? Can't she do whatever the Kommodor wants?"

Marphissa smiled. "Once we see what the Syndicate battle cruisers are doing, and deal with them, I will let Kontos see if he can catch some freighters. The Syndicate military transports will probably have too big a lead toward the jump point by then, though."

"Captain, the Syndic flotilla also broke orbit about the primary world," Lieutenant Castries said. "They seem to be coming around for an intercept aimed at our transports."

"It looks like you called it right, Kommodor," Geary said. "Captain Desjani, as soon as that Syndic flotilla steadies out, I want you to go meet it, ready for a fight."

She smiled again, even wider. "You know, I have simple needs," Desjani said. "Give me a battle cruiser and an enemy to fight, and I'm good."

"I'm glad that I could make you happy," Geary said. "But they still have to shoot first."

"Incoming transmission from the Syndic flotilla, Captain."

The CEO who appeared was a younger man with a lifetime's worth of arrogance on his face. "This is CEO Grandon of the Syndicate Worlds to the Alliance forces operating illegally in Syndicate Worlds space. This star system is part of the Syndicate Worlds. We are dealing with internal matters, engaging in pacification efforts against small bands of terrorists who have preyed on the peaceful workers of this star system. Our actions to enforce law and order are legal. You are threatening aggression against us in clear violation of the treaty that the Syndicate generously agreed to in order to end the late war. Do not mistake our generosity for a lack of resolve. Outside interference in our internal affairs will not be tolerated. We will defend Syndicate Worlds space! If you do not turn about and depart this star system, we will inflict grievous damage on your pathetic forces and the fault will lie with you. Forthepeople, Grandon, out," he finished, blurring together the phrase "for the people" as if it were meaningless words he had to recite.

"I think they're going to fight," Desjani said. "This guy actually seems to think he can beat us."

"He does," Kommodor Marphissa said. "I know this type. From a powerful family, no one has ever told him no and not suffered for it. He's done nothing on his own but thinks he achieved everything by his own superiority. This is his first real effort against a real problem where his name can't get him whatever he wants. His command training was on simulations configured to ensure his easy victory no matter the odds."

"The Syndics actually set up simulations that way?" Desjani asked in disbelief.

"I remember seeing simulations like that in the Alliance fleet before the war," Geary said. "The admirals always wanted to win."

"People," Marphissa said with a nod to Desjani.

"People," Desjani agreed. "What's the matter, Admiral?"

She'd noticed his disquiet, of course. "I'm thinking this all looks too easy," he said, touching his comm controls. "All units, this is Admiral Geary. Maintain a sharp watch for any unusual activity. We were surprised at Indras. We won't be surprised here. Geary, out."

It took a few more hours to see, but the second Syndic battle cruiser coming in from the jump point from Kukai had altered its vector as well to intercept the Alliance battle cruisers.

From *Dauntless*, the battleships and transports were behind and to the left, their relative position slowly drifting farther left as both formations grew farther apart on vectors for different objectives. The Syndicate flotilla was off the starboard bow and a little beneath it, remaining fixed in that relative position as it swept closer, aiming for a direct intercept. The second Syndic battle cruiser, above and farther to starboard, also seemed to hang unmoving despite having accelerated to point one three light speed as it aimed to reach the Alliance formation at the same moment as the Syndic flotilla.

"If I split our fire between both battle cruisers, we'll cause some damage but aren't guaranteed to knock out both of them," Desjani said. "But concentrating all of our fire on one battle cruiser would leave the second to do whatever it wanted."

"The question is," Geary said, "if you knock out one, will the other stay to try to protect it, or will it run for safety?"

"It depends on who the commander is on the other ship," Kommodor Marphissa said. "Is the commander indebted to the CEO or a rival? Personal relationships drive a lot of such actions in the Syndicate."

"I'm understanding some aspects of prior engagements better now," Desjani said.

"Captain," the communications watch said with surprise, "we're getting a tight beam transmission from the second Syndic battle cruiser."

"Just the second one?" Desjani asked. "Is it clean?"

"Yes, Captain. No embedded malware. It's addressed to the admiral."

"Tight beam? So the Syndic flotilla won't be aware of it?"

"No, Captain. They won't see any trace of it."

"The commander of that ship might not like the odds and might want to make a deal," Marphissa said. "But that would mean they'd already disposed of the snakes on board that ship."

"Let's have a look at it, then," Desjani said.

Geary saw the tab for the message appear on his display, too. Wondering what the message would say, he tapped receive.

And stared in disbelief at the image that appeared.

He heard a strangled sound from Tanya Desjani as she saw the same thing on her display.

SEVENTEEN

THE man looking at him in the message had a face that had haunted his dreams since first assuming command of the fleet when it was on the verge of destruction. A face that was leaner now, hollowed out a bit by what must have been a long time on a barely adequate diet. His Alliance fleet uniform was battered, bearing old scorch marks and roughly mended rips. Damage the uniform must have suffered when *Repulse* was destroyed.

How could he be alive? And how could he be here at Kane?

"This message is for Admiral Geary," the man said. "From Captain Michael Geary, formerly commanding officer of *Repulse*. I, along with a lot of other Alliance prisoners, have been held in a Syndic prison. We just recently learned the war had ended. We escaped and seized control of this Syndic battle cruiser. We haven't mastered the controls, don't have a full crew, and don't have a full weapons load-out or full fuel cell reserves. Basically, we're depending on our hell lances. But we can help engage that Syndic flotilla. We've received orders from their CEO to hit you in conjunction with him, and have pretended to accept those orders, but instead we can target him.

"I . . . imagine you're a bit surprised to see me, Admiral. I admit I never expected to see you again. But here we are, and this time we have the upper hand. Let's get these guys. To the honor of our ancestors, Geary, out."

Admiral Geary stared at his display, momentarily speechless. Not far off, he heard Tanya Desjani reciting a prayer of thanks in a barely audible voice.

"Okay," Geary finally managed to say. "We've got six battle cruisers."

"That's your reaction?" Desjani asked.

"I'm a little stunned." He inhaled slowly and deeply. "Is this for real? Was that really him or a fake?"

"Analysis of the message says it's not a deep fake," the communications watch stander said. "Ninety-four percent confidence that's really Captain Michael Geary."

"How could a group of prisoners not only free themselves but also gain control of a Syndic battle cruiser?" Geary said.

Desjani hesitated. "That I can't answer. It seems impossible."

"External help?" Lieutenant Yuon suggested. "Maybe Alliance Marines or special forces? It makes sense that if there were prisoners being held in undisclosed locations that we'd try to free them."

"That's a plausible explanation," Geary said, "except that you'd think Captain Geary would've mentioned that. Kommodor?"

Marphissa shook her head. "It could be a trick. The Syndicate CEO would require acknowledgment of his orders. I'm not sure anyone from the Alliance could successfully pose as a Syndicate executive. You should check."

"Ask him something only Michael would know," Desjani said. "Something the Syndics wouldn't have thought to ask about during interrogations."

"Yeah. Good idea." He paused, still mentally off balance, his mind refusing to cooperate. "Any suggestions?"

She stopped to think. "The ghost in the home network?"

"That's a good one."

"And if it is a trap, we want them to think you're falling for it. Don't sound too skeptical."

"Right. Comms, can we keep this return message on a tight enough beam to keep the Syndic flotilla from knowing it was sent?"

"Yes, Admiral," the communications watch said. "There's enough separation that even as the message spreads its edges won't clip the flotilla."

"Good." Geary composed himself before touching the reply command. "This is Admiral Geary for . . . Captain Geary. It's . . . very good to hear from you. I'm afraid we need some confirmation to be sure you're you. Please reply with the name of the ghost in the home network. How were you able to gain control of a Syndic battle cruiser? And how did you fool the Syndic CEO into believing that you're a friendly ship? Please advise. Geary, out."

"That was kind of clumsy," Captain Desjani said.

"Yeah, well, forgive me for being a little off balance."

"We're still three light hours from intercept with the flotilla," Desjani said. "Fifteen hours at the current closing rate. That leaves time to exchange a few more messages with Michael, if it's him, before the engagement, and time to think about what to do."

As if mocking her optimism, an alert sounded on the heels of her words.

"Five more Syndic ships arrived at the jump point from Kukai," Lieutenant Castries reported. "Two battle cruisers and three heavy cruisers."

Geary watched the symbols for the latest Syndic arrivals appear on his display. When the new Syndic force had arrived at the jump point hours ago, they had quickly accelerated onto a vector with a clear objective. "They're pursuing the battle cruiser which Michael Geary may or may not be aboard."

"Looks like it," Tanya Desjani agreed. "From the way they ramped up their speed as soon as they left jump, they're trying to catch that ship."

"The Syndicate used that trick at Midway," Kommodor Marphissa said. "Ships pretending to be fleeing, other ships in pursuit. They were all part of an attempted trap."

Geary didn't say anything as he watched the new warships steady out on the intercept vectors they'd adopted hours ago. *Dauntless*'s systems had no trouble projecting the result. The battle cruiser that might have Michael Geary aboard had headed toward the primary world before altering vector to close on the Alliance ships, whereas the new Syndic warships had immediately gone for an intercept. The Syndics had also accelerated to higher velocities. At the rate Michael's ship was traveling, the new warships would intercept it about ten light minutes short of reaching the Alliance battle cruisers.

"If that's Michael, he should be speeding up," Desjani grumbled.

"He said his ship had low fuel cell reserves," Geary said. "Any significant increase in velocity might be beyond their means. But saying they were fuel limited could be part of the setup for a trap." He sat back, angry at his options. "What if we head to meet up with Michael's ship? How does that impact everything else?"

Tanya tapped her controls. "If we change this vector in order to intercept his ship, it will leave an opening for the other three Syndic battle cruisers to get past us."

In a stand-up fight, Captain Hiyen's four battleships could easily handle three battle cruisers. But the Syndics wouldn't be trying to engage the battleships. They'd try to get past the battleships to hit the transports, and might succeed.

"If they're trying to lure us out of position to protect the fleet assault transports," Desjani said, "they couldn't have configured the trap better. Michael Geary on a damaged ship that's low on fuel cells, and the only way we can protect him is if we abandon our duty of screening the Marine transports."

She'd said "us," but if it was a trap, it was aimed solidly at him, Geary thought. "If Michael Geary is aboard that ship—"

"He'd expect you to do your duty," Tanya Desjani said. "He knows the choices you face, and he wouldn't want you imperiling the mission on his behalf."

Geary nearly snapped at her, something about how could she know what Michael would want, but realized that Tanya knew Michael much better than he did, having served with him in the fleet. His own experience with his grandnephew had been limited to only a few short conversations before *Repulse* had been destroyed. "He was already abandoned once," Geary finally muttered.

"He volunteered his ship as the rear guard," she replied. "He did what needed to be done."

The clearly implied message was that he needed to do the same. He felt anger growing at Tanya for pushing him on this, before realizing that she was deliberately being the voice of duty so he could blame her rather than himself if Michael was lost again. "I know what I have to do," he said, his voice low. "How much closer can we get to the point where they'll catch the ship that claims to have Michael Geary aboard, without leaving the Syndics an opening?"

"Wait one, Admiral," Desjani said, running through options. "We can alter vector enough to get five light minutes closer without leaving an opening for the Syndic battle cruisers to get past us. That'll still leave us five light minutes away when the pursuing battle cruisers catch him."

Five light minutes. Roughly ninety million kilometers. Not that distant in terms of the immensity of space. Much too far distant to have any impact on what happened in terms of human actions. He'd be leaving Michael Geary to fight alone. Again.

How do you do it? Dr. Jasmine Cresida had asked him. *How do you give orders knowing that those who must obey them will die?*

He hadn't known the answer then. He didn't know what it was now. He only knew what he had to do to keep faith with all of those under his command. "Captain Desjani, alter the vector of this formation so we'll be five light minutes from the intercept point but still able to cover the transports."

"Aye, aye, Admiral," she said, her voice more subdued than usual.

There was nothing else to be done now, not with hours to go before any changes in the vectors of the other ships could be seen. Geary stood up, trying to sound unaffected by recent events. "I'll be in my stateroom for a while, Captain Desjani."

The stateroom proved to be just another place that held painful memories, though. Memories of the time just after he'd gained command of the Alliance fleet, and just after he'd been forced to watch Michael Geary's battle cruiser *Repulse* be destroyed as it held off Syndic warships trying to catch the rest of the Alliance warships. Memories of the brief conversations he'd had with Michael Geary before then.

This isn't easy, is it? Michael had said after volunteering *Repulse* as the rear guard, knowing that his ship would have no chance of surviving. *You do what you have to do, though, and it's up to your ancestors how it all turns out.*

He got up, heading out into the passageway. The members of the crew he passed all looked in high spirits, confident of victory. Thoughts of Michael Geary reminded him of attitudes in the fleet back then. Everyone he'd encountered had been confident only that they'd fight to the last, that sooner or later their ship would be destroyed with odds that they'd die as well. Confident that they'd never stop fighting while breath remained in them, even though after nearly a century none believed the war with the Syndics would ever end, let alone end someday in a victory. It had been the self-assurance of the already damned.

He'd changed that. No matter how many mistakes he'd made, he'd been able to change that. Maybe, if it was Michael Geary on that ship, he'd be able to change what seemed an inevitable outcome at this point.

There was often a short line to enter one of the worship rooms, but this time a few were open when Geary arrived. He went into one of the small rooms, sitting down to face a little table on which a single candle rested. Lighting the candle, he sat trying to sort his thoughts into a clear request for his ancestors. In the end, that request was the same one he usually made. *Please help me do the right thing and make the right decisions.*

Did he imagine a feeling of reassurance, a sense of resolve, that followed? Perhaps. With a silent thanks, Geary snuffed out the candle.

On the way back to his stateroom he did his best to relax, knowing that if he displayed tension it would cause tension among the officers and crew. They deserved better than that from him.

He also had to bat down waves of anger at the thought that the message might have been a fake, a false image of his grandnephew designed to trick him.

By the time Geary got back on the bridge his mood hadn't been improved by the images of the primary world forwarded to him. Bombarded from orbit multiple times by Syndic warships, and now being fought over, the wreckage visible in what had been cities and towns offered a sickening view of total war against those who'd dared revolt against the Syndicate Worlds. How many citizens of Kane had died because of those attacks?

Tanya Desjani nodded to him as he sat in his fleet command seat on the bridge. "I was thinking how well this was set up to be a trap for you."

"And?" Geary replied, knowing the single word sounded more abrupt than it should.

But she continued with no sign of being put off by his attitude. "The Syndics didn't know, couldn't have known, that you'd be here at this time, or that our ships would be in these formations with these vectors. You told me that you'd suggested Captain Duellos command this mission, so he could've been here, not you. And how could the Syndics have preplanned the arrival of those additional warships from Kukai? This looks like a perfect trap laid specifically for you, but how could the Syndics have been able to precisely predict all of the specific elements?"

He stopped to think, frowning. "They couldn't have. The Syndics here could've improvised a fake of Michael if they were planning to employ that someday against me, but the rest of it . . . no." Taking a slow, deep breath, he nodded to her. "Thanks, Tanya. That should've already occurred to me."

"It doesn't mean it's not a trap," she cautioned him. "It wouldn't be the first time that chance set things up to favor one side. And we still face the same physics. If we head to directly intercept the ship Michael may be on, we'll leave the other Syndic battle cruisers openings to get past us."

"Understood."

"Oh, and Michael sent us an update that said the ship he's riding has been named *Corsair* by the Alliance personnel aboard it."

"*Corsair*?" Geary asked. "That's not a traditional name for a battle cruiser."

She shrugged. "You know those Gearys. Always breaking rules."

"Admiral," Lieutenant Castries said. "Incoming message for you from, uh, *Corsair*."

Geary tabbed receive, seeing the same image of Michael on the bridge of the Syndic battle cruiser. The signs of stress on Michael were more pronounced this time, doubtless reflecting his own extended period on the bridge of the other ship, but also making the image appear to be more real. "This is Captain Michael Geary. My apologies, Admiral. I should've realized you'd need some confirmation. The ghost is Lyn. We were able to fool the Syndic CEO because we have someone aboard who could act the part of a Syndic officer. I mean . . . hell . . . we didn't capture this ship on our own. That was done by our former guards, a Syndic ground forces unit. They needed us to fly the ship for them, so we made a deal to get them home if they freed us. This is their commander."

The image of the other ship's bridge expanded to show more of it. In the background could be seen other Alliance personnel in uniforms of varying damage. In the foreground was a woman in the uniform of the Syndic ground forces. She had a hard face marked by a prominent scar on one cheek. "I am Executive Destina Aragon," she said. "My workers and I liberated your scion, Black Jack, and captured this ship. He said you'd respect his commitment to us. Our families and some of our friends are on the surface of the primary world here. If you are truly for the people, you will help us save them."

Michael Geary nodded. "We made a deal," he repeated. "Admiral, I know Syndic forces revolting seems pretty off the wall, but apparently it's happening since the war ended. I *am* in command of this ship. I see you've got a captured Syndic battle cruiser with you. I assume that's for some sort of false flag trick?"

He took a deep breath. "You know our current situation. I'm certain that those two battle cruisers on our tail will stay on vector to intercept us. The Syndics must be pretty mad at us for getting this far. But we can deal with them. I can do the math on what could happen if you come to meet up with us, leaving your main formation unscreened. The crew on this ship, those from *Repulse* and other Alliance ships and Marine units held prisoner with me, want to strike a blow here. We've got this. Geary, out."

Captain Desjani exhaled a frustrated sigh. "He's not asking for help. That's sort of like Michael."

"Sort of?" Geary asked.

"Michael often had a chip on his shoulder," she explained. "It was the Black Jack thing."

"Yeah, I got a taste of that before *Repulse* was lost." Geary shook his head. "Do you think it's him?"

"Ship's systems now say there's a ninety-six percent chance that transmission really showed him and isn't a fake." Tanya paused, thinking, her eyes on her display. "Yes, Admiral, I think it's him."

He turned to look back at Marphissa. "What about that Syndic officer, Kommodor? She's pretty blunt and outspoken."

"Aragon seems authentic," Kommodor Marphissa said. "The Syndicate will tolerate some plain speaking if executives perform well, and here she was speaking to you, an Alliance officer, not a Syndicate CEO. But she'd have to be screened to ensure she wasn't a snake in disguise and playing her role well. I would want to meet her in person."

"Do you think she's really in command of that ship?" Geary asked.

"No. If she was, she'd have been making demands, not asking you to respect the deal the other Geary made. Even if she was trying to pretend to be under his control she couldn't have helped phrasing her words differently."

"Michael wouldn't cooperate with a Syndic trick," Desjani said. "He's very stubborn, and even though he hated being a Geary he always tried to live up to it."

Geary sat back, eyeing his display. "What's your advice, Captain? We can maintain this vector until the Syndics closing on Michael can't get past us, but that'll mean letting them hit Michael's ship long before we can get there to help. I can split our battle cruisers—"

"No," Tanya said, shaking her head. "If we split the force the two pieces won't be individually strong enough to stop the Syndics going after *Corsair* or if they lunge for the transports. Admiral, we have to screen those transports."

"Yeah." He gazed at his display, the smooth curves through space that marked the paths of the various ships bearing a beauty at odds with the life-and-death nature of the motion they revealed. Saying the options out loud had helped make it clear that he didn't really have any great choices. "His shields look to be at full strength. If that is Michael Geary, and he handles that intercept smart, he might be able to avoid serious damage." Was he trying to convince himself of that argument, or trying to rationalize doing something he didn't want to do?

Geary tapped his comm controls, doing his best not to let his uncertainties show. "Captain Geary, this is Admiral Geary. We will proceed to support your unit while also screening the rest of the Alliance forces." That was an ambiguous statement, deliberately vague to prevent the Syndics from knowing exactly what he intended if despite Michael Geary's assurances this really was a trap. He'd worried how to say the rest as well, recalling how abrasive Michael Geary had been, and knowing that Michael's experience with fleet tactics dated to the days when they had consisted of charging straight at the enemy. "You are to prolong engagements with Syndic forces as much as possible so as to keep them tied down while my units approach to intercept." Phrasing it that way should make it sound as important a task as it really was without appearing to be sidelining Michael's ship. He added something else, with all sincerity and to keep the Syndics thinking he'd been taken in by their trick, if a trick it was. "Welcome back. You've been missed. To the honor of our ancestors, Geary, out."

The message done, and Michael Geary's fate possibly sealed, he sat back, rubbing his face. "Kommodor, what do you think CEO Grandon will do?"

Marphissa took a moment to reply. "If this is not a trick, he will have been informed by now that the lone battle cruiser is controlled by escaped Alliance prisoners and rebellious Syndicate ground forces. I think he will want to be in on the kill of such a target."

Her guess was proved right within half an hour, as CEO Grandon's flotilla altered its vector to also aim for an intercept of Michael Geary's ship.

"If they're trying to lure us in," Tanya Desjani said, "there's going to come a point where it's obvious they'll intercept *Corsair* well before we're in contact."

"And if they intercept it," Geary said, "they'll either have to drop the pretense that Michael Geary is in command, or inflict significant damage on their own ship. If it's a trap."

Desjani was manipulating her maneuvering display, frowning in thought. "Thirty-six point four minutes. Admiral, if they keep on their vectors after they're less than thirty-six point four minutes from intercept, we'll know they're committed to that. And at that point we'll definitely be able to hit them if they try to get past us to go after the transports."

"That's taking into account the time delay before we'll see what they did?"

She gave him a lowered brow displaying her annoyance at the question. But her voice stayed absolutely respectful. "Yes, Admiral, of course it does. If at thirty-six point four minutes prior to their intercept we still see them on the same vector, we can safely alter our vector to head for an intercept with them." Desjani made a face. "Which will leave Michael fighting on his own for about an hour."

"That's the best we can manage?"

"I'm afraid so."

"Then it will have to be enough." He'd meant to only think those words to himself, but they came out, sounding clearly on the bridge. Glancing about, embarrassed, he saw looks of determination in response to the statement. His half prayer had turned into an inspirational declaration.

"I almost feel sorry for CEO Grandon," Desjani said. "He thinks he knows the odds because he's just looking at the ships involved. But he's actually going up against two Gearys."

"Do you want to warn him?" Geary asked.

"No. I want to be able to see his face when he finds out what that means."

Hearing a laugh from behind him, Geary turned to see Kommodor Marphissa grinning at Desjani.

Strange times, indeed. But not so odd, when he thought about it. Both Tanya Desjani and Kommodor Marphissa hated the Syndicate Worlds. Whatever failures could be laid at the feet of Syndicate Worlds CEOs, they had been very successful at creating highly motivated enemies.

He managed to get a small amount of rest in the intervening hours, as well as something to eat. It was an old problem in space, remaining ready for too long because you could see the enemy coming. But since you could see the enemy coming for days, that led to exhaustion by the time you actually met up. In this case, the usual worries were magnified by fear that his decisions had doomed a man he'd already left to die once before.

As the last hour began before that thirty-six-point-four-minute moment of truth, Geary went back to the bridge. He knew he'd have been notified if anything significant had changed, but still felt reassured to take his seat and check his display. Both Syndic formations were still on intercept vectors with Michael Geary's ship.

From the perspective of *Dauntless*, *Corsair* had been growing closer but sitting on the same bearing broad off the starboard bow and a bit below. The Syndic formation from Kukai pursuing *Corsair* had started out farther toward *Dauntless*'s starboard beam and farther below, and slowly tracked closer to the bearing of *Corsair* as it steadily headed to intercept. CEO Grandon's flotilla, which had come from orbit about the inhabited world, had started out almost dead on *Dauntless*'s bow and below it, but since altering vector to aim for *Corsair* had tracked across the bow, rising and growing steadily closer to the same bearing. Unless someone changed their course and speed, in about an hour and a half, all three contacts would merge as both Syndic flotillas intercepted Michael Geary's fleeing ship.

"Why do you think he's still not accelerating?" Geary asked Captain Desjani, who of course was already on the bridge.

"He's at fifteen percent fuel cell reserves according to a status report he sent," she replied. "That's really low. He's probably holding back on any changes in velocity until the Syndics are on him so he can maneuver as much as possible while engaging them. That's what I would do."

"Same here. I just wanted to know if one of your contemporaries in the fleet would plan the same way."

"That's pretty basic, Admiral." She'd been gazing thoughtfully at her display, and now bent a questioning look his way. "I have a recommendation. We shift to a vector now that puts us on a direct intercept with Michael's ship—"

"But wouldn't that give the Syndics a small window to get past us?"

"—and ten minutes later shift back to our current vector." Desjani indicated her display. "With the time delays because of the distance between us, the Syndics will have to decide whether to lunge for that window almost as soon as we shift vector. If we shift back soon afterwards, and they've altered vectors to get past us, we'll still be able to catch them when we see their courses change."

He'd considered trying that before, but at that time the trick hadn't been feasible. "That's a great idea, Captain. It wouldn't have worked when we were farther apart because we couldn't have held the new vector for long without giving them an opening. But this close it'll show us whether they're actually after Michael Geary's ship without endangering our transports."

She passed him the maneuvering commands. As he did with every recommended maneuver, Geary spent a moment focusing on the movements to ensure his mind understood what was going to happen. No subconscious alarm bells rang to warn of any problem he might not have consciously spotted, so he gave the orders. "All units in Formation Zebra One, this is Admiral Geary. Immediate execute, all units turn port zero one seven degrees, down zero four degrees. I say again, immediate execute, all units turn port zero one seven degrees, down zero four degrees."

On the five battle cruisers, as well as the heavy cruisers and destroyers accompanying them, thrusters fired to pitch the bows of the warships to "port," which in the human conventions for maneuvering in space was turning away from the star, as opposed to starboard or starward, which was a turn toward the star. The thrusters also pitched the warships slightly "down," which humans measured in terms of the plane in which a star's planets orbited. As the main propulsion drives on all of the warships lit off, they bent the course of the warships so that Michael Geary's *Corsair* was just slightly to the left as seen from *Dauntless*, the relative positions of the Syndicate flotillas also shifting. As the Alliance warships steadied out on their new vector aimed directly at an intercept with Michael Geary's ship, it began sliding very slowly to the left since it was still aimed at an intercept point using the original course of the Alliance formation.

The nearest Syndicate flotilla, the one commanded by CEO Grandon that had come from the primary world, was less than twenty light minutes away. Geary ordered his formation back onto the original vector after ten minutes, waiting for the next seven minutes to see if the Syndics had reacted.

They didn't. The aimed intercept at Michael Geary's ship hadn't wavered at all. "They're really after him."

"It looks like it," Desjani said.

"Captain?" Lieutenant Castries said. "We've picked up an unencrypted transmission sent from the second Syndic flotilla. It was aimed at *Corsair*."

"Forward it to me, the admiral, and to Kommodor Marphissa," Desjani ordered.

An earnest-looking Syndic officer, one with signs of age as well as authority, spoke in words that combined command with appeal. "This is Executive First Rank Pyotr Zin, speaking to the workers aboard the misappropriated Syndicate Worlds mobile unit. We know that through no fault of your own you have been led astray by your leaders. Instead of serving the Syndicate Worlds and the interests of workers such as yourselves, those leaders have betrayed their oaths, their workers, and their families. They will surely reap the fate they deserve. But *you* do not deserve to share that fate. You have followed orders in the belief your leaders were loyal. If you comply now with the orders of duly appointed Syndicate authorities such as myself, you will not only be pardoned, you will be rewarded! You know your leaders have made common cause with the mass murderers of the Alliance," Zin added, almost seeming to spit the word "Alliance." "You can have no clearer sign that they have betrayed you and left your families unprotected against the warmongering Alliance and its human tools. Did the Alliance prisoners on your unit make promises to you? You know what the word of the Alliance is worth! Nothing! Your only chance is to obey my directions now. Take action against your false leaders and the Alliance ghouls among you. Destroy them, and you will be welcomed back into the arms of the Syndicate, you and your families once more protected by the Syndicate! Act now! Comply! For the people! Zin, out."

Hearing Marphissa burst into sardonic laughter as the message ended, Geary looked back at her. "You don't think he's sincere, Kommodor?" he said, making sure the question clearly sounded sarcastic.

"No." Marphissa's laughter turned into a scowl. "They never change. Even while he's trying to convince those workers to revolt against their leaders, he drops in a threat to their families at the end!"

"Will any of those, um, workers believe him, though?" Desjani asked.

"Of course not," Marphissa said with a dismissive wave of one hand. "They know they've already committed unforgivable crimes against the Syndicate, and they've been lied to by the Syndicate all of their lives. Even if they have regrets at this time, they know better than to expect mercy if they surrender."

"The offer might cause some tension on Michael Geary's ship, though," Desjani said. "The former prisoners from the Alliance might worry that the Syndics who've been helping them will listen to that offer."

"Yes," Kommodor Marphissa said, frowning. "But they have come this far. They must have worked out means to cooperate."

"I hope you're right," Geary said. They were so close to meeting up with *Corsair*, and yet still so very far away. In less than a hour Michael's lone ship would be attacked by three battle cruisers, five heavy cruisers, and seven Hunter-Killers. And all he would be able to do was watch.

Just as he had when *Repulse* was destroyed. The image in his memory kept coming back to torment him.

"Should I try to tell him what to do?" Geary muttered. He knew micromanaging a combat encounter from light minutes away was a recipe for disaster, but guilt was causing him to second-guess everything.

"No," Desjani said in a low voice. "Admiral, your grandnephew Michael never bought into the myth of Black Jack, including the heroic charges into the teeth of the enemy. He won't do that now, if only because he'll want to emphasize that he may be a Geary, but he's *not* Black Jack."

"Neither am I," Geary said, gazing at his display where the other warships were growing steadily closer to each other. "So you're saying he'll fight smart to spite me?"

"It's what he tried to do before," she said. "Sometimes even smart commanders have no good choices, like you at Grendel, and like Michael when *Repulse* was lost. Trust him, sir."

"Thank you, Captain Desjani. I will."

He still felt vast relief when the moment came at which the Syndics could no longer get past his own ships, and his entire formation swung onto a new vector aimed at intercepting what would hopefully still be a running fight when he got there.

"The Syndics know they have to kill Michael's ship fast, before we can arrive," Geary said. "They'll try to hit him hard on their first firing runs."

"Michael will know that," Desjani said. "Hopefully it'll help him predict their moves. We'll be there in thirty-five minutes."

"Admiral, we're receiving a message from CEO Grandon."

Geary watched an image of the Syndic CEO appear. Grandon looked just as arrogant, and just as confident, which tended to confirm Kommodor Marphissa's assessment that he'd never faced real-world challenges before. "Because the Syndicate Worlds strives for peace and the well-being of all," Grandon began, "I am taking the time to issue you another warning. Cease interference in the internal affairs of the Syndicate Worlds. If you persist in aggressive actions in violation of the peace treaty between our peoples, I will not be responsible for the subsequent loss of life. Forthepeople, Grandon, out."

Desjani shook her head. "He really seems to believe that. Is he just an idjit or does he know something we don't?"

"He may have guessed that our orders say not to fire the first shot at any Syndics we encounter," Geary said. "But I have proof that Alliance personnel are aboard *Corsair* because of the transmission from that other Syndic commander. If they fire on Michael's ship, a ship full of escaped prisoners from an undeclared location, prisoners who weren't released as called for by the treaty, that will be the Syndicate Worlds firing the first shots at Alliance personnel. I'll be legally permitted to retaliate with appropriate force."

But he was also legally required to try to avoid that outcome, and he didn't want a fight that might result in *Corsair* being destroyed. He touched his comm controls to send a response. "CEO Grandon, this is Admiral Geary. I am aware that there are Alliance personnel aboard the ship you are attempting to intercept. I will take all necessary actions to protect them if they are fired upon. This is not an internal matter for the Syndicate Worlds. I strongly advise you to reconsider your threatening actions. I repeat, I will act to protect the Alliance personnel aboard that ship if they are attacked. To the honor of our ancestors, Geary, out."

He didn't expect CEO Grandon to reply or to change his plans. Geary touched another control to speak to his own ships. "All units in Zebra One are to assume full combat readiness in five minutes."

Despite his wish that he could do more, he couldn't even plan what to do when he finally reached the Syndic warships. His actions would depend on exactly how the Syndics attacked Michael's ship and how Michael maneuvered in response to that.

He sat gazing intently at his display, the bridge around him silent as everyone focused their attention on the battle about to begin. The information he was seeing was still about a minute old as light crossed the gap between where *Dauntless* was and where Michael's ship was about to face a fight for survival.

The Syndic flotilla most recently arrived from Kukai would intercept Michael's ship a short time before the Syndic ships under CEO Grandon. As that moment neared, thrusters fired on *Corsair*, pitching the battle cruiser over to face the enemy. *Corsair* was still moving just as fast, but nearly backward now, her heaviest shields and armament directed against the attack.

Geary realized that he was holding his breath, waiting for the moment when *Corsair* would face more than two-to-one odds as the Syndic battle cruisers and accompanying heavy cruisers raked the lone ship. It would be a valiant (and hopeless) defense, with the outcome sure to be far worse for *Corsair*.

"*Corsair* has lit off main propulsion drives," Lieutenant Yuon called out. "Maximum thrust."

"I hope his inertial dampers can handle that stress," Desjani murmured.

"He must be redlining them," Kommodor Marphissa said. "If those dampers were made by a contractor who cut corners that ship is going to come apart any moment now."

With *Corsair*'s propulsion units roaring at full power the battle cruiser's velocity was dropping fast. The oncoming Syndic flotilla, aiming at the point where *Corsair* would've been if she hadn't begun braking and too close to make any but the tiniest shift in its own vector, tore past ahead of where *Corsair* now was. With *Corsair* out of range of both hell lances and grapeshot, the Syndics volleyed out missiles that strove to come around hard enough to hit their target. Several of the missiles came apart under the stress, but the survivors accelerated toward *Corsair*.

Corsair had abruptly shut off its main propulsion, though, flipping around and to the side to face the second oncoming Syndicate flotilla, main drives lighting off again as the ship lined up. As the missiles tried to adjust their vectors to get back on collision courses with *Corsair*, the battle cruiser's hell lances fired, picking off missiles as they struggled to compensate for the movement of the ship. No other type of ship could have managed the maneuver, but the immense thrust-to-mass ratio on a battle cruiser could pull it off.

Unable to dodge again in time as the second Syndic flotilla swept in to contact, *Corsair* kept on reaccelerating on her new vector. Her bow faced the attack by a single battle cruiser, two heavy cruisers, and seven small Hunter-Killers.

CEO Grandon's ships hurled out missiles, then hell lance fire and grapeshot as the ships raced past each other in the blink of an eye. *Corsair* fired back, but only with hell lances.

"*Corsair* concentrated fire on one of the heavy cruisers and was able to inflict minor damage," Lieutenant Castries reported. "*Corsair* took significant hull damage. Estimate she's lost two hell lance batteries. Her forward shields were knocked down and are rebuilding slowly."

"What about propulsion damage?" Geary asked, surprised at how unemotional his voice sounded.

"Half of his main drives have ceased putting out thrust, Admiral. There's a strong chance he's suffered damage to maneuvering thrusters as well."

The first Syndic flotilla was whipping around in a vast turn to try to engage *Corsair* once more before Geary's ships reached the fight, while the second flotilla had gone into a long climb up and over to hit *Corsair* again as quickly as possible.

Corsair was coming around as well, but more slowly, turning to head toward Geary's oncoming force. "Looks like he lost a lot of thrusters," Desjani muttered. "Admiral, we can't get to him before the stronger flotilla hits him again."

"We'll take out CEO Grandon first, then," Geary said, once more surprised that neither tension nor despair could be heard in his voice. "All units in Zebra One, this is Admiral Geary, immediate execute come starboard zero one three degrees, down zero two degrees. All battle cruisers are to concentrate fire on the enemy battle cruiser. Heavy cruisers and destroyers engage the enemy heavy cruisers." That would leave the Hunter-Killers free, but they could do little damage in a short time against *Corsair*.

For an instant he felt the strangeness of this, that in a time of supposed peace he was once again battling an enemy. Would the still-deadly legacy of the long war ever go to the final end it so richly deserved?

And then he was focused on the engagement again, watching, planning, and waiting. He didn't spare any part of his attention for praying that Michael's ship would survive, because it was too late for prayer now.

Corsair swung sluggishly about to alter vector as the stronger Syndic flotilla closed for the kill. "His forward shields are still short of maximum strength," Lieutenant Castries reported.

He'd have to watch it again, Geary thought despairingly. Have to watch Michael's ship be destroyed while he was too far off to help.

But as the two Syndic battle cruisers and three heavy cruisers swept into their final approach, all of *Corsair*'s main propulsion drives flared to life, her maneuvering thrusters all firing as well to pitch her onto a different vector.

Their firing run thrown off once more, this time by *Corsair*'s unexpected agility, the Syndic flotilla fired a barrage of hell lances at long range, scoring a few hits on *Corsair*'s amidships shields. More missiles were launched as well, leaping toward *Corsair*.

Tanya Desjani bared her teeth. "He faked them out, using the wounded bird trick."

That trick wouldn't have been enough to save Michael's ship for long if help hadn't been close. Not with the other Syndic flotilla moments away from another attack. However, as the new volley of missiles homed in on *Corsair*, Geary's formation whipped through CEO Grandon's flotilla, which had held its own vector, trying to reach *Corsair* for another attack, but three seconds short of its goal when the Alliance battle cruisers threw everything they had at CEO Grandon's flagship.

At the velocities the ships were moving, CEO Grandon's flotilla went from being thousands of kilometers away to being here in what seemed an instant, the moment of actual intercept and firing far less than a second long, automated systems triggering shots as the engagement lasted too brief a time for human reflexes to respond.

The Syndic heavy cruisers and the battle cruiser were arrayed to hit *Corsair*, their combat systems locked on, as Geary's ships hit them.

CEO Grandon's battle cruiser's shields collapsed in a flurry of brilliant light, followed by the remaining hell lances and grapeshot tearing holes in and through the Syndicate Worlds warship, the blaze of destruction briefly blocking sight of the ship's death throes. As the wreckage shot harmlessly past *Corsair*, one of the Syndic heavy cruisers, hit by the combined firepower of six Alliance heavy cruisers, cartwheeled helplessly through space, all systems apparently destroyed.

"No damage to any units of Zebra One," Lieutenant Castries reported. "It doesn't look like the surviving ships in that flotilla got in any decent hits on *Corsair*."

"Immediate execute, all units up one nine zero degrees, come starboard zero zero five degrees," Geary ordered, bringing the Alliance formation swinging up and slightly over in a vast arc to intercept the second Syndic flotilla.

The second volley of missiles fired at *Corsair* by that flotilla were in final approach as Michael Geary's ship tried to throw off their aim with frantic maneuvers while *Corsair*'s hell lances attempted to pick them off. One missile skimmed past close enough to detonate amidships, nearly collapsing the shields there. Another exploded just short of the stern.

"*Corsair* has lost some propulsion for real this time," Lieutenant Castries reported. "We can see the damage. One drive out completely, and another estimated down to fifty percent."

A third missile got close enough to detonate off the bow of *Corsair*, shaking the battle cruiser as it steadied out.

"Bow shields on *Corsair* have collapsed. They're not rebuilding. The bow shield generators must have been damaged or destroyed."

The flotilla formerly commanded by CEO Grandon now consisted of a single heavy cruiser and five Hunter-Killers. With the damage already inflicted on *Corsair*, Geary couldn't afford to give even that greatly diminished force a free shot. He called the officer in charge of the Fourth Heavy Cruiser Division. "Commander Easton, take your cruisers and the destroyers of the Seventh Squadron and finish off the remnants of the first Syndic flotilla. Don't let them get in another attack on *Corsair*."

Easton grinned. "Aye, aye, sir. We're on it."

The six heavy cruisers and eight of the destroyers peeled off as the main Alliance formation continued in a tight arc to catch the larger Syndic flotilla.

Geary spared a glance at *Corsair*'s status. Given time, her damage so far was survivable. But if the Syndics hit her again soon, the harm already done to *Corsair*'s maneuverability, propulsion, weaponry, and shields would likely doom Michael's ship. "*Dauntless*, *Daring*, and all destroyers, concentrate fire on the leading Syndic battle cruiser. *Victorious*, *Intemperate*, and *Pele*, concentrate fire on the second."

The Alliance battle cruisers ripped through the second Syndic flotilla, unloading everything they had at the enemy warships as the Syndics fired back. *Dauntless* shook from several hits, but no alarms sounded to warn of damage to the ship. Her shields must have held.

He waited, tense, for the results. If enough damage hadn't been inflicted on the Syndics, they'd destroy *Corsair* before he could engage them again.

"Yes!" Captain Desjani said, clenching a fist in triumph as the sensors provided the results of the engagement.

One Syndic battle cruiser was gone, only an expanding cloud of debris marking its destruction. The barrage from *Victorious*, *Intemperate*, and *Pele* had been strong enough to knock down its shields, leaving the Syndic exposed to hits, at least one of which must have caused the ship's power core to overload.

The second remaining Syndic battle cruiser had not only caught the full force of fire from *Dauntless* and *Daring*, but had passed close enough to *Daring* for that ship's null field to hit it, evaporating part of the Syndic ship's hull. The battle cruiser had broken into several battered pieces, one of which exploded as Geary watched. A few escape pods were fleeing the rest of the wreckage as the surviving crew sought safety.

The three heavy cruisers in the flotilla had avoided significant damage, but had abandoned their attack run on *Corsair*, swinging down and wide.

Geary checked his own ships for damage. Two of the heavy cruisers had concentrated fire on *Dauntless*, but hadn't gotten any hits through her shields. Both Syndic battle cruisers had targeted *Pele*, managing to get a few hits through into her hull. But despite having a missile launcher and a hell lance battery knocked out, *Pele* remained in fighting condition. The third Syndic heavy cruiser in the formation, though, had targeted the destroyer *Katana*, hitting the smaller ship hard. *Katana* had managed to remain with the Alliance formation, but had lost all weapons and shields.

He shifted his attention to the remnants of CEO Grandon's flotilla just as Commander Easton's heavy cruisers and destroyers tore through it.

The remaining Syndic heavy cruiser in that flotilla reeled away from the encounter, all systems knocked out and escape pods already lurching away from the crippled ship. Two of the Hunter-Killers had vaporized as their power cores overloaded, another three too badly damaged to stay in formation as the last two HuKs scattered in an attempt to flee independently.

"Let's get those last three heavies," Geary said, determined to ensure that the warships didn't get another shot at *Corsair*, and that the Syndicate Worlds paid the maximum possible price for the harm they'd inflicted on the people of Kane. And on his own force. *Katana* had lost sailors in a fight the Syndics had insisted on fighting.

The three heavy cruisers that remained from the second flotilla were swinging even wider and farther "down," as if trying to give themselves time to decide whether to make another run on the badly hurt *Corsair*. "Kommodor, what do you think they're doing?"

"The snakes aboard the surviving Syndicate ships won't let the crews break off and save themselves," Kommodor Marphissa said. "They're pushing the officers on those heavy cruisers to try to finish off the ship Michael Geary is on. But the officers know that's suicide."

"Why don't they try to kill the snakes?" Desjani asked as Geary brought his formation around to hit the heavy cruisers. "As it stands, they're going to die anyway while they try to decide what to do. Their only chance to get away was to run the moment they realized we'd taken out their battle cruisers."

"I assure you some of them are thinking the same thing," Marphissa said.

Easton's heavy cruisers and destroyers were overtaking and annihilating the two surviving HuKs as the Alliance battle cruisers steadied on their firing run against the three remaining Syndic heavy cruisers, which had abruptly come about hard to charge at *Corsair*. "Too late, scum," Desjani said as the battle cruisers and their accompanying destroyers charged across the remaining gap, *Katana* being ordered to swing wide to avoid being hit again even though the stricken destroyer stubbornly remained with the Alliance formation.

Dauntless shook slightly from a single hit as the battle cruisers ravaged the Syndics, shooting past in a bare instant of time.

"One heavy cruiser destroyed, one badly damaged and out of action," Lieutenant Castries said. "The third has sustained damage but is still maneuverable."

"Let's get him," Geary said. But before he could give the order for his formation to swing around again, the last Syndic heavy cruiser suddenly dropped its shields. "Are they surrendering? Are we getting a surrender message?"

"We're not picking up any messages from the last Syndic cruiser, Admiral."

"There are people dying aboard that cruiser at this moment," Kommodor Marphissa said, her voice somber. "I will guarantee that part of the crew is trying to gain control from the snakes and any loyal workers and officers."

"When will we—" Geary began, his words cutting off as the last Syndic heavy cruiser exploded, a warship and every human life aboard it turned into an expanding cloud of dust and debris.

"The snakes have rigged means to destroy the power cores if crews revolt," Marphissa said. "Those revolting must not have been able to stop the snakes from triggering that."

"Damn." It was one thing to defeat an opponent in a fair fight. It was another thing to see some of those opponents die at the hands of fanatics who wouldn't allow surrender. The crew of *Dauntless* seemed to share that feeling, radiating satisfaction at their victory but not uttering any cheers for the destruction of the Syndic flotillas.

However, *Corsair*, though crippled and battered, was still intact, and slowly moving to intercept the Alliance battle cruisers. History hadn't repeated itself.

All that was left in space to be dealt with were those fleeing transports.

"Kommodor," Geary said, "you may direct *Pele*."

"Thank you, Admiral. Kapitan Kontos, take your ship and try to catch some of those freighters. See how many you can capture."

"I understand and will comply, Kommodor!" Kontos responded. Moments later *Pele* peeled away from the other ships, accelerating after the freighters slowly trying to flee from Kane. It was the sort of thing battle cruisers were designed for, chasing down weaker ships.

"Commander Easton," Geary sent, "congratulations on dealing with the rest of that flotilla. Remain detached from this formation and use your ships to collect Syndic escape pods from their crippled and destroyed ships. Captain Michael Geary, join up with us. Do you require assistance?"

To his relief, Michael Geary responded, unharmed. "This ship is going to need a lot of work," he said, "but all systems are stable. I'd be grateful for damage control and repair assistance."

"We'll get some people and equipment over to you," Geary said. "That was a well-fought battle, Captain."

"Worthy of Black Jack himself?" Michael Geary asked with a grin.

"I certainly think so," Geary said, not responding to the needling since he felt so relieved to have saved Michael and his ship. "One of the shuttles bringing your ship assistance can return you to *Dauntless* for a meeting to plan future actions. You and that Syndic executive with you," he added, remembering that Kommodor Marphissa had expressed a desire to meet her face-to-face.

"Aye, Admiral," Michael said. "It'll be nice to finally meet you in person."

THE shuttle dock on *Dauntless* had a hushed air about it as those present waited for the shuttle ramp to drop. "He was my first failure," Geary murmured to Desjani. "Losing him and his ship was a hard blow at a time when I was very unsure I could do what I needed to do."

"Have you ever noticed that you judge yourself more harshly than other people do?" she replied. "That's usually admirable, but right now I hope you're thinking about how everything worked out thanks to your successes. And that we saved his butt this time."

The ramp came to rest on the deck.

Michael Geary's steps out of the shuttle had a tentative quality, like someone walking but unsure if they were dreaming or not. In person, the badly repaired damage and scorch marks on his uniform were even more obvious, as was the way the uniform hung a little loose on his frame because of weight lost while a prisoner. He looked over, seeing Geary and Desjani. Walking up to them, he saluted. "Captain Michael Geary, reporting."

Geary returned the salute, smiling. "I've seen your face a lot in my dreams. I didn't think I'd ever see it in real life again."

Desjani stepped forward, grasping Michael's hand. "Welcome back, brother."

He smiled at her. "Thanks, Tanya." The smile faded into puzzlement. "Brother?"

"It's a long story," she said.

Another figure came down the shuttle ramp, drawing everyone's attention. Desjani's hand went to her hip where a sidearm would have been holstered if she had been carrying one.

It was Executive Aragon. The holster that should have carried her own sidearm was empty. This close it was easier to see that her uniform also bore plentiful marks of combat damage. The large scar on one cheek seemed more prominent in person, as did her penetrating eyes and air of command.

Michael Geary gestured her to walk to where he was. "This is Executive Destina Aragon. Her soldiers were guarding the prisoners at the camp where I was."

"Why exactly did you rebel against the Syndicate Worlds?" Geary asked Aragon.

"We'd already taken heavy losses fighting for the Syndicate," Aragon said, studying him. "We were supposed to be sent home, having done our part. Instead, we heard orders were coming for the surviving workers of my unit to be sent to fight Drakon's soldiers. We knew that'd be suicide, so we decided to force the Syndicate to respect its deal with us. You're Black Jack? I brought your scion to you. Will you respect the deal I made with him?"

"That's my intention," Geary said.

Kommodor Marphissa stepped slightly forward. "What's your home star system, Executive?"

"Anahuac," Aragon replied. "We're Tigres. What are you?" she added, looking over Marphissa's uniform.

"Kommodor Marphissa of the free and independent Midway Star System. Your families were brought here as hostages for your obedience?"

"Yes," Executive Aragon said as if expecting to be doubted. "They're down there."

"I believe you," Marphissa said. "The Syndicate did the same thing at Iwa. We brought Alliance Marines to stop the fighting on the surface of the planet. They'll save your families. They like killing snakes."

"Not as much as I do," Aragon said. "Alliance Marines? You trust them? Do you have beer to motivate them?"

Gunnery Sergeant Orvis, as usual standing not far from Kommodor Marphissa, attempted without complete success to smother a smile.

"Let's go talk things over in private," Geary said. "Captain Desjani, have Dr. Nasr meet us in the secure conference room so he can check over Captain Geary."

The small procession headed for the secure conference room, Gunnery Sergeant Orvis and a couple of Marine sentries following at a discreet distance, Michael Geary still looking about him as if unsure he was really back on an Alliance fleet ship, and Executive Aragon walking as if she expected a bullet in the back at any moment.

"Get General Carabali and Colonel Rogero linked in," Geary ordered. The battle cruisers were close enough to the main body again for a real-time conference. "You two, do you need anything to eat or drink?"

"I'm fine, Admiral," Michael Geary said despite having sat down with obvious relief.

Executive Aragon only shook her head, remaining standing.

Dr. Nasr came in, hastily checking over Michael Geary, frowning as he studied medical instrument readings.

The virtual presences of Colonel Rogero and General Carabali appeared, Rogero gazing with surprise at Aragon.

"So," Geary said after introductions, "we have a damaged but still-usable battle cruiser carrying a large group of Alliance former prisoners of war, as well as Executive Aragon's force of ground soldiers."

"The deal," Michael Geary said, "was that they'd capture the ship, we'd fly the ship to get them home, and after we dropped off the Tigres we would be given the ship and could try to get back to Alliance space. But we found out about the families being sent here, so Executive Aragon asked to modify the deal to bring her unit here. Since it looked like Midway might be a refuge before we tried sneaking and fighting our way across Syndic space, I agreed. We're very low on fuel cells and only had working hell lances when it comes to weapons, so it wasn't like we were in great shape for a long trip home."

"We'd been assigned guard duty at an orbital prison camp that officially didn't exist," Executive Aragon said. "Supposedly we'd be sent home soon. But we found out we were getting different orders, and decided if we were going to die, we'd die with our teeth in the neck of the Syndicate."

Kommodor Marphissa leaned forward, a grim smile on her lips. "I know that feeling. How'd you take the battle cruiser?"

"It had a skeleton crew. Snakes. Waiting for the full crew to arrive. It was also going to transport us to here when it got the full crew. When we found out our families and a fellow unit of Tigres were already here, we came anyway to see if we could free them."

"How many are you?" Colonel Rogero asked.

"Three hundred seven," Aragon said. "That's all that's left of us."

"Only three hundred?" Desjani asked. "Why'd the Syndics even bother moving such a small unit?"

Aragon turned cold eyes on Desjani. "Because we're Tigres. We're tough. Even the Syndicate knows our value."

"But you didn't want to fight General Drakon's soldiers?" Carabali asked.

"That's right," Executive Aragon said. "We're tough, not stupid."

"I've heard of the Tigres," Colonel Rogero added. "Soldiers from Anahuac have an impressive reputation."

Aragon looked at Rogero. "You're one of Drakon's?"

"I have the honor of serving General Drakon, yes," Rogero said. "I command one of his brigades."

For the first time, Executive Aragon looked impressed. "You must be pretty tough, too. Tell them. We can do anything they ask of us."

"What's the situation on the surface?" Geary asked Carabali.

The general activated some controls where she was, a curved map appearing next to her virtual presence. Since the human presence on the primary world had been mostly confined to one shore of a continent, the map didn't have to cover anywhere near the entire planet. "The red markers are Syndic ground forces units. You can see they were scattered through these inland areas. Colonel Rogero tells me inland on that continent is riddled with subsurface volcanic tubes. From the messages we've intercepted and what we can see of ongoing ground operations, the remaining population on Kane seems to have withdrawn into those volcanic tubes and has been conducting guerrilla strikes at the Syndics, while the Syndic ground forces have been trying to find the Kane defenders and pry them out of their holes."

"Inland the terrain is rough and covered with dense vegetation," Colonel Rogero said. "Ideal defensive terrain."

"Since our arrival in the star system," General Carabali said, "the Syndic ground forces have all abandoned their search-and-destroy missions and are trying to get back to a perimeter on the edge of the ruins of this city." She pointed to a place on the map near one of the coasts. "From what we're seeing, Kane's defenders are harassing them as they retreat, slowing them down. Inside the perimeter we can see Syndic defenders intermingling with an obviously civilian population. Colonel Rogero tells me those will be primarily the 'snakes,' and the civilians, the families of the Syndic soldiers they're using as hostages. Getting inside the perimeter and taking out the snakes without the civilians being massacred is our biggest problem."

Geary sat back, thinking. Michael Geary had earlier raised the possibility of a false flag attack when he thought *Pele* was a captured ship. Maybe that idea would work on the surface of the planet. "Executive Aragon, you said a sister unit is already on the surface?"

"Yes," Aragon said. "The 1234th. We're the 1233rd."

"Can you pass as part of the 1234th?"

Executive Aragon narrowed her eyes at Geary. "If our comrades with the 1234th go along with us. They will, I think."

"Do we know where the 1234th is on the surface?" Geary asked.

Colonel Rogero nodded and pointed to a place on General Carabali's map. "Here, Admiral. Like the rest, they've been pulling back toward the Syndic perimeter. At the pace they've been managing, they should reach it a little after we arrive in orbit."

"We were going to cut them off," General Carabali said. "Surround them before they could reach the perimeter. But if we let them through, along with Aragon's people, we could have a nice Trojan horse thing going. This might offer a good way to simplify the challenge of getting to those snakes without losing a lot of the hostages."

"Get us inside and we'll protect the families," Aragon vowed.

"Your numbers will be limited," Colonel Rogero pointed out. "Even if the members of the 1234th join in fully. Do you think you could open the perimeter to some of the Alliance Marines?"

"Marines?" Aragon gave Carabali a distrustful look. "Why?"

"Because," Rogero said, "that will free you Tigres to defend your families, while the Marines have a snake hunt."

"We kind of like killing snakes," Aragon said. But she paused to consider the idea. "How do we keep those Marines from killing my people when they go snake hunting?"

"I brought malware," Colonel Rogero said. "Get it into the Syndic command net and it'll cause snakes to display special markers on the Marine combat systems."

Aragon grinned. "Nice. But, still, we're talking Alliance Marines. I don't need to get 'accidentally' shot by Marines."

"My Marines," said Carabali, her voice stiff, "will not shoot at anyone who does not have a 'snake' marker or who does not shoot at them."

"So you say. I have no guarantee, though."

"I will personally vouch for General Carabali and her Marines," Geary said. "If sent in with orders not to shoot at any Syndic soldiers who don't open fire first, but to engage snakes whenever encountered, that's what they'll do."

Aragon looked at him, nodding. "If Black Jack guarantees it, that is enough."

"You need to try to convince the workers in the other ground forces units to surrender or at least stop shooting," Colonel Rogero urged her. "Let them know you're guarding their families as well as your own. Tell them they will be treated well if they surrender. They should have heard about General Drakon's mercy for workers who surrender."

"I was thinking, Admiral," General Carabali said, "can we let the Syndic soldiers surrender to Colonel Rogero rather than to Alliance

Marines? That might make a big difference in their willingness to stop fighting."

"It would make a big difference," Aragon said. "The Alliance won't be trusted. One of Drakon's officers, though, would be."

"Let's do that, then," Geary said. "Executive Aragon, if your unit backs up Colonel Rogero, and you get your sister unit to do so as well, it will allow him to disarm surrendering Syndics once the fighting stops without using the Marines."

"That would be best," Rogero said. "Between us, Executive Aragon, we might be able to save the lives of a lot of those workers as well as the lives of their families."

Aragon waved one hand in agreement. "Consider it done. I need to get back to the mobile forces unit and brief my people. Send me details when you have them. You have enough shuttles to drop us?"

"Easily," General Carabali said.

"Then I need a ride." Aragon looked about her, focusing on Michael Geary. "You coming?"

"Yes," Michael Geary said before anyone else could reply. He struggled to his feet, looking at the others. "It's my ship. My crew. I need to be there."

"Understood," Geary said. "There shouldn't be any more fighting in space, but I understand where you're coming from."

"Gunnery Sergeant Orvis," Desjani said. "Can you and the Kommodor escort Executive Aragon to the shuttle dock? I need to say something to Captain Geary before he leaves."

Aragon hesitated, with a suspicious look toward Desjani, but went with Orvis and Marphissa. Colonel Rogero and General Carabali made quick farewells and their presences vanished. Dr. Nasr, frowning, slapped some med patches on Michael Geary. "You need more basic nutrients and some immune stimulants. Do not overdo it."

"Sure, Doc," Michael said. "What'd you need, Tanya?"

"I need you to come back with us in one piece," she said as Dr. Nasr left. "Your sister Jane is waiting at Midway with her ship *Dreadnaught*.

She always believed you were still alive. Your picture isn't up at the family home's shrine. So don't get yourself hurt now when we've finally got you back."

"Okay, okay." Michael Geary paused. "How do you know my picture isn't up at the shrine back home?"

"We were there before we left."

"We?"

"Um . . . the admiral," Desjani said, waving toward him.

Geary stood up, feeling awkward. "Captain Desjani and I are married. That status doesn't exist aboard this ship, of course."

Michael Geary stared at him for several seconds as if paralyzed, then abruptly laughed. "Black Jack, the perfect officer, married his flagship's captain?"

"We are fully professional on this ship," Desjani insisted.

"Knowing you, Tanya, I don't doubt that. But . . ." Michael laughed again. "Every time I didn't do something right, I'd be told that Black Jack would never do that. You *are* human, aren't you? I wish I'd known that growing up." He looked at Desjani. "That's why you called me 'brother.' Welcome to the family, sister. Is Jane okay with it?"

"We're cool," Tanya said. "Battle sisters, you know."

"Great. I should get to the shuttle dock before Destina gets too worried."

"Is there something going on with her?" Desjani asked.

That brought another startled look followed by a laugh. "With her? You mean me? If I made a move on Destina Aragon she'd rip my arm off and beat me bloody with it. But she has honor. She's a good officer, believe it or not. And I respect that, even if I didn't owe my freedom to her. But an Alliance officer getting involved with a Syndic, even an ex-Syndic? Never happen."

"Honore Bradamont is married to Colonel Rogero," Desjani said.

"What?" Michael Geary looked dazed. "There have been a lot of changes since I was captured."

"You have plenty of time to catch up," Desjani said. "Let's get you back to your ship. You've got plenty of repairs to oversee."

◈

FROM orbit, to the naked eye, Kane was a lovely planet, large oceans of brilliant blue dotted with small continents covered with luminous green vegetation. The nightside showed the red glow of active volcanoes in a number of places, while the dayside sky was streaked with banners of volcanic ash mingling with the clouds.

The naked eye couldn't see that the cities and towns of Kane were mostly in ruins, pitted by craters from orbital bombardment. But it would have noticed that the nightside betrayed no artificial light advertising human presence. The remaining people on Kane were still in hiding, and the soldiers on the surface were also trying to avoid being spotted.

"This is Admiral Geary to all Syndicate Worlds personnel on the surface of the planet. Your warships have been destroyed. Your transports have fled. You have no means of escaping and cannot defend yourselves against bombardment. Colonel Rogero of the free and independent Midway Star System is here at the orders of General Drakon. He will accept your surrender. Everyone who surrenders will be treated humanely. Everyone who fights will be taken down. Your choice is clear. To the honor of our ancestors, Geary, out."

He sat back in his seat on *Dauntless*'s bridge, watching his display where scores of shuttles from the assault transports were dropping down through the atmosphere, heading for different landing zones. "General Carabali, did we get confirmation from Kane's government that they're going to halt action while our forces land?"

"Yes, Admiral." Carabali was still aboard *Typhoon*, coordinating from low orbit the action of her Marines as they landed at spots hundreds of kilometers apart. "President Rian Wake has ordered their senior surviving officer, Colonel Mako, to stand down all operations. They don't want to get in the way of us wiping out the Syndics."

"Good. Have Executive Aragon's troops landed yet?"

"They're dropping now, Admiral. We were able to link to their armor. It's limited access, so no intrusions can enter our net from them, but we can sit on the shoulder of *Aragon* and her senior officers. And Rogero is with them. I've got a company of Marine force recon dropping near them, ready to get inside the Syndic perimeter as soon as those Tigres give us an opening."

"Looks good," Geary said. He called Captain Hiyen aboard *Reprisal*. "Any luck spotting decent targets for bombardment?" The battleships had not only the widest range of orbital bombardment projectiles, but also the best targeting systems for them.

Hiyen shook his head. "Not if you want to avoid killing the civilians. I'm sure there are concealed positions, but we haven't spotted them. If the Marines do, we can take out any strong points for them."

"All right. You've got a good picture on our Syndics, right? The Tigres?"

"Yes, Admiral. They're clearly marked on our displays. We won't drop anything on them."

"I hope that Executive Aragon is as tough as she looks and as smart as her mouth," Captain Desjani said. "Otherwise we might lose a lot of those civilians."

"I'm hoping that, too," Geary said, watching as the first shuttles began dropping off Marines and Tigres. He activated the display that would let him get first-person perspectives from the Marines, hoping that he wouldn't have a front-row seat to further tragedy on a planet that had already seen far too much of it.

EIGHTEEN

THE view from Executive Destina Aragon's battle armor was of dense brush rising above head height in varying shades of green and brown, interspersed with some kind of tree-bushes that loomed even higher, their thickets of thin limbs too weak to support climbers.

Aragon was moving forward cautiously, a low-strength identification signal pulsing on her helmet's heads-up display.

The view from Colonel Rogero's armor was much the same. If not for the individual markers on the helmet display it would've been impossible to know where the other soldiers were.

The commander of the Marine recon companies was behind Aragon's soldiers and Colonel Rogero, moving blindly through the brush, and maintaining separation from the "friendly Syndics" only thanks to his link with their armor systems.

Aragon came to an abrupt halt as another figure in battle armor appeared in front of her, weapon leveled.

She flipped up her face shield and so did the soldier facing her. On the improvised link to the Syndic armor Geary couldn't hear them, but it was obvious that the reaction of the other soldier started with relief and welcome but quickly shifted to worry and anger.

"They're yelling at each other," he said, trying to grasp the idea that two soldiers with life on the line in the middle of a war zone would be arguing so vehemently, hands waving and fingers pointing.

"As long as they're talking," Kommodor Marphissa said.

More figures in Syndic battle armor appeared out of the brush, some beside Aragon and others beside the new soldier. Colonel Rogero arrived, giving Geary a new perspective on the same argument and a chance to see how heatedly Aragon was debating with the others. Face shields were popping open as additional soldiers joined in the argument.

It gradually became apparent that Aragon was winning the argument as she gestured to Rogero, and the new soldiers slowly lowered their weapons, staring at him. Hope began to appear on faces that had been haunted by the certainty of doom.

General Carabali called in. "It's going well."

"It's taking a long time," Geary said.

"That's not a problem, Admiral. I'm coordinating the actions of the other Marine forces with what happens there. The commander of the Marine recon companies just informed me he's gotten the come-forward request from Colonel Rogero. This will decide things."

Colonel Rogero and Executive Aragon had both turned to point as the Marine commander shouldered aside some brush and came into view. Geary marveled at the courage that had taken as dozens of weapons held by the new soldiers leveled on the Marine. Aragon was yelling again, and Rogero seemed to be speaking calmly.

"They're telling these new Syndics we're their best hope if they want their families to live," the Marine reported. "That Executive Aragon has got a mouth on her. I wouldn't want to be chewed out by her. Yeah. They're coming around. These guys thought they were walking dead, and now they're seeing a chance for them and their families."

The debate continued for what seemed to Geary far too long, but eventually the entire group started moving again at a faster pace, trotting through the brush, sharp-edged leaves and branch tips continuously scraping along their armor. He wondered what it would be like trying to move through that brush without battle armor to protect face and arms and hands. The leaves looked hard enough to slice through clothing.

It felt incredibly claustrophobic as well as strange. Geary was used to being able to see for literally billions of kilometers in all directions. But among this vegetation he could barely see beyond the armored face shields.

He noticed that a symbol on Aragon's face shield had altered. The unit identification. She and her soldiers now appeared to be part of the other unit.

"Diversionary attacks starting at other parts of the Syndic defense perimeter," General Carabali reported. "The Syndics are dug in and well concealed. It'll be rough if we have to dig them out."

"Should the battleships drop rocks on any of the positions?" Geary asked.

"No, sir. Not yet. We don't want to push forward now. We want the, uh, snakes to be focused on these places and to think they're holding out against us."

The brush Aragon and Rogero were walking through abruptly vanished, giving way to a mowed area where nothing stood higher than a centimeter off the ground. Beyond were the tangled ruins of what had been outlying buildings of a city.

Linked in to the Syndic net through their new friends, Aragon's and Rogero's displays showed scores of Syndic soldiers hidden among the ruins.

"Colonel Rogero is activating the malware he loaded onto the Syndic command net," General Carabali reported.

Suddenly, new markers appeared. Some of the so-called snakes hadn't been visible on the normal combat displays. Now they were, and every snake had a bright symbol next to their marker.

Aragon, her soldiers, Colonel Rogero, and the Tigres of the other unit raced across the open area, exactly like tired, scared soldiers who'd finally reached safety.

The Marines following them had paused, still fully concealed by the high brush.

Aragon and Rogero stood to the side as a couple of snakes in armor approached the commander of her sister unit, issuing orders. Even through the link and the covering armor Geary could sense the tension in the defenders.

"Ramping up diversionary actions," General Carabali reported. "The battleships are going to do several pinpoint rock drops."

Geary saw heads snap around in the direction of the far side of the Syndic perimeter as the roar of battle rose and the ground shook beneath the feet of the soldiers.

Aragon and a group of her soldiers stayed at the perimeter, pretending to be trying to fix problems with their armor, as most of the Tigres hastened off toward an area where many civilian markers were clustered, accompanied by Colonel Rogero. Confronted by more snakes, the Tigres with Rogero opened fire without hesitating, killing them, and ran onward, depending on speed to overrun all of the internal security service agents before they could alert their superiors or start massacring the hostages.

Aragon and those with her suddenly did the same, gunning down the snakes at her location on the perimeter, Aragon firing her weapon directly into the face shield of one at close range. The regular Syndic soldiers there stood gaping in surprise as Aragon and her Tigres leveled their weapons, holding the soldiers at gunpoint. There wouldn't be any time wasted with arguing and convincing here.

The Marine recon force came racing across the open area and through the gap opened in the Syndic defenses.

"Rogero's broadcasting to the entire Syndic net," General Carabali reported. "Telling them the hostages are being protected, and that Marines are inside the perimeter but will only target snakes and anyone who fires at them. Telling them the 1234th has already revolted and been guaranteed good treatment by General Drakon, and that anyone else who surrenders to him will receive the same treatment. And that he, General Drakon's officer, will protect them from the Marines. This is when we find out how bad it'll be, Admiral. If the Syndics decide to keep fighting, we'll have a hard time of it. But better troops than these would have trouble keeping on with the fight under these conditions."

General Carabali proved to be right. Their morale already in tatters, enraged with the security service agents who'd dealt death on an accusation or a whim, the Syndic soldiers began slaughtering the snakes among them before the Marines could reach their positions, then huddling defensively as the Marines raced past, their weapons silent.

As the inside of the perimeter collapsed, the defenses facing the Marines still outside fell silent except for shots aimed at the snakes among them.

Securing the entire area, and slowly disarming the Syndic soldiers who surrendered to Colonel Rogero and the Tigres with him as he moved to different parts of it, took a long time.

And then things got very tense again.

"Admiral, we have a situation," General Carabali reported. "Colonel Mako with some of the Kane defensive forces is trying to enter the former perimeter. He and his soldiers seem intent on slaughtering the surrendered Syndics."

"Get Rogero over to meet Mako, and link Mako in with me," Geary ordered.

The image of an angry, stubborn man in battered battle armor appeared before Geary. "We are grateful for your assistance," Colonel Mako said, "but now you will stand aside and let us deal with those who committed atrocities against our people."

"You don't give orders to me," Geary said, knowing he had to assert dominance quickly. "Look up. You'll see battleships in orbit. Look around. I've got a lot of Alliance Marines ready to act on my command. Now, let's discuss this. We don't want to fight Kane's defenders."

"Kane will not become a vassal of the Alliance," Colonel Mako insisted.

"You know that's not what will happen. We came here at the request of President Iceni and General Drakon to assist Kane. We will leave once the job is done. Kane will remain free."

"Then let us wipe this stain from our world!"

Colonel Rogero had arrived, coming face-to-face with Colonel Mako. "You know me, Mako! We gave promises to those who surrendered. You know General Drakon's policies!"

"Do you know the things they did?" Mako growled. "These people you gave promises to?"

"The snakes among them are all dead! You can come see that for yourself. There will be no killing of the helpless, Colonel. That is what the Syndicate does."

"Do you think they can change, Rogero? They all served the Syndicate."

"So did I, Colonel Mako. And so did you." Colonel Rogero looked beyond Mako to the ragged defenders of Kane behind him. "How many of you others served the Syndicate? Do you know the families of those workers are here? Those workers fought knowing if they faltered the snakes would kill their family. Would you have done differently?"

Mako's rage was lessening. "I would like to see these families. To see if this is true."

"I will take you to them," Colonel Rogero said. "But no shots must be fired. I have given General Drakon's mercy to these workers who surrendered. Do you want to face Drakon's wrath?"

"General Drakon does not rule here. Neither does the Alliance. We have nothing left to lose but our freedom. *No one* will dictate to us what we will do."

Geary turned to Marphissa. "Kommodor, can you link in with

Colonel Rogero? It looks like we have a big problem that hopefully the two of you can fix."

Hours passed, the situation on the surface stable, but Marines, surrendered Syndic soldiers, and Kane's defenders all eyeing the others with growing nervousness. Knowing the odds of trouble were growing with each minute, Geary was relieved when Rogero and Marphissa called him again.

Unfortunately, their expressions were not those of a pair that was about to report success. Both looked tired and frustrated. "We have an apparently unsolvable problem," Colonel Rogero said. "Kane will not permit any surrendered Syndicate soldiers on their planet. President Wake is not as openly bloodthirsty as the others, merely insisting 'something' will happen if the soldiers remain on the surface. But all refuse to compromise. If we withdraw the Marine guards and leave all of the surrendered soldiers on the surface, those Syndicate soldiers will be massacred. But of course we cannot leave the Marines, because then they would be seen as an Alliance occupying force."

Great. Geary massaged the bridge of his nose as he thought. "*Pele* captured five freighters, right?"

"Six," Marphissa said.

"They can hold all of the surrendered soldiers, can't they?"

"If they're packed in," Kommodor Marphissa said. "It wouldn't be comfortable, but it would be survivable."

"Then why can't we load the surrendered soldiers on those freighters and take them to Midway?" Geary asked.

Colonel Rogero shook his head, looking like someone repeating an argument for the hundredth time. "Because of the families. Those Syndicate workers will not leave their families undefended on the surface of Kane. I can't blame them for that. Even the families wouldn't be safe if left without guards."

"Kane won't commit to guarding them?"

"No. In fact, Kane refuses to offer any assurances of their safety. If we try to evacuate the soldiers without their families, the soldiers will riot. We'll probably have to kill a lot of them," Rogero said with calm certainty.

"The only way to suppress the riot would be killing?" Geary said, shocked.

"These are Syndicate workers," Kommodor Marphissa said. "Held on tight reins all of their lives. When the reins snap, they run amok. I've seen it."

"So have I," Rogero said. "So there's our problem. We can't leave the surrendered soldiers on Kane, but we can't take them off Kane. And we simply don't have enough transport to bring out the soldiers and the families at the same time."

Geary felt an old headache returning. "And Kane refuses to bend even though they've won."

"Exactly. They want blood, Admiral. The blood of the soldiers who invaded their world."

Something teased at Geary's mind. He held up a hand to stop something else that Rogero was about to say, trying to grasp at whatever was hanging just beyond his comprehension. Soldiers who invaded their world. That was it. Why . . . ?

He suddenly knew. "Executive Aragon and her people did not invade this world. They didn't engage in any actions on Syndic orders on this world. They weren't even Syndic when they landed as part of our force."

Rogero stared at Geary, then at Marphissa. Both nodded. "Maybe that's the wedge that can solve the unsolvable problem," Colonel Rogero said. "Let us pursue that and get back to you. I'm going to get Aragon here as well."

Another hour, while Geary watched the immense force at his command, knowing he couldn't solve this problem with it unless he was willing to kill a whole lot of people.

Finally, Rogero and Marphissa called back, showing wary expressions of success. "That did it, Admiral," Rogero reported. "Since Executive Aragon's soldiers never attacked Kane, and helped defeat the Syndicate forces here, Kane is willing to let Aragon's unit remain, fully armed, to protect the families of the Syndicate soldiers. Executive Aragon has agreed to do that. And the surrendered soldiers will trust Aragon's people to defend their families until we get transports back here for them."

"And Midway can take all of them?" Geary said. "You've got room?"

"A great deal of room," Colonel Rogero said. "The Syndicate built a lot of large facilities on outlying islands on Midway, facilities that have never been activated or occupied. Supposedly they were for a massive buildup if the enigmas attacked, but everyone believed they were really intended to someday support a huge invasion force aimed at the enigmas. Those facilities can, at least temporarily, hold all of the soldiers here and their families. And if some of them want to go to star systems associated with us, such as Taroa, they'd probably be welcomed there."

"Fantastic." Geary looked at Rogero and Marphissa. "Now what's the thing you haven't told me yet?"

Kommodor Marphissa met his eyes and spoke steadily. "In order to gain Kane's agreement, I had to offer one more thing. That I would strongly recommend to President Iceni that she give the battle cruiser captured by Executive Aragon to Kane, so this star system would have a powerful defense against more attacks."

He'd been so afraid of hearing an impossible demand that Geary almost laughed when he heard the reality of it. "That's fine with me. I was wondering what to do with that battle cruiser."

"It was promised to Captain Geary," Kommodor Marphissa pointed out.

"I don't think Alliance law permits individual ownership of battle cruisers," Geary said. "And I don't think Captain Geary will object to having to relinquish it to Midway to do with as it desires. But can Kane support a battle cruiser? And do they know it was pretty badly damaged?"

"No," Marphissa said. "Midway will have to carry out some repairs, and subsidize at least part of the crew and a good part of the operating costs, at least for a few years. But I believe President Iceni will agree to do that since it will benefit Midway to know Kane has that kind of space defense."

"I have no objection to doing it," Geary said.

"Then we've got a deal," Colonel Rogero said with relief.

"Let's get final agreement and get this done as fast as possible," Geary said. "We'll shuttle the captured Syndics up to their freighters and get out of here. Kommodor, I'm going to detach *Pele* to escort those freighters, if you don't object."

"No objection, Admiral," Marphissa said.

He sat back, relieved, but realized he had to make another call.

Michael Geary was still on the bridge of the captured Syndic battle cruiser. "Yes, Admiral?"

"You haven't gotten too attached to that ship, have you?" Geary explained the deal.

"I don't have any problem with that," Captain Geary said. "I guess." He looked around. "It's funny. Syndic design features are a little odd in places. We'll all feel better back on Alliance ships. But I'll still miss *Corsair*. You say Executive Aragon is being left here?"

"Until transports return from Midway to pick up her, her unit, and the families of all of the Syndic soldiers. By the time those transports get back to Midway again we should be gone."

Michael nodded, frowning. "Then I should make a formal, respectful farewell to Executive Aragon. Me and the other senior Alliance personnel on this ship."

"We can get a link set up."

"It should be in person, Admiral. Out of respect. We owe our freedom and probably our lives to her." Michael Geary slowly smiled. "It's what Black Jack would do."

Geary snorted a laugh. "You and Tanya Desjani are two of the only people who are allowed to say that to me. All right. You can take down one of the shuttles, but I warn you that on the trip back up, that shuttle is going to be packed with Syndics being hauled to those freighters."

"A crowded shuttle flight?" Michael Geary smiled again. "We've been in prison for a while. We can probably handle tight quarters in a shuttle."

Geary laughed once more. "Make sure you ask Aragon if she needs anything from us. I owe her, too."

The loading was as rushed as everyone could manage, first the surrendered Syndic soldiers brought up to the freighters that *Pele*'s prize crews had brought back into orbit, then the Marines handing over security of the families to Aragon's Tigers and being shuttled back up to their transports. In response to Aragon's request, Geary sent down to the planet a large amount of Marine field rations as well as other supplies the Tigres and the families needed until they could be evacuated from Kane as well.

His second-to-last act while in orbit was to call President Rian Wake. "I personally guaranteed to those soldiers that their families will be safe," Geary said. "And my family personally owes a debt to Executive Destina Aragon. I hope my meaning is understood."

"Nothing will happen to them," President Wake promised, her voice betraying her own weariness. "Kane has suffered enough. We don't need to make more enemies, especially among those who helped us defeat the Syndicate invasion. Just please make my job easier and ensure Midway sends transport back as quickly as they can. The less time those remnants of the invasion remain on this planet the better."

The last call was to Aragon. "Executive Aragon, I wanted to extend my personal thanks to you. If you ever need anything, try to get word to me or another Geary."

"All I did was make a deal," Aragon said, eyeing him. "It benefited us as much as it did your scion."

"Nonetheless, that deal saved my grandnephew, and you played straight with him all the way. My family is in your debt. May the light of the living stars shine on you. You've brought honor to the memory of your ancestors."

Aragon laughed, shaking her head. "You Alliance types. Okay. I'd be a fool to turn down a someday offer of help from Black Jack himself. You look after that fool grandnephew of yours. I didn't save his butt so he could get it blown off in another fight. And . . ." She straightened, saluting him. "Thank you for saving my unit, my sister unit, and our families. The debt flows both ways. If you ever need the Tigers, let me know. For the people."

An hour later, the freighters shepherded by battle cruiser *Pele* broke orbit, heading for the jump point for Midway. Soon after, Geary's task force followed, rapidly overtaking and passing the slow freighters.

It felt like a great success, but he wouldn't know for certain until he saw how the leaders of Midway reacted to what had happened at Kane.

"THAT was certainly a dramatic return, Admiral," President Iceni said, smiling at Geary.

He'd brought the task force back, knowing the newly captured battle cruiser with them would raise a stir the moment it was identified as not being *Pele*. His report on the outcome of the mission, along with notice that the shiploads of surrendered Syndic soldiers were on the way escorted by *Pele*, had been met with only muted acknowledgment. But Ambassador Rycerz had greeted him warmly once he'd made it back to the fleet and boarded the *Boundless* once again. The rescue of the Alliance prisoners had both given a firm legal backing to Geary's actions and given the Alliance a substantial stick to beat the Syndics with in discussions about the peace treaty. Moreover, both President Iceni and General Drakon were in good moods as well.

Jane Geary had reacted to the return of her bother with sisterly affection, scolding him for worrying everyone and taking so long to get back. The former prisoners of war on *Corsair* had been distributed among ships in the fleet for at least temporary berthing, Michael Geary being sent to *Dreadnaught* where his sister could keep an eye on him and catch him up on events.

Far less pleasant had been memorials for the dozen sailors who had died aboard the destroyer *Katana*. After the far heavier losses in some battles (such as at Unity Alternate), "only" a dozen dead would seem easier to handle. But Geary found himself just as downhearted when he contemplated a dozen lives that had been cut short. "I'll never get used to it," he confided to Tanya.

"That's good," she said. "Anyone who can just blow off the deaths of people under their command doesn't deserve command. During the war we got used to losing people, but the good officers never got used to their people dying. You know what I mean. Even that Syndic Executive Aragon was worried about losing more of her 'workers.'"

"Yes. And to save them she saved Michael." He shook his head. "I never thought I'd end up owing a family debt to a Syndic officer, even if she is a former Syndic."

"That is going to be weird," Desjani had conceded. "But I have a feeling that Aragon will only call in that debt if she really, really needs it."

That had been yesterday. Now, once again, Geary sat in the ambassador's office, Ambassador Rycerz and Dr. Cresida on the same side of the table. Dr. Kottur had once again reported that he could not attend due to a health issue.

On the other side, facing them, were once more the virtual presences of President Iceni, General Drakon, and Kommodor Bradamont.

"Thank you for agreeing to another meeting," Ambassador Rycerz began.

Iceni smiled again briefly. "It was the least we could do given the favor you've rendered to an associated star system. Admiral, I've decided to honor Kommodor Marphissa's conditional promise to Kane and will return the battle cruiser to that star system as a gift."

"If they've harmed any of the Tigres or the families," Geary said, "I hope you haul it back here again."

"We just might," Iceni said. "Our reputation, like your own, is worth more than a single battle cruiser. Colonel Rogero also committed to the safety of those people. We'll get them off Kane. Now, Ambassador Rycerz, please outline your proposed new offer."

Rycerz flashed a smile of her own. "You asked for two Alliance hypernet keys. I was sent here with an offer that included no Alliance hypernet keys. You understand, I hope, that if I'm perceived as having given in to your demands, the Alliance won't ratify the agreement. On the other hand, I understand that you cannot be seen as giving in to Alliance demands, and must have something to show you demonstrated your independence, as well as the means to sustain your economy. Admiral Geary tells me the costs of supporting the new battle cruiser for Kane will be borne by you as well, increasing our interest in properly rewarding Midway for its vital role in maintaining freedom and stability in this region of stars.

"In light of these factors, I propose a compromise. One Alliance hypernet key in exchange for allowing us to modify your gate and use the hypernet here."

"One key?" President Iceni asked, eyeing Rycerz. "So you can say we demanded two but you only gave one?"

"And so you can tell your people that we offered none and you demanded one," Rycerz said.

President Iceni stroked her chin, watching Rycerz. "I assume that you know hypernet keys can be duplicated."

"Can they?" Rycerz asked, her voice sounding innocent of any pretense.

Iceni's smile stayed in place this time. "I see. But regardless of what we tell others, I need to know that will not create any claims of deal breaking from the Alliance."

"The agreement will contain nothing about duplicating hypernet keys," Rycerz said. "Is there a need for that?"

"No need at all. Why should it address hypothetical issues?"

General Drakon frowned at Rycerz. "So you're deliberately leaving a loophole for us to exploit."

Rycerz shook her head. "I've said nothing of the kind. I've simply asked if the issue needed to be addressed."

"Fair enough," Drakon said, also smiling.

Geary, watching him, thought again that Drakon's smile was the sort of expression that with only minor changes could be either reassuring or frightening.

"But," Rycerz continued, "given the magnitude of my concession, I'm hoping that Midway has something to offer that will provide the sense of a balanced deal to the Alliance. The Senate has to approve this deal. Kommodor Bradamont indicated there might be such a thing at hand."

General Drakon nodded. "Kommodor Bradamont brought her proposal to us, and President Iceni and I both saw merit in the idea. There's a Syndicate research facility at a star named Kahiki not far from here. We've taken possession of it."

Ambassador Rycerz's eyes watched him closely. "What kind of research?"

"Theoretical long shots that might yield something of use in dozens of areas. Due to its isolated location, Kahiki was deemed safe for the most cutting-edge research funded by the Syndicate."

Dr. Cresida, who'd appeared zoned out earlier, had fastened her attention on Drakon.

"What are you offering in relation to that?" Rycerz asked, her voice cautious.

"We can't exploit the potential of much of what Kahiki holds," President Iceni said. "But, if someone with substantially more resources were given access to it, they might gain some valuable insights."

"Which they'd be expected to share," General Drakon said.

"That's . . . an intriguing offer," Ambassador Rycerz said.

"Here's some of what they're working on," Drakon said, gesturing over the table. A virtual paper list appeared on the table in front of Geary, Rycerz, and Dr. Cresida.

After struggling to comprehend any of the topics listed, Geary looked at Cresida, who was studying her copy intently.

"Dr. Cresida?" Ambassador Rycerz asked.

Cresida looked up, blinking. "Interesting."

"Are they of value?"

"Yes." Cresida nodded, looking back at the list. "I mean, this is indeed theoretical research into some extreme concepts. Many of them might lead nowhere. But even failures would be extremely valuable in what they'd tell us. I'm not a specialist in some of these areas, of course."

"Should the Alliance help fund this effort?"

"Absolutely." Dr. Cresida looked at the paper again. "Absolutely," she repeated.

"I think we have a deal," Ambassador Rycerz said.

That brought another smile from Iceni. "Good. The best deals are those that offer equal benefit to both sides. I believe that is what we have. Once we finalize a few details, our gate experts can talk to your gate experts about the next steps."

"Excellent," Ambassador Rycerz said.

After Iceni's and Drakon's virtual presences had left, Bradamont lingered to salute Geary. "Thank you for getting my colonel back safely to me, sir."

Ambassador Rycerz beamed at her. "They understand now, don't they? That I really am in charge here?"

"No," Bradamont said, shaking her head. "They still think he runs the Alliance, but is doing so behind a screen. Even his time leaving Midway to go to Kane is to them simply more proof of how Admiral Geary is maintaining the pretense of answering to you rather than you answering to him."

"You're joking."

"No, I'm sorry, I'm not. That's how they view the universe, and everything they see is filtered through that. But they also view Admiral

Geary as an, um, enlightened leader in their own mold, which is why they remain willing to deal with the Alliance as long as the Alliance is perceived to be Admiral Geary's kingdom."

"Fine." Ambassador Rycerz had apparently developed yet another headache.

This mission, Geary thought, seemed to produce a bumper crop of headaches.

After Bradamont's virtual self had vanished as well, Rycerz turned to Dr. Cresida. "Doctor, I'll get you connected to Midway's gate technicians as quickly as we can once the deal is finalized. Let the absent Dr. Kottur know that we're going to be proceeding. Keep me informed of important actions."

Dr. Cresida tilted her head to one side as she considered the last statement. "Do you want to know when we deactivate the safe-collapse system on the gate?"

"What?" The ambassador stared at the doctor. "You're going to deactivate the safe-collapse system?"

"We have to," Cresida replied in a matter-of-fact way. "Otherwise that system would block our attempts to entangle the gate with the Alliance hypernet."

"Why did Dr. Kottur never mention that to me?"

"I don't know. He was supposed to."

"Yes," Ambassador Rycerz said in the manner of someone keeping tight control of her feelings. "I want to know when the safe-collapse system is deactivated. And when it has been reactivated. And exactly what is wrong with Dr. Kottur that he keeps missing these meetings."

"I'll inform Dr. Kottur of that," Dr. Cresida said. "I do think there's something wrong with him." Having made that ambiguous statement, she left.

The ambassador made a quick call. "Colonel Webb, we have a complication. It turns out the scientists will have to deactivate the safe-collapse system on the hypernet gate in order to do their work."

Webb frowned. "That creates a window for real trouble if anyone knows of it."

"Exactly. I want to keep that information held tightly among those who need to know. And I need you to keep an eye and an ear out for any signs that anyone is taking too much interest in the state of that safe-collapse system." She gestured to Geary. "Keep the admiral informed as well. Have you spotted anything we should be aware of?"

"Nothing much. There's been a lot of access of the files on the aliens. Everything that's known about them. But that's hardly suspicious when we're getting ready to head into their space. Our science team has been monitoring the hypernet gate and analyzing the operating system, but that's their job." Colonel Webb made a face. "Oh, and Dr. Macadams. He keeps demanding things. Get the original translator from the other ship, as if I could overrule an admiral. Trying to block any socializing between his people and anyone else on the ship."

"Is he trying to hide something?" Ambassador Rycerz asked.

"The living stars only know," Colonel Webb said. "And questions about the status of the work on the hypernet gate." He paused. "Which now looks particularly interesting. I assumed it was just because we couldn't head for alien space until that part of the mission was done. But in light of what you just said . . ."

"Keep an eye on him, Colonel," Rycerz ordered. "He's surely figured out that I'm slowly edging him out of his job."

"How are your people holding up, Colonel?" Geary asked. "This duty must be pretty boring for them."

"It's nothing we haven't been through before," Webb said. "Hurry up and wait, you know. They're working out, running through sims, the usual things. I admit they can't wait to get moving, and really envied your Marines getting to go have some fun at Kane."

"I'm not sure I'd call it fun," Geary said. "What about that bug? Did you learn anything more about it?"

Webb looked at Ambassador Rycerz.

Rycerz made an angry gesture. "We found another, in this office, while you were at Kane. Which I suppose rules out anyone on any of the ships you took with you."

"But otherwise," Colonel Webb said, "no fingerprints at all, electronic, manufacturing, software, anything. Even the materials have been mixed from a variety of sources to be generic so we can't identify any particular source."

"But someone with access to the ambassador's office," Geary said.

"Or someone who has access to someone who has access to this office and made them an unknowing carrier of the bug," Webb said. "Which really doesn't narrow it down at all. What about that Dr. Cresida? She's an odd fish, and it's obvious she doesn't like you at all."

"No, she doesn't like me," Geary said. "But I think she really wants to see if she can make this gate entanglement work. And she's been in here for important meetings, so why would she need to plant a bug?"

And that, unfortunately, was where they had to leave it.

The next day, Midway approved the deal, and the technicians and theoreticians began their work.

NINETEEN

"**THEY'VE** deactivated the safe-collapse system on the hypernet gate." Ambassador Rycerz looked as angry as Geary had ever seen her. "They did it this morning, and I only now found out by accident."

He had just met her aboard *Boundless* once more. "Maybe that's the reason for this urgent meeting that Dr. Kottur summoned us to."

"It had better be. Every time I meet him the man is pleasant and easy to talk to, but his behavior when he's not with me is getting more than annoying." They walked together through the passageways of *Boundless*, toward the section where the science offices were.

As they reached the door to Dr. Kottur's office, Geary could see Dr. Bron approaching. "Do you know what this critical meeting is about?" he asked Bron.

Dr. Bron shook his head, looking annoyed. "He said it was absolutely vital before the attempt to dual-entangle the hypernet gate. We should be preparing for that now, but this has called us away and is delaying the attempt."

"We were told we had to meet with Dr. Kottur at exactly 1210 ship's time," Ambassador Rycerz said. "Why?"

Dr. Bron gave them a hapless look. "I'm sure Dr. Kottur must have a good reason."

"It's a quarter to twelve now," Rycerz said. "I have no intention of standing around for almost half an hour waiting on Dr. Kottur."

Dr. Bron leaned closer to the door to examine it. "It's locked, on a timer. It'll release at exactly 1210."

Ambassador Rycerz rubbed her nose, her unhappiness growing. "Why does he think we need these kinds of dramatics?" She tapped the door alert, waiting for Kottur to respond, then tapped it again, harder. "And does he think the admiral and I have nothing better to do but wait outside his door?" Pulling out her personal pad, she tapped a link. "Captain Matson. The door to Dr. Kottur's stateroom is on a time lock. I want it opened now."

Geary could hear the voice of *Boundless*'s captain reply. "I'm ordering an override of the time lock, Madam Ambassador. You should get a green open light in less than five seconds."

It actually took only two seconds before the time lock blinked to zero. "Thank you, Captain," Ambassador Rycerz said.

Since Dr. Bron seemed hesitant to enter, Geary pushed open the door, leading the way inside.

He stopped when he saw Dr. Kottur sitting slumped at his desk. Kottur's eyes were closed, and he didn't move. A small, empty glass sat on the desk before him.

Dr. Bron ran forward with a small cry of shock, grabbing Kottur's arm and neck, feeling. "There's no pulse, no respiration. But he's still warm and no stiffness has set in. It must have happened less than an hour ago. We have to—"

His words cut off as another audible click filled the room, perhaps a circuit set to detect the presence of the others. A virtual image of Dr. Kottur appeared, standing beside the chair, his usual comradely smile firmly in place. "I know you're wondering why I called you together," he said, his smile growing a bit. "I've always wanted to say that, just like an old-style detective. Let me start by apologizing for what's about to

happen. I really do regret the necessity of my actions. But I had to ensure you all knew the reasons for them, and why they were required for
the sake of all humanity."

Dr. Kottur's image gestured outward. "For a long time, humanity
could take comfort in knowing only it existed as a truly intelligent species. When the discovery was made that other such species existed, it
became clear that the universe and the forces which rule it, in their
wisdom, had placed such species on widely separated stars. Intelligent
species are not made to coexist. It violates the laws of nature."

Geary stared at the image of Dr. Kottur, feeling a growing sense of
dread though he didn't know exactly why.

"Look at Old Earth," Dr. Kottur continued, still smiling as if this
were a collegial meeting to discuss minor matters. "Humanity's cous-
ins, other intelligences like the Neanderthals, were either absorbed
into humanity, or exterminated. That's how it has to be. The enigmas
understand that. They want to exterminate us. And the homicidal cow
creatures understand as well. They make no secret of it."

Kottur raised one hand to wag a finger at his audience as if they
were a lecture hall filled with students. "But the spider wolves are more
clever than that. They know what must be, but they pretend to be our
friends because they've seen how fiercely humanity will defend itself
against open enemies. They want to infiltrate human space and human
society, becoming a common presence, their claws and tentacles gaining access into all of our systems. With what purpose? To do what nature demands. When they are ready, humanity will die in a single
night. Or be reduced to perpetual slavery. Or perhaps turned into doc-
ile sources of food for the maws of the spider wolves.

"How could I let that happen? This mission was so badly miscon-
ceived that it had to fail. The forces of the universe needed an agent to
act on their behalf."

"What the hell . . . ?" Ambassador Rycerz whispered, her expression
increasingly aghast.

Dr. Kottur's image pointed to his desk. "At exactly 1200 ship time,

I sent a command to the hypernet gate, which has had all of its protective software disabled preparatory to the attempted realignment. That command contains the program to cause a maximum destructive output when the gate collapses. The gate will be destroyed, producing a nova-force blast that will destroy everything in this star system. But I'm afraid that you won't witness that event. Even though there shouldn't be any possible means of preventing it, I don't want you all suffering or making futile efforts. This ship will itself be destroyed in only a couple of minutes."

Kottur's image paused, the smile briefly wavering. "I truly am sorry that you're all going to die, along with everyone else near this star. It's unfortunate. I couldn't even attend the meetings with those from Midway, knowing that I'd have to be the agent of their deaths. And worried that they might see through me. But my actions are necessary, you see. A few millions or billions of lives are nothing compared to the greater good. Compared to the future of humanity. Please don't run around wasting your final moments in futile efforts to stop my last project. There's nothing you can do. As for me, I wouldn't want any panic on your parts to result in painful injury to myself, so I will drink from this small glass on my desk, and very quickly fall into a slumber from which my spirit will depart my body. I don't fear that! No, I'm certain of my reward. But I am sorry you all must die, and wanted you to understand why it had to be."

The image vanished.

"Oh my ancestors," Dr. Bron whispered, his voice strained by disbelief. "We're doomed."

Maybe it was because of his experience with time-delayed communications, but Geary grasped a vital fact before the others. "We weren't supposed to enter this room until 1210. That's . . . twenty minutes from now."

"Twenty minutes." Ambassador Rycerz whipped out her personal pad again. "Captain Matson! I want everything on this ship capable of sending an external transmission shut down *now*!"

Matson took a few seconds to reply. "I don't understand—"

"There's no time to explain! Shut down your transmitters!"

"Power them down," Geary called. "Kill all power to them."

"Got it," Matson said. "I'll call you back as soon as it's done."

Geary had only a moment to wonder if they'd get the transmitters shut down in time before he realized that was only one of their problems. "He said *Boundless* would be destroyed within a few minutes of us entering his room."

Rycerz and Dr. Bron both stared at him. "How could he destroy an entire ship of this size?" Rycerz asked.

"Unless he somehow smuggled aboard the parts for a nuclear weapon, the only means of being sure of that would be sabotaging the ship's power core," Geary said.

Rycerz hit another link on her pad. "Colonel Webb! Dr. Kottur has set up something to destroy this ship within a few minutes of 1210. Admiral Geary thinks he may have sabotaged the power core, but it's possible he smuggled weapon components aboard."

Colonel Webb didn't require even a few seconds to absorb the news. "We're on it! I'll inform you of whatever we find."

"What happens if we can't stop that message from being sent?" Rycerz demanded of Dr. Bron.

Bron shook his head, looking dazed. "We'll be dead."

"Can't we reactivate the safe-collapse system?" Geary demanded.

"No. No. It would take too long to do that. The collapse would be well underway before the system finished reinstalling."

"We have time he did not intend us to have," Rycerz said, pointing at Dr. Kottur's body. "We need to use that. There must be something else we can do!"

"There's nothing else that *I* can do!" Dr. Bron said.

Geary tried to sound calm even though he'd seen the damage that a collapsing gate could do to ships and worlds in the same star system. "The only thing we could have done if we had time was to get every ship as far from the gate as possible in the time left before it collapsed and hope the energy had spread out enough for our shields to handle. But with only about twenty minutes left, we can't even do that."

"Assuming our own ship doesn't explode at any moment," Rycerz said. From the way she was looking at Dr. Kottur's body, she would have killed him then and there if he weren't already dead. "The escape pods . . ."

"We couldn't get far enough away to be safe from a power core explosion that soon on a ship this size," Geary said. "And the rest of the people on *Boundless* would barely have time to reach the pods before the ship blew. Besides, if the gate goes down, the pods will be no protection at all."

"We need to warn everyone in the star system," Dr. Bron began. "No, our warning wouldn't arrive until just before the shock wave hits," he added, sounding as if he was about to cry in frustration. "Wouldn't it be better to let them die without knowing what was coming?"

"I still need to tell my ships," Geary said, pivoting to reach the nearest comm panel. His ships, *Tanya . . . Ancestors how can I save Tanya.* "*Dauntless.* Fleet command priority."

Tanya Desjani was in her stateroom when she took the call, gazing at him with a look of curiosity that changed to concern in a moment's time. "What happened?"

He told her. "We're too close to the gate. If we can't stop that transmission—"

"I'm seeing transmitters still active on *Boundless*," Tanya snapped as she checked her display. "How long does it take them to kill power to their transmitters?"

Geary looked at Rycerz, who growled an obscenity as she hit her comm pad again. "Captain Matson! Why aren't your transmitters shut down?"

Matson sounded frustrated. "Something is blocking the power-down commands. My technicians are trying to— What? Why are they accessing the power core? Madam Ambassador—"

"Colonel Webb is acting on my orders. The power core may have been sabotaged. Get those transmitters shut down! Colonel Webb!" Rycerz called, hitting that link again. "I want every transmitter on this ship shut down as quickly as possible by any means necessary!"

"Yes, Madam Ambassador!"

"Dr. Bron!" Rycerz spun to focus on the unhappy scientist. "Why can't you do something?"

"There isn't anything . . ." Bron said, his voice trailing off.

"Kottur planned this well," Geary said. "Captain Desjani. I want active jamming of any signal from this ship. Link the whole fleet into the jamming if necessary to get enough power behind it."

"Yes, sir," Desjani said. "How will I get any more word from you?"

"I'll send you an all clear by flashing light from *Boundless*."

"Yes, sir. Consider it done."

He had a moment as her image vanished to realize those might be the last words they ever spoke to each other. But they couldn't waste time with more words.

Two of Colonel Webb's "honor guard" came running into the room, checking portable scanners as they moved about the room. "All clear in here," one reported to the ambassador. "If he has a nuke, it's nowhere near this room."

"How about the power core?" Rycerz demanded.

"Colonel Webb has our hack and cracks checking the operating system while the rest of us search for bombs, ma'am."

"Then keep searching."

Captain Matson called in, anger warring with frustration in his voice. "We can't power down the transmitters. They won't respond. I've ordered the power links physically severed."

Geary checked the time. "We have one minute until noon. Kottur said he'd sent the message ten minutes before 1210, so that's our deadline."

"Unless he lied about that, too," Dr. Bron said.

A faint vibration rumbled through the ship. The first signs of a power core going unstable?

Matson called in again, outraged this time. "Those maniacs with Webb are blowing up my transmitters!"

"Good," Ambassador Rycerz snapped at him. "They're trying to save all of our lives." Turning to Geary, she held up her pad where the time was displayed. "It's noon. Let's hope Colonel Webb found whatever Kottur was planning to use to destroy this—"

The lights went out.

As an emergency light flared to life to give them illumination again, Dr. Bron turned to run.

Geary grabbed him. "If the power core was going to blow, we'd already be dead."

"What does this mean, Admiral?" Ambassador Rycerz asked, her voice rigidly controlled.

"It probably means they shut down the core to keep it from blowing," Geary said. "If sabotaging the power core was Kottur's plan, shutting it down will give the crew time to go through the operating system and find any malware." Another vibration ran through the hull. "The transmitters will have battery backups, so they'll still need to be taken down."

The sound of feet running down the passageway was followed by Colonel Webb himself bursting through the door. "All transmitters shut down by physical destruction," he reported to Rycerz. "Two of them were sending something. The ship comm techs said it looked to them like some sort of malware had taken control of the communications system."

"Did you stop the transmissions in time?" Rycerz demanded.

Webb shook his head. "I don't know, Madam Ambassador."

"I've got the fleet actively jamming transmissions from *Boundless*," Geary said.

Colonel Webb nodded, his expression somber in the limited light cast by the emergency illumination. "There are methods of getting through that," he said. "As I'm sure you're aware, Admiral. We found malware in the power core control system. My people are still analyzing it but it looks like it would've caused an overload despite every safeguard built into the core system." He gazed at Rycerz. "Ambassador, whoever provided the malware used for this had access to the very best, or worst if you will, available. Which means they might've used a transmission method that could get past the fleet's jamming."

"It's 1205," Dr. Bron said, his voice faint. "We'll find out whether the worst happened in about fifteen minutes."

They all turned as someone else entered the room. "Dr. Bron?" Dr. Cresida looked about her, dispassionately taking in the sight of Dr. Kottur's body. "Is he dead? I received a message from Dr. Kottur to come here at 1210. Can you explain the situation here?"

Her expression barely altered as Dr. Bron raced through an explanation, causing Geary to wonder at Jasmine Cresida's self-control.

"Oh," Dr. Cresida said as Bron finished, her voice revealing as little emotion as her expression. "You've stopped the threat to the ship? Good. I wouldn't worry about any danger to the hypernet gate."

"Dr. Cresida," Ambassador Rycerz said, her voice almost trembling, "do you know of something we can do to stop the gate from collapsing even if that message was able to transmit?"

"No. Because the gate will not collapse." Dr. Cresida turned her gaze to each person around the room. "I'm certain of it."

"Why?" Colonel Webb demanded.

"Because I distrusted Dr. Kottur. I distrusted this mission, thinking it might be cover for an attempt to expand control over this region, or to threaten the Dancers, or to attack the enigmas. Something aggressive. So I broke into his private files to see if Dr. Kottur had secret orders." Her gaze grew defiant as she spoke. "I found the destructive gate collapse program in there. Very well hidden, but I was looking for very-well-hidden items. I didn't know what use Dr. Kottur intended to make of it, but I don't think such a program should ever exist or be used. I went through it and deleted every command line, every set of instructions. All that was left were the shell, a user interface that no longer connected to anything, and disconnected code segments. I added enough junk data to return the file to the same size, then I resaved it, looking as if it was still intact."

Geary couldn't remember if he'd been breathing, but he suddenly inhaled fast and deeply. "You're sure that Kottur couldn't have spotted your deletions and repaired them?"

She shook her head. "Kottur wasn't that good at coding. His scientific skills were mostly in the area of academic politics. I could tell he hadn't written the original program, which was beyond him. Even if he'd spotted the damage I did, he couldn't have repaired it." Her eyes focused intently on Geary. "I recognized the hand behind a lot of that code. It was my sister's. Whoever put together that program used the original code written by Jaylen."

Ambassador Rycerz seemed to be trying to regain her composure. "Which means whoever helped Kottur get that program had access to the original in highly classified Alliance files."

Colonel Webb nodded, his eyes on Dr. Cresida as if he was reevaluating whatever he'd thought of her. "Like I said, Ambassador, whoever it was had access to the worst malware out there. The Alliance has got a serious internal problem."

Which wasn't exactly new information, Geary thought, but when news of this got back to Unity there'd be some more hell to pay. "Did Kottur need any help aboard this ship to get the malware planted?"

Webb grimaced. "Possibly. He could've done it alone. All he had to do was download the malware in the right places and it would've done the rest. But an accomplice, or more than one, would have made that easier. Madam Ambassador, we should assume there are others on this ship who helped Kottur. My people are going to find them."

Ambassador Rycerz spoke again, this time in a fully controlled, formal voice. "Keep me informed, Colonel Webb. Dr. Cresida, we, and the entire Alliance, owe you a debt that is impossible to ever adequately repay."

"I didn't do it for you," Dr. Jasmine Cresida said. "I didn't want my sister's work misused." She glanced at Geary again. "I'll be honest that

I suspected the program might've been provided by the military. Or some secret government agency. That's why I waited to see who would try to use it, and how."

Dr. Bron turned a look of pure hatred on Kottur. "He timed this so we'd know what was going to happen, but have no chance to do anything to save anyone! Just so he could try to justify himself for what he was doing! And then apologizing for dooming us as if that would make it all right? If we hadn't come in early, if the ambassador hadn't ordered his lock overridden, we'd probably all be dead now. I trusted that man! I liked him! He was always smiling!"

Smiling faces, Geary thought. He should've remembered that warning.

"How could he have tried to do that?" Dr. Bron wondered, bafflement warring with his rage. "He tried to kill us all!"

"You did say he apologized," Dr. Cresida said, her voice dry.

The lights came back on, happy shouts rising in the passageway as others reacted to the power returning. "The power core must be safe again," Colonel Webb said.

"We'll have to brief Captain Matson on all this," Ambassador Rycerz said. "Is it possible to revive Dr. Kottur?"

"Why bother?" Bron said, kicking Kottur's leg.

"If we can revive him, we can interrogate him and perhaps learn who helped him in this," Rycerz said.

"On it," Colonel Webb said, going to the comm pad that had powered up again as well. "Medical emergency! This compartment! We need emergency care here as quickly as possible!"

"What do we tell the medics?" Geary asked, his mind latching onto the security aspects of the situation. "What do we tell anyone?"

Rycerz gave him a long look, her lips twisted as she thought. "Even though it's been resolved without real danger, we should keep this between us and Captain Matson. Oh, Admiral, you told someone aboard your ship?"

"Captain Desjani," Geary said. "She won't say anything if I tell her it's confidential."

"Good. I'll prepare a full report, so it'll be on the official record. But I ask each of you not to discuss this with anyone else. Dr. Kottur . . . attempted suicide because of personal matters."

"Why protect his reputation after what he tried to do?" Dr. Bron demanded.

"I'm not worried about Kottur's reputation," Rycerz said. "I'm worried about everyone else in this star system. A panic could erupt if they even knew an attempt had been made to collapse the gate and destroy everyone here. And the leaders of Midway might well withdraw their permission for the effort to realign the gate. That would partly serve the purpose of whoever was behind Dr. Kottur's sabotage."

"The ambassador is right," Geary said. "This mission can still be sabotaged even though Kottur's chosen method failed."

Dr. Bron breathed in and out slowly a few times, then nodded. "Right. We don't want to help him. Not one bit."

"Dr. Cresida?" Ambassador Rycerz asked.

"I will accept your request to not speak of this," Cresida said. "But, if we are to continue, we first need to go through the realignment programming with a fine-tooth comb, to be certain no malware or Trojan horses or other malignant code has been hidden in that."

"That's right!" Dr. Bron said, nodding rapidly. "It's supposed to be clean, it's been checked repeatedly, but if Kottur did this, maybe he had a backup plan. I'll get the team together. You'll assist, right? You're the best at this."

"I'll assist," Dr. Cresida said as medical personnel and equipment came swarming into the room. "I'll follow in a moment. After I say something to the admiral."

Wondering what Dr. Cresida intended, but willing to listen after learning she might have saved everyone in this star system, Geary followed her into the hallway.

"Admiral," Jasmine Cresida said, looking straight at him, "one thing coders have done since ancient times is add notes to their work, embedded in the code. Explanations, thoughts, sometimes even jokes and comments. At the end of the destructive collapse program that Dr. Kottur had, I found a comment that traced back to the original coding. It was written by my sister, and said, 'I have unwittingly unleashed from its bottle a genie that could destroy us all. I pray my commander and my comrades will have the wisdom to help humanity find a way to render that genie harmless.'"

Geary had to look away, painfully remembering Captain Cresida's optimistic enthusiasm. "That's what I would have expected," he finally said.

"And what you told me to expect," Dr. Cresida said. "Proof of your word. For the record, I did believe you, because I wanted to believe you. I'm nonetheless glad to have found confirmation. Tell me something, Admiral. Do you have that program on your ship?"

Geary frowned at her, momentarily puzzled by the question. "Do you mean the destructive collapse program? No. Even though the safe-collapse systems are supposed to block it or at worst ensure a collapse doesn't give off damaging levels of energy, no ship in the fleet is supposed to have that aboard. It's never to be used, and it's never to be available to be used if someone gets their hands on it."

Dr. Cresida studied him. "But some form of that program was used at Unity Alternate."

"Yes. I don't know where Victoria Rione got her copy of it. All physical evidence was of course destroyed, so there was no way to learn the answer afterwards. She had a lot of software that she wasn't supposed to have."

"Fortunately for us all." Dr. Cresida turned to go. "Don't thank me for stopping the destruction of the gate here. You gave me back my sister. We're even." She walked away without another word.

THE next day, at the time Midway's gate was to be entangled with the Alliance hypernet, Geary was on the bridge of *Dauntless*, watching the gate a few light minutes distant. The technicians were in a ship much closer to the gate, able to correct any problems within seconds. Tanya Desjani was on the bridge as well, along with the primary watch standers, all interested in observing the historic event. Of them all, only Tanya knew how close they'd come to disaster the day before.

He'd been in an earthquake once, feeling the solid ground suddenly ripple and heave beneath him like a living thing. That was the closest he could come to describing what he felt as the gate entangled with another hypernet. The universe, reality, seemed to wrinkle and flex before subsiding again with only a lingering sense of a fading vibration that was impossible to describe.

"That was weird," Lieutenant Castries breathed.

"But did it work?" Desjani asked.

"Good question," Geary said.

A few minutes later, they received a message from the science team at the gate. "From Dr. Cresida. 'Now I am become Schrödinger, entangler of hypernets.'"

"What does that mean?" Desjani asked.

"I think it means it worked," Geary said, grinning with relief. "And it means after they finish some tests, we can head for Dancer space."

Tanya Desjani nodded. "You know, Admiral, it hasn't been easy so far, but I have a feeling things are probably going to be harder from this point on."

"You're probably right, Captain."

"I'm always right."

ACKNOWLEDGMENTS

I remain indebted to my agent, Joshua Bilmes, for his ever-inspired suggestions and assistance, and to my editor, Anne Sowards, for her support and editing. Thanks also to Robert Chase, Kelly Dwyer, Carolyn Ives Gilman, J. G. (Huck) Huckenpohler, Simcha Kuritzky, Michael LaViolette, Aly Parsons, Bud Sparhawk, Mary Thompson, and Constance A. Warner for their suggestions, comments, and recommendations.